INVITATI

"Would your family be ... ... we'd spent time together?" Adam asked.

"I'd say that's incontestable," Melissa sighed. "Furor would be a better description of my father's reaction." She sat against the door on her side of the cab.

With a wry smile, Adam commented, "If you sat any farther away from me, you'd be on the outside of this cab. Scared?"

She gave him a withering look. "Of whom?"

"Well, if you're so sure of yourself," he baited, "slide over here."

She controlled the urge to lean into him, when his long fingers stroked the back of her neck. "What does it take to get you started?" she asked idly, voicing a private thought.

"One spark of encouragement from you." He flicked his thumb and forefinger. "Just that much, honey." She couldn't muffle the gasp that betrayed her.

"Move over here," he taunted. "Come on, see for yourself." Tempting. Seductive. Enticing her. An invitation to madness.

* * *

"A scintillating literary perfume redolent with romance."
—*Romantic Times*

"A truly satisfying read from beginning to end. AGAINST ALL ODDS is not to be missed."
—Donna Hill, author of DECEPTION

"AGAINST ALL ODDS is a perfect read on a rainy night!"
—*Literary Times*

"Gwynne Forster continues to scale the mountain toward greatness with this contemporary, ethnic retelling of the Hatfield and McCoy feud . . . a sure bet."
—Harriet Klausner for America Online

ROMANCES ABOUT AFRICAN-AMERICANS!
YOU'LL FALL IN LOVE
WITH ARABESQUE BOOKS FROM PINNACLE

SERENADE (0024, $4.99)
by Sandra Kitt

Alexandra Morrow was too young and naive when she first fell in love with musician, Parker Harrison—and vowed never to be so vulnerable again. Now Parker is back and although she tries to resist him, he strolls back into her life as smoothly as the jazz rhapsodies for which he is known. Though not the dreamy innocent she was before, Alexandra finds her defenses quickly crumbling and her mind, body and soul slowly opening up to her one and only love, who shows her that dreams do come true.

FOREVER YOURS (0025, $4.50)
by Francis Ray

Victoria Chandler must find a husband quickly or her grandparents will call in the loans that support her chain of lingerie boutiques. She arranges a mock marriage to tall, dark and handsome ranch owner Kane Taggart. The marriage will only last one year, and her business will be secure, and Kane will be able to walk away with no strings attached. The only problem is that Kane has other plans for Victoria. He'll cast a spell that will make her his forever after.

A SWEET REFRAIN (0041, $4.99)
by Margie Walker

Fifteen years before, jazz musician Nathaniel Padell walked out on Jenine to seek fame and fortune in New York City. But now the handsome widower is back with a baby girl in tow. Jenine is still irresistibly attracted to Nat and enchanted by his daughter. Yet even as love is rekindled, an unexpected danger threatens Nat's child. Now, Jenine must fight for Nat before someone stops the music forever!

Available wherever paperbacks are sold, or order direct from the Publisher. Send cover price plus 50¢ per copy for mailing and handling to Penguin USA, P.O. Box 999, c/o Dept. 17109, Bergenfield, NJ 07621. Residents of New York and Tennessee must include sales tax. DO NOT SEND CASH.

GWYNNE FORSTER

Against All Odds

PINNACLE BOOKS
KENSINGTON PUBLISHING CORP.

PINNACLE BOOKS are published by

Kensington Publishing Corp.
850 Third Avenue
New York, NY 10022

First Printing: September, 1996

Printed in the United States of America
10 9 8 7 6 5 4 3 2 1

Acknowledgment

To my lovely daughter-in-law, Margaret Dougherty Acsádi, who willingly and efficiently fulfills my requests for research assistance; to my dear stepson, Peter Forster Acsádi, whose encouragement and support mean so much to me; and in memory of my dear friend, Lily.

One

Melissa Grant hung up the phone. Anxious. Her graceful brown fingers strummed her desk. She'd had to expand her business in order to stay ahead of her competition, but months would pass before she got the results that she anticipated. Until then her financial status would be precarious at best. Her banker knew that and—because her first loan hadn't been fully paid—had denied her request for a second one. Now she stood a good chance of losing her business. She knew when she came to New York that she could expect tough competition, but she had worked hard and established one of the top executive search firms, and she'd done it in less than five years. She had taken stock of her resources and decided that she had three alternatives, all of them unattractive. She could put her personal funds into her MTG Executive Search firm—something she'd been taught in business school never to do; she could borrow the money from her father; or she could take the lucrative Hayes/Roundtree account. Bankruptcy was preferable to discussing a loan with her father, Rafer Grant, and only trouble could come from any kind of involvement with a Roundtree. Adam Roundtree's executive assistant, Jason Court, had called her with a request that she find a manager for "Leather and Hides," the division of Hayes/Roundtree Enterprises, Inc., that tanned leather and made leather goods. She noticed the light on her phone.

"MTG." She leaned back in her desk chair, twirling a slingshot that she won in a charity raffle. "Hello, Mr. Court. I'm not sure I'm the person you want for this job. I don't know a thing about leather."

"In other words, you don't want the contract," he said as though surprised. Adam wants MTG. He thinks your firm is the best, and Adam is used to having the best. Think it over. I can raise the fee by twenty percent, but no more."

Melissa hung up and buzzed her secretary for the Roundtree file.

"Here you are." Kelly put the folder on Melissa's desk. "I thought you said you wouldn't take that job for all the bullion in Fort Knox."

"That was yesterday. The bank just refused my request for a loan." She scanned the few pages. "This must be a mistake." She checked the figure on the last page. "He's offering more money than I ever dreamed of asking for a search. I can find a manager who'll suit him—I don't doubt that, but the consequences could be . . . explosive. Probably hell to pay."

Kelly frowned. "I don't get it."

"Someday when we have a few hours to throw away, I'll tell you about it." Melissa weighed the pros and cons. If she took the contract, she would no longer have a financial problem and, when she listed a firm on the New York Stock Exchange as one of her clients, her ability to attract fat accounts would be guaranteed. She looked over the papers, corrected the fee, initialed it, and signed the contract without giving herself a chance to change her mind. Her signature was unreadable, and she didn't doubt that Adam Roundtree would inscribe his name beneath hers. But when he found out . . . when they all found out! Talk about dancing with the devil!

She walked over to her bookcase, scanned a shelf of business and reference books, and selected a volume of an encyclopedia with the intention of learning about leather tanning. The afternoon sun glared in her face, and she lowered the blinds, wondering absently why Adam Roundtree worked for Jenkins and

Tillman, a New York real estate firm, rather than with his family's Hayes/Roundtree Enterprises. Had he left northern Maryland and come to New York to escape his parents as she had? From what she'd heard of him, she doubted it. Men of his reputation didn't run from anything or anybody. She put the book in her briefcase, sat down, and lifted the receiver.

"Would you please send this signed contract to Jason Court at Jenkins and Tillman?" she asked her secretary. "Get a messenger, and mark the envelope confidential. I'll be leaving in a minute." She pushed her tight curls away from her olive-toned face and completed her final task of the day.

Melissa walked out of her office, two blocks from Wall Street, and into the sweltering early July heat, her discomfort intensified by the high humidity for which New York City was famous. She didn't wait long for a taxi, sat back and took a deep breath, grateful that she'd escaped the rush hour madness. Ten minutes later, getting a taxi within a mile of Wall Street would be impossible.

Adam Roundtree sat in his New York office reviewing reports from Hayes/Roundtree Enterprises, Inc. The Maryland-based company belonged to his family, handed down to them by his maternal grandfather. Jacob Hayes hadn't believed that his gas field would produce indefinitely, and it hadn't, but he'd lived modestly and ploughed his money into a hosiery and a fabric mill, the leather business, and the newspaper. His foresight had enabled him to pass considerable wealth to his children and grandchildren. Adam appreciated his social station and the wealth that he'd inherited, but he wanted his own kingdom, wanted to build his own legacy for his children—that is, if he ever had any. His father's recent death meant that he had to take an active interest in the family business, including management of the leather factory, which his father had skillfully nurtured. His mother possessed a sharp mind, but his grandfather had thought it improper for a young woman to work, and she'd never used her university education. His younger brother, Wayne, a journalist, had his hands full running the newspaper. No help there. So the onus was on him. It would mean working two demanding jobs, but he'd do it.

He summoned Jason Court for a progress report on the search for a manager of the Leather and Hides division. Adam had just gained full partnership in what was now Jenkins, Roundtree, and Tillman, and he had worked hard for it. He didn't see how he could manage a leather tanning and manufacturing business located in Frederick, Maryland, from his office opposite the World Trade Center in New York.

"Come in, Jason, and have a seat. What have you got for me?"

"I have a contract with MTG for your signature." Adam slapped his right knuckle into the open palm of his left hand.

"Nothing else?" If Jason felt pressured, he didn't show it.

"I got the contract by messenger twenty minutes ago." He handed it to Adam, who didn't even glance at the papers but fixed his concentration on the man opposite him.

"How much time did you allow? A week ought to be more than enough for a firm that knows its business. I need that position filled yesterday. Make that clear." He signed the contract and handed it back. "Thanks, Jason." Adam watched his executive assistant as he left the room. The man was his perfect complement; he liked working with him. A sharp mind and a cool head. But he didn't like doing business by mail with an anonymous nonhuman entity, because he wanted to know with whom he was dealing, see him, size him up, and know what to expect. He called his secretary.

"Olivia, would you arrange a meeting here with the president of MTG tomorrow morning, if possible? I don't like dealing with a faceless company." He walked around to Jason's office, next door to his own.

"Tell me something about this fellow who heads up MTG. I've asked Olivia to have him come over here tomorrow morning, and I need a line on him."

He watched Jason lean back in his chair with a half smile playing around his mouth.

"Adam, the president of MTG is a woman."

"A woman?" He quickly veiled his astonishment; no one was going to accuse him of bias against women or any other group.

"Yeah. And she's a no-nonsense person and a good-looking sister, to boot. She's feminine, but she's the epitome of efficiency, a thorough pro. I figured the fact that she wears a skirt wouldn't bother you."

"It doesn't. I take it from your reference to the sisterhood that she's African-American." Jason nodded. "Well, all I want is for her to bring me a first-class manager."

"She will."

"She'd better."

When Olivia opened his office door, Adam stood. The tall, light-skinned woman approached him slowly and confidently, the epitome of self-possession. Cool, laid-back, and elegant, she didn't smile as she made her way, seeming to saunter, across his vast office to where he stood. Stunned. Poleaxed. She stopped a few feet from him and, flabbergasted as he was, he could nonetheless detect a complete change in her—could see the catch in her breath, the slight droop of her bottom lip, the acceleration of her breathing, and the widening of her incredible eyes just before she lowered them in what was most certainly embarrassment. Woman. She was certainly that. He managed to erase the appreciative expression from his face just as she looked up, her professional demeanor restored, and offered her hand.

"I'm Melissa Grant. It's good to meet you."

His eyebrow quirked, and then a frown stole over his face as he walked to the leather sofa and offered her a seat. She took the chair beside the sofa. Amused, he told her, "The name Grant is anathema to my family."

"As Roundtree is to mine," she coolly shot back.

If he had needed a damper for the desire that she'd aroused in him the second she walked through his door, she'd just provided it. Ordinarily he didn't mind getting a fast fever for a woman, stranger or not; he didn't have to do anything about it. An unexpected sexual hunger assured him that he had the virility a man his age ought to possess, but he didn't like this powerful assault on his senses, the jab in his middle that he'd just gotten in response to Melissa Grant. He wouldn't have liked it if her name hadn't been Grant. Making sure of his ground, he asked her, with seeming casualness, "You're not by chance related to the Frederick, Maryland, Grants, are you?"

"I'm Rafer Grant's daughter, and my mother is Emily Morris Grant. I assume you're Jacob Hayes's grandson."

He had to admire the proud lift of her head, the way in which she fixed her gaze on him, and he didn't doubt her message: if her being a Grant was bothersome, it was his problem, not hers. His desire ebbed and, in spite of himself, his mind went back to his fifteenth year and to Rafer Grant's beautiful and voluptuous sister, Louise, and the way in which she'd flaunted his youthful vulnerability. The memory wasn't a pleasant one, and he brought himself back to the present and to the business at hand. What he felt right then wasn't desire but annoyance at himself.

Assuming his usual posture with a business associate, he pinned her with an unwavering gaze. "What have you managed so far?" He knew his tone was curt, brusque; he made it so deliberately. He wouldn't give her the satisfaction of knowing that she'd gotten to him so easily.

"What do you mean?"

He detected a testiness in her voice. If she had a temper, he'd probably know it soon. "I mean, what have you come up with so far?" He imagined that those were storm clouds forming in her eyes, but he didn't have to imagine that her excessively deep breath bespoke exasperation. He repeated the remark and leaned back to observe the fireworks.

Her cool response disappointed him. "Mr. Roundtree." She

punctuated his name with a slow turn of her body toward him and paused while she seemed to weigh her next words. "Mr. Roundtree, I signed that contract less than twenty-four hours ago. If I were a magician, I'd be in a circus or perhaps in the White House where miracles are expected. You couldn't be serious, because the contract gives me one month." He was accustomed to women who smiled at him at least occasionally, but not this one. Just as Jason had said, she was all business, and he had just made a tactical error. He'd practically demanded what he hadn't put in the contract, solid evidence that he'd let his emotional response to her interfere with his professionalism, something he'd never done before. He wouldn't do it again, he promised himself, resenting his slip.

He nearly gasped as she stood abruptly, preparing to leave. Nobody terminated an interview with him. Nobody. And neither would she. He stood and began walking toward his office door, but she stopped before reaching it and held out her business card.

"I'm giving you this in case you feel you need to speak with me in person again. My office is as close to you as yours is to me. Otherwise . . ." She pointed to the telephone. "This has been most informative. Good-bye."

His gaze lingered on her departing back. Was this more evidence of Grant contemptuousness for a Roundtree? Or was she telling him that he'd been out of order in requesting that she come to his office for a business meeting rather than suggesting lunch at a neutral place? If the lady disliked his having called rank on her, she had good cause. He should have invited her to lunch.

Adam answered his intercom. "Yes, Olivia. Well, get Di-Campino to translate those papers. She claims to know Italian."

"She's out today."

"Really? This is the third time this week. Get a replacement."

He heard Olivia's deep sigh. "Adam, I think Maria is pregnant, and the love of her life is unprepared to honor that fact."

"Well, hell, Olivia." He knew his secretary was waiting for him to pounce on the subject of males who mistreat females, and he didn't keep her waiting. "A man shouldn't impregnate a woman if he's unprepared to make a commitment to her and to their child. He's obligated to marry her. Deliver me from these modern-day Johnny Appleseeds. It's one thing to leave a legacy of apple trees, but it's something else to produce a bunch of fatherless kids. Find out what she needs and let me know." He knew without seeing her that his secretary's face bore a smile.

"Yes, sir. But I can tell you now that she's going to need shelter pretty soon, because her father has threatened to kill her. He says it's an affront to the Blessed Virgin for a good Catholic girl to get pregnant out of wedlock."

He threaded his fingers. "Well, get her a place, and whatever else she needs. And tell her that if the guy doesn't marry her before she begins to show, she should stay away from him."

"Yes, sir. I figured you'd help her."

"Did you, now?" He switched off the intercom and turned on his closed-circuit television. He needed a quote on cowhide futures. He'd thought his life was in order and his career in advance of where he hoped to be at this stage of his life. When his father passed away unexpectedly six weeks earlier, all of that changed. He was the elder son, and he had a responsibility to his family but, in truth, he didn't want to leave his firm. Leather and Hides had always been the most profitable unit of Hayes/Roundtree Enterprises, and it was in trouble and didn't have a manager. He didn't believe in promoting the person who had been on the job longest—he went after the best man, even if he was an outsider, and he wanted the best product. His thoughts went to Melissa Grant. She had impressed him with her professional manner. He smiled. Professional after she recovered from the surprise they both received when they met. He wondered what his family would think of Ms. Grant.

What had she done? Melissa sat back in her desk chair and tried to imagine the possible fallout from her signature on that contract when Adam's family found out about it, not to speak of her father's behavior when he learned of her reaction to Adam Roundtree's blatant, blistering masculinity. He haunted her thoughts, as he had done since she first looked at him. A big man. Self-possessed. And he was very tall, very dark, and very handsome. Thinking of him unsettled her, and she recalled that her entire molecular system had danced a jig when she laid eyes on him. But he was like the fruit in the Garden of Eden—one taste guaranteed a fall from Grace. Until today, as far as she knew, the Grants and Roundtrees and the Morrises and Hayeses before them hadn't communicated by mouth or letter in her lifetime or her parents' lifetime. Yet three generations of them had lived continuously within twenty miles of each other. And if today was an indication, their contact now wasn't likely to be pleasant. They had been the bitterest of enemies since Moses Morris, her maternal grandfather, accused Jacob Hayes, Adam's maternal grandfather, of cheating him out of a fortune nearly seventy years earlier. Whether she did it to assuage a sense of guilt, she didn't know, because she didn't examine her motive as she lifted the receiver and dialed her mother.

"Why are you calling in the middle of the day, dear?" Emily Grant asked her daughter. "Is anything wrong?"

"No," Melissa said, groping for a plausible explanation. "I haven't answered your letter, and I thought I'd better make up for that before I forgot it. How's Daddy?" Her mother's heavy sigh did not surprise her.

"Same as always. I'll tell him you asked." The voice suddenly lacked its soft, southern lilt. "I know you're busy, dear, but come home when you can. And take care of yourself. You hear?"

Melissa hung up, feeling no better than before she'd made the call.

Melissa arrived at her apartment building that evening just as her friend, Ilona, reached it. She had met Ilona—a blond, vivacious, and engaging Hungarian with a flair for wit, conversation, and romance . . . and who admitted to fifty years—in the mail room just off the lobby. Until she'd met her, Melissa had never known anyone who kept a salon. You could always meet an assortment of artists, musicians, singers, dancers, and writers in Ilona's bachelor apartment. Most were European; all of them were interesting.

"Melissa, darling," Ilona said in her strong accent, "come with me for a coffee for a few minutes." Ilona drank hot espresso even on the hottest day.

"Okay, but only for a couple of minutes." They rode the crowded elevator in silence and didn't speak until they were inside Ilona's place.

"What's with you, darling?" Ilona called everybody "darling." "Who is the man?" Laughter tumbled from Melissa's throat, the first genuine merriment she'd felt since signing that contract.

"With you, it's always a man, Ilona. This time, you guessed right." She recounted her meeting that morning with Adam Roundtree.

"I don't understand," Ilona said.

"If I had passed up that contract, I might have had to declare bankruptcy. Now . . . well . . . Ilona, Adam Roundtree didn't know who I was, but when he found out, I could see the light dimming in his eyes. You see, back in the 1920s his grandfather and my grandfather pooled their money to prospect some unproductive Kentucky oil fields for natural gas. For some reason,

my grandfather pulled out, and six months later, Jacob Hayes
brought in gas. My grandfather claimed that the gas field belonged to both of them, but he lost the court case. The townspeople gossiped, and years later Adam's mother sued my family
for slander and won an apology. It's a mess. As far as I know,
the Hayes-Roundtree clan and my folks hadn't spoken in seventy years—until today when I met Adam Roundtree. You can't
mention their names in my father's house."

"And how do you feel about all this?"

"I don't carry grudges." Her weak smile must have reflected
her grim mood; for once, Ilona had no clever response. Ilona
brought their espresso coffee and some frozen homemade
chocolates, explaining that she hadn't made them and that she
never cooked.

"If I had been wearing my glasses this morning, I'd have
been better prepared for what I saw when I got close to Adam."
She thought that glasses didn't become her and wore them
only when absolutely necessary. Her laughter floated through
the apartment. "The truth is that if I could have seen him, I
wouldn't have been foolish enough to get that close to him."
She rose to leave, but Ilona detained her.

"Darling, what are you going to do about this man?"

Melissa shrugged. "Avoid him as much as possible."

"I'm sorry you feel that way," she said, "but I'd never give
up on that man."

"I'd like to see more of him but, knowing what I know, that
wouldn't be smart. I'd better go."

Melissa left Ilona and went home to get her dinner and review some contracts. Her face heated as she remembered what
she'd felt when she got a good look at Adam. He'd made her
feel . . . Recalling it embarrassed her. His smooth sepia skin
invited her touch, and when she'd looked into his warm brown
eyes, eyes that had a natural twinkle, she sensed herself being
lulled into a receptive mood, receptive to anything he might
suggest or do. Although twenty-eight, she had never experienced such a reaction to a man. His big frame had towered

over her five feet eight inches, but she hadn't been intimidated. Power. Flagrant maleness. He exuded both. Adam Roundtree was handsome . . . and dangerous. His eyes continued to twinkle, she recalled, even when his tone became cool.

Melissa arrived early at her office, drank a cup of tasteless machine coffee, and settled into her work. At about eight thirty, she answered her secretary's buzz.

"Yes, Kelly."

"Mr. Roundtree insists that he won't speak with anyone but you, and that if you refuse to talk to him, he'll void the contract. He says he knows other executive search firms; he's serious."

Melissa remembered Jason Court's deference to his boss. Void their contract? "Just let him try it," she told Kelly. "Put him on." She let him wait a second, but not so long as to seem rude. "How may I help you, Mr. Roundtree?"

"My name is Adam, Melissa, and you may help me by assuring me that you don't palm off your clients on your assistants. I'm paying enough to be able to speak with you directly. You left my office before I had an opportunity to tell you what you can trade off. I know what the contract says, but we may have to give a little, because I can't wait for a manager until you've checked every guy who's been close to a cow. Could we meet somewhere for lunch tomorrow, say around one thirty?"

"Does that mean I can check every gal who's been near a pig or an alligator?" she asked, alluding to other sources of leather. She heard him snort, but before he could answer, she agreed to meet him. "One o'clock would be better for me, and I like a light lunch. How about Thompson's?" He had to compromise, she figured. And why couldn't he discuss it right then? Adam's voice interrupted her thoughts.

"Alright. Thompson's at one. And Melissa, leave your armor in your office."

"Will do. And you leave your tough guy personality in yours."

"See you tomorrow." He hung up, and she thought she heard him make a noise. It couldn't have been a laugh. Maybe he had a hidden soft side, but if he did, she didn't want to be exposed to it—what she'd seen of him was more beguiling than she cared to deal with.

Melissa walked into her co-op apartment in Lincoln Towers, three blocks from Lincoln Center for the Performing Arts, closed the door, and thanked God for the cool, refreshing air. She got a glass of orange juice from the refrigerator, took it into the living room and drank it while she watched the six o'clock news. After a few minutes her mind wandered to Adam Roundtree, and she switched off the television. She disliked driven, overachieving, corporate males. Gilbert Lewis had been one, a man with a timetable for everything. After "X" number of dinners, movies, and taxi rides, you either went to bed with him, or you were off of his list. She had told him to get lost when he gave her his stock ultimatum. She had stupidly fallen for him, and his attitude had hurt, but she'd kept her integrity. And now there was Adam Roundtree, a man whose impact on her when she met him was far more profound than any emotion Gilbert Lewis or any other man had ever induced.

Melissa wouldn't have admitted that she dressed with special care that morning, had the red linen dress that she wore only when she wanted to make an impression not been proof. If her parents knew she planned to have lunch with Adam Roundtree, they'd have conniptions. She'd never been able to please her father, and her mother only said and did that which pleased her husband. She stared at herself in the mirror and saw her mother's grayish brown eyes and her father's mulatto coloring—the result of generations of mulatto inbreeding—and prayed that that was as much like them as she'd ever be. One thing was certain—if her business went under, she would con-

sider it to have been due to her own shortcomings, not the
fault of some imagined enemy that could be conveniently
blamed the way her father always blamed the Hayeses and
Roundtrees for his succession of failures. She let her curly
hair hang down around her shoulders in spite of the summer
heat, picked up her briefcase, and went to work.

She arrived at Thompson's promptly at one to find Adam
leaning casually against the cashier's counter at the entrance
to the restaurant. Punctuality fitted what she'd seen of his personality, and it was a trait she admired. His piercing gaze and
that twinkle in his eyes fascinated her, and she realized she'd
better get used to him—and quick—or he'd be laughing at her.
She shook his hand and greeted him with seeming casualness,
but the feel of his big hand splayed in the middle of her back
as he steered her to their table was a test she could have happily
forgone.

Melissa's heavy lashes shot upward, and she gasped in surprise at the dozen yellow roses on their table. She glanced
quickly at Adam, opened the attached note, and read: "My
apologies for not having done this Tuesday rather than ask you
to come to my office. Forgiven? Adam."

Unable to associate the man with the soft gesture, she
merely stared at him.

"Well?"

Melissa glanced downward to avoid his piercing gaze with
its suggestive twinkle, certain that he discerned the flutter in
her chest.

"Thanks. It's a lovely gesture."

Immediately he replaced his diffidence with his usual businesslike mein.

"Well, did you bring it?"

"Did I bring what?" she asked. His tone was jocular, but
she wasn't certain that it depicted his mood. She suspected

that, with him, what you saw and even what you thought you heard might mislead you.

"Did you bring your armor?" She wanted to glare at him but didn't trust herself to look straight into his eyes long enough to make it effective.

"It's always close by," she told him with studied sweetness, "but I'm not wearing it out of deference to your sensitive, gentle self." He laughed. The dancing glints in his eyes matched both his softened face and the smile that framed his even white teeth, and hot sparks shot through her, his transformation very nearly electrifying her. He broke it off at once, and she had the feeling that laughing wasn't something that he did often.

"When did you last laugh?" She watched him quirk an eyebrow and then frown.

"Not recently. What made you ask?"

She narrowed her eyes, squinting to get a good look, and shrugged her shoulder. "You didn't seem comfortable doing it." He laughed again, and she realized that he surprised himself when he did it.

Melissa controlled the urge to laugh along with him, reminding herself that she couldn't afford to be captivated by his mercurial personality—they were there to discuss business. *Her* business. He sat erect suddenly, all semblance of good humor banished. She needn't have been concerned, she told herself, because he had his own techniques for keeping people at a distance. And right then, his method was to serve his charm in small doses.

"Why did you need to see me in person?" she asked him. Did the twinkle in his eyes become brighter, or was she mistaken? She wished she could look somewhere else.

"My father managed Leather and Hides in his own way, ignoring the latest techniques and machinery. He made a good product, the best, but he's gone now, and he didn't leave a manual. I need a manager who can deal with that, who can make the business a state-of-the-art operation without sacrificing the quality that my father achieved. And I want an increase in productivity. We need to work together if I'm going to get what I'm looking for."

"What are you willing to give up?"

He listed several traits that she considered minor.

"Okay. Now I'd like to eat my salad." She looked down at her food and began to eat, but she knew he was glaring at her.

"Melissa, do I automatically ring your bell, or are you planning to carry on this ridiculous family feud?"

"I could ask you that."

"You ring something, alright, but I'd hardly call it a bell. As for the rest, I chart my own course. I alone decide what I think and how I act, and my criteria for judging people don't include reference to their forebears."

"I can buy that. But with all their weaknesses, parents and siblings are very important, and it isn't easy or comfortable to turn one's back on them." She could have kicked herself for that statement—after all, her thoughts about her family were not his business. "Why are you staring at me?" she asked him.

He seemed momentarily perplexed. "I didn't realize I was. My common sense tells me I'd never forget a woman like you, but there's something . . . Do you get the impression that we've met before . . . under unusual circumstances?"

"No. To my knowledge, I saw you yesterday for the first time. Why do you think we met somewhere else?"

"Just a feeling I have. When you were speaking softly about your family, your voice reminded me of someone and something special. Forget it. It's probably just my imagination. Well, I've enjoyed our lunch, Melissa. Are you going to take my calls, or will I have to use blackmail again?"

She didn't look at him. With that teasing tone, she could imagine the expression in his eyes. "Blackmail. But try something more original next time." They both laughed, and she realized she liked him.

* * *

Adam told Melissa good-bye and walked briskly toward his office. In spite of the heat he didn't want to go inside. He had a strange and uncomfortable feeling that something important was about to occur. It was like smelling a storm in the scent of the wind. Melissa Grant did not fit a mold, at least not one with which he was familiar. She wasn't beautiful, but something about her grabbed him, embedded itself in him. He'd often wondered if he would ever feel for a woman what he'd felt the first time he saw her, wondered whether there would ever be a graceful, intelligent woman who'd bring him to heel. He had an irritating certainty that she could. She'd made him laugh, too, not once but three times, and it had felt good. The loud horn blast of a red Ford alerted him to the changing traffic light, and he stepped back to the curb and waited under the blazing sun. Melissa respected him, he reflected, but she wasn't afraid of him, and he didn't know many men about whom he could say that. But she was a professional associate, *and she was a Grant.*

Several days later at their regular Monday morning conference, Adam questioned Jason Court about Melissa. He wanted to know what progress she'd made, but he had other queries, too.

"Jason, why did you choose MTG for this search? I'm not displeased, just interested." He had to know exactly what Melissa's relationship was to Jason, and he scrutinized the man for any shred of evidence that he had a personal interest in her.

"MTG placed me in this job, Adam. I presume since you've just met her that my predecessor negotiated the terms. Anyway, she impressed me with her efficiency and manners. She's thorough. She's competent. If you answer all of her questions truthfully, you won't have a secret when she's through with you."

"Oh, I don't doubt that." So there was nothing personal between them. Good. He recalled her reaction to him when they met; if any other man was interested in Melissa Grant, he was out of luck.

Adam watched Jason tilt his head to one side, as if making certain of his words, before he said, "She's not bad on the eyes, but she's nearsighted as all hell. Man, she can't see a thing from a distance of five feet, and when she does wear glasses, they're on top of her head instead of on her eyes." Adam couldn't control the laughter that erupted from his chest. His head went back, and he laughed aloud, causing Jason to gape at him, apparently stunned.

"What's so funny, Adam? That's the first time I've heard you laugh in the four years I've been working for you."

Adam stood, effectively terminating the meeting. "You don't want to know, Jason. Believe me, you don't." He went to his office, closed the door, and enjoyed a good laugh. The morning she'd come to his office, Melissa hadn't seen him clearly until she was close enough to touch him, and what she saw must have sent her hormones into a tailspin. At least it was mutual.

The flashing phone lights brought him out of his heretofore unheard-of indulgence in reverie. "Roundtree." He'd hoped it was Melissa calling to say that she had found a prospect, but it was his younger brother, Wayne.

"I've engaged a search firm to find a head for Leather and Hides, Wayne. Yes, I know you're not keen on headhunters, but it's the most efficient way to get the kind of person we want." He didn't mention that he'd hired Melissa Grant to do the job; time enough when the bimonthly report circulated. He wasn't ready to take on Wayne and his mother, especially his mother, about dealing with a Grant or a Morris. Mary Hayes Roundtree would go to her grave despising the Morrises and Grants. Such a waste of emotion! He got up from his desk and began to pace. Wayne was asking a lot of him. The telephone cord reached its limit and halted Adam's pacing.

"You're suggesting that I leave my firm here in New York and spend three months in Frederick reorganizing Hayes/ Roundtree Enterprises? But I've just been made full partner,

Wayne—this is hardly the time to amble off for a few months leave of absence. I know you have your hands full with the paper, but I'll have to give this some thought and get back to you."

A leave of absence. He could do it, though he disliked leaving his department in the hands of another person, even Jason Court. But what choice did he have? Wayne wouldn't suggest it if there was a way around it. His brother couldn't continue to manage both the leather factory and the newspaper. He needed that manager. He walked around to Jason's office, thinking of the fallout when their families learned of that contract.

That question plagued Melissa as she prepared and ate a light supper and mused over the day's events. The telephone ended her reverie, and one of her father's demands greeted her hello, shattering her good mood.

"Daddy, I know you think my business is child's play, but it has supported me well for five years, and I've never asked you for help. Can't you at least credit me with that?" Wrong tactic, she knew at once: independence was precisely what he sought to deny her. "I can't leave my business and go back home. And I don't want to."

"Your mother needs you," he replied, emphasizing the words this time as if to say, "You wouldn't dare disobey me."

Scoffing, she ignored his words. She didn't wonder that her brother, Schyler, had taken a job overseas to avoid the emasculating effects of their father's dominance, overprotectiveness, and indulgence.

"Daddy, I'm running a business here. I hire three people full time. I can't close my business like that"—she snapped her finger—"and leave them and my clients stranded. I have contracts to fulfill."

"But your mother's been feeling poorly, and I want you to

come home. You don't have to work—I'll take care of you. You come home."

"Don't my responsibilities mean anything to you, Father?" Melissa wanted to kick herself—he knew she always called him Father when he managed to make her feel like a small child.

His answer didn't surprise her. "What's an employment agency? Anybody can run that. You come home where you belong." Why had she expected anything different? He could as well hire a companion for her mother, and if she went home, he probably wouldn't even realize she was there. And if her mother needed anyone, it was her husband, the man who ignored her at home but played the besotted husband in public.

Her father hadn't wanted a girl and had ignored her, but he doted on her brother, and her mother seemed to love whatever and whomever her father loved, because she hadn't the will to confront or defy her domineering husband. Resentment coursed through her. No matter what she did, her father wasn't satisfied with her. And now he demanded that she give up the life she'd made for herself. For as long as she could remember, she had done everything she could to please him, but whenever he needed something he imposed on her, never on his precious Schyler.

"I'll go down and see Mother," she told him, "but I'll have to come back." He hung up, and she knew he was furious, but for once she didn't care. Immediately shame and remorse overcame her for having thought unkindly about her family. Family was important—Rafer Grant held that premise sacred and had taught her to do the same. She mulled over her father's suggestion; perhaps moving back to Maryland might not be such a bad idea. She could care for her mother, and computers and fax machines would enable her to run her business from there. She'd also have lower overhead, and she'd be away from the temptation of Adam Roundtree.

Two

Several days later, frustrated by the poor caliber of the applicants she'd contacted, Melissa answered the phone without waiting for her secretary to screen the call.

"MTG."

"Melissa? Adam. You must have guessed that it was me. Otherwise you wouldn't have picked up, right?" What had come over him? She'd had the impression that he didn't joke much, but that if he did, his words had an important, second meaning.

"Well?"

His voice carried a tantalizing urgency that challenged her to open up to him, but the very idea put her on guard, and she shifted in her chair. He had to be thirty-four or -five and couldn't have reached that age without knowing his effect on people, especially women. Well, if he wanted to play cat and mouse, fine with her, but she was not going to be the mouse.

"Sure thing," she bantered. "Didn't you know that I'm a psychic?" She wasn't, but let him think about *that*.

"You disillusion me. I thought you answered because you're on my wavelength, but I've been wrong a few times. How are you getting along?"

"Just fine."

"You have some good prospects? That's great."

"I don't have any prospects, but I'm just fine." Silence greeted her delicate laugh. "Adam, what happened to that sense of humor you had a minute ago? Don't tell me that it only operates at somebody else's expense?" Before he could reply, she asked him, "You wanted something?"

"I told you. I want to know how you're getting along with the search."

"Adam, when I have a candidate, I'll contact Jason Court."

"Are you saying you prefer speaking with Court?"

Melissa's sigh, long and deep, was intended to warn him of her exasperation. "I'm assuming that you're too busy to deal with so insignificant a matter as a head hunt." Where was her brain? How could she have told him that he was paying her an exorbitant fee for an insignificant service?

Adam's thoughts must have parallelled hers, because he spoke in clipped tones. "I didn't realize you thought so little of the service you provide." Did his voice reflect bitterness? She wasn't sure.

"I'm sorry, Adam. It wasn't my intention to imply that I don't take your needs seriously."

"Now you see why I dislike discussing business on the telephone. If I had been looking at you, I wouldn't have mistaken your intent. Have lunch with me, and let's straighten this out."

"Adam, I don't see that there's anything to straighten out. Anyway, you probably won't enjoy lunch with me. I don't care much for power executives and two-hour lunches."

He spoke more slowly, and his tone suggested that he didn't like what she'd said. Why did the worst in her always seem to come out when she talked with him? She reckoned that, no matter how much the corporate giant he was, he had feelings, and she didn't want to hurt him.

"I take it you don't care for executive men. Why?"

"It isn't that I dislike them—I understand them."

He winced, and she had no trouble figuring out what he'd thought of that. Not much.

"I wasn't aware that we were all alike," he replied with pronounced sarcasm. Then he asked her, "Melissa, when you signed our contract, did you know I was a member of the Hayes-Roundtree family in Beaver Ridge, Maryland?"

"Yes, I knew." She'd been expecting the question and had wondered why he hadn't asked earlier. That was one thing she had decided she liked about him—he didn't waste time speculating if he could get the facts. "I run a business, Adam, and I try to give my clients good service. If I think I can find them the kind of employee they want, I take the job. I don't hold one person responsible for what another did." The words had barely left her mouth when she realized her mistake.

His low, icy tone confirmed it. "Moses Morris's accusation was false and unconscionable, and that was proved in court."

"I'm sorry I alluded to that. I'd rather not discuss it. As far as I'm concerned, the matter was over seventy years ago."

"No. You won't state where you stand on that issue, though you know it's important. You'll evade it just like you walked out of my office without completing our discussions the day I met you. Avoid the heat, lady. That way you can stay calm, unruffled, unscathed, and above it all."

She couldn't tell from his voice whether she had angered him or saddened him, but she wouldn't let him browbeat her. "You're very clever to have learned so much about me in the . . . let's see, two and a half hours that you've been in my presence. The arrogance of it boggles my mind, Adam. Well, let me tell you that I hurt as badly as the next Joe or Jane, and I bleed when I get cut, just like you do."

"Look, I didn't mean to— Melissa, this was a friendly call. I wanted to get to know you. I . . . We'll talk another time."

Her gaze lingered on the telephone after she hung up, annoyed with herself for having revealed such an intimacy to Adam. She could hardly believe that he'd been so accurate. She'd gotten out of his office that morning to preserve her professionalism, but for reasons other than he'd said. His effect on her had been mesmerizing, and she'd had no choice but to flee or lose her poise. She couldn't allow him to regard her as just so much fluff—she headed a flourishing business, and she wanted that fact impressed on him.

Adam replaced the receiver with more care than usual and stared at the blank wall facing his desk. He didn't want to feel compassion for Melissa; she'd made a solid enough impression on him as it was. It was one thing to want her, but if he also began to care about her feelings, he'd be in trouble. He had close women friends, but he didn't allow himself to become emotionally involved with them. One woman had taught him to need her, to yearn for her, but foolish boy that he'd been, he had believed her seductive lies and gone back for more. Her full breast and ripe brown nipples were the first he'd ever seen. She had guided his lips to them while she stroked him, and he'd gone crazy. How could he have known that she only wanted to humiliate him? After nineteen years her vicious laughter still rang in his ears. *Not again.* Yet his life lacked something vital: a loving woman with whom he could share everything, the deepest desire of his soul; a home warm with a woman's touch, devoid of the chrome and black leather sofas that decorators loved. And children. He shook his head. Just so much wishful thinking.

He left work late, grabbed a hot dog from his friend, who sold them at a corner pushcart, and made his way to the Metropolitan Museum of Art. He enjoyed the concerts there. People went because they appreciated the music, not because it was the chic thing to do, and they didn't applaud halfway through a piece. At intermission he strolled out to the hallway for a stretch and a look at the crowd. Was he seeing correctly? He wouldn't have thought that Melissa would attend a concert alone. Maybe she was waiting for someone. He watched her, undetected, and saw that she didn't have a date. Just as he decided to speak to her, she looked directly at him, surprise mirrored in her eyes, and flashed him a cool smile.

* * *

Melissa watched Adam walk toward her, a gazelle in slow motion, and resisted the urge to smile. He must collect women the way squirrels gather nuts, she mused. She told herself not to be captivated by his dark good looks, his blatant masculinity, but she sucked in her breath as he neared her and wished that she'd taken off her distance glasses at the beginning of inter- mission.

She couldn't hide her surprise at seeing him there alone. What had happened to the New York City women that such a man as Adam Roundtree attended concerts by himself? She decided not to comment on it, not to rile him, since he seemed more relaxed, less formal than previously, though she sensed a tight- ness about him. Her heart lurched in her chest as his slow, captivating smile spread over his handsome ebony face. She wasn't a shy person, but she had to break eye contact with him in order to control her reaction. When her glance found him again, he had nearly reached her, and she had to steel herself against the impact of his nearness. *What was wrong with her?*

Adam held out his hand to her, and she took it, but they didn't shake—though that was what he seemed to have in- tended. Instead he held her hand, and they looked at each other. His gaze burned her until her nervous fingers reached for the top button of her blouse. What is it about him? she asked herself. He spoke first.

"The auditorium is barely half full. Why don't we sit to- gether for the remainder of the concert?" She didn't want to sit with him, and she didn't want him holding her hand. Tremors ploughed through her when he touched her. She eased her fingers from his—feeling as though he'd just branded her—opened her mouth to refuse, and had half turned from him when another familiar voice caught her at- tention. Gilbert Lewis sauntered toward them.

"Yo, Melissa. I saw you sitting by yourself. I'm going for a drink, mind if I join you?" The man glanced up at Adam. "Or are you busy?" She wondered if he would have suggested it had she been alone.

"Excuse me, Gilbert. I'm with Mr. Roundtree." She watched Gilbert Lewis walk away and thought how long she'd waited for that small measure of revenge. Small, but priceless. If a man saw a woman with Adam Roundtree, he knew he didn't have an iota of a chance. The lights blinked, signaling the end of intermission, and Adam touched her elbow to guide her to their seats. She stepped away, but he trapped her.

"Have a good look at me, Melissa, so that you won't try this trick with me again. I'm not accustomed to being used, Melissa, because nobody dares it. If you didn't want that man's company, you could have told him so. You said you're with me—and lady—*you are with me.* Let's get our seats before the music begins." He walked them to their seats. Chastened, she explained.

"Adam, if you knew how much that scene meant to me, you wouldn't grumble."

His tone softened. "Are you going to tell me?"

She laughed. "You're a hard man, aren't you? Not an inch do you give."

His shrug didn't fool her that time, because his eyes denied the motion. "If it suits you to think that, I wouldn't consider disabusing you of the idea." At least he smiled, she noted with satisfaction. They took their seats, and she turned to him as the curtain opened. "You realize, of course, that if I didn't want to sit with you, I'd be over there somewhere, don't you?" She nodded toward some empty seats across the aisle. He patted her hand, and his words surprised her.

"I should think so. If you were the type to allow yourself to be steamrollered, you'd be less interesting."

They stepped out of the great stone building, J. Pierpont Morgan's grand gift to the city, and into the sweltering night. Several men removed their jackets, but not Adam. Her glance shifted to him, cool and apparently unaffected. She wondered how he did it. She had the impression that he didn't allow anything, including the weather, to interfere with his adherence to the standards he'd set for himself.

The swaying trees along the edge of Central Park provided a welcomed, if warm, breeze as they walked down Fifth Avenue, but as though they had slipped into private worlds, neither spoke until they reached the corner and waited for the light to change.

"It's early, yet," Adam observed. "Let's stop somewhere for a drink." If he hadn't been staring down at her, she reasoned, saying no would have been easier. But a smile played around his lips almost as if he harbored a delicious secret—she didn't doubt that he did—and the twinkle in his eyes dared her to be reckless.

She voiced a thought that tempered her momentary foolhardiness. "Adam, if anybody in Beaver Ridge or Frederick saw us walking together, they'd be certain the world was coming to an end."

"Why?" he asked, taking her arm as they crossed the street, "we're not holding hands." She was grateful that he wasn't looking at her and couldn't see her embarrassment, but she needn't have worried, she realized, because his thoughts were elsewhere.

"Melissa, why did you agree to find a manager for me if you knew who I was?"

"What happened between our grandfathers was unfortunate, Adam, and it is one legacy that I don't intend to pass on to my children. I've never been able to hate anyone, and I'm glad, because hatred is as crippling as any disease. Believe me—I've seen enough of it. Anyway, why shouldn't I have taken your business?" she hedged, unwilling to lie. His large retainer had been her salvation. "I operate a service that you needed and for which you were willing to pay." She looked up at him and added, "It's tempting to walk through the park, but that wouldn't be safe even with you. How much over six feet are you, Adam?"

"Four inches. How much under it are you?"

"Four inches." He stopped walking and looked down at her. "How much under thirty are you?"

"Two years." Her lips curled into a smile. "How much over it are you?"

"Four years." He grasped her hand and threaded her fingers with his own.

Each time she was with him, he exposed a little more of himself, she realized. His wry wit and unexpected teasing appealed to her—she liked him a lot. Pure feminine satisfaction enveloped her. Here was a man who was strong and self-reliant, sure of himself, who didn't need to blame others for his failures, if he had any. She shook her head as though to clear it. Adam Roundtree could easily become an addiction. And she knew that part of his appeal was his contrast with her father. Adam was direct, fair, but her father tended to be manipulative, at least with her. Adam was a defender, but for all his accomplishments, Rafer Grant was a user.

"Where are we going for this drink? We're walking toward my place, but we could go over to Madison and find a cafe or bar. There's no reason to go further out of your way."

"Stop worrying, Melissa. I recognize your status as my equal—well, almost." A glance up at him told her that the twinkle carried humor. "We *are* walking my way. I live on Broadway just across from Lincoln Center." When she showed surprise, he slowed his steps.

"Where do you live, Melissa?"

She laughed. "Four blocks from you, in Lincoln Towers."

They took the bus across Central Park, stopped at a coffeehouse on Broadway, and idled away three-quarters of an hour.

"How long have you lived away from home?" he asked between sips of espresso.

"Since I left for college. A little over ten years."

"Do you miss it?"

She thought for minute. "No. I guess not. Our home life was less than ideal." Hot little needles shimmied through her veins when his hand reached across the tiny table and clasped hers, reassuring her. She knew right then that he'd protect her if she let him.

"I'm sorry." His words were soft. Soothing. She wouldn't

have thought him capable of such gentleness. "That must have been difficult for you," he added.

"Oh, it wasn't all bad. From time to time, I got lovely surprises that brightened my life."

"Like what?"

"Let's see. The occasional rose that I'd find on my dresser. The little crystal bowl of lavender potpourri that would appear in my bathroom. Books of poetry under my pillow. I remember I was so happy to find 'The Song of Hiawatha' there that I read it and cried with joy half the night."

His strong fingers squeezed hers in a gentle caress. "Who was this silent angel?"

"My mother."

His perplexed expression didn't surprise her, but she was glad that he didn't question her further. He looked at her for a moment, then shook his head as though dismayed. "Ready to go?"

She nodded. As they left, he took her hand, intensifying her wariness of him and of what she sensed growing between them.

"Walk you home?" he asked her. She wanted to prolong the time with him but thought of the consequences and tried to extricate her fingers from his, but he held on and then squeezed affectionately. Warmth flowed through her, a warmth that strengthened her, invigorated her, and enhanced her sense of self. She noticed couples, young and old, among the late evening strollers, some of whom were obviously lovers, enraptured, in their own world. Some seemed to argue, to be ill at ease in their relationship. Others appeared to have been together so long that complacency best described them, but they all held hands. Like small children clutching their security blankets, she mused. When they reached the building in which she lived, Adam assumed a casual air and looked down at her, silently awaiting a signal for his next move. What a cautious man, she thought as she prepared to head off any gesture of intimacy on his part. Though wary of the guaranteed effect of his touch, she extended her hand.

"It's been nice, Adam. Since we've just had coffee, I won't invite you for more. Maybe we'll meet again."

His displeasure wasn't concealed by the dancing light in his eyes, she noted. "Are you always so cut and dried?" When I'm nervous, yes, she thought. Without waiting for her answer, he went on. "Your tendency to dismiss people could be taken as rudeness. Why are you so concerned with protecting yourself? Trust me, Melissa. I can read a woman the way fortune-tellers read tea leaves. You'd like this evening to continue, but you've convinced yourself that it wouldn't be in your best interest, and you have the fortitude necessary to terminate it right now. I like that."

He grinned. She hadn't seen him do that before, and she couldn't decide what to make of it. Why didn't he leave? She didn't want to stand there with heat sizzling between them. Tension gripped the back of her neck, and her hair seemed to crackle with electricity when he took a step closer. She moved, signaling her withdrawal from him, and he pinned her with the look of a man who knows every move and what it symbolizes. His brazen gaze told her that her reprieve was temporary, that he knew she was susceptible to him, and that he could easily get her cooperation in knowing him more intimately. Her blood raced when his right hand dusted her cheek just before he nodded and walked away.

Melissa closed her apartment door, leaned against it, and sighed with relief. Adam Roundtree was quintessential male. An alluring magnet. But she wasn't fool enough to ruin her life—at least she hoped not. But the uneasy feeling persisted that Adam Roundtree got whatever he wanted, and that her best chance of escaping him was if he didn't want her. Just the thought of belonging to a man like him was drugging, a narcotic to her libido. With his height, fat-scarce muscular build and handsome dark face, and those long-lashed bedroom eyes with their brown hazel-rimmed irises, he was a charismatic knock-out. Add to that his commanding presence and . . . A long breath escaped her. She recalled his squared, stubborn chin and the personality that it suggested and concluded that if he softened up and stayed that way, he would be a trial for any woman. She heard the telephone as she entered her apartment, and excitement boiled up in her at the thought that Adam could be calling her from the lobby.

Her hello brought both a surprise and a disappointment. "I thought we agreed that you wouldn't call me again, Gilbert."

"You suggested it," he said, "but I didn't agree." At one time she couldn't have imagined that this man's voice would fail to thrill her or that her blood wouldn't churn at the least evidence of his interest.

"You don't say." His weary sigh was audible. Women didn't dangle Gilbert Lewis, and she found his impatience with her disinterest amusing.

"Well, if you didn't agree, what's your explanation for this long hiatus? Do you think I've been twiddling my thumbs waiting to hear from you?" She didn't approve of toying with a person's feelings, but where Gilbert was concerned, she didn't have a sense of guilt—if he had feelings, he hadn't made that fact known to her. She grinned at his reply.

"Honey, you don't know how many times I've tried to reach you, but you're never home. Let's get together. I'm giving a black tie party next Saturday, and I want you to come. And bring Roundtree." The latter was posed as an afterthought, but she knew it was the reason for his call. Ever the opportunist, Gilbert Lewis had called because he wanted to meet Adam Roundtree. He had no more interest in her that she had in him.

"And if Adam has other plans, may I come alone or bring someone else?" She had evidently surprised him, and his sputters delighted her, because she'd never known him to be speechless.

"Well," he stammered, "I've always wanted to meet the guy. See if you can get him to come." She imagined that her laughter angered him, but he was too proud to show it. When she could stop laughing, she answered him.

"Gilbert, you couldn't have been this transparent four years ago. If you were, there must have been more Maryland hayseed in my hair than I thought. Be a good boy, and stick to your kind of woman. I'm not one of them." She hung up feeling cleansed. What a difference! Her thoughts went to Adam. That man would never expose himself to ridicule or scorn.

Minutes after he left her, Adam sat at a small table in the Lincoln Center plaza drinking Pernod, absently watching the lighted waters spray upward in the famous fountain. Across the way, the brilliant Chagall murals begged for his attention, offering an alternative to his musings about Melissa Grant, but he could think only of her. His strong physical reaction to her mystified him. He sipped the last of his drink, paid for it, and walked across the street to his high-rise building.

"This has to stop," he muttered to himself. He'd never mixed business with pleasure, but when they'd reached her apartment building, he had wanted more than the coffee she refused to offer or a simple kiss—he'd wanted her. She would never know how badly. Sound sleep eluded him that night. Another new experience. Like a flickering prism, Melissa danced in and out of his dreams. Awakening him. Deserting him. And waking him up again.

Adam walked into his adjoining conference room promptly at eight o'clock to find coffee and, as he expected, his senior staff waiting for him. Their normal business completed, he detained them.

"Where might an abusive man look for a woman who'd defied him and escaped his brutality?" he asked the group. Anywhere but a small town was the consensus. He returned to his office and began redrafting plans for a women's center in Hagerstown, Maryland, an unlikely place for one. His secretary walked into his office.

"Are you planning to open another one?" He nodded, explaining that "this is more complicated and more ambitious than our place in Frederick."

Her gaze roamed over him, with motherly pride, it seemed. "If you need help with this, I'll work overtime at no cost to you. It's a wonderful thing you do for these poor women, supporting these projects from your private funds."

He leaned back in his big leather chair. "I can afford to pay you, Olivia, and I will. You do enough for charity."

"Pshaw," she demurred. "What I do is nothing compared to the help you give people. These homes for abused women, that hospital ward for seriously ill children, and the Lord knows what else. God is going to bless you—see if He doesn't."

He shook his head, rejecting the compliment. "I'm fortunate. It's better to be in a position to give than to be on the dole." Abruptly he changed the topic. "Olivia, what do you think of Melissa Grant? Think she'll find me a manager for Leather and Hides?"

"Yes. She seemed very businesslike. Real professional. Anyhow, I trust your judgment in hiring her. When it comes to people, you don't often make mistakes."

Adam slapped his closed left fist into the palm of his right hand. Not in the last fifteen years, he hadn't, but the thought pestered him that where Melissa was concerned he was ripe for a blunder of the first order.

Melissa. He had the sense that he'd been with her before. She reminded him of a woman he'd danced with in costume one New Year's Eve. He'd been dancing with the woman, but at exactly midnight she'd disappeared, leaving an indelible impression. As farfetched as it seemed, whenever Melissa spoke in very soft tones, he thought of that unknown woman. Perhaps he'd wanted the woman because she was mysterious. His blood still raced when he thought of her. Warm. Soft. He'd like to see her at least once more. Yet he wanted Melissa. He rubbed the back of his neck. His elusive woman was at least two, maybe three, inches shorter than Melissa, but he couldn't dismiss the similarity in allure.

He picked up the business section of *The Maryland Journal* and noted that the price of sweet crude oil had increased more rapidly than the cost of living index. His folks were no longer in the natural gas business and had sold their property in Kentucky, so fuel prices didn't concern him, but every day his family had to combat the scandal brought on by Moses Morris's unfair accusation of seventy years earlier. Anger toward the Grants and Morrises surged in him as he reflected on how their maltreatment had shortened his grandfather's life and embittered his mother. His passion for Melissa cooled, and he strengthened his resolve to stay away from her.

He dictated a letter pressuring Melissa to find the manager at once, though the contract specified one month. He rationalized that he wasn't being unfair, that he was in a bind and she should understand.

Several hours later Adam told himself that he would not behave dishonorably toward Melissa or anyone else, that he should have investigated MTG and identified its president. He tore up the letter and pressed the intercom.

"Olivia, get Jason for me, please." Melissa hadn't been in touch with Jason, and that riled him. He paced the floor of his office as he tried to think of a justifiable reason to telephone her. Finally, he gave up the idea, left his office and went to the gym, reasoning that exercise should clear his head. But after a half hour, having conceded defeat, he stopped as he passed a phone on his way out and dialed her number.

Adam held his breath while the phone rang. She's in my blood, he acknowledged and wondered what he'd do about it.

"Melissa Grant speaking."

"Have dinner with me tonight. I want to see you."

She had dressed when he arrived at her apartment. He liked that, but he noticed her wariness about his entering her home.

He didn't put her at ease—if she didn't want to be involved with him, she had reason to be cautious, just as he had. It surprised him that she didn't question why he'd asked her to dinner, and he didn't tell her, reasoning that she was a smart woman and old enough to divine a man's motives. He'd selected a Cajun restaurant in Tribeca, and it pleased him that she liked his choice.

"I love Cajun food. Don't you think it's similar to soul food?"

He thought about that for a bit. "The ingredients, yes, but Cajun's a lot spicier. A steady diet of blackened fish, whether red or cat, would eat a hole in your stomach. Reminds me of my first trip to Mexico. I'd alternate a mouthful of food with half a glass of water. I don't want that experience again. Come to think of it, that's what prompted me to learn to cook."

"You cook?"

He knew she wouldn't have believed it of him, and neither would any of his staff or business associates. "Of course I cook, Melissa. Why should that surprise you? I eat, don't I?"

"Aren't you surprised that we get on as well as we do?" she asked him. "Considering our backgrounds, I'd have thought it impossible."

He let the remark pass rather than risk putting a damper on a pleasant evening. Later they walked up Seventh Avenue to the Village Vanguard, but neither liked the avant-garde jazz offering that night, and they walked on.

Adam took her arm. "Let's go over to Sixth Avenue and Eighteenth or so. The Greenwich Village Singers are performing at a church over there, and we may be able to catch the last half of the program. Want to try?" She agreed, and at the end of the concert, Handel's *Judas Maccabeus,* he walked with her to the front of the church to shake hands with two acquaintances who sang with the group. While he spoke with a man, his arm went around her shoulder, automatically, as if it belonged there, and she moved closer to him. He glanced down at her and nodded, letting her know that he'd noticed and that

he acknowledged her move as natural, but he immediately reprimanded himself. He'd better watch that—he'd been telling
the man with whom he spoke that Melissa wasn't available,
and he had no right to do it.

"That was powerful singing," he remarked, holding her arm
as they started toward the front door. She nodded in agreement.
"That mezzo had me spellbound." He tugged her closer.

"Would you have enjoyed it as much if you hadn't been
with me?" She looked up at him just before a quip bounced
off of her tongue. She'd never seen a more serious face, but
she had to pretend that he was teasing her.

"I doubt it," she joked, "you're heady stuff."

"Be careful," he warned her, still serious. "I'm a man who
demands evidence of *everything.* If I'm heady stuff, you're one
hell of an actress." His remark stunned her, but she recovered
quickly.

"Oh, I've been in a drama or two. Back in grade school,
it's true, but I was good." Laughter rumbled in his throat, and
he stroked her fingers and told her, "You're one classy lady."

Melissa looked around her as they continued walking down
the aisle of the large church toward the massive baroque front
door and marveled that every ethnic group and subgroup
seemed to be represented there. She stopped walking to get
Adam's full attention. "Why is it," she asked him, "that races
and nationalities can sing together, play football, basketball,
tennis and whatever together, go to school and church together,
but as a group, they can't get along? And they make love
together—what's more intimate than that? You'd think if they
can do that, they can do anything together."

"But that's behind closed doors," he explained. "Two people
can resolve most anything if there's nobody around but them,
nobody to judge them or to influence them. Take us, for in-
stance. Once our folks get wind of our spending time together,

you'll see how easily a third person can put a monkey wrench in a relationship."

Melissa quickened her steps to match those of the man beside her. He must have noticed it, because he slowed his walk. Warmth and contentment suffused her, and when he folded her hand in his, she couldn't make herself remove it. Was the peace that seemed to envelop her the quiet before a storm? She couldn't remember ever having felt so carefree or so comfortable with anyone. Adam was honorable, she knew it deep down. But that didn't mean he wouldn't leave her to cope alone with the problems that they both knew loomed ahead if they continued to see each other.

As if he'd read her thoughts, he asked her, "Would your family be angry with you if they knew we spent time together?"

Looking into the distance, she nodded. "I'd say that's incontestable. Furor would be a better description of my father's reaction." She tried to lift her sagging spirits—only moments earlier they had soared with the pleasure of just being with him. He released her hand to hail a speeding taxi, and didn't take it again. She sat against the door on her side of the cab.

With a wry smile, Adam commented, "If you sat any farther away from me, you'd be outside of this cab. Scared?"

She gave him what she intended to be a withering look. "Of whom?"

"Well, if you're so sure of yourself," he baited, "slide over here."

"I read the story of 'Little Red Riding Hood,' " she told him solemnly, careful to maintain a straight face.

"Are you calling me a wolf?"

She was, she realized—and though he probably didn't deserve it, she refused to recant. "You used that word; I didn't. But I bet you'd be right at home in a wilderness." Or most other places, she thought.

She controlled the urge to lean into him, when his long fingers stroked the back of her neck. "Don't you know that men tend to behave the way women expect them to? Huh? Be careful, Melissa. I can howl with the best of them." Tremors of excitement streaked through her. What would he be like if he dropped his starched facade?

"What does it take to get you started?" she asked idly, voicing a private thought.

"One spark of encouragement from you." He flicked his thumb and forefinger. "Just that much, honey." She couldn't muffle the gasp that betrayed her.

"Move over here," he taunted. "Come on. See for yourself." Tempting. Seductive. Enticing her. The words dripping off of his smooth tongue in an invitation to madness. She clutched the door handle and prayed that he wouldn't touch her.

"Melissa."

She clasped her forearms tightly. "I'm happy right where I am." Her heart skittered at his suggestive, rippling laughter.

"You'd be a lot happier," he mocked, "if you closed this space between us."

"Speak for yourself."

"Believe me, honey," he purred, "I'm doing exactly that." If she didn't control the impulse, her fingers would find his and cling.

He took her key to open her door for her and held it as though weighing the consequences of alternative courses of action. After a few minutes during which he said nothing and she was forced to look into his mesmeric eyes while she fought rising desire, she had the impulse to tell him to do whatever he wanted—just get on with it. But seemingly against his will, as if he pulled it out of himself, he spoke.

"I'd like to spend some time with you, Melissa. I don't have loose strings in my personal life nor in my business affairs. I need to see whether our friendship, or whatever it is that prevents our staying away from each other, will lead anywhere. I'm not asking for a commitment, and I'm not giving one. But there's something special going on between us, and you know it, too. What do you say?"

"We'll see." Even if she hadn't already learned a lesson, she had good cause to stay away from Adam. The most optimistic person wouldn't give a romance between them a chance of maturing, because no matter how they felt about each other, their families' reactions would count for more. So that settled it—she wouldn't see him except with regard to business. But how could she be content not knowing what he'd be like if she let herself go and succumbed to whatever it was that dragged her toward him? Oh, Lord! Was she losing sight of the storm that awaited her when Rafer Grant learned of her passion for Adam Roundtree?

Adam awakened early the next morning after a sound and refreshing sleep. He'd made up his mind about Melissa, and as usual he didn't fight a war with himself about his decision. That was behind him. He suspected that given the chance, she'd wrestle with it as any thinking person in her circumstances would, but he didn't plan to give her much of a chance.

He scrambled out of bed as the first streaks of red and blue signaled the breaking dawn, showered, poured coffee from his automatic coffee maker, got a banana, and settled down to work. He liked Saturday mornings, because he was free to work on his charities, the projects whose success gave him the most pleasure. The Refuge, as the Rachel Hood Hayes Center for Women that was situated in Frederick was commonly known, had become overcrowded. He had to find a way to enlarge it and expand its services. His dilemma was whether to continue financing it himself or seek collaborative funds. If it were located in New York City or even Baltimore rather than Frederick, raising the money would be fairly simple, but corporations wouldn't get substantial returns from humanitarian investments in Frederick, and he couldn't count on their support.

He looked out of the window across Broadway and toward

the Hudson River, knowing that he wouldn't see Melissa's building. He had had years of impersonal relationships and loveless sex, and he had long since tired of it. After the humiliation of that one innocent adolescent attachment, he'd sworn never to be vulnerable to another woman. The lovers he'd had as a man had wanted to be linked with Adam Roundtree and regarded intimacy as a part of that. They hadn't attempted to know or understand him. Hadn't cared whether he could hurt or be disappointed. Hadn't dreamed that a hole within him cried out for a woman's love and caring. But Melissa was different. He sensed it. He *knew* it. He pondered what his mother would think of Melissa. She'd probably find reasons to shun her, he mused, and none of them would have anything to do with Melissa herself. Mary Hayes Roundtree was bitterly opposed to the Morris/Grant people for having vilified her family's name without cause. And he suspected that Melissa's fair complexion might bother her, too—his mother liked to trace her roots back to Africa, and she ignored all the evidence of miscegenation that he could see in the Hayes family. A muscle twitched in his jaw. He couldn't and wouldn't allow his mother's preferences and prejudices to influence his life.

He spent an hour on his personal accounts, then lifted the receiver and dialed her number.

"Hi. I mean, hello."

He could barely understand the mumbled words. "Hi. Sorry to wake you, but I've been up for hours. Want to go bike riding?"

"Biking?" The sound resembled a lusty purr, and he could almost see her stretching languorously, seductively. "Call me back in a couple of days."

"Come on, sleepyhead, get up. Life's passing you by."

"Hmmm. Who is this?" He had a sudden urge to be there, leaning over her, watching her relaxed and inviting, seeing her soft and yielding without her defenses. Her deep sigh warned him that she was about to drop the receiver.

"This is Adam." He heard her feet hit the floor as she jumped up.

"Who? Adam? Bicycle?" A long pause ensued. "Adam, who would have thought you were sadistic?"

"I didn't know I was. Want to ride with me? Come on. Meet me at the bike shop in an hour."

"Where is it?"

"Not far from you. Broadway at Sixty-fifth Street. Eat something."

"Okay."

They rode leisurely around Central Park, greeting the few bikers and joggers they encountered in the still cool morning. Melissa knew a rare release, an unfamiliar absence of concerns. It was as if she had shed an outer skin that she hadn't known to be confining but the loss of which had gained her a welcomed freedom. She looked over at the man who rode beside her, at his dark muscular legs and thighs glistening with faint perspiration from their hour's ride and at the powerful arms that guided the bike with such ease. From her limited experience, she had always believed that it was the man who wanted and who asked. She shook her head, wondering whether she was strange, decided that she wasn't, and let a grin crease her cheeks. Self-revelation could be pleasant.

"Let me in on it. What's funny?"

"Me." She replied and refused to elaborate, watching him from the corner of her right eye. He slowed their pace and headed them toward the lake. At the shed he locked and stored their bikes and rented a canoe for them. He rowed near the edge of the lake. The ducks made place for them amidst the water lilies, and some swam alongside the canoe, quacking, seemingly happy to provide entertainment. Melissa looked around them and saw that, except for the birds, they were alone. The cool, fresh morning breeze pressed her shirt to her skin, and she lowered her head in embarrassment when she realized he could see the pointed tips of her breasts. Her rest-less squirming seemed to intensify his fixation with her, and she had to employ enormous self-control to resist covering her breasts with her arm.

"Don't be shy," he soothed, "let me look at you. I've never before seen you so relaxed, so carefree."

"If you saw it all the time, you'd soon be fed up with it," she jested in embarrassment. "And maybe worse. One Latin poet, I believe his name was Plautus, said that anything in excess brings trouble."

His half smile quickened the twinkle of his eyes, and her hands clutched her chest as frissons of heat raced through her. "I prefer Mae West's philosophy," he taunted. "She said too much of a good thing is wonderful. You stick with Mister What's-his-name's view." Melissa stared at him. Did he know what he'd just done to her?

His eyes caressed her while she squirmed, rubbed her arms, and moistened her lips. As though enchanted, he dropped anchor and let the boat idle.

"You're too far away from me. If I wasn't sure this thing would capsize, I'd go down there and get you."

"And do what?" she challenged. Heat seemed to radiate from him, and she shivered in excited anticipation.

"When I finished, you'd never think of another man. You know you're playing with fire, don't you?" She wrinkled her nose in disdain.

"Keep it up," he growled, "and I'll go down there to you even if this thing sinks." The air crackled and sizzled around them, and she fought the feminine heat that stirred in her loins. Sweat poured down her face as his hot gaze singed her, but she struggled to summon a posture of indifference. Nose tilted upward and chin thrust forward, she teased him, her voice unsteady.

"Planning to rock the boat, are you? Well, if you let me drown, the Morrises and Grants will have your head."

She thrilled from head to toe as his laughter washed over

her, exciting her. "I'm scared to death, Melissa. I'm shaking in my Reeboks." Her right hand dipped into the lake as a duck swam by, and she brought up enough water to wet the front of his shirt.

"Lady, what do you think you're doing?"

"Cooling you off." She hoped she'd made him give her some room. She hadn't. He looked at her steadily and spoke without a trace of humor.

"If you think I'm hot now, Melissa, you're in for a big surprise."

Adam watched as her eyes widened and knew she was at a loss as to how to handle him. He regretted that—he wanted her to handle him and to enjoy doing it. He pulled up the anchor and began rowing. The trees heavy with green leaves and the quiet water provided the perfect background against which he could appreciate her beguiling loveliness. His fingers itched to replace the breeze that gently lifted her hair from her shoulders and neck, and his lips burned with the impulse to taste her throat, to . . . They had the lake to themselves. If he dared . . . He raised his gaze from the water surrounding them and caught the naked passion unsheltered in her eyes. Watched, flabbergasted, as she licked her lips. Desire sliced through him, and he had to fight to rein in his rampant passion.

He rowed back to the shed, surrendered their boat, and retrieved their bikes. He was in control, he assured himself. He could stop the relationship, walk away from it anytime he chose. Or he could have until he'd seen the heat in her eyes and the quivering of her lips—for him.

He stood in front of the building in which she lived, looking down at her, trying to keep his hands to himself. She squinted at him and licked her lips. Did she want him to . . . ? He ran his fingers over his short hair in frustration.

"Melissa, I . . . Look, I enjoyed this." He settled for banality, when what he needed to tell her was that he wanted her right then. She smiled in an absentminded way and responded to his meaningless remark: "Me, too."

Maybe he'd spend some time with Ariel on Sunday and get his desire for Melissa under control. Abstinence wasn't good for a man. He smiled grimly as he bade Melissa good-bye, admitting to himself that self-deception wasn't good for a man, either. The next morning, Sunday, it was Melissa whom he called.

Three

A soft sigh escaped Melissa when she awakened and realized that Adam wasn't with her, that she'd been dreaming, and that the glistening bronze male who'd held her so tenderly was an illusion. Had she leashed her emotions so tightly these past four years that her defenses against masculine seduction were weak and undependable, that a man, who'd never even kissed her, could take possession of her senses? She didn't think so. What was it about Adam? She reached for her glasses, looked at the clock, decided she could sleep another hour, and turned over. Wishful thinking. She answered the ringing phone.

"Hello," she murmured, half conscious of the seductive message in her low, sleepy tones.

"So you're awake. Thinking about me?"

"No," she lied. "I was thinking about the weather."

"First female I ever met who gets turned on by thoughts of the weather."

She frowned. He was too sure of himself. Then she heard his amused chuckle and couldn't suppress a smile, then a giggle, and finally a joyous laugh.

"Want some company? I want to see you while you're so happy. You're uninhibited when you first wake up, aren't you?"

"Why did you call?" She twirled the phone cord around her index finger and waited while he took what seemed an inordinate amount of time answering.

"I didn't intend to—it just happened. How about going to the Museum of Modern Art with me this afternoon? There's a show of contemporary painters that I'd like to see, and browsing in a museum is my favorite Sunday afternoon pastime. What do you say?"

"Depends. I'm going to church, and then I'm going to shoot pool for an hour." After his long silence, she asked him, "Are you speechless? Don't tell me I shocked you. Women do shoot pool, you know."

"Surprised, maybe, but it takes more than that to shock me. Should I come by for you, or do you want to meet me?"

"I'll meet you at the front door of the museum. One thirty."

She hung up and immediately the telephone rang, sending her pulse into a trot in anticipation of what he'd say.

"Mama! Are you alright? Why aren't you going to church this morning?"

"Oh, I am, dear, and I'm just fine. I wanted to say hello before your father and I leave home. Schyler called. He just got a promotion to vice president and head of the company's operations in Africa. I knew you'd want to know." They talked for a few minutes, but Melissa's pleasure at receiving her mother's call had ebbed. Her parents took every opportunity to boast of her brother's accomplishments. She hoped she wasn't being unfair, but if they boasted about her, she hadn't heard about it.

Melissa's status within her family was far from her thoughts while she roamed the museum with Adam. She could have done without many of the paintings, she decided, but an hour among them was a small price to pay for a stroll with Adam in the sculpture garden. She had to struggle not to betray her response when he slung an arm around her shoulder as they stood and looked at a Henry Moore figure, splayed his long fingers at her back as they walked, and held her hand while he leaned casually against a post, gazing at her with piercing intensity—letting her see that his plans for them included far greater intimacy than hand-holding. She had to conclude that Adam Roundtree was a thorough man, that he left nothing to chance. He'd said he wanted to find out if there could be anything between them, and he clearly meant it. He was also stacking the odds. He might need proof, but she knew they had the basis for a fiery relationship, and he couldn't want that anymore than she did, but he was in a different position. He was head of his family, and his folks might not try to censor him as hers surely would, but she couldn't believe he'd be willing to drag up those ancient hatreds.

Adam let his gaze roam over Melissa. Her wide yellow skirt billowed in the breeze, and he could see the outline of her bra beneath her knitted blouse. Her softly feminine casual wear appealed to him, made her body more accessible to his touch, his hands. He grasped her arm lightly. "I've got a friend in Westchester I'd like you to meet. Come with me." He sensed her reluctance before she spoke.

"I have to be home early—I've got a lot to do tomorrow."

"Come with me," he urged, his voice softer, lower. Persuasive. "Come with me." He watched her eyelids flutter before she squinted at him and insisted that she should go home. He knew she wanted to escape the intimacy between them, but he was determined to prolong it.

"I'll take you home early. Come with me."

She went.

They boarded the train minutes before its departure. Melissa didn't know what to make of Adam's mood, and his invitation to join him in a visit with a friend perplexed her. She was certain that he hadn't planned for them to go to Westchester when he'd called her that morning.

"Are we going to visit one of your relatives?"

Adam draped his right ankle across his left knee and leaned back in his seat. "If that were the case, Melissa, I'd warn you.

I would never spring a member of my family on you unexpectedly, and I think you know that. Winterflower is a very
special friend. You'll like her. She has an aura of peace about
her that's refreshing—the best preparation for the Monday
morning rat race that anybody could want. I go up to see her
as often as I can."

"How old is she?" She could see that the question amused
him.

"Oh, around fifty or fifty-five, I'd say. But I could be way
off—I don't make a habit of asking women their age."

"I got the impression from what you said a minute ago that
she's different. Is she?"

"In a way. Yes. Winterflower doesn't fight the world,
Melissa—she embraces it." He shrugged elaborately. "Flower
defies description . . . you have to experience her." So he had
a tonic for the New York rat race after all, she mused, pleased
that the woman wasn't his lover.

A tall Native American woman of about fifty greeted them
with a natural warmth. Adam introduced them, and Melissa
liked her at once.

"What are you two doing together?" she asked Adam before
telling him, "Never mind, it will work itself out. But you'll
both hurt a lot before it does."

Melissa watched, perplexed, as Adam hugged the woman
and then admonished her. "Now, Flower, I do not want to
know about the rough roads and slippery pebbles ahead, as
you like to put it. You told me about them three months ago."

The woman's benevolent smile was comforting, though her
words were not. "You're just coming to them." Melissa had a
strong sense of disquiet as Flower turned to her and extended
her hand. "It's good that you are not as skeptical as Adam is.
You complement him well."

Adam snorted. "Flower, for heaven's sake!"

Flower held her hands up, palms out, as though swearing

innocence. "Alright. Alright. That's all—I'm not saying anything else."

They walked around the back of the house to the large garden and seated themselves in the white wooden chairs. Adam moved away from the two women and turned toward the sharp decline that marked the end of Winterflower's property, impatiently knocking his closed right fist against the palm of his left hand. He didn't need Winterflower or anyone else to tell him that Melissa was well suited to him, that she could be his match. She was unlike any woman he had ever known. Independent, self-possessed, and vulnerable. He didn't turn around—he was vulnerable himself right then, and he'd as soon she didn't know it.

Winterflower served a light supper. The late, low-lying sun filtered through the trees, tracing intricate patterns on them, patterns that moved with the soft breeze and seemed to cast a spell over the threesome, for they ate quietly.

Melissa spoke. "Are you clairvoyant, Flower?"

Winterflower nodded. "I see what chooses to appear. Nothing more." Melissa nodded. Not in understanding, but acceptance.

"Why were you surprised to see Adam and me together?" She thought her skin crawled while she waited for what was without doubt a reluctant reply.

"I've been associating the two of you with the end of the year." Winterflower nodded toward Adam, who frowned. He may not agree, Melissa decided, but he didn't suggest that the woman's words were foolish, either.

Winterflower's soft voice reached Adam as if coming from a long distance, intruding in his thoughts. "How is Bill Henry?"

Adam shifted in his chair, aware that her mind was again on the metaphysical. "He's well enough, I suppose. I haven't been home to Beaver Ridge recently, and I haven't spoken with him by phone since I last saw you."

"You will learn something from him," she told Adam. "He has taught himself patience, and he has stopped racing through life. Now he has time to reflect, and soon his heart will be overflowing with joy." She looked from one to the other, nodded, and relaxed as though affirming the inevitable. "And he is not the only one." Then she turned to Melissa. "Ask Adam to bring you back to see me."

Adam stood and hugged his friend. "See you again before too long." Melissa shook hands with Flower and thanked her.

"You're very quiet, Melissa," he said, as they trudged downhill toward the train station. "Was I mistaken in bringing you to visit Flower?"

"No. I'm glad you did." She appeared to pick her words carefully. "You seemed different with her."

He couldn't help laughing. "Melissa, I expect everybody's different around her. She's so totally noncombative, so peaceful. Life-giving. Sometimes I think of her as being like penicillin for a virus."

"But she's also unsettling."

He slid an arm across her shoulder and drew her closer. "That's because you were fighting her good vibes."

"Oh, come on!" she said, and he thwarted her attempt to move away by tugging her closer.

"Now, you're fighting *my* vibes."

"Adam," she chided, "you could use a little less self-confidence."

He squeezed her shoulder. "Be reasonable. Nothing would lead me to believe that you like wimps." She wiggled out of his arm. "Go ahead. Move if you want to. You still know I'm here." She reached up and pulled his ear, delighting him with the knowledge that she needed to touch him.

"Feel better?"

"About what?"

"About giving in to your desire to have your hands on me?"

From the corner of his eye, he saw her frown dissolve into a smile, and he stopped, grasped both of her hands in his, and stared down at her.

"You're delightful, even when you're trying to be difficult." Her eyes narrowed in a squint, and she wet her lips with the tip of her tongue in a move that he now realized as unconscious. His breath quickened. "You make my blood boil." She parted her lips as though to speak but said nothing, and his passion escalated as she merely looked down the tree-lined street, escaping the honesty of his gaze. He held her hand as they walked to the train.

"Somehow I can't picture you with a close personal friend like Flower," she said as they seated themselves on the train. "You belong to the modern era; she doesn't."

"She does," he corrected. "Winterflower is her tribal name. She is Dr. Gale Falcon, a history professor, but she manages to stay close to her origins. My uncle, Bill Henry, introduced me to her. She and I can sit on her deck for hours at night without saying a word, yet we're together. I value her friendship."

"She's clairvoyant."

"Oh, yes," he confirmed, "but that stuff works only if you believe in it."

"And you don't?"

His cynical laugh challenged her to accept his premise. "It implies that life is guided by fate, that whatever happens to you is preordained. I can't accept that. Life is what you make it."

His hand covered hers to assist her as they left the train, and her inquiring look drew a grudging half smile and an unnecessary explanation. "I don't want you to get lost."

"If I get lost, it will be deliberate."

"I'll bet," he shot back. His arm around her shoulder held her close to him as they walked through Grand Central Station. The eyes of an old woman who pushed a shopping cart of useless artifacts beseeched him prayerfully. Melissa thought that he would give the woman a dollar and continue walking. Instead, he stopped to talk with her.

"What do you want with the money?" The woman seemed to panic at the question. "What are you going to do with it?"

"Well, I need some food for myself. . . ." She paused, as though uncertain. "And for my cats, please."

"Where are your cats?"

"In my room on Eleventh Avenue." The woman looked into her hand and gasped at the bills he'd placed there. He bade the woman good-bye, and within a few paces a man asked him for money.

"Are you planning to buy a drink?" Adam asked him.

"No, sir," the man replied. "I'll take groceries. Anything, so long as I can feed my kids. You wouldn't have a job, would you?" Melissa's heart opened to Adam, and she didn't fight it, couldn't fight it, as she watched him write down the man's name and address before giving him money. It made an indelible impression on her that he didn't ignore the outstretched hand of a single beggar, and she couldn't dismiss the thought that he might not be as harsh and exacting as he often appeared. She was unable to avoid comparing Adam's response to people in need with her father's behavior when accosted by beggars, whom he despised.

"You're quite a woman, Melissa," Adam told her as they walked to her apartment door. Her eyebrows shot upward. "You're straightforward," he went on. "No roughness around the edges. A man knows where he stands with you. And you're not a flirt." A smile creased his handsome cheeks. "At least not with me. And I like that. I like it a lot." His gaze roamed over her upturned face, as if he searched for clues as to what she felt. He pushed a few strands of hair from her forehead and then squeezed both of her shoulders, letting her know that he wanted more than he was asking for.

"You're not entirely immune to me, though," he told her in a near whisper, "and I like that, too. Good night, Melissa."

Melissa upbraided herself for having spent the day with

Adam. She couldn't fault his decorum, though: no cheap shots, no attempt at intimacy in spite of the almost unbearable sexual tension. He could brighten her life. Oh, he could, if he chose to do so. But he wasn't for her, and she intended to make sure that, in the future, Adam Roundtree would be just a business acquaintance. She sighed, remembering having made that resolution on two previous occasions.

After leaving Melissa, Adam strode quickly up Sixty-sixth Street to Broadway, crossed the street, and entered his building. Melissa was beginning to tax his self-restraint. He rubbed the back of his neck in frustration. Aching want settled in his loins when he thought of her high firm breasts, her rounded hips, and those long, tapered legs. He stopped undressing. It was one thing to desire an attractive woman, but it was quite another to be captivated by her because she was special, because she had an allure like none other. It bore watching, he decided, pulling off his shorts and getting into bed. Careful watching.

But she was there when he closed his eyes. Deeply troubled, he sat up in bed and turned on the bedside lamp, fighting a feeling he hadn't had for years. For all his wealth, his phenomenal success as a realtor, and his meteoric rise in the corporate world, his life lacked something. An emptiness lurked in him, a void that begged to be filled with the sweet nectar of a woman's love.

Three evenings later Melissa rushed to find her seat before the concert began. She hated being late and had been tempted not to renew her subscription to the museum's summer concert series, because it meant fighting the rush hour traffic in order to be on time. She shivered from the air conditioning and rubbed her bare arms as she realized belatedly that she'd left her sweater in her office. It would be a long, uncomfortable evening. As she weighed the idea of leaving, a garment fell over her shoulders, and large hands smoothed it around her arms. She looked down at the beige linen jacket that warmed her, felt the gentle squeeze of masculine hands on her shoulders, and fought not to turn around. But she couldn't resist leaning back, and when his hand rested softly on her shoulder, she tapped it lightly to thank him. So much for her resolve to avoid a personal relationship with him.

They left the concert together, stopped for coffee at a little cafe on Columbus Avenue, and though there was no discussion of it, she knew he'd walk her home. Maybe this time he wouldn't leave her without taking her in his arms. But when they entered the lobby of her building, she shuddered at the sight that greeted her. Wasn't it like her father to appear unexpectedly, giving himself every advantage? Rafer Grant rose from a leather lounge chair and walked toward them. He stopped, gazed at Adam, and fear ripped through her as his mouth twisted the minute he recognized the man whose family he detested.

"What is *he* doing here with you? Is this why you can't come home and look after your mother?" He didn't give her a chance to reply. "How could you consort with this . . . this man after what he and his kin did to our family? Aren't you ashamed of yourself?" Adam's arm steadied her.

Her voice held no emotion. "Hello, Father. I needn't say that I'm surprised to see you. There's no reason for you to be displeased. Adam—"

He interrupted. "Adam, is it? I'm shocked and disappointed at your bringing this man here to your home. It's disloyal, and I won't stand for it."

Adam pulled her closer to him, possessively and defiantly. "How are you planning to prevent it? This isn't the Middle Ages when you could have her shackled to the foot of her bed. She's an adult, and she can do as she pleases."

"It's alright, Adam." She was used to her father's harangues, having endured his reproofs and censure for as long as she could remember, but until now no one had called him to task for it—not her mother nor her brother. She needed her father's approval—it seemed that for most of her life she'd striven for it. Yet she couldn't remember a time when he'd praised her. She reached toward him involuntarily, but he waved her aside, glared at Adam, and marched huffily out of the building without having told her why he'd come.

She looked up at Adam, trying to read him. "I'm sorry you were exposed to this, Adam. My father never wanted a daughter, and sometimes I think he's not sure he has one. At least that's how he acts." She'd meant it in jest, but Adam's dour expression told her that he was not amused. Upon reflection, she wondered if her father might be more caring if she showed him that his opinion of her didn't matter. Should it matter so much, she pondered, as she and Adam walked without speaking to the elevator, her hand tightly enclosed in his.

At her apartment door he held his hand for her key, and she gave it to him and watched him open her door. Inside, Adam asked her, "Does your father always behave this way with you, or was he disrespectful because you were with me, a Roundtree?"

"Both. He's that way when I do something that displeases him," she explained, "which is fairly frequent."

"How does he act when your brother displeases him? Or does that ever happen?"

She hesitated; even though she was displeased with her father and ashamed of his behavior toward her, she couldn't criticize him. Especially not to a man whom he considered an enemy.

"Adam, my brother doesn't displease my parents." Then as the implications of her words hung between them, she joshed, "He's the good kid.

"Come on in the kitchen with me while I make some coffee." She had to change the subject—she didn't want Adam to see her as an ineffectual person. They were business associates, and she'd better remember that. She gave him a mug of coffee, and when he nodded in approval after having sniffed it, she was glad she'd made it strong.

"I like it straight," he told her, when she offered sugar and cream. "I also like your taste. I wouldn't have thought that beige and a dark gray would be so comfortable to look at, but this kitchen is attractive. Of course, the yellow accents don't hurt."

Her surprise at his interest in colors must have showed, because he shrugged and explained, "I dabble in watercolors." Then he asked her, "What's your hobby?"

She hesitated. "I go to a library in Harlem on Saturday mornings in the winter and conduct a children's story hour."

"That's not a hobby, Melissa. That's volunteer work. What's your hobby? I mean, what do you do for fun, just to please yourself?"

She didn't reveal that part of herself to acquaintances. Only her mother knew of her secret pleasure, though she hadn't let her mother read her verses. A desire to share herself with Adam welled up in her. She didn't look directly at him. "I like to write poetry. When I was at home, before I went to college, I used to sit in my room writing poems, and if I heard my father or brother roaming around or calling me, I'd hide what I was writing under my mattress."

His grim expression disconcerted her. "You don't think much of poetry writing?" He stood, his gaze boring into her. "I was thinking that I've known you less than a month and yet I know you better than your family does." Lowering her eyelids, she tried to veil her emotions from his probing stare. Her sudden self-consciousness must have been evident to him, for his casual posture suddenly changed. As though attempting to rein in an uncustomary wildness, he jammed both hands in his pants pockets and rocked back on his heels before turning swiftly and heading toward her hallway. Her ingrained courteousness overcame her diffidence, and she followed to see him out. At the door he turned to her.

"It's too bad that my presence caused you problems with

your father. I expect you have enough trouble with him without having to explain why you were with me." She sensed that this impatient, demanding, and sometimes harsh man could be gentle, tender, and he would be that way with her. Her gaze drifted up to his face to the yearning, the fiery passion in his eyes and unconsciously she moved to him.

"Adam. Oh, Adam." Both of his hands reached out and wrapped her into his embrace. Her senses reeled at the feel of his big hand behind her head, positioning her for the force of his mouth. Heat shot through her when his marauding lips finally took possession of her, imprisoning her in a torrent of molten passion. He nipped her bottom lip and quickly, as if she'd waited a lifetime to do it, she opened for him and welcomed his hot tongue into every crevice of her hungry mouth. She reveled in the savage intensity with which he loved her, crushing her to him, then caressing her with a gentleness that belied the strength of his ardor. She opened her mouth wider, and as if he sensed a deeper need in her—one that he wanted to fulfill—his hand stroked her bottom then pulled her up until the seat of her passion pressed against the unmistakable evidence of his desire.

More. She needed more. To be a part of him, to crawl inside of him. One hand moved to his head to increase the pressure of his mouth on hers while the other caressed his face and neck. Frantically she undulated against him. His groan warned her to stop it, but she couldn't make herself move from him. The feel of his hard chest against her tender, sensitive breasts, his hands moving slowly over her back, and the intimacy of her position against him enticed her closer. She wanted . . . His hands gently separated them and held her from him. When she dared look at him, she saw his difficulty in maintaining control. Honest to a fault, as always, when she could restore her equilibrium, and without thought to sparing either of them, she told him, "If you hadn't waited so long to do that, it might have been easier."

He released a grudging laugh. "Easier? You're kidding.

Woman, kissing you *is* easy—it's the consequences that'll sure as hell be rough." He continued to let his gaze roam indolently over her, and she knew his passion hadn't cooled.

She backed away from him. What had she been thinking about? If she had doubted that an involvement with Adam would rekindle the hatred between their families, her father's behavior when he saw them together was proof. Adam folded his arms and leaned against the wall, obviously judging her reaction to what had just happened.

"I see you intend to break off personal relations between us. I agree that we ought to at least decide if we want to go where we seem to be headed, but I hope you know that breaking it off and staying away from each other will be easier said than done." He brushed her cheek with his lips and winked at her. "I'll call you."

"At my office on business only," she quickly interjected. His raised eyebrow did not signify agreement.

She closed the door, drew a deep breath, and sat down to assimilate her feelings. One minute she had thought he'd walk away from her as usual, but in the next she was reeling from the jolt of his strength and passion. She knew that trouble lay ahead of her, so why was she already anxious for that telephone call? A famous actress once said that she'd have swum the Atlantic to be with her man—I still don't know exactly why, Melissa reasoned, but I sure am in a better position to guess.

Two days later, one day short of the month allowed in her contract, Melissa decided that she'd found a candidate with flawless credentials, one whom Adam couldn't reject. As was her custom, she escorted the candidate, Calvin Nelson, to his potential employer. Jason Court liked the man and assured her that his boss would. Adam hired Nelson after an interview that confirmed Melissa's opinion that Adam was hard, but fair, and that he had a keen mind. And her relief was nearly palpable when Adam made no allusion to the intimacy they had shared the previous Sunday evening.

"You're African American and so is Mr. Court," Calvin Nelson commented to Adam. "When I saw you, I was sure I wouldn't get the job, that you wouldn't hire a man who wasn't African American for such a high position in your company."

Furrows creased Adam's brow as he leaned back in his chair and weighed the words. The man was open, unafraid to speak his mind; he liked that. "I'm an equal opportunity employer, Calvin. What I want in an employee is competence, integrity, and honor. I don't give a hoot about a person's sex or ethnicity." He stood and shook Calvin Nelson's hand. "Welcome to Hayes/Roundtree Enterprises, Calvin. Oh, yes. We use first names here and in Maryland. Let me know what I can do to help you get settled in Frederick."

Jason shepherded Melissa to the reception room so that Adam could speak privately with his new employee. She blinked to make certain that her eyes weren't betraying her when Adam followed them and told Calvin to make an appointment to see him the following morning.

"Let's get some lunch," he called to them, pausing by his secretary's desk. "Olivia, call Thompson's and tell the maitre d' I'm bringing three guests."

Melissa couldn't hide her surprise at Adam's odd behavior. "I thought he'd want to talk to Calvin alone, Jason. And another thing, I didn't say I was free for lunch." Her resentment flared at his cavalier disregard for her preferences, forcing her to squash what would have been a rare display of temper. One kiss didn't give him the right to take her for granted.

"He's marking his territory," she heard Jason say.

"What do you mean by that?" she asked him and warned herself to be calm—an agitated person didn't think clearly.

Jason nodded toward his boss. "He just told me to stay out of his territory, meaning you."

She reflected for a second. Jason had given her an appreciative glance. More than one, in fact, but she hadn't thought that Adam noticed.

"How can you say that? I haven't given him the right to do that."

Jason's shoulder flexed in a quick, careless shrug. "You don't have to give it to him. Adam doesn't wait for doors to open—he opens them himself. You believe what I'm saying. A man knows when another tells him to back off from a woman. Melissa, I have never lunched with Adam. Unless he has an important client, he doesn't go to lunch. He has a sandwich and coffee at his desk. You're the reason he's going to Thompson's."

She turned on her heel and headed for the elevator, but Jason must have guessed her intention, because he detained her. "Melissa, it isn't smart to belittle Adam. You wouldn't get away with it, and there's no point in making an enemy of him. Besides," he grinned lazily, "the food at Thompson's is first class. Worth a try." She looked up as Adam approached the elevator with Calvin Nelson. His disapproving scowl told her that he knew what she'd threatened and dared her to do it. Jason looked from one to the other. He didn't know that she and Adam were more than business associates, she remembered, forced a smile and got on the elevator.

Adam stopped abruptly as they walked out of the restaurant, and his companions stared while he greeted a woman with such warmth that neither of them doubted she was a close friend.

"Ariel! What a pleasant surprise!" A smile drifted over his face. He shook hands with his guests, excused himself, and left with the elegant woman. Jason's knowing look confirmed what Melissa knew: Adam had repaid her and had enjoyed doing it.

"He's not vindictive," Jason said, so that only Melissa heard, "but he believes in letting you know how he feels about a thing." They waved Calvin Nelson good-bye.

"What is this about?" she asked Jason.

"Melissa, surely you know that Adam has cut you away from the pack. He knew you intended to leave his office with me and without telling him good-bye, and he didn't like it. You didn't show much enthusiasm for his company, and he's just let you know that he isn't pining for you."

"Who was she?" She hated herself for having asked him, but she had to know.

"I don't know," he replied, "but I don't think she's anyone special, because she made a pass at Nelson but, well . . . you never know."

Melissa swore to herself that she hated Adam, that he was just another of the four-martini corporate types she disliked. She wished that it was Jason Court who attracted her, but *Adam was the one.*

Adam settled down to work on that August morning, after telling himself that he'd done the smart thing in not calling Melissa over the weekend. They'd moved so fast in the short time they'd known each other that he figured he'd better step back and take stock of things, decide what he wanted. Maybe he'd been wrong last week in not asking her if she wanted to lunch with the group, but she'd been wrong in threatening to walk off in a huff, too. He flicked on the intercom.

"Yes, Olivia. Sure. Put him on." He lifted the receiver of his private phone. His eyes widened in astonishment at Wayne's incredulous request. Could he get away for a few weeks, go down to Beaver Ridge, and settle the strike at the hosiery mill? It was becoming increasingly clear that, except for Wayne's newspaper, the family businesses had been held together by the force of their father's personality, rather than by his managerial abilities.

"That's asking a lot, Wayne. I'll need an office manager for the time I'm gone, and it may be a few days before I can get one. I'll get back to you." He hung up and called Melissa, and the anticipation he felt as he awaited her voice surprised him.

"MTG." His customary aplomb seemed to have deserted him, and seconds passed before he could respond in his usual manner.

"Melissa, this is Adam. I need an office manager right away. Can you get one for me without Jason having to spend hours drafting a contract? I'm in a hurry for this." He walked around his desk cradling the phone against his left shoulder while he squeezed his relaxer—a plastic object that he kept in his top drawer—with both hands.

"Why do you need one? If your secretary can't manage your office, maybe you should be looking for one of those, not an OM."

He hoped that his deep sigh and long silence would warn her that he didn't have time for games.

"Well?" she prodded.

"Melissa, would you please stop while you're ahead? When I say I want an office manager, that's what I want. If you can't attend to that without lecturing me about how to run my business, I'll try another service."

"Yes, sir. Whatever you say, sir. Just fax me a job description," she needled, her tone cool and sarcastic.

Olivia's voice came over the intercom, and he realized he hadn't turned it off. "My Lord, Adam, what could she have said to make you mad enough to break the telephone? And I didn't know you knew those words." Her chuckle didn't relieve his boiling temper.

"I'm sorry, Olivia, but Melissa Grant strips my gears, and she gets a kick out of doing it."

He turned off the intercom, grabbed Betty—as he called his relaxer—leaned back in his chair, and squeezed the plastic object. What was it about her, he pondered. Why did that one woman get to him that way? She could make him madder than anybody else, and she could heat him up quicker and make him hotter than any woman. If he couldn't get her out of his mind, maybe the solution was to take her to bed and get her out of his system. He dropped the relaxer, pushed away from his desk, and put a hand on each knee as if to rise, but didn't. That could work either way, and if it brought them closer together, what would he do then?

Adam locked his hands behind his head. She questioned his motives and grilled him about his decisions—*nobody* did that, not even his brother, his closest friend. He could get the response he wanted from most people with just a look, but not from Melissa. Was her attitude toward him part of the old Roundtree-Grant antagonism, or was it just Adam and Melissa, a part of the storm that seemed to swirl around them and between them even when outward calm prevailed? His intelligence told him it wasn't their last names and that their family ties were irrelevant. He sat up straight, his nerves tingling with excitement. Melissa was worth the cost of getting her.

Melissa began the search for Adam's office manager, deliberately looking for a man, because she knew he would expect her to find a woman. He'd repaid her for threatening to defy him in the presence of Nelson and Court. Well, she'd give it back to him. Nobody put her down and got away with it, she vowed, still smarting from the warm greeting he'd given that woman at the restaurant.

Within an hour after speaking with Melissa, Adam received another call from Wayne.

"Adam, one of the older workers discovered what appears to have been foul play or, at best, an uncommon accident in the Leather and Hides plant. Nearly seven hundred pounds of cattle hides that we've earmarked for women's shoes and luggage have been given chrome tanning rather than vegetable tanning, and the lot is now too soft and too elastic for its intended use. These valuable hides will have to be made into cheaper and less profitable items, and we haven't been able to trace the error to any worker."

"Do what you can, Wayne. I'm working on getting that manager."

He hung up and phoned Melissa. "How's the search for my OM going?" She was peeved with him, and he knew why, so he kept his tone casual and friendly. He didn't want her to have an excuse to needle him.

"Don't worry. I've been working on it ever since you made the request an hour ago. When I find one, I'll notify Jason."

He couldn't resist correcting her, but he kept his tone gentle. "Melissa, Jason Court is not in charge of this—I am. Please remember that." He hung up and stared at the phone. Somebody ought to tell her that he never walked away from a challenge. And she was that . . . in more ways than one.

Melissa walked into Adam's office the following morning with his new office manager, a forty-six-year-old man who had impeccable references. She entered his suite with her head high and defiance blazing across her face.

"Good morning, Mr. Roundtree. I've got the perfect person for you. Adam Roundtree, this is Lester Harper." Adam narrowed his eyes and glared at her for what seemed an interminable minute. Abruptly he extended his hand in a welcome to Lester.

"Have a seat, and tell me about yourself."

"Well, Miss Grant said I'm just what you need, so I thought—"

Adam interrupted, pulling rank, Melissa thought.

"We'll see about that," Adam said, spreading his hands in exasperation. His lips tightened as he ground his teeth and looked Melissa in the eye. "If you'll excuse us, please."

Her triumph dissolved into remorse as she realized that he'd practically ordered her to leave them alone. Shivers sprinted along her nerves when his twinkling eyes delivered an icy rebuke. She was teasing a tiger, she realized belatedly, and his whole demeanor told her that he wouldn't be soothed until he got proper recompense. His gaze held her, refused to release her even when she struggled to look away. And she had no doubt of their message: *retribution is mine* was their promise.

The day passed too slowly. He had to let her know what he thought of her smart trick, bringing him a man when she knew he would have preferred a woman or anyone less officious than Lester Harper. The man was bound to try lording it over Olivia, and Jason had winced at the sight of him. Clever, was she? Well, he'd see about that! He sighed heavily. She infuriated him—but, heaven help him, he wanted her.

She answered her door uneasily around seven thirty that evening, knowing intuitively that her caller was Adam. What had possessed her to toy with him, she asked herself, as she slipped the lock.

"You aren't surprised to see me?"

"Not very." Why tell him she'd known he'd come after her? When he stepped inside the door without waiting for an invitation, she wouldn't let him see her eager anticipation of his next move, nor her erotic response to the danger and excitement that his determined look promised her. Goose bumps popped up on her arms, and she rubbed them frantically. He didn't give her time to regroup.

"Come here to me," he growled as if he'd waited long enough. She thought she didn't move, but she was in his arms, his fiery mouth moving over hers, possessively, unbelievably seductive. Her hands moved up to push at his chest, but instead they wound themselves around his strong, corded neck. She felt him growing against her just as he stepped back, though he didn't release her.

So he was holding back, was he? He'd fire her up, but he wouldn't let her know how she affected him. Darn him, he

wouldn't play with her and do it with impunity. She pulled him
to her and held him so tightly that he could release himself only
if he hurt her. And she knew he wouldn't consider doing that.
She felt him then, all of him, and she gloried in his male
strength, his heat and energy until his fire threatened to over-
whelm her. Now it was he who wouldn't let go, he who groaned
while he spun her around in a vortex of passion, he who held
the loving cup and tempted her to drink from it. And how she
wanted that sip. But she couldn't take the chance—there was
so much at stake. And he didn't intend to commit to her, he'd
all but said it. It wasn't Gilbert Lewis whom she was facing;
that relationship had been child's play. Adam's gaze warned her
that he intended to go all the way, and even with her nearsight-
edness, she couldn't mistake the storm raging in his eyes.

"I think we're being reckless." She spoke softly as if she
could barely release the words. "Adam, there would be the
devil to pay back home if my family knew what we're doing."
She hoped her words didn't make her appear as foolish to him
as she did to herself.

"We're of age, Melissa." He didn't sound convincing, she
noticed, sensing that his folks would also be furious. "And
why do they have to know?" She moved back, farther away
from him.

"I refuse to have a secret, back door affair with you or any
other man, Adam, and I'm surprised you'd want something
like that. I wouldn't have thought it your style."

His right index finger moved back and forth along his
square jaw, a sure sign of frustration. "You're right. I don't
want it. My one brief experience with a secret affair, if you
could even call it an affair, was disastrous. But then I was
only fifteen." Her eyebrows shot up. He'd started early. When
she was fifteen, she hardly knew what boys were for.

They hadn't moved from her foyer. "Come on in." He followed as she glided into the living room.

"Melissa, I'm relocating for a couple of months. That may
cool things down between us, and if it does, I expect it will be

for the best." She couldn't argue with that, nor could she understand why it pleased her that his heated look belied his words.

"You're right again," she said. "It would be for the best. I think we ought to avoid each other so we don't reopen those old family wounds, because I don't want to stir up that mess."

"Neither do I." He walked a few paces, turned around, and let her see the desire in his eyes. "But I want you." A note of finality laced his tone.

His words sent tremors racing through her, but she maintained her composure. "And you always get what you want?" she goaded.

He shrugged. "Why should I want something and not get it if all that's required is effort on my part? I go after what I want, Melissa. I work hard—I leave nothing to chance, and I get what I go after."

"This time you may get what you don't want," she told him, seeing in her mind's eye the ugliness on their horizon.

Adam walked home oblivious to the light misty rain. The minute Melissa had opened her door, she had guessed his reason for being there, and her demeanor had become that of a defenseless person at the mercy of a Goliath. Not that he'd been taken in by that. She could defend herself with the best of them. But she'd parted her lips and squinted at him, and he'd lost it. Getting her to him had been the only thing he'd cared about. He weighed the chances of dashing safely across Broadway against the light, noted the speeding cabs, and decided to wait. Thinking about it now, he admitted that his reason for going to Melissa had nothing to do with the office manager. He'd needed to see her. His displeasure about Lester had been a weak excuse.

Four

Adam closed and locked his office door, spoke at length
with Olivia, took the elevator down to the garage, got into his
newly leased Jaguar, and headed for Beaver Ridge. He hadn't
told Melissa where he would spend the next two months or
so, because he wanted to find out whether a complete break
would have any effect on their feelings for each other. He
couldn't imagine that they'd lose interest though, because a
mutual attraction as strong as theirs had to run its course. He
loved to drive and had missed having a car, which he considered more of a nuisance than a convenience in New York, but
he'd forgotten the frustration of driving bumper to bumper.
After more than four hours in heavy traffic, he turned at last
into Frederick Douglas Drive, the long roadway that marked
the beginning of his family's property.

Wayne met him at the door of the imposing white Georgian
house that Jacob Hayes had built for himself and his heirs
sixty-five years earlier. Remodeled and modernized inside, it
was home to Adam as no other place ever would be. He could
close his eyes and see every stone in the huge, marble-capped
living room fireplace. As a youth he'd slipped numerous times
out of the room's large back window that oversaw his mother's
rose garden and, as many times, the thorns had ripped his
pants. He had loved the solitude that its many rooms assured
him, and cherished the stolen fun he'd had with his brother

when they secluded themselves in upstairs closets or the attic away from parental eyes. Coming home was a feeling like no other.

He and Wayne exchanged hugs in the foyer that separated the living and dining rooms and slapped each other affectionately on the back, appraising each other with approval, before Wayne took one of Adam's bags, and they climbed the wide staircase to Adam's room.

"What do you know about the new manager you hired for Leather and Hides? I'm sure you investigated his references. From what I've seen of him, he's competent . . . but, well, can we trust him?"

Adam rubbed the back of his neck. "He came with excellent references, but if you're suspicious . . ." He let the thought hang. Wayne's question raised a possibility that he hadn't considered. He went to find his mother, to let her know he'd come home.

With several hours remaining before dinner, Adam decided to visit Bill Henry, his mother's younger brother. He figured he'd be seeing a lot of his uncle. If any man had come to terms with life, B-H was that man. And with a stressful two months ahead of him, he was going to need the relief that B-H's company always provided. He entered the modestly constructed, white clapboard house without knocking. When B-H was at home, the door was always unlocked, and in summer the house was open except for the screen doors. It amused him that his wealthy uncle chose to eschew the manifestations of wealth, while his neglected investments made him richer by the minute.

"Why're you home in midsummer, Adam? You usually manage to avoid this heat." Not only did Bill Henry take his time speaking, Adam noted—his uncle, though still a relatively young man, did everything at a slow pace.

"Wayne asked me to come home. I expect you've heard about the near fiasco at Leather and Hides. I hope it was a simple error, but I'm beginning to suspect that someone wants to sink Hayes/Roundtree Enterprises. We don't know who's masterminding it, or even if that's the case, but one of our employees had a hand in it. It couldn't have happened otherwise."

Bill Henry rocked himself in the contour rocker that he'd had designed to fit his six-foot four-inch frame. "What kind of mix-up was it?"

Adam related the details. "That's burned-up money, B-H." He wiped the perspiration from his brow. If Bill Henry chose to live close to nature, he could at least have something handy with which his guests could fan. The man must have sensed Adam's discomfort, for he passed an old almanac to his nephew, and Adam made good use of it.

"Any new men on the job?" When Adam shook his head and then looked hard at him, as though less certain than he had been, B-H probed.

"Anybody mad at you?"

Adam shrugged. "I've thought of both possibilities, and I've got some ideas. But I can't act until I'm positive. In the meantime I'll install a variety of security measures. If you have any thoughts on it, give me a call."

Adam took his time walking the half mile back home in the ninety-six-degree heat. A new man was on the job, but what did that prove? He had no reason to suspect Calvin Nelson. The man was too experienced to have permitted such a blunder, so he couldn't have known about it. If it was deliberate . . . But why would he want to do such a thing? Unless . . . Adam didn't want to believe that Melissa would engineer the destruction of his family's company, that she would participate in industrial sabotage, producing the perfect candidate for the job. One who could destroy his family's livelihood. No, he didn't believe it. But she was a Grant, and there had never been such a mishap at Leather and Hides in the plant's sixty-five years. Not until Calvin Nelson became its manager. It was a complication that he'd prefer not to have and an idea that he couldn't accept.

He didn't want to think about Melissa, but he couldn't get her out of his head, because something in him had latched on to her and refused to let go. He'd taken a chance in letting her think their relationship was over. If she knew him better, she'd know that he finished what he started, and that she was unfinished business. He meant to have her, and leaving her for two months only made it more difficult. Melissa was special, and she appealed to him on many levels. He liked her wit, the way her mind worked, her composure, the laid-back sexy way she glided about. And he liked her company. He was tired of games, sick of hollow seductions, disgusted with chasing women he'd already caught just because good taste demanded it. It was always the same. A woman allowed him to chase her until she decided enough time had elapsed or he'd spent enough money, and then she let herself be caught. He never promised anything, but she'd go to bed and then she chased him. He was sick of it. Done with it. Melissa didn't engage in such shenanigans, at least not with him, and that was part of her attraction. He wondered if she'd miss him.

A phone call from her father was reason for apprehension, though Melissa had learned not to display her real feelings when his treatment of her lacked the compassion that a daughter had a right to expect of her father. But when her father called her office and began his conversation with a reminder of her duties to her family, she knew he was about to make one of his unreasonable demands. She geared herself for the worst, and it was soon forthcoming.

"Melissa, you've been ignoring your mother," he began, omitting the greeting. "I'm taking her to the hospital so the doctors can run some more tests. They can't find anything wrong with her, but anybody can see she's not well. Your mother's getting weaker every day, and I want you to come home." She didn't want to argue with him. She had talked with her mother for a half hour the day before, and Emily Grant hadn't alluded to any illness, though she had said that she got tired of taking test after test just to please her husband. But Melissa knew that her father's views about his wife's health would be the basis on which he acted, not the opinions of a doctor.

A strange thought flitted through her mind. She had never heard her father call her mother by her given name. Did he know it? It was my wife, your mother, she, her, and you. She didn't want to go back to that depressing environment. It wasn't a home, but a place where trapped people coexisted. Her brother had found relief from it by taking a job in Kenya.

"Father, I have responsibilities here." She'd told him that many times, but he denied it as many times as he heard it.

"And I've told you that if you come home, I'll support you." She didn't want that and wouldn't accept it, but if her mother needed her, she couldn't ignore that. Annoyance flared when he added, "And I need a hostess and someone to accompany me on special occasions. Your mother isn't up to it, or so she says. She isn't up to anything."

She terminated the conversation as quickly as she could. "I'll call you in a day or two, Father, and let you know what I can do." Why hadn't she told him no? That he could hire someone to help with her mother. Wasn't she ever going to stand up to her father, stop begging for his approval? She closed her office door, kicked off her shoes, and began analysis of her financial situation to determine the effect of a move to Frederick, Maryland. Her father was insensitive in some ways, but she'd never known him to lie. Maybe her mother didn't want to worry her by admitting that she was ill. She thought for a while. Yes, that would be consistent with her mother's personality. Three hours later she walked down the corridor and knocked on the door of two lawyers who'd just begun their practice. If they agreed to her proposal, she'd move her business to Frederick. Later that afternoon she telephoned Burke's Moving Managers and set a date.

Melissa entered her apartment that evening and looked around at the miscellaneous artifacts that had eased her life and given her pleasure for the five years she'd lived there. She loved her home, but she could make another one, she rationalized, fighting the tears. Ilona's phone call saved her a case of melancholy.

"Melissa, darling, come down for a coffee. I haven't seen you in ages."

"You saw me yesterday when I was hailing a taxi. Give me a minute to change."

Ilona hadn't indicated that she had a guest, and Melissa winced when she saw the debonair man. A boutonniere was all he needed to complete the picture of a Hungarian count. Melissa had dressed suitably for one packing to leave town with all of her belongings, but not for the company of an old-world gentleman. At times she could throttle Ilona.

"You and Tibor remember each other, don't you?" Ilona asked with an air of innocence that belied her matchmaking, as she placed three glasses of hot espresso and a silver dish of chocolates on the coffee table. They nodded. Melissa suppressed a laugh. She was glad he didn't click his heels, though he did bow and kiss the hand that she'd been tempted to hide behind her. After a half hour of such dullness that not even Ilona's considerable assets as a hostess could enliven, Tibor bowed, kissed Melissa's hand once more, and left. Ilona turned to Melissa.

"He is crushed, darling. He has been begging me to invite you down when he is here, so last night I promised him that if he came over this evening, I would ask you, too. I couldn't warn you to wear something feminine, because then you'd give me an excuse not to come down. But Melissa, darling, you could have showed him a little interest." At the quirk of Melissa's eyebrow, Ilona added, "Just for fun, darling. A real voman is never above a little harmless flirtation." The more Ilona talked, the stronger her accent became.

"Ilona, you spend too much time thinking about men. I've—" Ilona interrupted her, clearly aghast at such blasphemy. "Melissa, darling, that's not possible. Ah . . . wait a minute. What happened with that man?"

"Nothing happened. He built a fire, and he's going away for a couple of months. Before you ask, the fire is still raging."

Melissa looked with amusement at Ilona's open-mouthed astonishment. "You mean he didn't take you to bed? What kind of man is this?" Both shoulders tightened in a shrug, and her palms spread outward as if acknowledging the incredulous.

"He's your kind of man, Ilona, believe me." She grinned as Ilona shrugged again, this time in disbelief. "Anyway, that's irrelevant now. I'm moving back to Frederick."

"You couldn't be serious, darling. The town doesn't even have a ballet company—you told me so yourself. Who could live in such a place?" Ilona would have been a wonderful actress, Melissa decided, grinning broadly, as she took in her friend's mercurial facial expressions and impassioned gesticulations. And all because a town of forty thousand inhabitants didn't have a resident ballet company.

"I've decided to try it for two years." She had to keep the uncertainty out of her voice. Ilona would pick it up in seconds and start punching holes in the idea. "My mother isn't well," she went on, "and . . . Look, I've made the arrangements, and if you hadn't called, I'd be packing right now." Melissa watched Ilona's eyes widen.

"Really? Well, darling, you know I don't do anything laborious, but I'll help you pack. This is terrible. I hate to see you go but . . ." She paused, and a brilliant smile lit her face. "Maybe you will find there the man for you."

Melissa couldn't restrain the laughter. Was there a scenario into which Ilona couldn't inject romance? "Thanks for the offer, but my biggest problem is finding a tenant. I'll pack my personal things, but the movers will pack everything else."

"You're not selling your apartment?"

Melissa wondered at her keen interest. "No. I'm going to rent it unfurnished for two years. If I find life in Frederick intolerable, I'll move back here."

Ilona beamed. "I have a friend who would take your apartment for two years. That would suit us both, darling. Your place would be in good hands, and I'd be assured of seeing him every night, even if New York got two feet of snow. Shall I tell him?"

Melissa couldn't contain the peals of laughter that erupted from her throat at the gleam in Ilona's green eyes. "Sure thing," she told Ilona when she recovered. "Tell him to call my office tomorrow morning."

Two weeks later Melissa sat on a bench facing Courthouse Square in Frederick, exhausted. It hadn't occurred to her that finding an office in her hometown would be so difficult. In the short time since she'd made her decision, she'd arranged to share her secretary with the lawyers who had offices down the hall from her own in New York, made similar arrangements in Washington, D.C., and Baltimore, and shifted her business headquarters to Frederick. With fax, e-mail, telephones, and the use of electronic bulletin boards, she had expanded her business while cutting her expenses in half. But coming back home also had its darker side. She hated that the bed she slept in was the one she'd used as a child, and her father, satisfied that he had her once more under control, ignored her most of the time.

Melissa's mother had remembered her daughter's love of

pink roses and had placed a vase of them in her room. A bowl of lavender potpourri perfumed Melissa's bathroom, and the scent teased her nostrils when she opened the doors of her closet. Emily Grant had greeted her daughter with a warm embrace.

"Welcome home, dear. I knew he'd keep after you till you gave in." Melissa returned the fierce hug, though she thought it out of character for her usually undemonstrative mother.

"I'm not sure you've done the right thing, coming back," Emily continued, "but I'm glad to see you. I've missed you."

"I missed you, too, Mother, and I hope we'll get to know each other again. It's been a long time since I lived at home."

"Over ten years. I know you'll be busy, but you come see me whenever you have time." Thereafter Melissa saw little of her mother, who, she recalled, preferred the solitude of her room and who, she'd decided, looked the picture of health.

She unfolded *The Maryland Journal,* checked the real estate ads, and walked four blocks to investigate the one office that might suit her needs. With its attractive lobby and wide hallway, the redbrick, five-story building enticed her as she entered it. The office suite that she liked had high ceilings, large windows, parquet floors, and a comfortable adjoining office for her secretary. Her excitement at finding exactly what she needed ebbed when she learned that the building was owned by the Hayes-Roundtree family. Unfortunately, if she wanted prime space, she'd have to take it.

She didn't mind renting from Adam's family, although she knew her father would explode. How could he harbor such intense hatred? It wasn't even his war. He hadn't known about the feud until he met her mother, but he'd since used it to justify every disappointment, every failure he'd had. She had to shake her guilt for having thought it, but she rented the office nevertheless. For the sake of peace, she had sacrificed her feeling for Adam and come home, but there were limits.

Raised eyebrows greeted her when she introduced herself to her office neighbors: a Grant renting from the Roundtrees.

She'd almost forgotten about small town gossip. One friendly woman who introduced herself as Banks told her, "I see you've emancipated yourself. Good thing, too—when hell breaks loose, everybody will sympathize with the good guys." Melissa grimaced. She didn't need an explanation as to who the good guys were.

Melissa didn't have long to wait for an indication of the problems that her move into that building would cause. Her cousin Timothy stood at the corner light as she left the building, and she smiled as she walked toward him.

"Hi," he greeted her. "I heard you'd come back home, but what the hell were you doing in there? That's the Hayes Building." Cold tension gripped her as she noted his angry frown.

"Where else can you find decent office space in this town?" Her attempt to dismiss it as irrelevant didn't please him.

"You've been gone a while, but the rest of us have been right here watching them flaunt their money. Find some other place. Why do you need an office anyway? Uncle Rafer said you were coming home to be with Aunt Emily."

"Long story," she said, unwilling to explain what she considered wasn't his business and waved him good-bye.

He yelled back at her. "Get out of that place. You're just going to start trouble." I seem already to have done that, she thought, her steps slow and heavy.

Melissa worked late the next evening, arranging the furniture, books, and fixtures that had arrived that morning from New York. That done, she decided to acquaint herself with one of her new computer programs, but she had just begun when the screen went blank, the lights in her office flickered, and darkness engulfed her. She didn't have a flashlight and hadn't bothered to locate the stairs, and a glance at her fourth-floor window told her that the moon provided the only relief from darkness. She didn't get a tone when she lifted the telephone receiver, so she prepared herself mentally to spend the night there and tried to remember where she'd put her bag of Snickers.

"If you don't have a lantern or flashlight, go into the hallway and stand right in front of your door. I'll be along shortly with light."

She looked toward the loudspeaker as tremors shot through her, and she struggled to still the furious pounding of her heart at the sound of Adam's voice. She hadn't known that he had come home to Beaver Ridge, only that he'd left New York. It had to be Adam. She couldn't mistake anyone's voice for his— no other sounded like it. Did he know she was there? Would he be glad to see her? She opened the door and waited.

The air conditioning was off, but goose bumps covered her bare arms, and chills streaked through her as the lights approached. He stopped a few feet away.

"Melissa! What— What are you doing here?" Her eyes beheld his beloved face before taking in the length of him, as though assuring themselves that it was he. "Melissa— Am I hallucinating?" He took a step closer.

"Adam— Adam, I . . . I'm standing in front of my new office."

"My God!"

He didn't want her there. Why had she thought he cared for her even a little? She wanted to back up, but the eerie, unsettling atmosphere and the shock of seeing him kept her rooted there. Her gaze followed the two lanterns as they neared the floor, and then she looked up at him walking to her, a determined man whose motives she didn't need to guess.

"My administrative assistant didn't say she'd rented this suite. Tell me why you are here." He stood inches away, so close that she breathed his breath and smelled his heat.

"I—" He stepped closer, and her hand went to his chest. "I— Adam!" Quivers began deep inside of her when his hands grasped her shoulders, pulling her closer, and then wrapping her to him. She couldn't wait for his mouth, but stood on tiptoe and pulled his head down until his lips reached her moist kiss. She refused to let herself remember that he'd told her good-bye. She had him with her, and she had to have what he was offering her. Her parted lips took him in, and with unashamed ardor she sipped from his tongue's sweet nectar and fitted herself against his hard body. He thrust deeply into her mouth as though rediscovering her seductive honey, and she arched her hips into him. Her shameless demand must have threatened his control, for he eased the kiss and lightened his caress.

"I take it you're glad to see me," he said, a smile softening his face. He looked down, saw the two lanterns, and laughed as he reached for them. "Sweetheart, you're so disconcerting that I forgot about the blackout. There may be some more tenants waiting for me. Come on."

She couldn't believe he'd said it. "Adam, you just kissed me as though we'd never get another chance, and now you're acting as though you only patted your dog."

The man grinned. "I don't have a dog. Pets never appealed to me, and I don't think of Thunder as a pet. He's my friend."

She gaped. "Who the devil is Thunder?"

"My stallion. Try not to be outraged, Melissa. For a moment there, I gave myself the choice of moving away from you and cooling things down or seducing you into letting me put you on the floor. You do not belong on any man's floor, Melissa—so cut me a little slack, will you? Now tell me why you have an office in this building."

He showed surprise at her explanation.

"I'm glad I worked late tonight. You would have been here alone if I hadn't. We don't have night watchmen in our buildings here, and most people don't stay after hours, so if you plan to work after seven, notify my secretary."

"Your secretary? Is this where you'll be spending the next two months?" He nodded.

"Good Lord!" She didn't want to know that instead of

avoiding each other, their respective moves guaranteed that they'd be together more frequently now than ever.

The first repercussion from her having moved into the Roundtrees' office building greeted her when she got home. News that a Grant had rented office space in the Jacob Hayes Building wouldn't need wire service. She'd bet everybody in Frederick knew about it before dark. Rafer seemed to have been waiting to pounce.

"Now you've done it. You've really done it. You've moved into that building, and you're paying them good Grant money. Haven't they done enough to us? Don't you have a bit of pride?" He paced the length of the foyer, turned and glared at her. "I assume you're paying rent. You ought to be ashamed of yourself."

"I'm paying rent, and it's *my* money, not Grant money." She had expected his anger, but not his constant harassment. Rafer put his thumbs in the watch pocket of his vest, paced as he did when he had a judge to admire him, and told her, "I want you out of the Hayes Building tomorrow and not a day later."

Melissa looked at him, snugly wrapped in the splendor of his self-righteousness, and knew two things: if she didn't have her own home within two weeks, she'd go crazy; and she was going to learn not to care what her father said or thought. Her cold smile conveyed the message that the Melissa who returned home was different from the one who'd left ten years earlier.

"You're a lawyer, Father," she reminded him, "so I'm sure you know the penalty for breaking a lease without provocation."

The following morning Rafer used different tactics. He arrived at her office minutes after she did and, with her office door ajar, lectured her for not being attentive to her sick mother, who Melissa suspected wasn't sick, and demanded that she leave her office and go home.

She wouldn't dignify it with an answer, she decided, and was about to close the door when she heard her friend Banks's voice.

"Well, I'll say, Mr. Grant, you're a real sweetheart. I always ignored the things people said about you, since I figured nobody was all bad—but, honey, you make me rethink my philosophy."

Melissa recalled having witnessed her father's upbraiding once before. She heard Adam's voice again and knew that as long as she was in her office, she'd have peace. But she had no doubt that she'd pay when she got home. Her father would never let her forget that, because of her, Adam Roundtree had ordered him off of Hayes-Roundtree property.

She'd known he'd come. He walked through her open door at six o'clock that evening, an hour after the normal end of the workday, as if he'd expected her to be there. He closed the door.

"You'll get more of that when you get home, won't you?" he said without preliminaries. "Does he get violent?"

Alone with him, worn out and vulnerable after her father's antics, she crossed her arms beneath her breast. "Yes, he'll have his say, but he's never been violent nor showed a tendency toward it." Her words must have reassured him, because he became less tense.

"I hadn't realized that your mother is sick. How is she?" A half laugh that was little more than a sigh slipped through her lips, and her shoulders flexed in a shrug as she pushed the frizzy hair away from her temple.

"I don't think my mother's sick. As far as I can see, she's the same as always. She stays in her room as much as possible and doesn't disagree with anything my father says or does. But I have noticed that when he's away she comes out of her room more often, even goes shopping."

"You came home because Rafer asked you to, or maybe he demanded it. But can you live in the house with him?"

She fidgeted with a rubber eraser and avoided his eyes. "I'm looking for a small house. I love the Federal town houses like the ones on North Court and Council, but I don't believe anybody would sell me one of them."

He inclined his head. "You're right, but it's a moot point, since they're never for sale. Whoever has one is keeping it. Some of those houses have been held by the same family since the Civil War. Have dinner with me this evening."

She sensed that he wanted to postpone the time when she'd have to deal with her father, and asked, "Why do you want us to have dinner together?"

His incredulous look brought bubbling laughter from her throat, and in her amusement she didn't notice the change in him. The breath escaped her in a sharp gush as he drew her into his arms. "Wha—" Her hands clutched the lapel of his jacket and then tried to pull him closer to her. His answering sigh encouraged her exploration of him, and her fingers eased first into the tight curls at the back of his head and then found their way inside his jacket, roaming over his chest and shoulders.

He broke away from her, walked to the window and turned his back to it, facing her. "Melissa, I'd thought that if we didn't see or speak with each other for a couple of months, if we were out of touch, we'd either lose interest or discover that what we felt was more than the physical. But instead, here we are. How can you ask why I want to have dinner with you? I want you and I want to find out whether it's mutual."

How could he have a doubt? Surely, he knew . . .

"Do you want me?" he persisted. She knew that his relaxed, casual stance as he leaned against the wall was misleading, and she sensed his vulnerability, that by asking the question he had exposed himself to an extent unnatural to him. Her pride wouldn't let her lie, so she hesitated, searching for a way around it. He held her glance, waiting.

"Adam," she began in a hesitant voice, "what I want or don't want may prove irrelevant in this case." His eyes dared her to look away, and she couldn't doubt the importance that he attached to her answer.

"Irrelevant? That may be, but I don't think so. I'm not asking what you plan to do about it. I just want an answer—yes or no."

The fire in his eyes set her lips to trembling in anticipation as both fear and excitement clutched at her. If she said no, would he ignore it and attempt to seduce her? And if she said yes, when would he claim what she told him was his? She kicked at the half empty box of items that she planned to place on her desk and in its drawers.

"Well?"

"You . . . you know I do. Why are you forcing me to say the words? Will saying what you want to hear satisfy you?"

He walked toward her, shrouding her in his captivating aura, a male animal stalking his certain mate. "Say it, Melissa. Say the words. Tell me that you want me."

"Yes. Yes, I want you, and you've had plenty proof of it. But nothing can come of it. My father is out of joint because I rented an office in your building. What do you think his reaction would be if we . . . if I—"

"If we became lovers?" he interrupted. "Can't make yourself say it? Well, I don't share your fear. Rafer is concerned about himself, his family name, another loss to the Roundtrees. Not about your virtue, I'm afraid. A man who loves his children doesn't ridicule them in public. I'm sorry to say this, sorry if it hurts you, but it's true. If you go on trying to please him, you won't have a self to give. He doesn't deserve you. I'd hoped we could have dinner together, but if you don't want to—"

"Where would we eat?" The smile in his twinkling eyes stole her breath.

"I know just the place."

* * *

Adam stopped the car at Rafer Grant's front door, put the car in park, turned and looked at Melissa. She was preparing to get out quickly and leave him sitting there, as he'd known she would, and his right hand stilled her departure.

"Melissa, when have I ever left you to walk to your door unescorted? You underestimate me."

She opened the door. "Please, Adam, not tonight. I'm not ready to do battle with him. I enjoyed dinner. Good—"

In an abrupt move, he took her gently to him. "You may refuse me permission to see you to your door, but not this—I'm taking this." His kiss was hard and quick, but he knew he'd shaken her. He stayed there until the front door closed behind her and a figure, no doubt Rafer, approached her. He wanted to go into that house, to shield her from her father's unkind words, from the torrent of abuse that awaited her. For the first time in his adult life, he faced what he regarded as an insurmountable barrier, but he refused to consider the one certain way around it, and he wouldn't back away. She was in his blood.

Adam headed for Beaver Ridge, pensive and restless. He didn't fool himself. If he had to see her every day, his desire for her would grow, not diminish. He cursed—since when had he spent so much time thinking about one woman? Bitter laughter spilled from his lips when he reminded himself that no woman had stood against him as she had. With any other one, he would have long ago plucked the bud, sated himself, and gone his way. It was the reason that sophisticated women had suited him. This one was different, very different. She would want it all, and he wasn't ready to spring for that.

He realized that he hadn't driven home, that Bill Henry's house was at the next turn. He parked, remembered with considerable relief that it wasn't necessary to lock the car, and started up the modest walkway.

"Well, what brings you here tonight, Adam?" His uncle's voice came from a corner of the shadowy front porch, hidden from the light of the moon. "Come on up. Mosquitoes are hiding ever since I lit one of those lemony candles that Winterflower insists on sending me. 'Course, you didn't come here this time of night to discuss mosquitoes. I was in town this evening—heard an awful lot of whispering about you. What's her name?"

He regarded his uncle with affection. A tall, powerfully built and energetic man with smooth dark skin and a pencil thin mustache, he had been Adam's childhood idol. B-H had had time to listen to his dreams for the future while his father strove to preserve the family legacy. He'd never wanted to be like his uncle though, because Bill Henry didn't care about money or building empires; he was a seeker of contentment.

"What's her name?" B-H asked again, and Adam noted that as usual he didn't mince words, nor was he reluctant to get personal.

"Her name is Melissa Grant, and she's head of the search firm that located my newest Leather and Hides employee for me, the one I probably ought to suspect."

B-H nodded. "I see. And you think she might be in cahoots with this fellow—"

"The fellow we're speaking about is my manager of Leather and Hides," Adam cut in. His uncle released a long, sharp whistle.

"So you think she wants to sink the business? I know you'll handle that one way or another, so that's not all that's bothering you." When Adam didn't respond, B-H allowed a considerable amount of time to elapse before he asked, "Are you talking about Emily Morris's daughter?"

Adam swung around. "Yeah. Why?"

B-H stood and walked toward the front door, signaling the end of their conversation. "Just watch your step. There hasn't been a real blitzkrieg around here in over thirty years, and it looks like we're in for one. Stop by again soon."

Meals in the Roundtree home had always been a time of family bonding, and Adam raced down the winding stairs knowing he'd find his mother and brother waiting at the breakfast table. It was one of the reasons why he didn't eat breakfast in New York. He couldn't get accustomed to being alone at a breakfast table. Mary Roundtree didn't spoil her sons, but she gave them as much mothering as they would tolerate. In Adam's case that wasn't much.

"It's so good to have you home, Adam. Sit down, and I'll get your breakfast." He was about to tell her that he'd get it, when he remembered the tradition that she dictated what the family ate for breakfast. She couldn't prevent their eating junk for lunch, she told them, but she could put a good, healthful breakfast in them. Adam had noticed Wayne's unusual silence, but he waited until their mother left the room before inquiring about it.

"What's on your mind, Wayne?" The brothers occasionally went fishing or played tennis on Saturday mornings when both were at home, a carryover from their boyhood days. "It's too hot for tennis. How about spending some time with me at the office?"

"I'd rather we went over to Leather and Hides. Last night while you were out, Nelson called to report another vat of improperly tanned calf skins. He was so outraged that I've begun to wonder if he's involved in this."

They discovered nothing at the factory that Calvin hadn't reported. Adam was more certain than ever that he was dealing with sabotage, because someone had brought formaldehyde from a locked cabinet in the basement up to the third floor and added it to the chrome tanning when zirconium salts should have been applied.

"What's the damage?"

"We'll have to find a buyer for this glove leather," Adam told Wayne, "and we won't be able to fill our orders for first-quality shoe leather. Whoever's doing this is trying to destroy the family's reputation along with the business. Somebody on our payroll is at the bottom of this." As if he didn't have enough to think about: he had to know whether Melissa had a role in it, whether she'd selected someone whom she could depend on to wreck the business. He didn't want to believe her capable of it, but the possibility existed, and his desire for her wasn't going to overrule his common sense. "I'm going to the office to think about all this. I'll let you know what I decide."

Adam closed his office door, locked it, and stretched out on his luxurious leather sofa. He'd come to appreciate the solitude that living alone afforded, and he could only be assured of that total separation from others on Saturdays or Sundays in his office. Sunday was out—small town people went to church on Sundays, and if you had any standing in the African American communities of Frederick and Beaver Ridge, you'd better be there. To go to one's office was to risk being labeled an infidel, and the brothers and sisters did not associate with nonbelievers.

He turned over on his stomach and remembered that he hadn't eaten lunch, but food wasn't what he wanted. He wanted Melissa. He had to see her, but where could they be together without the wrath of their families or the speculations of gossip mongers? He couldn't go to her house, and she wouldn't be welcome in his, and if they went to a public place, the news would float back to their families within the hour. Did he dare even to telephone her? He sat up. For himself, he feared nothing, but he didn't want to trigger her father's mean behavior. He paced the floor, but with each step his desire to see her, to be with her, intensified. She'd said that her father was never violent. He dialed her number.

To his chagrin, Rafer answered. "This is Adam Roundtree. I'd like to speak with Melissa, please." He hadn't hesitated to identify himself, because surreptitious behavior wasn't his style.

"What do you want? Isn't it enough that your family stole her birthright? Now you're after *her!* I won't allow it."

He listened to the man's discourteous remarks with as much patience as he could muster. "If you won't allow me to speak with Melissa, please tell her that I—" He broke off when he heard Melissa's voice.

"Give me that phone. How could you speak that way to another person, Daddy, especially when that person is calling me at the place you said would be my home? If I came back, you promised this would be my home. You listen to me, Daddy—if I'm at home, I should be able to receive calls and entertain my friends without your interference. So it's clear that I'm not home now, but I soon will be." She disregarded her father's stunned expression, aware that she had never before defied him to his face, and turned her back.

"Adam. I apologize for my father. You wanted to speak with me?" Her spirits rose as the deep timbre of his voice warmed her heart.

"I would have preferred not to call, but I had no choice. I want to see you. Where can we meet?"

Melissa looked at her father, saw the veins that protruded at his temple, the rapid breathing that always accompanied his moments of extreme displeasure. When she tried to please him or when, as now, she finally defied him, his reaction was the same.

"Pick me up in a half hour," she told Adam, hung up, and waited for the inevitable. She figured her father needed at least one minute's worth of verbal explosion, gave it to him, and went to her room.

Adam strode up the steps and rang the bell at Rafer Grant's front door. He was certain that Melissa had planned to wait for him on the front steps and had arrived ten minutes earlier than agreed in order to forestall her. He greeted Rafer with as much civility as he could, looked up and saw Melissa coming down the stairs, a vision in a wide-skirted dress of buttercup yellow and knew that, if he had to, he'd take far greater chances in order to be with her.

He took her hand, turned, and looked Rafer Grant in the eye. "Good night, Rafer." The man's whipped expression said that he'd gotten the message, clear and unmistakable: Adam Roundtree did not hide his actions from *anyone*.

Neither spoke, and both knew that their relationship had changed, because each of them had risked something in order to preserve it. Adam drove two blocks, aligned the Jaguar with the curb, parked, and turned to her. She had to know that he'd needed to see her or he wouldn't have called, that her defense of him to her father had heightened his desire to possess her, to be one with her. He reached for her and took her to him hungrily, shocked at first to realize how badly he'd needed to have her in his arms and then stunned by the ardor with which she returned his kiss, clung to his embrace. Again, a nagging memory pestered him: where and when had he known her before?

She nestled in his arms, and he held her there as he marveled that words seemed unnecessary, that they seemed to belong together. Yet he knew that it couldn't be. He wasn't ready for it, not with her, not with a woman who might be guilty of the epitome of treachery, not with the daughter of a man who hated him. Reluctantly he released her. He had to get his emotions into harmony with his brain. Her hand remained on his chest, warm and sweet, and he wanted to pull her back to him. To feel again her soft breast against his chest and her eager mouth welcoming his tongue. He ignored his craving for her and started the engine.

Her words reminded him of what she faced, of what they both faced because of their attraction. "I pray to God that I never have to stand between you and my father. Nothing would have convinced me that he was capable of such acrimony if he hadn't directed it to me, if I hadn't been the butt of it. I've seen a house that I want, and I'll be moving as soon the deal is closed. I shouldn't have let him persuade me to come back here, but fate seems to have had a hand in it, so I'm not knocking it."

"Fate is an excuse people use, Melissa. I don't believe in it," he said, working hard at combating his vulnerability to her.

"I know. You told me that."

He knew that their circumstances troubled her, as they did him. He could feel it, but he couldn't relent and comfort her. His desire for her already neared fever pitch, and he had to keep his counsel, had to resolve the problems at Leather and Hides. He couldn't—wouldn't—think beyond that.

He drove toward Baltimore and stopped at an elegant little mom-and-pop restaurant just on its outskirts, where they were unlikely to encounter anyone from Frederick or Beaver Ridge. But as they entered, Adam saw his brother, Wayne, at a center table with a woman whom he didn't know.

"Do you see someone you know?" Melissa asked.

"My brother and a companion." He sat back, looking in Wayne's direction until his brother acknowledged his presence. That accomplished, he opened the menu and concentrated on what he'd eat.

"So much for privacy. I doubt we'll get any before you move into your house." He couldn't bring any humor to his chuckle. "And then we'll have more privacy than will be good for us." He could tell from her reply that she didn't have her sense of humor with her right then.

"Will your brother come over here? Do you think he'll join us?"

A smile touched the corner of his mouth. Her feelings about additional company couldn't have been clearer. She didn't want any, at least not his brother's.

"Wayne wouldn't engage me in a public confrontation, Melissa. My brother and I respect each other." They ordered cold minted pea soup, Maryland deviled crab cakes, salad, and peach cobbler a la mode for dessert. Adam contemplated the soup in which he normally delighted, but which he could not enjoy. He had looked forward to being with her as they'd been that Sunday with Winterflower, but he knew she wouldn't let down her guard, that Melissa Grant wouldn't drop her public persona so long as they were under his brother's watchful eye.

Heat pooled in his middle when she idly stroked his left hand.

"Will Wayne be angry with you?"

He realized then that she had a deep concern for his family's reaction to their being together. He told the truth.

"Wayne is angry, and he will continue to be for some time."

He watched, fascinated, as the gray of her eyes lessened and the brown grew more striking. Obviously appalled, she exclaimed, "Don't you care?"

"Every bit as much as you do, I assure you," he replied, "but I try not to allow the opinions of others to dictate my behavior."

"Doesn't *anything* get to you?"

"Sure. You get to me, Melissa. What do you suggest I do about it?"

She glanced anxiously toward Wayne.

"Don't be provocative. We're not alone." No, they weren't. But if there had been no one around them, it would have made no difference. The communion he needed with her couldn't be expressed in words. Frustrated and fearing that he'd spoiled the evening for her, he squeezed her hand and suggested that they leave.

"I'm not a masochist, but the longer I sit here with you, the more I'm beginning to feel like one." Tenderness for her surged within him, and he longed to cherish her for the world to see, to protect her from the berating he knew she'd get at home because of him. Their circumstances chafed him, its reality like bile in his mouth. He wanted to kick something.

When they got back to her parents' home, he parked and

cut the motor. Her hand reached toward the door, and he told
her in a voice soft but firm, "Don't even think it, Melissa. I
went in and got you, and I'm taking you back in there." He
took her key, opened the door, stepped inside, and took her
into his arms. Her passionate trembling when his fingers
streaked down her cheeks and her neck nearly cost him his
self-control. He didn't consider whether he had an audience,
didn't think of that, only that he needed her fire, her woman's
heat, her total surrender.

Blood pounded in his brain as the heady scent of her desire
tantalized her nostrils. The slight movements of her hips
against him stunned him and then, as though giving in to her
feelings and dismissing caution, her action became rhythmic
undulations that sent blazing heat to his groin. At his swift,
powerful erection, her arms tightened around him, and she
sucked his tongue into her mouth and gave herself to him. He
nearly buckled from the force of his desire. He demanded, and
she gave. Gave until the blood coursed through him like a
rising river rushing out of control; gave until he thought he'd
lost possession of his big muscular body as it quivered with
rampant passion; gave until the salt of her tears brought him
back to reality, and he released her. He stood for long minutes
looking into her eyes, looking for the woman that he wanted
her to be. Looking for himself. At last he forced a smile, ran
his hand over her frizzled curls in a gesture of affection, and
left her.

The next morning, Sunday, he got out of bed at eight o'clock
after having slept barely three hours. Frustrated because she
was who she was and at himself because of the dilemma he'd
gotten into, he had to settle at least one thing. What was her
tie to Nelson? To his relief, it was she who answered his telephone call. He greeted her warmly before asking, "Melissa,
did you know Calvin Nelson before you interviewed him for
my company?"

He had to admit her genuine surprise at his question. "I

met Nelson the day before I brought him to your office. Prior to that he was a name on my computer screen. Why?"

"I needed to know."

"If you doubt my integrity, say it right out."

"If I find fault with you, Melissa, I'll tell you to your face."

"Watch your step," she shot back, her voice cool and businesslike. He hung up. He'd annoyed her, and he hadn't solved one thing.

Melissa dressed for church in a white seersucker dress and white low-heel sandals. Disconcerted by Adam's odd question, she told herself that it couldn't mean anything, that a man couldn't kiss a woman as he'd kissed her the night before unless he at least respected her. She stopped by the breakfast room for a cup of coffee and found her father seated at the table deep in thought, his place setting undisturbed.

"Good morning, Daddy."

"You're a traitor," he began with obviously controlled fury. "You know Jacob Hayes stole your birthright and that every one of his descendants has laughed in our faces, flaunting their millions at us. And you have the nerve to go consorting with Adam Roundtree, parading yourself with him right in front of me. You've got no shame and no family pride. I ask you to come home and look after your mother, and what do you do. You open an office in a Roundtree building and walk out of my house with Adam Roundtree holding your hand. You're—"

Melissa couldn't listen any longer. She left the room without having gotten the coffee and started up the stairs. For the first time, she wondered about her father's unnatural hatred for the Hayes people. He isn't a Morris, she reflected; he only married one. "I'm tired of this."

Banks knocked on Melissa's office door the next morning and walked in with two cups of coffee and a box of powdered sugar doughnuts. Except for her beloved Snickers, Melissa confined her junk food intake to late night snacks, but that morning she ate two of the doughnuts, arousing her friend's curiosity.

"Most mornings, I can't get you to eat half of one of these things. What's got into you?"

"How does tall, dark, and handsome sound?" Melissa asked, in an attempt at jocularity as she idly braided the curly hair that hung over her right ear.

Banks gulped her coffee. "You're sweet on Adam? Good Lord! Why don't you just drop the bomb and start World War Three?"

Melissa shook her head, conceding her dilemma. "My father is outraged because I went out with Adam Saturday night, says I've disgraced the family, and that Adam's motive in seeing me is suspect. I enjoy being with Adam, and I'm sick of this ridiculous feud, but I can't let my family down, Banks. I can't betray my folks."

Banks removed the cigarette from the corner of her mouth, and when she didn't see an ashtray, put it out against the sole of her shoe. That done, she settled into the room's most comfortable chair and looked at Melissa. "I don't know how meddlesome you allow your friends to be, but you might as well learn right now that I speak my mind. So if you don't want to hear it, push the rest of my doughnuts over here and tell me to leave."

Melissa returned her friend's steady gaze. "If you've got the guts to say it, I can take it."

"Well," Banks began after a long pause, "have you ever wondered whether Moses Morris, your grandfather, just stood silently and naively by while Jacob Hayes took him to the cleaners? Do you think a man smart enough to swing a loan for a high-risk venture with no capital behind him was stupid enough to let another man soak him? Think, Melissa. That was nearly three-quarters of a century ago, when most of the black people in this country didn't have a reason to go to a bank."

She lit another cigarette, puffed it, and sent a perfect smoke ring drifting its way to extinction. "And what about the court ruling, Melissa? Don't you think that has any validity? From what I read of it, the jury consisted of ordinary people living in the county here, and none of them stood to gain anything. You can read the trial record in the library on Market Street, or you can read the newspaper reports preserved in some of those glass cases in City Hall." She laughed, though it was more of a snort. "Or you can take the town tour that old lady Aldridge sells the tourist; she never fails to mention it. The Hayes-Morris feud is almost as famous around here as the one between the Hatfields and the McCoys." She glanced at Melissa to gauge her reaction. "I like it," she joked, not bothering to veil the mockery. "I like the fuss the townspeople make over it. It legitimates us black folk as social beings."

"Anybody would think you invented sarcasm," Melissa said, her tone conveying admiration.

Banks feigned modesty. "Aw, shucks, you know I didn't invent it, honey. I just know how to make good use of it."

She extinguished her half smoked cigarette in the manner previously adopted. "You know, Melissa," she continued when she saw that Melissa didn't object to her candid words, "all this sounds like jealousy to me, like your grandfather wanted to kick himself for his own rash behavior. Even *I* know you don't bring in gas or oil overnight. If he took his money out of that speculative venture before the find, he didn't have a claim. And, honey, if you let this ridiculous grudge keep you from a man that just about every woman within driving distance would like to have, you're doing yourself a disservice. And you're crazy. Plain looney." She crossed her leg and swung it. "Her highness, Mary Roundtree, is going to see red. Ha. Serve her right. She always was too highfalutin for me." She sighed and got up . . . a bit dramatically, Melissa decided. "I'm going back to work, Melissa. You can tell me what you think about this at lunch."

* * *

An afternoon several days later, Melissa put the keys to her new house in the pocket of her slacks and began the ten-block walk to her parents' home. She hoped the workers would complete the renovations within a couple of weeks, because she needed her own place, and soon. Her father had stopped speaking to her, and her mother stayed in her room reading the world's great books, the purpose of which Melissa sensed was to legitimate her refusals of Rafer's company, if indeed, it was she who did the refusing.

Her mother welcomed her visits, but rarely went to Melissa's room. Melissa had begun to suspect that Emily Grant would do most anything to avoid her husband's anger. Did that account for the times when she'd find chocolate under her pillow, a pink rose in her bathroom, or a book of verse on her night table? But never a word of it from her mother. Or when, as a child, she'd find a new doll or other toy in her drawer or closet. She had attributed that to her love of surprises and had thought that her mother knew that and catered to it.

She couldn't help pondering Banks's caution of her loyalty to her parents, especially her father, an allegiance that her friend believed to be misplaced. Why shouldn't she enjoy Adam's company? He hadn't hurt her in any way, and even with her limited knowledge of men, she knew he was honorable. Proud and at times arrogant, perhaps, but honest. Yet she hadn't been able to forget how he'd queried her about Calvin Nelson nor the questions he'd asked: how well and how long she'd known the man. She disliked the subtle implication that she might have recommended a personal friend after taking a retainer for an executive search. The more she thought of it, the closer she came to getting mad.

She walked into the house, went to the telephone, and called him. "Why did you ask me the other day how long I'd known Calvin Nelson before I brought him to you? I've been thinking about that, and I do not like the insinuation."

"I told you not to worry, that I was covering all bases."

"What kind of an answer is that?" The lilting cadence of his voice always thrilled her, but waves of joy washed over her at the sound of his deep, vibrant laugh, a wondrous sound that he so rarely let her hear. He must have heard the warmth in her voice, must have detected how well his brief answer had charmed her.

"I want to see you tonight."

She wouldn't let him bend her to his will. "I don't think so. What did Wayne have to say about our being together last weekend?"

"Don't let that concern you," he replied with evident lack of concern. "He means well. They all do—Rafer included—in their way. What time should I call for you?"

The man wasn't accustomed to hearing the word no, and as Jason Court had warned her, he didn't like it when he heard it. Well, he should know by now that she was as independent as he. "Not tonight, Adam," she insisted. "A war broke out in our house after you left here the other night."

"You mean I'm not worth your defense of me?"

She heard his laughter and figured it was time he got some of his own. "You've got the courage to come to my house and create a storm. Well, suppose I come by for you at, say, seven o'clock tonight. Be ready." She hung up. And you can be sure, she murmured to herself, that I'll ring your bell at a quarter to seven.

She grabbed the phone before its second ring. "What's the matter? Chicken?" she asked. But Adam was not the caller.

"Melissa, this is Timothy Coston, your cousin Timmy."

She sat down, glad that she hadn't said more and that she hadn't called Adam's name.

"How are you, Timmy? I'm surprised to hear from you."

"Yeah. I guess you are. I hear you have an employment agency. That's what your dad said, and I'm looking for a job." Some more of her father's shenanigans.

"I locate executives for corporations, Timmy. I don't run an employment exchange, but if I happen upon an opening, I'll keep you in mind. I'm in the Hayes Building. Send me your CV." She terminated the conversation as quickly as she could. She would not hire her cousin no matter what her father said or did. She'd lose control of her business, and her father would have been the instigator.

Five

Melissa's breath stuck in her throat as she waited at the front door of the Roundtree house. She had never before stepped on the property, hadn't even had a clear view of the house, though, like most of the area's residents, she'd heard about its sumptuousness. She'd been taught from early childhood that the place was off limits. To her relief, no wild, vicious dogs barked furiously and snarled at her feet, which, as a child, she'd imagined was the reason for her father's stern edict that she, Schyler, and their cousin Timothy avoid the place. She listened for footsteps, heard none, and pressed the bell again. The doorknob turned, and she released her breath at last, only to suck it in sharply when the door opened and Mary Roundtree faced her. Lord, she hadn't counted on this.

"Good evening, Mrs. Roundtree. I'm Melissa Grant." The woman's manners matched her regal bearing. "Hello, Melissa." Though her voice was pleasant, it lacked warmth, Melissa noted.

"Won't you come in? I assume from what I've heard that you wish to see my son, Adam." What had she expected, Melissa asked herself—small towns and secrets were incompatible.

"Thank you. Would you please tell him I'm here?" She reflected on their behavior toward each other, so pleasant and so civilized. A stranger would have gained the impression that they had always been on friendly terms, but those were the first words they had ever exchanged. She stood straighter with her shoulders squared, faintly amused at the barely leashed anger she saw in Adam's mother's eyes. Parental possessiveness wasn't limited to her father. Mary Roundtree turned to leave, and Melissa heard Adam's footsteps as he loped down the stairs. She looked up with a start. Would she ever get used to his arresting, masculine good looks? She stared into the depth of his gaze until the sound of his mother's throat clearing restored her presence of mind.

As she stood there admiring him, she wished she could enjoy their relationship without reservation. There was so much about him that she liked. Cherished. If he had spoken, if he had said one word, she would have quickly gotten herself in hand, but he didn't speak, merely ambled toward her without taking his gaze from hers. She backed up a step and tried to shake the tension, but it flooded the room like a powerful, invisible chemical and settled over her. Again Adam's mother cleared her throat, and he turned to her.

"Mother, this is Melissa Grant. Melissa, my mother." Mary Roundtree nodded, told Melissa good night, and left them. Melissa watched her walk away and couldn't help thinking that the woman could give her father lessons in manners.

She relaxed within the arm that he slid around her waist, nestling her to him as he opened the door for them to leave. She wanted to turn around, to know whether Adam's mother watched them, but he didn't give her the chance.

"How'd you get here?" he asked her, looking about for a car.

"Towne car service. I'd have been in a pickle if you had forgotten and gone off."

He walked around to the driver's side, got in, and turned to her. "So you got even. Why is it that I'm not surprised? Don't be too proud of yourself, though. The last time anybody in my house reprimanded me was the day I finished high school. And I only got it then, because I'd brought a girl home the evening before when my parents were out. That was the number one no no around here, but I never gave them the satisfaction of knowing that we only sat in the kitchen and drank root beer." He started the ignition. "Let's go."

She slid comfortably down in the bucket seat. "I figured if you'd made my father mad with me, you wouldn't mind a little turbulence in your own household. You call that getting even? Tut-tut."

He looked down at her and grinned. She could give as good as she got. Soft, but strong. Clever. He liked that.

She stole a peek at the man as he glanced over his left shoulder, swung into Route 70, and revved the engine. Her heart lurched at the sight of him sitting behind the wheel of that powerful car, strength emanating from him. She looked away from him at the passing scene. With her glasses in place, her eyes skimmed the late summer cornfields as he sped past them, and she wondered whether a woman awaited the lone man who trudged through a field toward an old farmhouse. She longed for the day when she'd have a man of her own, one who loved her so much he couldn't stay away from her, one who would never be content with her sleeping in any room but his. One different from her father. A man who wouldn't be too proud to love a woman with every atom of his being.

"You're unusually quiet. Maybe you're not pleased with yourself, with your little devilment?"

She marveled that he wasn't annoyed by what she'd done. Or was he showing her that she couldn't dent his unflappable cool, that she wasn't of such importance that her little misdeed would make him mad?

"Do you think your mother's angry?" she asked.

"You betcha. Mad as hell." He took his attention from the highway long enough for a quick glance at her.

"And you don't mind that's she's mad?"

"Of course I mind." She detected impatience and something like sympathetic understanding in his voice. "What do you take me to be? That woman is my mother, and I care about how she feels. But I'm a man, and that's my home, so I don't seek anybody's permission and don't expect anybody's condemnation about what I do there." He reached over and patted her hand.

"What would you do if I abducted you, took you to my lair and kept you there for a couple of weeks?"

She saw that he'd ended that topic. She turned toward him, and her eyes dared him to do it.

"Well?" he prodded

"Grin and bear it," she joshed. His warm, throaty laugh that seemed to come from deep inside him sent frissons of heat racing through her. If he knew how much ground he could cover with just a laugh, she reckoned, the man would be unbearable.

Darkness encroached as he turned off the highway and into the only asphalt side road that she'd seen since leaving Beaver Ridge.

"We've passed plenty of them," he told her when she commented. "Don't tell me I've cast a spell on you, closing your mind to all but me." He laughed, and she imagined that her face mirrored her startled reaction. He did it often now, and she thought back to the day shortly after they met and the first time she'd heard his laughter. He'd been stunned at himself. Now he seemed to enjoy it, as though it released something that had been dammed up inside him. He stopped the car, got out, took her hand, and began walking up a gravel path. Melissa looked up at him, perplexed. Where were they going in the darkening woods? A strain of happiness wove through his laughter and swirled magically around her, exhilarating her like a warm twilight breeze frolicking in her soul. She gave herself over to the moment and let his joyous mood infect her.

They paused at an old mill lodged a few feet above the dawdling waters of a once busy brook, and his arm slipped around her shoulder while the moon let them see their reflection in the clear stream below. Melissa wanted to lean against him, but she didn't. If he had squeezed or patted her the tiniest bit, she would have moved toward him, but his large warm hand on her bare arm evidently didn't communicate to him the feeling it gave her. She moved away. Men were not meant to be understood.

"What's over there?" she asked, pointing to a footpath that led into dense woods.

"Not much of interest this late in the year, but in the spring you see a lot of trails littered with wildflowers and small streams alongside them. It's idyllic—a man's best ally if he's got a woman he wants to sweet-talk."

"I can't imagine you'd need help."

"Of course not." And you're proof of that, his eyes mocked. In spite of the lectures she gave herself, she knew she was becoming increasingly susceptible to Adam, but she told herself that she wasn't going to sell out her family by having an affair with him. And he was going to stop kissing her, too. Then his strong but gentle fingers reached for and squeezed hers, and she slipped a little farther into his universe, his world of riveting tension and longing.

Hours later, as he parked in front of her parents' home, she reflected on their evening together. Not once had he alluded to anything personal between them. Not one sexual innuendo. Not a single pass. And yet his twinkling eyes had held such fire and his smiles had triggered such excitement in her as to make her wonder whether he had special powers. He had made no effort to seduce her—but captivate her, he did. She told herself that she wouldn't kiss him good night, that he didn't deserve it. She had learned that he loved to read, liked football, tennis, horses, Mozart, Eric Clapton, and Duke Ellington, and disliked atonal music, baseball, washing dishes, and strong, gusty winds. Yet he hadn't even hinted at what he felt about her. Well, if he was satisfied with an evening of impersonal togetherness, so was she. And she'd show him.

"Adam, you haven't told me what you think of your new office manager. How's he doing?"

He took his hand off of the doorknob, turned, and looked at her in a way that suggested her question was not in order. "He's efficient and competent, but I think Jason's getting tired of him."

"Why?" So, she surmised, a problem did exist, but she wouldn't have known about it if she hadn't asked.

"The man doesn't accept supervision well, especially from someone he considers beneath him."

"He thinks Jason is beneath him?"

"Yeah. Lester's a snob, Melissa. To him, anybody who didn't go to Yale is illiterate. Jason was graduated from Morehouse and got his master's degree at Georgetown. I'm sure the reason they haven't clashed is because Jason is boss when I'm not in the office, and he just calls rank on the man. Anybody who pushes Jason too hard usually regrets it. I think Lester knows that, and he likes having a good income."

"He didn't behave that way with me, but then he was looking for a job. I'm surprised at his snobbishness, though, because several of the references I checked suggested that until Lester was in his late teens, a lot of that Mississippi mud found its way between his toes."

Adam cut short a laugh. "So you do check references?"

Melissa whirled on him. "What do you mean by that question? I run an honest, efficient operation. I've placed executives in some of the most successful businesses in this country, and I want to know how you get the temerity to suggest that I don't have integrity." She jumped out of the car, and he caught her just as she reached the front steps of the house.

"Don't get so riled." He paused as though weighing his next words. "Riled isn't the word—I've noticed that little if anything upsets you, or if it does, you don't show it. Where business is concerned, I don't insinuate anything, Melissa. If something needs saying, I say it. You can be sure that if I have a complaint against an executive hired through MTG, I'll tell you."

She handed him her key, and he opened her front door and walked in with her. Rafer stood in the middle of the foyer, facing them, his face mottled with rage.

"Now that you've discovered this house, you can't seem to stay out of it," he told Adam. His derisive tone and dismissive glance at Melissa was evidently calculated to annoy Adam. Melissa stepped toward him. "Daddy, if you want to bait Adam, please do it outside so he'll have as good a chance as you at winning a case of assault and battery." She heard them snort, but she wouldn't let that prevent her from having her say. It was overdue. "I am twenty-eight and self-employed, and I've established my business without help from anyone. I'm not used to your concern for my well-being after all these years of disregarding me, and I wish you'd stop it." She turned and kissed Adam, well aware that she surprised him when she pressed her lips to his in a lingering caress. "Good night, Adam. I had a lovely evening. Good night, Daddy."

Shivers streaked down her back as she walked up the stairs to her room, aware that they both stood as she'd left them, staring in her wake. Why had she kissed Adam when she had told herself that she wouldn't, not even if he tried to seduce her into it? She closed her bedroom door and turned the key. This was merely the beginning. Her father's pride was his most damning trait, and she had just embarrassed him, exposed him in front of Adam Roundtree. She'd pay. Oh, she'd pay plenty. She reflected on her brother's comment that their father wasn't a bad person, only a pathetically insecure man, and that he'd give anything to know what accounted for it.

* * *

Adam got into his car and drove off. He neared the house hoping his family had turned in for the night. He needed to be alone, to think over the evening's events, beginning with his turmoil before he'd brought Melissa home. He had promised himself that never again would he let a woman scramble his brain and hijack his hormones. But another woman *had* gotten inside of him, one who could be his family's enemy, who could have engineered the sabotage of his family's business, who could be the greatest actress since Waters or Barrymore. He'd strung her along all evening, touching but not caressing, drawing her to him while making sure that she didn't get close, and talking about any and every thing except the two of them. It had been hard work.

Adam shook off the autumn chill as he entered the wide foyer of his home and continued upstairs to his room for the privacy he needed. But as soon as he closed his door, his mother knocked and, like her elder son, she didn't skirt the issue.

"Adam, why are you pursuing a relationship with Melissa Grant? Is it because you like her, or because you're suspicious of her? Do you mind telling me?" He knew that she found prying into his personal life distasteful and was certain that that accounted for her uncharacteristic diffidence. She wanted his answer to be that he was suspicious, but he wouldn't lie.

"I see her because I like her, Mother." He noticed that she tensed.

"But what about the problem at Leather and Hides?"

"I don't have any proof that she's in on it, and I'd give her the benefit of the doubt until I was certain even if I had never met her." He locked his hazel-rimmed, brown-eyed gaze on his mother's identical one. "That's the way I was raised." Her affectionate smile assured him that she understood and accepted the reprimand. He told her briefly of their confrontations with Melissa's father.

Mary Roundtree grimaced. "Why did she come here tonight? Were you expecting her?"

He smiled. "I think to show me what she went through with her father because I insisted on ringing her bell and going inside her house for her, as I would any other woman with whom I had a date."

"Well, she paid you back, and I have to admire her strength. Looks as if she has grit."

"Oh, she has plenty of that." He sighed, deep in thought, private thought. "And she has something else, too. A quiet dignity that hides a deep-seated vulnerability, a softness . . ." He rubbed his brow with his long, tapered brown fingers. "A sweetness that I haven't—" Suddenly reminded of his mother's presence, he was himself again. Quiet. Uncommunicative.

"You think a lot of her." He'd opened the door, and now she'd have her say. Alright, he'd listen.

"Do I? I'm not so sure."

"Well, you *feel* a lot for her—that's clear. What I can't understand is how you let it happen, knowing what you know." Her tone held deep bitterness. Adam shuttered his eyes, shielding his emotions.

"I care about your feelings, Mother, and I know what you think of Melissa's family. But if I conducted my personal life according to *your* wishes, nobody would be more surprised or disappointed than you. And you know there isn't an iota of a chance that I'd do that, so please save us both some heartache; don't get into this. I chart my own course." He walked over and kissed her cheek. "Good night, Mother. I'll see you in the morning." He mounted the stairs slowly. Where the Morris/Grant family was concerned, his mother was matched for intolerance and hatred only by Rafer Grant's attitude toward the Hayeses and Roundtrees. He wished he could see the end of it.

Adam stretched out in bed, wanting to clear his mind and go to sleep. The chirping crickets had as their backup a loud chorus of croaking frogs, familiar notes that had lulled him

into many of his most precocious childhood dreams. As though
back in time, he responded to the night music, and his mind
drifted to Melissa, cataloging her lush feminine assets. What
did she have that caused his pores to absorb her the way mush-
rooms drink water? Why did her woman's scent stay with him
always? And why couldn't he stop feeling her lips? He wiped
his mouth with his naked arm and turned over on his belly.
In every way that counted, she was the kind of woman he
liked, that was why.

His gut instinct told him she was honest, and he'd learned
to go with his instincts. But he wouldn't swear that he hadn't
let his emotions fog up his reasoning about Melissa. He had
to have some proof. Sleep. He'd be willing to pay for it.

Melissa showered, got ready for bed, slipped on a robe, and
knocked on her mother's door. What kind of marriage was it,
she wondered, when the couple didn't share a room, not to
speak of a bed?

Emily Grant opened the door, still dressed as though expecting guests for afternoon tea.

"I hate to disturb you, Mother, but I need to tell you what's
going on with me these days." She looked around her mother's
sanctuary. That's what it was, she saw, a hideaway, her mother's
own place with her own decorative taste, own things, and, especially, her own books. Unlike the foyer, living, dining, and
family rooms that had been decorated in dull, muted, and so-
cially correct tones by the most expensive interior decorator
Rafer could find, her mother's room shouted with joy in hues
of green, yellow, and sand with an occasional red or orange
accent. Melissa sat on a brilliantly patterned Moroccan leather
footstool and watched in surprise as her mother kicked off her
shoes, sat on her red chaise lounge, leaned back with both
hands behind her head, and waited. Had she been missing
something about her mother all these years?

"You know I came back home to be with you, to see you

through this terrible illness that Daddy described to me, don't you?" Her mother sat up as if waiting for the ax to fall, but she remained silent.

"Mother, I can't stay in the same house as Daddy. I've bought a place on Teal Street, and I'm going to move as soon as possible." She watched Emily walk over to a small antique cabinet and return with two brandy snifters and a bottle of cognac. I don't know my mother, she mused, accepting the drink.

"I've done a lot of thinking since you've come back," her mother began, "and I'm ashamed. I made unforgivable mistakes with my children, and if I got what I deserved, you'd still be in New York. Rafer doted on Schyler, and I did whatever pleased Rafer, even when I knew it was wrong. I parroted him until I had no self left, until I couldn't stand him or myself.

"I wish I had challenged him, for you, if not for myself. Instead I tried to comfort you with little presents, when what you needed was the solid support of knowing that your mother loved you. You needed my absolute defiance. I should have battled him over his treatment of you. I admired you for your strength in getting out and making a life for yourself. I missed you, but I was glad you left, and I prayed you'd find the love you'd been robbed of at home."

Melissa leaned forward, hoping that her mother couldn't see how astonished she was. She didn't want to appear censorial, but she had to ask. "Why didn't you leave him, Mother?"

"No woman in my family had ever been divorced, and I didn't want to be the first."

"Was there a chance of that?"

Emily sipped the brandy. "Oh, yes. There was more than a chance. If I had chosen to behave differently, we would have separated. And I've often thought I should have let it happen. I should have forced it myself. We would all have been happier."

Melissa knew from her mother's strained expression that she found the conversation painful. She emptied her glass, indi-

cated that she didn't want more and told herself to relax, to
listen even if the words she heard hit her like sharp darts shot
into her chest.

"Don't let him bully you."

Melissa gasped. She hadn't known that her mother knew
how her father treated her since she'd come home.

"And don't let him interfere in your life. I spoiled your
brother, because it was what his father wanted, and I didn't
stand up for you against Rafer when I should have. I don't
ask you to forgive me, because I can't forgive myself." She
stood and turned her back. "Would you unzip me, please? I
love this dress, but I hate back zippers—they're too much for
my short arms. Be glad you're tall." Melissa did as she asked,
then waited for her mother to face her.

"Why did Father have so little tolerance for me when I was
a child? I used to think he couldn't stand me." She fought
back the tears. "I tried so hard to make him love me, to make
him think I was special . . . like Schyler was special."

Cold fear gripped her as she waited for Emily's answer, but
her mother's deep sigh of resignation told her she'd have to
wait.

"And you're still trying. But we've said enough for tonight.
Someday, you'll know everything, Melissa. A lot of this furor
about Adam and his family is my fault. I'll say this much:
Mary Roundtree must be proud of Adam. I would be, if he
were my son. It's time we got some sleep. Good night, dear."

Her mother's words had pained her, but they had also given
her comfort. She wasn't sorry that she had made the move
from New York. Her financial position had improved, and she
had as many clients as she could serve. But most important,
she had just shared genuine intimacies with her mother, a first.
Her mother didn't disapprove of her relationship with Adam
as her father did and as Schyler might, and that could set them
against Emily. If she didn't stop seeing the man who was com-

ing to mean more to her than any other ever had, she could destroy her family.

Timothy's presence in her secretary's office when she arrived at work the next morning astonished her. He hadn't sent his curriculum vitae as she'd directed, but he expected nevertheless that she'd find work for him.

"Complete this and send it to me, and I'll see what I can do." As he strolled out of her office, it occurred to her that she could be years finding her cousin a job.

Two weeks passed and Melissa's house wasn't ready, but after her meeting with the roofer that afternoon, she figured that she'd be able to move in within a few days. The cool October nights came early now as the days grew shorter. She didn't have much confidence driving the secondhand car she had just bought, so she worked swiftly to finish her chores and get to her parents' home before nightfall. She noted the low-lying, dark clouds as she left the house and had no sooner begun the short drive than a torrent of rain pummeled the car's roof.

She drove by a middle-aged man who struggled against the downpour, his shopping bags nearly useless, remembered small-town neighborliness, backed up, and offered him a ride. When he opened the door, she recognized Bill Henry Hayes, though they hadn't been formally introduced, and held her breath fearing that he'd rather drown than ride in a Grant's automobile. He got in, and she introduced herself.

"I know who you are, Melissa, and I'm sure glad you came along. I didn't like the idea of my groceries littering this street." She wondered at his remarkable resemblance to Adam, most evident in his smile.

"I'm glad I happened along." She'd never been good at making talk, and for once she wished she was more adept at it, because she didn't want to appear unfriendly to Adam's uncle.

He turned to her. "You and Adam have just about lit up this

town. Anytime you see two African Americans stop each other in the street and start a long conversation, you can bet they're back on the Hayes-Morris saga. If the Ringling Brothers came to town tomorrow, they'd probably just break even. Our own show is better."

A sense of dread overcame her, and she wondered if she'd been foolish in stopping for him. She let her silence tell him what she thought of the town gossips.

When he spoke again, his voice had lost its merriment and warmth. "Answer me this. Do you mean to do Adam harm?"

She couldn't control the sharp intake of breath that betrayed her astonishment at his question. "Of course not." If her tone sounded bitter, she didn't care. "Is that what he thinks?"

The conciliatory timbre of his voice did nothing to soothe her. "Nobody knows what Adam thinks but Adam." At least he shoots straight, she admitted to herself.

"Yes, I know," she answered.

Bill Henry's deep sigh warned her that she could expect more. "I could ask you what he means to you, but I don't expect you're foolish enough to tell me. I don't know a finer man. Never have. If you're after him, you'd better be one hundred percent straight. As far as I know, Adam's never learned how to forgive deceit nor forget a wrong deed. He's hard, but he's a solid rock of a man. And he's never been known to use his power against a helpless person. I watch him sometime. There's a fountain of goodness deep in that man."

She wondered if he realized how nervous she had become. "Why are you telling me this, Mr. Hayes? Adam hasn't indicated that I'm special to him in any way. Furthermore, we haven't made a commitment to each other, and there's little chance that we will." She glanced quickly at him as they neared his house.

"Well, he's indicated his interest to me and to the rest of the family."

He must have noticed her astonishment, because he patted her arm when she asked him what he meant.

"Adam wouldn't flaunt his defiance of Mary's wishes unless the situation was extremely important to him, and he did that when he walked out of her house with you on his arm."

She parked, rested her right hand on the back of her bucket seat, and turned to face him. "What will everybody think about my driving you home? How much fallout should I expect?"

"I couldn't say, Melissa. It's been decades since I gave a hoot about what anybody said. My guess is that Adam will appreciate it. Mary won't. Rafer will behave as only he can. And Emily, well . . ." His voice softened perceptibly. "How is Emily?"

Alerted by the strangely melancholy tenor that his voice took on, she told him in greater detail than she otherwise would have that her mother hadn't been well and that it was because of Emily's health that she'd returned to Frederick. His long silence caused her to wonder about his reason for asking. Then his words and tone mystified her.

"I'm sorry," he said with a slow shake of his head. "I'm so very, very sorry. Thank you for the ride and for the chance to meet you. And please call me B-H." She hadn't realized that the rain had stopped until he got out, retrieved his shopping bags, and started toward his front door, trudging very slowly, she thought, for a man as young as he. She backed up, turned the car around, and started home. Something in addition to the fight over entitlement to that gas field had mired their families in hatred. She was sure of it.

"Are you declaring yourself as my competition?" Adam enjoyed putting Bill Henry on the defensive. It wasn't often the man gave anyone the opportunity to do that. His uncle had wasted no time telling him that "the lovely Melissa" had been his savior during the late afternoon downpour. He had the impression that B-H wanted his relationship with Melissa to become permanent, but he didn't want that encouraged. He hung up the phone, stretched out on his bed, and answered his beeper. A foreman at Leather and Hides had discovered more skullduggery. In the pretanning process, someone had failed to add the correct amount of lime to the sodium sulfide solution that gave the company's shoe leathers their distinctive quality.

Frustrated and angry, he beeped Calvin Nelson. "Meet me at my office in an hour. I need to talk with you." He sprang up from the bed, tucking his T-shirt into his jeans as he did so. He listened.

"Don't interrupt your wife's plans. I can drive by your house. Yeah. Twenty minutes."

They sat in Adam's office sipping coffee from one of the building's automatic coffee machines. "Cal, this is the fourth such incident at the plant since you took over as manager, and nothing like this had happened before. Do you know of a worker who might dislike or resent you, or who has a gripe of any kind?"

"I've been on the lookout for that, but . . . no, I don't think so. I circulate as much as I can, but it's impossible for me to be everywhere in that plant at once."

"I know that." Adam resisted the urge to ask him whether he had a personal connection to Melissa. "I think it's deliberate, and if it continues, whoever's doing it will succeed in trashing the plant's reputation. I want it stopped."

"Have you considered hiring an undercover man who knows the business? We could make up a job that would justify his roaming all over."

"Good idea. Thanks." Adam brushed his index finger back and forth across his square chin. Would a guilty man make such a suggestion? He didn't think so.

He wasn't prepared for the coolness with which his brother greeted him at breakfast the next morning, and he guessed rightly that Melissa was the issue.

"Cut me some slack, Wayne," he said with dwindling patience. "I'm not impulsive—you know that. And you also ought to know that I keep my own counsel. If I want a woman and she wants me, it's between us and no one else. And if I decide that I want Melissa Grant, she's the only one whose feelings and opinions will matter to me."

"But what about Leather and Hides? What about her family's seventy-year crusade to blacken our name? That means nothing to you?"

Adam disliked unpleasant arguments with his brother, but he refused to let Wayne censor him as Rafer had done Melissa. And he wouldn't tolerate a baseless indictment of her.

"If you've got any proof against Melissa, bring it to me, and I'll see her in jail." Good Lord, he hoped it wouldn't come to that. Less agitated now, he stopped pacing and sat on a stool at the breakfast bar. "Wayne, has she ever slandered a member of this family?"

His brother looked over his shoulder and returned Adam's probing stare. "Not that I know of."

Adam walked over to the window where Wayne stood, dropped a strong hand lightly on his shoulder, and spoke in a gentler voice. After all, they both were concerned about the family's welfare.

"You were always fair, Wayne. Why are you making her a scapegoat? What has she done? Get to know her. Then if you think she's poison, you'll be entitled to say so." He walked over to the refrigerator and took out a pitcher of orange juice. "Don't hope that I'll stop seeing her without good reason. The time I spend with her is the most relaxed, the ha—" He looked into Wayne's knowing eyes and bridled his tongue.

"Alright. Arrange a meeting with the three of us. Not dinner. That's too formal. Let's drive to Washington Sunday and catch the Redskins and Giants. I'll get the tickets. Does she like football?"

Adam shrugged. "I think so. I'll ask her."

"I'll be on my best behavior," Wayne assured him.

"You bet you will."

* * *

Forty minutes later Adam closed his office door, checked his messages, sat down at his desk, and picked up his private phone. "What happens between the time you lift the receiver and the time you say hello?" he asked Melissa. "I always get the feeling you're going to hang up without speaking. What are you doing for Halloween?"

"Hi, Adam. The answer to both parts of your question is 'nothing.' Before I met your uncle yesterday, I hadn't realized there were any poor Hayeses." His amusement must have been noticeable by phone, he figured, when she asked him, "What's funny?"

"Honey, B-H is rich." At her exclamation, he explained. "He's also a loner and a nature lover. His Vietnam experience changed his outlook on a lot of things. He came back, wounded, in 1963, and even though he'd nearly lost his life fighting at the behest of good old Uncle Sam, he had to risk it again in the civil rights movement before he could get a decent meal anyplace but somebody's house. He says he could handle that, but a year later something happened that alienated him from the family. Whatever it was left a big hole in him."

"Don't you know what it was?"

"I've asked, but the answer is always that some things are best left alone. Mother said he built that little house, and for years he isolated himself with his animals and his garden. He's back in the fold now, but he prefers his clapboard sanctuary. He doesn't have much use for money. Told me not long ago that what he wanted most in life wasn't for sale."

"You sure have raised my curiosity about him, and you make me feel kind of sorry for him, too."

"Save it—he doesn't accept pity. Want to watch the goblins with me tonight?"

"Where?"

"Melissa, you couldn't be as innocent as some of your comments suggest. We can watch from anyplace you want to, as private or as public as you like." He leaned back in the big, leather desk chair and twirled the telephone cord, hoping she'd throw him one of her little witticisms. A slender young boy— one of the many Adam had plucked from the jaws of the Goans and the Pirates street gangs—walked in and placed letters in Adam's incoming tray.

"Hold on a minute, Melissa." He addressed the boy. "Pete, I know you're memory challenged, but I gave you a tie, and you're going to wear it to work every day. I don't want to repeat this to you again. You're not a Pirate anymore. You're working on becoming a gentleman. Got it?"

"Yes, sir."

Adam waved the boy out of his office. "Now where were we, Melissa?"

"Adam, why did you call me?"

Adam laughed. He knew he'd done more of that since meeting Melissa than in his first thirty-four and a half years.

"Lady, you can ask some of the most astonishing questions. I like your company. Don't you need to know what's going on between us? I do. I want to see you, but when I leave you, I'm dissatisfied. I told you I don't walk away from problems— I solve them. And you, Miss Grant, are an enigma."

"I am not," she huffed. "What am I supposed to do when you come on with the hot stuff? If you'd keep your hands off of me, maybe we could get to know each other."

"What an ingenious piece of wisdom," he scoffed, rocking back and resting his crossed ankles on his massive oak desk. "Well, if you'd control your libidinous gazes, I might be more inclined to do that."

"Your ego's run amuck, mister. My libido doesn't know you're alive."

He rolled his eyes skyward. "Excuse me a minute, will you? I'll get back to you."

Melissa congratulated herself on having bested Adam. She closed the office door, and with the intention of hanging the

124   *Gwynne Forster*

remainder of the pictures that had arrived with her last ship-
ment of belongings from New York, she started to climb back
on the chair that she'd been using as a ladder when he called.

"Owee," she yelped, as strong hands circled her waist. He
pulled her to him, and she raised her knee. But at the same
moment that she would have attacked, she caught his scent.
"Adam . . . Adam, have you lost your—"

The words died in his mouth, but the lust swished out of
him when he stepped back and gazed into her trusting eyes.
Tenderness for her suffused him, and his instinct was to protect
and care for her. He relished her soft, womanly surrender, the
nuzzling of her warm lips against his jaw, the points of her
nipples teasing his hard chest. He covered her face with soft
kisses. Then with exquisite tenderness, he set her away from
him and kissed her, but didn't release her.

Her forehead grew hotter with the slight pressure of his lips
there, as he breathed erratically, telling her of his struggle for
self-containment.

"Adam . . . Oh, Adam . . ." The feel of his warm hand slid-
ing up and down her back, easing her tension, protecting her,
sent a different message to her senses than he intended. She
didn't want to be protected from him.

"It's alright, baby. I'll get it together in a second. If I told
you I didn't plan for that to happen, would you believe me?"

She looked at him, and her tongue darted out, moistening
her lips, as she moved toward him. He wrapped her to him in
a gentle hug, and she knew he was back in control.

"Would you believe me?" he persisted.

She let her head loll on his chest. "I don't think so. Maybe
you didn't intend for it to go that far, but you sure left your
office and came in here to give me my comeuppance."

"What about your libido? Think it knows I'm alive now?"
Her hand accidentally grazed one of his pectorals, and his demeanor changed, the playful tone gone. "Don't ever do that,
Melissa, unless you're planning to make love with me right
then and there."

"You don't take rain checks?" she asked, feeling devilish.

His gaze stroked her sensually, though his words were contradictory. "I usually smile if I'm joking." He pinched her nose. "You take that piece of information and use it wisely." His behavior disconcerted her. She wasn't used to that side of him.

"What do you say I drop by for you here around five thirty and we go goblin hunting tonight. Hmmm? No telling what we'll catch."

Six

"I'd forgotten that the lights in this town are always dimmed on Halloween. It's eerie walking behind a skeleton on these dark streets, Adam. Ghoulish things give me the creeps."

"Don't be such a namby-pamby." He draped an arm around her shoulder. "That's just a man wearing a costume, but if you're going to be chicken, we can turn around and follow that mummy we passed back there, see how many people he scares."

"Give me the mummy over this thing anytime. At least I can't see what's on the inside." They strolled along closely behind the shrouded figure for the next twenty minutes until the rising wind and the night's chill made their walk uncomfortable. Adam quickened their pace until he caught the mummy and tapped him on the shoulder. Melissa stepped back a few feet. Whatever was in those wrappings might be alive, but from its appearance, she wouldn't swear to it.

"You deserve the prize, Wayne, but I'll have to abstain from the vote."

"No problem. I still have six other chances." He nodded to Melissa. "You're not a judge, I take it?" he asked hopefully. Adam's incredulous look made an answer unnecessary, but he seemed compelled to make his point.

"Make sense, Wayne. This woman's scared of her shadow."

"Am not." She squinted at Adam, wanting to be certain that

he was aware of her displeasure. He gazed down at her, his brilliant smile tender and possessive. Warmed, secure, she stepped toward him, and jolts of pleasure rioted through her when his strong arm welcomed her.

"Then you're scared of the dark," he teased. "When you saw that skeleton, you were ready to dive into my pocket." Wayne looked from one to the other and laughed.

"Don't let him get your number," Wayne advised Melissa. "He's been known to wear a joke thin."

"I've already got her number," Adam argued. "She's only tough before sundown."

"Am not."

"Are, too."

"It ought to be a while before you two get this settled. Adam, I've got to frighten some more kids and shore up my position, since your ethics won't let you vote for me. See you later. Hang in there, Melissa." He darted into a darkened side street.

"Wayne wasn't antagonistic toward our being together. In fact, he was friendly."

"Melissa, my brother is my best friend. I hope he'd be civil to any woman I had my arm around. Besides, he probably doesn't even know how a mummy acts when it's angry. Let's go over to Banks's Watering Hole and get a drink."

You never had to guess when he'd finished with a topic, Melissa mused. "I don't mind. At least the town gossips will be spreading the truth for a change." She had a sense of devil-may-care when he squeezed her shoulder and pulled her closer to him.

"Many a lie has begun with the truth, but if that bothers you, I'll take you home."

"You're not calling me chicken twice in one night."

They walked into the crowded, noisy bar, and in less than a minute not a sound could be heard. Melissa released a long breath when she saw her friend, Banks, rushing to meet them.

"I see you two decided to stonewall it and defy the gossip mongers. Come on back here to my table, give 'em something else to talk about. Bill Henry stopped by here a few minutes ago asking for lemonade, and I had to rescue him from that little number posing over there at the end of the bar. Everybody's going to swear that your folks have me in their pocket, Adam. Not that I'd mind hanging out in such nicely lined pockets." She paused at a table and crushed her cigarette. "Sit down, and I'll get your drinks. What do you want?" They each ordered a gin sling.

"I hadn't connected this place with Banks. I take it her family owns it, since she's working here."

Adam looked around, certain before he did it that most of the other patrons were gazing at him and Melissa. Rafer's law partner sat at a nearby table eyeing them intently, and Adam figured that guaranteed Melissa another scene with her father. He lifted her hand and stroked its back gently, idly.

"The place belongs to Banks's father," he said at last, "but she never works in here. She's waiting on us as a courtesy. I can't imagine Banks waiting tables in a bar. The place would be out of business in weeks."

"Why?"

Adam smiled at some tantalizing, imaginary scene. "The first unfortunate Joe who couldn't resist temptation would have to explain his adolescent behavior to a judge. After she dumped whatever she had in her hands right on top of him, of course." Banks joined them with the drinks and sat with them until they'd finished. Melissa's eyes widened when her friend walked them to the door and told them good night there.

"What was that about?" Melissa asked.

Adam's shoulders jerked upward. "Beats me." Minutes later they understood as Rafer's car moved out of the parking lot and into the street at a pace well above the speed limit.

At Melissa's questioning glance, Adam told her, "Your father probably walked out just before we got there. She knew he was out there and wanted to make certain he didn't lose his temper in the Watering Hole." He walked with her to her door.

"I don't want you to come in tonight, Adam. There's no reason for me to flaunt you before my father. It's enough that I defy him. I know he's wrong in this, but I don't want to humiliate him." Scattered pellets of rain dampened her red designer jacket, a carryover from her New York dress-for-success wardrobe.

"I enjoyed checking out the goblins with you."

"Me, too," she replied, "and I'm not scared of my shadow."

"Are so," he teased, rubbing her nose with his thumb. He opened the door and kissed her quickly, so quickly that she didn't know whether her upturned face had invited the kiss or his finger under her chin had signaled his intent. She stared after him as he dashed through the raindrops to his car. Her father awaited her, but he only nodded when she greeted him, and she thought she detected sadness on his face.

Melissa got ready for bed, put on a robe, and knocked on her mother's bedroom door. She couldn't get used to her mother's open affection, and she cherished it in her heart. She must have been a difficult child for her mother, she mused, for she had been so concerned about getting her father's love and approval that she hadn't reached out to her mother, hadn't been responsive to her silent pleas for affection. She'd taken her mother's secret acts of love for granted, hardly ever acknowledging them.

"It's been years since I went frolicking on Halloween," Emily said. "From your father's temper when he came home, I assumed he saw you out with Adam."

Melissa nodded. "I guess he did, though we didn't see him."

"Do you love Adam, honey?"

"I don't know, Mama. But I feel so good when I'm with him. No matter what kind of shenanigan I pull off, what I say or do, Adam is equal to it or better." She couldn't help comparing Adam to other men she'd known. "When I was in undergraduate school," she recalled, "I went out with a guy a few times, but I couldn't get along with him, because every time I used a word with more than two syllables, he accused me of being uppity. After a while I did it just to annoy him. It didn't take me long to figure out that airheads weren't for me."

"Well, I presume Adam is well educated. Isn't he?"

"Oh, sure. He has an MBA from Columbia." Emily's happy smile jolted Melissa; her mother was a beautiful woman.

"I didn't realize you two had so much in common. The same degree should make you sympathetic with each other's work. It's a good basis for—"

Melissa interrupted her mother's wistful thought. "You shouldn't be counting on anything coming of this, Mama. We've got too many obstacles, and there's no commitment between us." She could see the disappointment mirrored on her mother's face.

"We haven't talked about things like this, and it's another way that I failed you. Did you ever love another man?"

Melissa thought back to the time when she would have given anything to be able to discuss Gilbert Lewis with her mother. The pain, the disappointment, had been severe, so much so that it had shoved her into womanhood. She had later marveled that the first man to whom she had been attracted should have displayed the kind of callousness toward her that her father did. She took her mother's delicate hand.

"I don't think I've ever been in love, although I once thought I was. I was naive until I discovered that he . . . well, he was sophisticated, successful, and not interested in any one woman. You know the type. After we'd gone out together for a while, he told me that if I wanted to continue seeing him, I had to go to bed with him. He gave me that ultimatum because he thought I was crazy about him. I told him to get lost."

Emily patted the edge of the bed, inviting Melissa to sit beside her. "You were hungry for love, the love you should have gotten right here at home or you wouldn't have reached out to a man who was obviously wrong for you. I hope you've gotten over it."

Melissa rested a hand on her mother's knee in assurance. "The only thing I'm carrying around from that experience is the lesson I learned, and the only thing I feel for Gilbert Lewis is contempt."

"And Adam?"

"Oh, Mama. They're nothing alike. Adam is honorable. I wanted to fall in love with Gilbert—or somebody, but I'm scared to death of loving Adam. I say I'm going to stay away from him, but if I know I'll see him, I can't think of anything else. He's so strong, so. . . . I can't explain it. When I'm with him, it's like lightning wouldn't dare strike." She heard her mother's deep ragged sigh and turned to face her. "What is it?"

"That last says it all, honey, because you've been afraid of lightning all your life. I just hope your feelings for Adam don't turn bitter in your mouth." That was the second time her mother had alluded to the misery a person could experience for having loved, Melissa recalled, and decided to risk the question that had nagged her for days.

"Mama, did you have an unrequited love?"

"No, dear. It was returned fourfold, but I was a victim of my own stupidity. He pleaded with me to marry him, but I did what my father wanted me to do. I married Rafer instead, and we've both suffered because of my cowardliness." Melissa's heart constricted as tears flowed untouched down her mother's cheek. Whatever she had expected, it wasn't this.

As if she had waited years to tell someone, had struggled in combat with her fate and then been whipped into submission before glimpsing freedom's light, the words rushed from Emily's mouth.

"Don't let the same thing happen to you. If you love Adam, take him. Don't let his family or yours get in your way, because if you do, you'll spend your life regretting it. I've been a good wife to your father, as good as he would let me be. I did what he wanted, loved what he loved, and went against everybody and everything that he didn't like. He favored Schyler, so I did, too, and I'm sorry. I did all that trying to prove to myself that I loved Rafer."

Breath whirled sharply through Melissa's lips, and she stared at her mother, stunned beyond words. How could she have known this woman for twenty-eight years and yet not known her at all? How could she not have seen the sadness, the suffering? She shifted at her mother's side, uncomfortable because in many ways she, too, had seen the world through Rafer Grant's eyes. Silence hung between them until, after a time, Melissa questioned her mother.

"Good Lord! I never dreamed— What happened?" Melissa knew from her mother's sigh of relief that she had been awaiting what she feared would be a harsh verdict.

"Our parents threatened armed conflict to keep us apart, and they succeeded. I should have known that our fathers, pillars of the community, wouldn't engage in a public battle, but I believed them and broke my engagement to Bill Henry. God alone knows what that did to me."

Air swished from Melissa's lungs. Stunned, she repeated, *"Bill Henry?* You mean—?"

"Yes. Bill Henry Hayes. And Rafer never lets me forget that Bill Henry was my first choice, my first love." Melissa could not miss the silent confession, *and my only love.*

Melissa clasped her mother around her slim shoulders in belated comfort. Encouraged, Emily leaned against her daughter and expressed her concern for Melissa's fate with Adam. "If you tie up with your father about this, I doubt I'll have the strength to go against him. I never have, and it's probably too late for me to start—weakness is habit forming. But you fight for what you want, Melissa. Either you walk the whole mile for him and step over every obstacle or you'll end up like me. If I had the chance again, I'd face an army in order to be with Bill Henry."

Melissa hugged her mother and went back to her room. She stood by the window, pulled the curtains aside, and stared at the night. Small wonder that her father harbored such hatred for the Hayes-Roundtree family, that he opposed any contact between Adam and her with such vehemence. The alleged loss of a family fortune to Hayes and his descendants wasn't half the cause of Rafer's furor. A more personal, ego-shattering ordeal nurtured his rancor. His wife's heart belonged to Bill Henry Hayes. Always had and always would. Melissa could understand that with those two insults, her father couldn't help being irrational about the Hayeses and Roundtrees. She turned away from the window. What made him irrational about her?

The next day Melissa moved into her new home, a small, three-story house that wasn't the Federal she'd wanted, but a more modern facsimile. She raced from the basement to the top floor and stood at the edge of the stairs, panting for breath. The doorbell jarred her out of a self-congratulatory mood, and she loped with some anxiety down the two flights. Surely her father wouldn't leave his office just to bait her.

"Adam . . . what? How did you know I'd moved?" She stood back to let him enter.

"I called your office to ask if you'd like to see the 'Skins and Giants with Wayne and me this weekend, and your secretary told me where you were. I didn't know this place was for sale, but there's no reason why I should have. I left my real estate cap in New York." His glance swept around the foyer and living room, then across the hall to the small dining room.

"What's the kitchen like?" She walked with him to the little room at the end of the hallway and pointed with pride to the modern kitchen she'd had installed. "This is a nice house. What did Rafer say about your moving?" Neither his stance nor the heat in his eyes suggested an interest in Rafer Grant's views.

"He didn't know about it until I'd made a binding down payment, and my father doesn't believe in wasting money."

Adam had stepped closer in order to hear her murmured words, his eyes blazing with passion. She moved backward a step.

"How come you're here in the middle of the day?" She looked away to avoid seeing the come-hither look in his twinkling eyes.

"You asked me a similar question at least once before, and I told you that I intend to find out what we've got going for us. Quit faking, Melissa. The football game, this house, and any other excuse we can find for being together be damned. I'm here because I want to be alone with you, and you invited me in because you want the same."

She looked at the hand he extended toward her in silent invitation and opened her arms. If she'd expected a searing kiss, a sample of his torrid passion, he surprised her. His arms enfolded her gently, carefully as if she would splinter like fine porcelain. Soft kisses on her cheek exacerbated her longing for the sweet pressure of his mouth, until she stopped fighting for passion and enjoyed his gentle loving. Her heart fluttered as she savored the thrill of his embrace, his tender stroking of her back and arms. His strokes and caresses continued until she curled into him as her senses drank in his sweet onslaught of loving. She looked up at him, and a smile eclipsed her face when she glimpsed the soft adoration in his eyes. He had cherished her, had given her something of himself, perhaps for the first time, because he'd never before made her feel like that. As if he hadn't wanted to take, only to give. She closed her eyes and let her head loll against him, ashamed that she had tried to move him to a frenzied passion when he'd wanted only to share what he felt.

His twinkling eyes brightened when he smiled at her. "I'd better get back to work. It isn't even lunch hour." He glanced up at the sculptured molding on the high ceiling. "When you've finished decorating, this place will look great. I'm glad you moved. Every time I've brought you home, I've had to fight the urge to go in your house and protect you from harassment, because I know it's due to me that your home life's been unpleasant." She turned to face him fully and wrapped her arms around him, but he hugged her and quickly disengaged himself. She smiled, loving her ability to arouse him.

"You've changed, Melissa, but your father hasn't accepted it. You were in New York on your own and you succeeded where many have failed. That would give you or anybody confidence and a right to demand treatment as an adult. You won't tolerate from your folks what you once did, but Rafer apparently hasn't realized that. I can't figure out his behavior."

"Long story." She wasn't going into that. "When is that game you want me to see?" Adam's laugh held little humor, and Melissa sensed his displeasure at her having changed the subject. Didn't he realize how often he did the same?

"Sunday. Will you go? Wayne's coming along." Both of her eyebrows jerked upward.

"Oh, yes, you did say that. If you'd said B-H would be going with us, it would make more sense to me. Why Wayne?"

"He wants to get to know you, and I want him to. What's wrong with that?" he asked.

"Nothing. It should be fun."

Adam knew he'd better leave while he could. He wasn't surprised at what had taken place between them, but he hadn't planned it, and he certainly hadn't known he would behave with her as he had. That would bear examination when he had the time and privacy. He could have used the phone to invite her to the game, but he hadn't. He admitted to himself that even though they'd been together for three hours the evening before, he'd gone there because he had needed to see her. He knew he teetered dangerously toward caring deeply for her, but swore that it wasn't going to happen. Still he had to admit that if he found that she wasn't involved in the sabotage of his leather manufacturing company, he'd probably go after her. He didn't let himself dwell on their families' certain reaction. Whether to tell her about the problem at Leather and Hides and how much to disclose bore heavily on his mind. He needed to share it with her, but he also had to be cautious.

"I hate to put a damper on this peaceful moment, Melissa, but I have to tell you something. Someone has been damaging leathers at our factory, and one of the reasons I came back to Beaver Ridge was to find the culprit." Her eyes widened in surprise. "So far, we don't have a lead," he went on, "but we know the person either works there or has an accomplice who does." He didn't tell her when it began.

"Oh, Adam, I'm so sorry. This must be terribly expensive. I can't imagine who would do it. You don't have any serious competitors. You have to get at the bottom of this." She seemed genuine in her expressions of regret and concern, but he still scrutinized her for any clue that would point to her guilt and couldn't find a single one.

He noticed her untidy appearance and looked down at the beige and brown tiles she'd been setting. "If I wasn't dressed, I'd help you with that. Why don't I bring over a batch of Clara's crab cakes or whatever you'd like this evening and do that for you?"

Her mouth dropped open at his suggestion. "You'd do that? Thanks, but I wouldn't want to inconvenience you."

He laughed. Didn't she think him capable of manual labor? He told her, "Don't give it a second thought, Melissa. I'm not in the habit of volunteering to inconvenience myself. Setting those tiles for you will give me pleasure." His steady gaze must have been warm and inviting as he'd meant it to be, because she folded her arms and rubbed them with her hands. Feeling wicked, he added, "And so will you."

"You'd think Nelson Mandela was coming here, the way I'm acting," Melissa muttered, trying to settle the butterflies in her stomach. Confound it, she couldn't even put on a decent dress. Nobody got dolled up to put in a floor and hang pictures. Disgruntled that he'd see her looking frumpy twice in a day, she compromised and topped a pair of army combat fatigues with a tight-fitting, scoop-necked lavender sweater and went to answer the doorbell.

She couldn't contain her amazement. Adam Roundtree in jeans and an open-necked jogging shirt. "I didn't know you could look like this. Scruffed up, you're . . . well"—she scratched her temple as she searched for the right word—"you know . . . human, more accessible. I don't know. You're different." His stare knocked her off balance. She would never have expected the message she read in his eyes. He quickly shuttered his gaze, but in that brief, open moment, she saw him as she never had, as he'd never permitted her to see him. Vulnerable. And hurt.

She needed to make amends for her seeming callousness, to heal him. But a vision of the trouble ahead, of her mother's life flashed through her mind, and she wanted to suppress and to deny the compassion, the tenderness, that he wrung out of her. She pushed the warning out of her conscious thoughts, and her right hand lifted seemingly of its own volition to caress his jaw. He stood, wordless, while she stroked his jaw, his gaze sweeping her face repeatedly as though seeking some truths, some answers that she alone possessed.

Shaken, she stepped closer to him with her eyes narrowed in a squint and her womanly need to banish his anguish unguarded. "What is it, Adam? What have I said?" But he stepped back, away from her, as though unwilling to forgive her and loath to accept her succor.

"Adam?" His pained stare drilled her as surely as any bullet ever pierced its target.

"I'm human, alright. As you once said, I bleed just like you do."

She saw the change in him—from anguish to need—and without thought as to the meaning of her feelings or the implications of what she did, she opened her arms to him. "Adam, tell me what's the matter, what I've done."

He didn't try to stifle the groan that could have been torn

from his soul, so violent, so wrenching, as he rushed into her outstretched arms, aware that he was giving her more of himself than he had ever given to another human being. He let her hold him while he drank in her murmurings, her soothing words that declared her respect and her appreciation of him as a man. Abruptly he covered her mouth with his own, curtailing her outpourings in a powerful, ravishing kiss. His fever for her blazed, but he got a grip on his emotions and dragged himself out of the clutches of desire.

Her glance locked on his face, but even as she continued to hold him tight, he read in her eyes repudiation of what they'd just shared and saw her uncertainty and her fear that she'd gone too far. He wouldn't deny the pleasure of being in her arms, and he wouldn't belittle what he felt. He believed in facing the truth even if it hurt, because you couldn't solve a problem unless you knew precisely what it was, unless you understood its nature and what caused it. And he had a problem.

"Melissa, where are we headed? I can't guarantee that if I have another angry exchange with Rafer, I won't fight back. It's against my nature to let a man impose on me with impunity. But he's your father and you love him. I don't want you between us." He set her away from him, though he was loath to separate from her, and pointed to the bag of food that he'd placed on the table by the door.

"Want to eat now, or after we finish? Me, I'm hungry right now, and the scent of those crab cakes makes my mouth water. How about—" He turned abruptly toward the door, alerted by the sound of footsteps, and braced himself for another encounter with Rafer Grant.

Melissa opened the door to her father, who looked past her to her guest. Adam sensed Melissa's discomfort in what was becoming an all too frequent occurrence, but he didn't give quarter. He'd known instinctively that the caller would be Rafer. By some ruse the man seemed to know just when he needed to be reminded of what could happen if he let himself get too close to Melissa. He let her take the lead.

"Is anything wrong with Mama?" Adam didn't believe he'd previously witnessed such courteous and thinly veiled antagonism. She could hold her own, alright, he thought with pride.

"No more than usual. You know why I'm here, and you know I don't want him hanging around you. This is why you moved, isn't it?" Adam stepped closer to her.

"I moved so you and I could live in peace, Daddy, and we wouldn't be a constant source of annoyance to each other. I'm tired of so much unpleasantness, and I'd appreciate it if you'd leave now." Tension gripped Adam as Rafer's nostrils flared, and his eyes shone with hostility.

"He's turned you against your family. After all they've done to us, you're throwing yourself at him. You can flaunt him in our faces, but you won't give your own cousin Timmy a job. You will regret this. I promise you. You'll be sorry."

Adam stared at the closed door. He pitied the man. Loyalty and love couldn't be had on demand and especially not from your child. That had to be earned from the child's birth onward. He turned to Melissa, saw that she had hung her head, and knew that their evening was shot: no friendship could flourish in an environment of suspicion and hatred. Rafer would gladly see him dead, and he and Melissa had misgivings about each other. Why couldn't she have been someone else? He took the bag of food in one hand and grabbed her arm with his other one.

"Come on, let's eat and get this floor fixed."

Melissa prowled around in her basement after Adam left. Her father had a knack for spoiling her pleasant moments with Adam, and she foolishly let him do it. But she couldn't turn her back on her father, and now that she knew that a deep, personal hurt fueled his anger, she judged him less harshly. She shouldn't attend that football game with Adam and Wayne.

In her view she and Adam were behaving as fatalists do, as if they had no control over the course of their lives when neither of them believed that. But she'd promised, she rationalized, so she'd go.

Melissa supposed that where Wayne was concerned, she was on trial, but she wouldn't give him the satisfaction of behaving as if she knew it. She sat between them aware that her body language was that of a woman with two casual male friends. Indeed, until Adam looped his arm around her shoulder, an onlooker wouldn't have known which of the two she cared for. She moved closer to him.

"Mind your manners, Melissa. My women do not root for the New York Giants," Adam said.

"In other words your women just go along with whatever you do. Sweet little things. My men do as they please. If they were patsies, they'd bore me." She watched her warm breath furl upward until it dissipated in the cold November air.

"Your *men?*" His sharp whistle split the air. "Tell me more." She ignored his taunt.

"If the Giants lose, you owe me," he challenged, apparently warming up to the easy banter.

"How much? Or should I say, what?"

Adam's gentle laughter warmed her inside, and she noticed that it brought a quick glance from his brother. "Me thinks you don't trust me," he replied in a voice that suggested she might be foolish to do so.

"Sure I do, but you can be very imaginative sometimes, and I'd as soon not be the victim of your agile mind. So no blind bets. What's the wager?"

"You're smart to get it up front," intervened Wayne, who had been silent until then. "I recall that when we were hellions in our teens and about to scale a neighbor's barbed wire fence, Adam bet me that my pants would tear worse than his. I forgot that he was high jumping in gym class and took him on. It wasn't only my pants that got torn, but he breezed over that six-foot fence as though it wasn't there and had the gall to suggest that I should have been wearing my thinking cap when I bet him. It's best to stay on your toes when you're dealing with Adam."

Anticipating a Redskins' score, Wayne jumped up but quickly sat down, his jubilation short-lived, when the perfect pass slipped through the wide receiver's outstretched hands. Melissa patted his shoulder. "You poor baby. Well, at least you finally got a chance to stretch." When the next play resulted in a Giants' interception of the Redskins' pass, Melissa soothed, "I'm sorry. I wanted my boys to win, but I didn't want them to romp all over your guys."

Wayne grumbled, "Get her to cool it, man." But Melissa knew from Adam's warm laughter that their outing was going as he'd hoped, had perhaps even known it would. His response reassured her.

"I'm congratulating myself on not having insisted that she take that bet, because I'd planned to ask her to put up a few months of her time as collateral."

Melissa sat forward, alert, when Wayne asked Adam, "What were you planning to wager?"

Her breath stuck in her lungs while she waited for Adam's answer, staring as his shoulders bunched in a half hearted shrug.

"Myself." Air zinged through Wayne's teeth in a loud whistle.

At halftime Adam stood and wound his scarf more tightly around his neck. "I'm going for coffee. Would either of you like anything else? Peanuts, maybe?" Melissa nodded agreement, wondering why Adam would deliberately leave her alone with Wayne. Adam's brother seemed friendly enough, but how would he behave once they were alone? She was still a Grant. In the heavy silence a less self-possessed person might have resorted to small talk or rambling, but Melissa didn't say anything. She knew Wayne would take advantage of the opportunity, so she waited for him to speak.

"Do you love him?"

Taken aback, she turned toward him, thinking that bluntness must be one of their family traits. "Adam doesn't know the answer to that question, Wayne, and you shouldn't know before he does."

"Do you know the answer?"

She noticed that his voice wasn't hostile, and from his relaxed manner he didn't appear to want to aggravate her. So she answered him honestly.

"I try not to think about it. I haven't faced it. I don't know how your family has reacted to the friendship between Adam and me, but because of it my father barely speaks to me."

"Scared?"

"You could say that. Maybe."

"Adam is a different man when he's with you. If I didn't see him laughing and teasing with you with almost childlike enjoyment, nobody would make me believe it. Well, the jury's still out, but I have a feeling that if the two of you break up, it won't be due to any outside force or faction."

"What do you mean?"

"I know the hostility between our families worries you. It plagues all of us, but it won't be the cause of permanent cleavage between you and Adam. Only the two of you can ruin your friendship."

She stared at him. "How can you be so sure?"

"Melissa, I know Adam. And you're not a patsy, either." He paused. "Adam hasn't told me anything about you. Where'd you go to school?" She told him, adding that her degree was a master's in business administration. Several people sitting below them turned around when Wayne's whistle pierced the air.

"So you two have the same degree. This gets more interesting all the time. Hold on, I'll get that for you." He reached between their seats and retrieved her umbrella. "What's this thing for?"

"We're supposed to have rain or snow, and I hate getting wet when I'm not dressed for it."

He laughed. "Cover all bases, do you? I thought we weren't expecting a change in weather until after midnight. Are you another of these people who leaves nothing to chance? If you are, Adam's meticulousness probably doesn't bother you. It can wear on me."

She looked up as Adam placed a tray of coffee in her lap. Wayne took it from her, removed the lids, and gave her and Adam each a cup. They drank their coffee and nibbled the nuts in companionable silence, but Melissa had the impression that Wayne had warmed up to her. He held his empty cup for her peanut shells and took her own empty cup before Adam could reach for it.

Melissa pulled up the collar of her coat to ward off the late fall chill as they walked to the car. Adam's arm snuggled her close to him, and his gloved fingers toyed with her cold nose, and she had a delicious feeling that he cherished her and was protective of her. Excitement wafted through her, and she reveled in Adam's attentiveness, though he always showed concern for her. His openness with it in his brother's presence lit up her whole being.

When they reached the car, Adam slapped Wayne's shoulder. "You drive back."

"You're ordering me to chauffeur so you two can make out in the backseat."

Adam attempted to stare Wayne down, feigning distaste for the presumptuous remark, but Wayne protested. "I'm telling it like it is, brother."

Melissa couldn't help but marvel at their camaraderie. Maybe a brother and a sister couldn't be that close, she surmised. Or maybe the environment in which she and Schyler had grown up hadn't been conducive to that kind of love and affectionate exchanges.

When Wayne eased the Jaguar toward MacArthur Boulevard

and Route 270 to Frederick, Adam leaned back in the seat, winked at Melissa, and announced that he was sleepy.

"Watch your step back there, Melissa," Wayne warned. "He's a fox that I wouldn't let anywhere near my chickens."

"You sound downright friendly," Adam said in a voice that Melissa thought strained and tension-filled. The silence weighed on her, for she knew that if Wayne bothered to reply, both she and Adam would know his reaction to their relationship.

Wayne turned off the radio. "I am. To both of you." She didn't know what response she'd expected from Adam, but he didn't say that he was glad nor did he thank his brother. But as she mused over their afternoon and evening, she concluded that Adam hadn't brought Wayne and her together in order to gain his brother's approval, but to give him a chance to make a more informed opinion of her. What a man.

"Let yourself out at Beaver Ridge, Wayne. I'll take Melissa home. If Rafer sees the two of us anywhere near that house on Teal Street, he'll lose control for sure."

Wayne reduced the Jaguar's speed as he entered the town limits, glanced into the rearview mirror and spoke as though surprised. "I thought you'd moved, Melissa."

"She moved," Adam said, "but Daddy's omnipresent gaze sweeps a very wide area." Annoyance at the sarcasm in his voice jerked her out of her reverie and out of his arms.

He made no effort to bring her back to him, and she slumped in the seat. Another lovely evening had been derailed by that ridiculous feud.

Adam secured the front door and walked down the lengthy and richly carpeted hallway toward the family room, where he knew Wayne waited for him. About halfway there he glanced toward a portrait of Jacob Hayes that had hung there ever since he'd known himself. The old man's intelligent eyes with their piercing and unsmiling twinkle always seemed to follow him when he passed. He stared at his grandfather's likeness until he heard Wayne call to him, shook his fist at the old man and walked on, less purposefully than usual.

"You've got your work cut out for you."

"Meaning?" Adam knew he'd have to talk with Wayne about Melissa, but he didn't intend to discuss her merits or lack of them. Not with Wayne or anyone else.

Wayne whistled. "Touchy, aren't we? What I mean is you haven't won her, but you can get her, though, because she is susceptible to you. Your problem is you've got her kin and our mother to deal with, and by the time they wear you out, you may say the hell with it."

Adam walked over to the bar, got some ice cubes, and poured two fingers of bourbon over them. He twirled the amber liquid around in the glass in what Wayne had to recognize as a means of gaining time while he thought out his next words. He didn't intend to seek his brother's opinion of Melissa, but he couldn't resist asking, "But not you? You're saying that I don't have to deal with you?" He smiled at Wayne's elaborate shrug, his brother's signature gesture.

"You two were made for each other."

Adam quirked an eyebrow in disbelief. "You're not even skeptical?"

"I liked what I saw of her, and I know you well."

"In many respects, yes, but not in this context."

Wayne paced the floor with uncharacteristic deliberateness, his hands in his pockets. "I may not know what you want in a woman, but I know what you ought to be looking for, and I've gained a good sense of Melissa's personality. She's the perfect foil for your tough cynicism. She's patient, determined, and independent, but she's soft, too. And she's smart. She respects you, but unlike a lot of people who know you, she's not afraid of you. And she wants you. She's the woman for you, alright."

Adam shuttered his eyes. "Damned if you haven't become clairvoyant. Good night." Halfway down the hall, he turned and walked back to the family room where he found Wayne drinking the untouched bourbon on ice. "I'm glad you like her. Shows you that the words Morris-Grant and Satan aren't necessarily interchangeable. A lot of times, maybe, but now you'll acknowledge at least one exception."

Melissa mulled over the afternoon and evening events, unable to fall asleep. Adam Roundtree was not a wishy-washy man. He knew where he was going, but he hadn't revealed it to her. Whatever he'd planned to do about their relationship, he'd guarded as closely as a miser does his money. She knew he had to consider his family just as she worried about the reaction of her father and brother, but she didn't doubt he'd decide independently of anything his folks said or did. So what accounted for his halfhearted courtship, his reluctance to go after what she knew he wanted? She had a niggling feeling that Adam's caution about her went beyond concern for the ruptured relationship between their families.

She had always been able to arrive at a decision and stick to it, but this time her head and heart were at odds, and where Adam was concerned, both exerted a powerful pull. She didn't fool herself: she loved being with Adam. But he's a Roundtree, an enemy of your family, her mind cautioned. He's a strong man with the temerity to stand up to your father, whom you've never known to back down, her common sense replied. And he makes you feel what you've never felt before, makes you want what you've never wanted before and what you know you can hardly wait to have, her unreasonable heart argued. She turned over in bed, exhausted by her mental struggle.

She sat up in bed and pulled the pale yellow bedding up to her shoulders. If only she'd switched off the phone. Surely her father wouldn't interrupt her sleep to harass her about Adam. At the sound of her mother's soft voice, she knew intense relief.

"I'm sorry to disturb you, dear, but I figured you hadn't

gone to sleep. Your father's nephew—you know, Timmy, called this afternoon. He said you asked him to fill in a questionnaire and send it to you, but he said the questionnaire doesn't have anything to do with him. Call him, dear. He's called a few times since you've been home, and he always asks about you. Do what you can for him, honey."

"I will, Mama, but not at the expense of my hard-earned reputation. I wish Daddy hadn't started this."

"Well, you know how he is," Emily soothed. "Do what you can." Melissa hung up, frustrated and angry at her father for having interfered in her business.

Melissa put the pillow behind her back, propped her elbows on her knees, and tried to think. She'd try to help him, but how could she if he didn't do what she told him to do? I don't think he wants a job, she told herself. He wants to hang out in my office and get paid. No way.

Seven

A call from her New York secretary several days later sent Melissa scurrying to New York City. Before she'd agree to find an executive position for an employee of Jenkins, Roundtree, and Tillman, she'd have to make certain that the man's efforts to relocate weren't calculated to hurt Adam. She wouldn't work for him without first interviewing him and finding out why he wanted to change jobs. The slow, bumper-to-bumper taxi ride from La Guardia Airport into Manhattan and the impatient horn-tooting of the drivers reminded her of the things she disliked about New York. Still, she had missed its museums and galleries, the little West Side bistros, its music—classical, jazz, and unclassifiable, the multitude of bookstores, and the ever-changing street scenes.

She registered at the Drake Hotel, settled in, called the secretary she shared with Crow and Ankers, and arranged for an appointment with a man she discovered was Jason Court's assistant. She plodded across the modest-sized but beautiful room and looked down on Park Avenue, killing precious time while she gazed unseeing at the speeding cars, the fur-coated women of leisure, and the corporate males who were too macho to put on an overcoat as they went out to lunch in the thirty-six-degree weather.

Ordinarily she'd be making notes for the next day's interview, researching the type of business or industry in which the man wanted to work, but she did none of this. She paced the floor. If she didn't take the job, the man would get assistance elsewhere. If she worked for him and succeeding in placing him, how would it affect Adam?

She had to pull herself out of that mood. Ilona answered at the phone's first ring. "Melissa, darling, you became sick of this place with no ballet and came back to civilization? Where are you?" At Melissa's reply, she complained, "Darling, you should have stayed with me. We need to have a good talk."

Melissa knew she wouldn't have contemplated such a thing. She had heard Ilona recount her escapades and seen her swoon over thoughts of her past lovers so many times that she could put on the show herself. She didn't relish being Ilona's captive audience in a bachelor apartment. They agreed to meet for dinner at a restaurant on Columbus Avenue, a choice Melissa regretted when she recalled light, happy times there with Adam early in their relationship.

Melissa dressed in a chic, brown ultrasuede business suit, complemented it with a cowl-necked orange cashmere sweater, brown suede shoes and brown leather briefcase, put on her Blass vicuna coat, and stepped out into the morning cold. It didn't even take a day for me to revert to form and turn back into a New Yorker, she admitted to herself as though it was an indictment. Where else do women dress with a briefcase instead of a pocketbook?

If the man had been tardy, if he had behaved condescendingly toward her, or if she had disliked him for any reason, she could in good conscience have refused to take the job. But as she had once told Adam, her criteria for accepting a client were whether she thought she could fulfill the terms of agreement and whether her integrity would be compromised in any way. She signed the contract and collected her mail, went back to the Drake, packed, and got a flight to Frederick via Baltimore.

Within a few days she'd located three firms that began aggressive bidding for the man when it was learned that he had worked for Adam Roundtree and that it was his decision to leave. Wary of corporate spying, she called Adam.

"So that's where you've been," Adam said. She had to know that her having left town without a word displeased him. They were not committed to each other, and she wasn't obligated to inform him of her whereabouts, but they were more than friends. Or were they? He'd been vexed and a little hurt and had refused to ask her secretary where she was. Her reply told him she'd detected his annoyance.

"Adam, when I left here, I didn't know what the man wanted nor when he wanted to leave Jenkins, Roundtree, and Tillman. I'm telling you, now that I have the facts, because it's the decent thing to do. I haven't placed him, but I can offer him one of three firms, all of which are anxious to get him, and one of them is your competitor. I hesitate to introduce him to your enemy, and I want to know what you think."

A muscle tensed in his jaw. She hadn't understood his comment on her whereabouts. Well, so much the better. "Dan's my best middle-level salesman, but if he wants to leave my shop, he can go. If you don't place him, someone else will, and I'd as soon you got the profit."

"I was planning to place him, but I wanted you to know. My question was where to put him." Her long pause alerted Adam to the possibility that her next words might not please him, and they didn't.

"Adam, I think you should know that your biggest competitor is trying to raid your shop."

"Not to worry. Ken Bradley is less of a competitor than he thinks." Still, he didn't like the man enticing away one of his most valuable employees.

"You told me not to tell you how to run your office, but I think you ought to get back to New York for a spell." His antennae up, he tried to figure out what she'd left unsaid.

"Are you saying—"

"I turned down two offers of a contract to get Jason Court away from you. The fat cats in New York think that because you're not there, you're a sitting duck."

Adam bristled, angry at himself because he might have left his flank unprotected. "If they think I'm not in control of my office, they're a pile of bricks short of a full load. I'll get up there. Thanks. Oh, Melissa," he added in an afterthought, "I should be back in a few days. Stay out of mischief."

"Stay out of . . . Me? Do what?" she sputtered. "You're full of it, Adam. Just keep it up. One of these days you're going to get a hole in your sails." Her laughter floated through the wire to him.

"Don't sweat over the thought, baby. With any luck, you'll be in the boat with me when it happens. I can't wait to drown with you. In fact there are times when I can think of little else." He waited, hoping to get her sharpest dart.

"I hate to be the bearer of bad tidings, but you'd better look forward to a long life, sweetie"—she emphasized the *sweetie*—"because I'm a survivor." A riot of sensations darted through him at the sound of her husky giggle. She wasn't satisfied to challenge him, she had to entice him as well. But he'd have his day.

"Any man with an iota of sense knows when he gets an invitation to try harder, Melissa." Insinuation punctuated his words. "And ignoring opportunities, however thinly veiled, is not something I do. See you when I get back."

He buzzed his secretary. "I need to be in New York tomorrow morning at eight o'clock. Do what you can to get me a plane out of here tonight. If necessary, phone Wayne and ask him to call in some favors." He leaned back in his chair and stroked his chin. Would a person who would double-cross him have done as Melissa had, and would she risk his asking her not to place Dan? He had yet to find any solid evidence that Melissa lacked integrity. But how else could the sabotage at Leather and Hides be explained? What if her warning was a ruse to get him away from Frederick? He tossed his head to the side and grasped his chin with his tapered brown fingers, pensive. How had he allowed himself to crave a woman he wasn't sure he could trust?

He walked into his suite of New York offices the next morning to find things as he'd left them. Olivia hovered about, obviously happy to see him. "You look good, yourself," he said in response to her compliment. "I want to speak first with Jason and then with Lester." He assured Jason that his arrival unannounced did not indicate a lack of confidence.

"I've been told the raiders are busy. Any truth in it?" Before Jason spoke, his slow nod and straight-in-the-eye stare gave Adam the assurance he needed.

"Plenty, but as far as I know, you don't have anything to worry about. Dan wants to leave, and that's for the best. He's in love with Virginia, and she's engaged to marry another guy. He figures he can get another good job easier than she can, and he doesn't want to be around her anymore."

Adam's whistle alerted any of the staff who didn't already know it that the boss was in his office. "He's in love with his secretary? How long's that been going on?"

Jason shrugged eloquently. "Since the minute he first saw her, though she didn't reciprocate the feeling, but he didn't give up until she got engaged."

"Well, hell! I'm sorry to see him leave, but you're right—no point in staying around her, unless he's a masochist. What about you? My source also tells me they're after you."

"I've had several feelers and a couple of offers. But if I wanted to move, man, you'd be the first to know it. I believe in hanging out with the champ, Adam, and from where I sit, you're it."

Adam had to hide his relief. "What about Lester?" Jason's jaw hardened, and Adam worked hard at squelching a laugh.

"He rings your bell, does he?"

Jason grimaced. "I'd bet my AT & T stocks that Lester rings his mother's bell."

Adam laughed outright. "Not to worry, Jason. Nothing lasts

forever." He made a mental note to give Jason a raise. Loyalty was very important to him and deserved reward. He spoke with Lester and decided that when he returned to the office full time, he wouldn't keep the man, held a staff meeting, and satisfied that his employees weren't contemplating leaving him, headed back to Frederick that afternoon.

Why such hurry to get to Beaver Ridge? he asked himself. He hadn't even bothered to go to Thompson's and get his favorite pastrami sandwich or to Sognelle's Cajun Kitchen for some hot ribs and boudin, and he wouldn't get any of either until he got back. He settled into his business-class TWA seat. "It's time I had a talk with myself," he acknowledged. "She's the reason I'm in a hurry. I misjudged her this time, and . . ." Disgusted with himself, he opened his briefcase and tried to work. "Hell, nobody's going to scramble my brain like this." He closed the file and looked at his watch. Another couple of hours; if he was lucky, she'd be home.

He phoned her from the airport. "Have dinner with me."

"And hello to you, too, Mr. Roundtree."

He shrugged off her gentle rebuke. "At least you recognized my voice. I hope you don't have other plans. Do you?" When she didn't respond immediately, he continued. "What time shall I come for you? I'd like an early dinner, if possible." She asked if he'd skipped lunch.

"You might say that." Let her think what she liked. He wanted to see her. He went home and telephoned Wayne. Now for another test.

"Anything untoward happen at Leather and Hides last night?"

"Nelson patrolled with the new guard last night, but they didn't see or hear anything suspicious. He thinks the culprit is trying to lull us into complacency. How'd it go in New York?"

He hadn't realized that he was holding his breath. "Clean as fresh snow, but it was a good idea to check the place out, and I intend to do it more often. I'll be in touch."

* * *

Melissa stared at the molding in her ceiling, while the dial tone menaced her ear. She had good reason to meet with Adam, she told herself, since she'd placed Lester in Adam's office, and the man might be the cause of his problems. The telephone operator's tinny voice got her attention, and she hung up. But she dallied beside the pantry door with her hand resting on the cradled wall phone. What was the use of lying to herself? She wanted to be with him. She hadn't seen Adam for a week, not since she'd gone to the football game with him and Wayne. And their tepid parting had frustrated her and thrust her into a whirlpool of confusion, leaving her more than ever at sea about their relationship. The fault had been hers. She couldn't overcome the deepening conflict between her feelings for Adam and loyalty to her family. And her inner struggle had intensified, she realized, because she'd become more sympathetic to her father since learning why he was so irrational about the Hayeses and Roundtrees.

They didn't know how to greet each other, so they stared in silence. Finally she smiled and his arms opened to her. But Adam held her to his side, unwilling to risk the escalation of desire. She leaned away and looked up at him, but he let her see a bland expression and joked, "You know the old adage, 'an ounce of prevention . . .' and so forth. We're supposed to be going to dinner, and I'm hungry, but if you want to hang around here, my two appetites are equally demanding right now." Desire pooled in his loins at the double meaning implied in her lusty laugh, and he set her away from him.

"I'll get my coat. Have a seat." He didn't move.

"You do that, Melissa." He watched the devil-may-care way she walked, turned his back, and tried to think about the problems at Leather and Hides, but those thoughts didn't lessen the heat in him. She returned quickly, too quickly. One look at her—scented as she was with a subtle but extravagant perfume and bundled up past the neck, waiflike to thwart the cold—and he struggled against man's most primitive impulse. I'm in danger here, he admitted to himself and sought to introduce some levity into the situation.

"I can hardly see you in all that stuff you've got on." His gaze stroked her face; not pretty but strangely beautiful.

Melissa's shoulders hunched in anticipation of the outside temperature. "I don't like to be cold."

"No reason why you should be. I'll keep you warm."

"Said the spider to the fly," she shot back, gazing up at him as though to confirm his meaning. He watched her teasing look dissolve into awareness and knew that he hadn't reduced the tension, but worsened it.

"Let's go while we can still walk."

"Where are we going?" He helped her into the passenger's seat, awed as she struggled to sit down with what could pass for decorum.

"Wherever you like."

He gazed down at her. "If you're so afraid of getting cold, why are you wearing your skirt a yard above your knee? And it's so tight, you could hardly sit down. Didn't you ever hear of comfort?" Her glare might have been meant to shame him, but he held his course.

"You've practically hidden your neck and face, and they're least likely to feel the cold, but your lower precious parts are left to freeze." He tapped his forehead with a long index finger. "Universities ought to give courses in deciphering the female enigma, and the male students should be forced to take them."

"If you're not happy with the way I look," she huffed, "I'll get out and go right back in the house, and I'll stay there." The breath from his laughter fogged the mirror.

"You look great to me, always do, and like I said, it'll give me great pleasure to warm you."

He drove to the mom-and-pop restaurant where they'd once encountered Wayne and found comfortable seats in the nearly empty but charming room. Melissa smoothed the red and white checkered tablecloth, wondering whether is was the time to open a discussion of what they seemed to have been avoiding.

"Aren't you going to tell me about your trip? How did you find things?"

He took his time answering. "Thanks for the tip. You were right about the raiders, but my people are loyal to me. Go ahead and do what you can for Dan—he's in a difficult situation." She wondered why they spent precious time talking about his staff, her staff, and a myriad of unimportant, impersonal things. He must have shared her exasperation at it, for he reached across the still empty table, grasped her fingers, and asked her, "Did you miss me, Melissa?" But before she could answer, what passed for a laugh escaped him.

"You didn't have enough time for that. I was only away overnight." Their locked fingers appeared strange to her, as if they didn't belong together. She wanted to tell him about her mother and Bill Henry, but couldn't force herself to do it, because she didn't want to hide behind that tortured relationship. When she looked at him, sensations swirled within her at the brilliant twinkle in his eyes. He tipped up her chin, and she brushed his hand aside.

"I missed you."

"But you didn't miss me when *you* were away for a week. How was that?"

Melissa squinted at him, frowned and bit her bottom lip. "Are you trying to pick a fight? Or what?" His wry smile brought a catch to her throat.

"Not me. I'm a peaceful man. I figure that at this stage there ought to be some honesty between us."

"Adam, the kind of honesty you want is not good for your ego. How about you being honest?"

That grin should have warned me, she thought, when he said, "No problem. I want to make love with you, and I don't feel a bit casual about it."

"Oh," she blustered. "Is that a direct pass?" Adam laughed.

* * *

The waiter's long awaited arrival interrupted them, but Adam returned to the subject. "I've said before that you can't be as naive as you sometimes seem. You shy away from intimacy until I drag you into it. Why is that?"

"Adam, you enjoy digging into my personality and my life, but if we sat here until doomsday, I wouldn't learn one thing about you that everybody else doesn't know." His look was one of funereal solemnity.

"That's because I ask; you don't."

She placed her fork in her plate, leaned back in the booth, and looked directly into his eyes. "Have you ever been in love?"

"No, but I've been close to it." Her eyes widened in surprise, and he wondered how deeply she felt, but he didn't ask her. She'd veiled her emotions. Even her eyes told him nothing. He switched topics, hoping to smooth over whatever damage his answer might have caused.

"You never told me what you thought of Wayne as a mummy hell bent on frightening every kid in Frederick." Relief and something akin to joy settled over him when her eyes lit and a smile broke out all over her face. But when she said, "Oh, Adam, you're wonderful," he had to caress her and maneuvered to her side of the booth, squeezed her quickly, and feathered her cheek with his lips. Frissons of heat exploded in him as her hot gaze drank in the warm affection that he knew was reflected in his eyes. Oh, the wonder of her! His heartbeat accelerated and his senses whirled when she lowered her gaze, obviously embarrassed at her inability to hide her response. They finished the meal in contented silence.

He wanted to share with her his deepening concern about the sabotage at Leather and Hides. He needed desperately to confirm her loyalty to him. But if she were guilty of betrayal, he would have tipped his hand. And even if she were innocent, if one of her relatives had a hand in it, to whom would she be loyal? He needed to know that she stood with him, and he needed her. Badly.

He parked, walked with her up the short cemented path to her house, and stood looking down at her, hands jammed in his coat pockets and his back braced against the outer wall of the house. His breath hung in his lungs as she reached into her bag for her keys, then hissed through his lips when she didn't hand them to him, but opened the door herself. He straightened up, and tugged at her ear with his gloved hand. "It was a lovely evening, Melissa, and an informative one." He brushed her cheek. "Good night." He didn't feel much like whistling when he got into his car, but he thought he'd better, because it was the only way he had right then to blow off steam. He knew his whole body had telegraphed to her his desire to be with her, to make love with her, and it hadn't escaped her, either. She was obviously less sophisticated than he'd thought—hard working, intelligent, her own woman, but afraid to take a chance. Concern for the reaction of their families wasn't stopping her from seeing him, nor from responding to him whenever he put his hands on her. So what had kept her out of bed with him?

He parked, secured the house, went into his room and closed the door, knowing that he faced a long, restless night. If he did the smart thing, he'd drop it, but he hadn't gotten where he was by accepting defeat. He wanted her, and he had no intention of giving up.

Ten minutes after Adam left her, Melissa answered her door-bell thinking it might be him. Her father glared at her.

"At least you sent him home. If you can't leave those people alone, you can consider yourself no longer a member of my family. No kin of mine is going to consort with them."

Anger paralyzed her tongue, and she stammered in frustration. Finally her calm restored, words that had long wanted release spilled from her lips, and she faced him defiantly and more resolutely than ever before. "You never treated me as a member of your family, and if you read me out of it, I won't lose a thing. I might even gain something."

No blow struck him, she noticed and marveled that a father could be so cavalier about his daughter's feelings. His only reaction was the lifting of his forehead and the movement of his jaw. He wasn't used to the posture she'd assumed with him.

"They've already turned you against us," he said. "Even your cousin Timmy is more loyal to us than you are. But you mark my word, young lady, you're going to be sorry for this. You're just like your mother."

She spoke in a gentle tone. There was no point in beating a dead horse. "If I am, I don't consider it a disadvantage. Is that why you've never loved me, never wanted me?"

"Did she tell you I didn't want you?"

"No. I feel it. I've always felt it." He looked into the distance and pursed his lips as though reminded of an unpleasantness.

"It was what came before you that I didn't want. A man can stand just so much."

"What did it have to do with me? Any eyes can see that I'm your daughter."

He quirked an eyebrow and in icelike tones informed her, "I've had no reason to doubt your mother's virtue. But once she had you, she didn't care about anybody or anything else."

Melissa stared at him in disbelief. "How can you say that? Both of you ignored me." He didn't deny his share in it.

"After your brother, Schyler, was born, I had to make your mother concentrate on him. She was too wrapped up in you. A baby, especially a boy, needs all of its mother's time." She didn't comment on that. Clearly he either couldn't or wouldn't tell her why he had rejected her. Indeed, he didn't appear to realize that he'd done it. She reached for the doorknob simultaneously with him.

"Good night, Father." He appeared to hesitate, but he only said, "Good night."

* * *

Adam jumped out of bed at the sound of his beeper and switched on the light beside his bed. Damn. Two thirty in the morning.

"Roundtree." He sat on the edge of his bed, while Calvin Nelson recounted the havoc he'd just discovered at Leather and Hides. Zirconium salt had been applied with great care to the grain side or upper leather intended for the manufacture of fine shoes, so that the tanning process produced a white rather than bluish, more elastic, leather used for such shoes. Some of the hides could be retanned with chrome salts and used for lower-grade clothing, Calvin told him, but most of that expensive lot had been rendered useless.

He rested his elbow on his knee and dropped his forehead in his hand. "Any leads?"

"Sorry, Adam. Not a one, but I'll keep after it."

"I know you will." He got back in bed. He'd been two hundred and fifty miles away the night before, and nothing untoward had happened. But tonight while he was a couple of miles away . . . He sat up. Was somebody trying to frame Melissa? From the time she came back, the saboteur had usually struck when he was with her, and nobody who was as smart as she would incriminate themselves with such strong circumstantial evidence. The possibility that he might have found a clue that didn't implicate her enabled him to get to sleep.

Adam ambled into the dinning room the next morning to find his mother, brother, and Bill Henry waiting for him. Mary Roundtree had called a family conference, and Adam's surprise at Bill Henry's presence was evidence that he hadn't been consulted. He took his place at the table, and they knew his restrained good morning was nothing less than censure.

"Don't tell me you've taken to eating soul food, B-H?" He needled his uncle whom he regarded as a health nut. "What's the matter, sick of alfalfa and bean sprouts?" It didn't surprise him that his comment wasn't lost on his mother. She had always been able to detect his anger no matter how subtly he expressed it.

"I called the meeting, Adam, because we have to put an end to this destruction of Leather and Hides. I'm going to be honest with you. I believe this problem started because of your flirtation with Melissa, and that it'll continue as long as you're seeing her. The Morrises and Grants are out to destroy us."

He had to suppress his irritation. "What proof do you have, Mother? And let's get it straight that I am not flirting with Melissa Grant. I'm involved with her."

Her lips curled in anger. "You know I don't have any proof. But I'm an intelligent person, and I know that the problem began when you hired her to find the manager, and it intensified when she just happened to move back home after a little absence of nine or ten years."

Adam leaned forward, planted both elbows on the table—in a gesture that he recognized as one of defiance since his mother counseled that no part of the human body should touch the top of the table during a meal—and supported his cheeks with his fist. Then he sat up straight and articulated his words with Churchillian accuracy.

"If anyone present wants my job as CEO of Hayes/ Roundtree Enterprises, Inc., that person is welcome to it, and I can get back to New York and take care of my business." His glance swept the table. "No takers? Well, that settles it." He rose without having eaten or drunk anything and addressed his mother.

"Mother, I consider myself responsible for our family and its affairs, and I'll sacrifice a lot for our family, but I won't walk away from Melissa Grant unless I have proof"—he folded his right fist and slapped it into the open palm of his left hand—"unless I have indisputable proof that she isn't worth my . . . my attention. If none of you has proof, I don't want to hear this kind of talk again. How would you feel, and

what would you do if you were in my place?" He walked to
the door, but paused there as Wayne began to speak.

"I spent some time with her and Adam a couple of weeks
ago, and I thought she was nice. In fact I rather liked her. If
the Grants are involved in this, she doesn't have to know about
it. I know you can't look at a person and tell whether she's
honest, but she impressed me as being straight. But like I said,
it was a first impression."

Adam walked on as though impatient for fresh air and failed
to remember his overcoat until he'd driven halfway to his office. Wayne's endorsement had been weak and grudging compared to what his brother had said to him about Melissa.

Bill Henry Hayes finished his high-cholesterol breakfast, his
first such meal in over twenty years, and walked around to
the sideboard for another cup of mint tea. He leaned against
it and commanded his sister's attention. "Some things never
change in this family. The people come and go, but the men-
tality manages to stay a little below moronic, especially about
people's private lives. You two are acting as if Adam isn't
Adam. He can take care of himself and his business, too. I
met the young lady, and I like her. I like her a lot, in fact."
His gaze drilled his sister.

"You're ready to do the same thing to Adam and Melissa
that these feuding families did to me over thirty years ago.
You can't control other people's lives. Mary, I'd like you to
guess what you would have done if anybody had so much as
hinted that you couldn't have had John Roundtree. I doubt the
United States Marines could have kept you from him. You
watched what they did to me, and you're willing to see the
same thing happen to your firstborn child. I suggest both of
you consider the hell Rafer is putting Melissa through because
of Adam."

"What about her mother?" Wayne asked.

Bill Henry set his cold tea on the table. "She's one person who won't stand in their way."

Should she walk or drive the short distance to her office? Normally she walked, but dark clouds hovered ominously above and the weather forecast hadn't made clear the severity of the coming storm. Finally she decided to walk, but as a precaution she put a flashlight and a bag of Snickers in her briefcase. Banks joined her a half block from the office building.

"I see your folks had a miniconference at the Watering Hole last night. Seemed kinda strange that you and Miss Emily didn't join them."

Melissa waited until they were inside the warm lobby before commenting.

"Take your time," Banks offered in a tone that suggested she was handing Melissa a gift. "Your teeth make such original music, Melissa. If mine danced around like that every time they got cold, I'd invent some mouth muffs. How'd you happen to miss that confab last night?"

"Easily. I didn't know anything about it, and since I was probably the reason for it, I'm not surprised that I wasn't invited. As for Mother, none of them would expect her to go. Who was there?" Melissa marveled that her friend's brow furrowed as though she was in deep thought, trying to recall what Melissa knew she had carefully memorized.

"Let's see, now," Banks drawled. "Your mother's sister Mable, your father, his brother Faison and sister Louise, her husband and her son Timmy. Uh . . . oh, yes, and Louise's sister-in-law." As if she'd just had successful acupuncture for excruciating pain, Banks beamed at her and declared, "I think that's all."

Amusement buoyed Melissa as she entered the elevator. Too bad her mother hadn't known about the clandestine little meeting. She might have gone just to spite them, and Banks could have enjoyed relating it even more.

Banks got off at the third floor. "Sure you don't want some of my hot doughnuts?" she called over her shoulder.

"I want some, but I'm not going to eat any," Melissa replied, her tone laced with regret as she continued to her office on the fourth floor. The elevator door closed, and her lips pursed in disapproval. Though she liked Banks, she disliked gossip. For the local African American citizenry, the Watering Hole and the church were the vats in which gossip fermented. You could hear all about the righteous folk in church circles, but at the Hole you could get the goods on everybody, the devout included. That was one of the things she'd been happy to miss in New York. Your neighbors couldn't discuss your affairs, because they didn't know anything about you, and few cared enough to speculate.

She checked her e-mail, called her part-time secretary in Baltimore, and got the same message from each source: a Texan named Cooper needed a ranch manager. For persistence, the man rivaled Adam, she thought, not a little irritated. If she didn't answer, he should know that she wasn't interested. All she knew about a ranch, she'd learned from Clint Eastwood movies and romance novels. She put a cassette in her tape recorder, but before she could begin dictating a letter refusing the job, her phone rang.

"MTG. Melissa Grant speaking."

"I'm surprised you're in this morning. It's been snowing for fifteen minutes, and the streets are already white. It might be a good idea to leave." Her gaze followed the twirling pencil in her left hand. He'd spin me around like that if I let him, she mused. She tossed the pencil across the desk.

"Adam, do you think James Earl Jones ever identifies himself when he makes a phone call?" His chuckle warned her that her barb had missed the mark.

"He shouldn't have to. I doubt there're many people who wouldn't recognize that voice, and you can bet his significant other wouldn't be among the few who didn't. If a man has an intimate relationship with a woman, she ought to recognize everything about him."

"Humph. If the male ego needed physical space, men would be scarce as dog feathers. What size hat do you wear, Adam?" She leaned forward, placed her elbows on her desk, her palms beneath her chin and waited.

"I've never worn a hat. And no matter what you say about my ego, you recognized my voice."

"Yeah, but that's a defense mechanism," she teased, eyeing the window and the swirling snow.

"Against what?" he demanded, his testiness sizzling through the wire.

"Against being mistaken for a significant other," she replied, getting up to lock her door because she knew what would happen if she didn't. But to her chagrin, the cord's length didn't allow that precaution.

"What man would be so pea-brained as to hang such a non-descript title on you? You come under the heading of woman, babe." When he got casual and flirtatious like ordinary mortal men, she told herself with some amusement, she'd better watch her nervous system.

"Still there?"

"Haven't moved a fraction of an inch."

"I suggest you go home before you have trouble maneuvering your car through that snow."

"I didn't drive this morning," she said and would have liked to bite her tongue.

"Then you ought to consider putting on your boots and hiking it home. This stuff's getting bad."

She straightened up and weighed the folly of staying there for the sake of annoying him against getting home in reasonable comfort. She hung up and looked around for her bag of Snickers. If she ignored his advice, she could wind up bedeviling herself rather than Adam. Her door swung ajar, and she gazed up into a pair of fierce brown eyes, not a bit surprised that he was making sure she left the building before the weather worsened.

"Just as I thought. Settling in for the day, were you? I'm asking everyone to leave within the next thirty minutes. The storm is getting heavier by the second, and I'm going to turn off the heat to make certain everybody gets out of here. You'd get yourself snowbound just to vex me."

"Tut-tut! Really, Adam. You could do something about your tendency to be overbearing. Just a wee bit of improvement there would do wonders for your personality."

He had to struggle not to laugh. He'd seen Melissa in many moods and with a number of facial expressions, but he couldn't recall her having previously shrouded herself in innocence. Her serene countenance and angelic eyes proclaimed her blameless, and she even lowered her gaze, he noted, and folded her hands in her lap to enhance the effect.

He grinned down at her. "You're a dirty fighter, but you're one hell of a woman. Come on, let's get out of here." He took her coat from the coat tree and walked over to her with it. She pushed her chair back from the desk and glared at him. Then she reached in her desk drawer, pulled out a brown paper wrapper, and handed it to him.

"Have a Snickers while you find your way down off of your high horse." Her smile dared him as she leaned back in her chair and crossed her knees, displaying her endless legs to the greatest advantage. He swallowed the saliva accumulating in his mouth, glanced back at the open door, and rubbed his dampening palms against his pant legs.

"One of these days you're going to find out who you're playing with."

"Anytime, Mr. Roundtree."

He couldn't believe the transformation in her. Her smile had become sultry and her teasing blatant. He had to control the inclination to whistle. He'd regarded her as laid-back and cool, touchable but unavailable. Maybe he'd been right, but he was certain now that her dress-for-success suits and Brooks Brothers ties disguised a wild siren. He threw the coat to her.

"Melissa, this storm is intensifying. You may be satisfied with candy for supper, but I'm not, and I'm not going to leave you alone here in an unheated building. So come on." She looked toward the window, then back at him, and he could see her judging the weather and knew the minute she decided to cooperate. She stood, began to put on her coat, and he reached out to help her, but she brushed past him, pulling his nose as she did so.

One spark. Her touch was as tinder to dry grass. His left arm imprisoned her shoulder and his right encircled her waist as he brought her into the heat of his body. He stared into her eyes, eyes that asked him for all that he could give a woman, and every nerve screamed for the release of himself within her. He had to summon every vestige of willpower that he possessed to resist opening himself fully to her, revealing every nuance of himself, for he knew that if they started loving each other, neither one of them would call a halt to it until they had sated themselves. He tried without success to focus his attention on the rattling of a partially open window somewhere down the hall. Having given in to his feelings, he stood with his back to her desk holding her, soaking up her warmth. Warmth he hadn't realized he needed so badly. Finally the tapping of a woman's stiletto heels in the corridor brought him back to himself, and he released her.

"Melissa, we have to do something about this and soon. If we continue to see each other, I don't give us much chance of avoiding it. You know, we're mature adults, and we're supposed to know what we want and don't want. You're as familiar as I am with the circumstances past and present that are against any lasting relationship between us, but logic isn't what were dealing with here. We want to make love with each other, *and we will*. We both know that."

She locked her office door and walked along with him. Uncommunicative. "Let me guess," he said, frowning. "You're

wondering whether Loraine saw us when she passed the door."
Her eyes widened and she sucked in her lip. "Yes, Loraine.
Nobody else in Frederick wears four-inch heels. By tomorrow
night, half of the town will have heard her own version of it
and the other half will have gotten it secondhand. I hope
you've got better things to worry about."

When they reached his car, he brushed the grainy snow from
the door and scraped the windshield. She remarked that
Frederick didn't have any underground garages and few indoor
ones, and that not having them was an inconvenience in bad
weather.

"It's just as well," he replied, laughter taking the punch out
of his words. "I'd hate for our first time to be in the backseat
of a car."

"You're awfully sure of yourself," she grumbled. "For the
last twenty minutes, you've been acting as if you're the one
who decides this. But let me tell you: contrary to what that
song says, *everything depends on me.*"

Adam glanced at her as the Jaguar's skidding wheels fought
his efforts to get them home. "You're grumbling, but I see
you're not disagreeing with me." He got out, opened the trunk,
took out the two army blankets that he kept for emergencies,
and threw them under the spinning wheels.

"I've used sawdust and dry leaves, but I never heard of
anybody using blankets. Where'd you get that idea?"

Adam breathed deeply and adjusted himself as the car
crawled away from its temporary prison. He got out and put
the wet blankets back in the trunk. It didn't surprise him that
she'd chosen not to respond to his challenge, because he had
learned that she wouldn't let him push her into a corner. He
looked over his shoulder as the car chugged into the main
street and the snow pelted its windshield. "You will learn,
Melissa, that I'm innovative. If it doesn't work one way, I go
at it another way, and I usually manage to do what I set out
to do and finish what I start."

He noticed that she adjusted her skirt, folded and unfolded

her hands, and shifted away from him toward the passenger's door. Let her squirm. The sooner she realized that they were destined to be together, even if temporarily, no matter what their families said or did and no matter what happened at Leather and Hides, the sooner he'd get on with his life. He stopped in front of her house.

"I'll come around and get you. There's no point in both of us getting our feet soaked."

"Would you like some coffee?" She didn't look at him as she spoke, and he wondered whether she was eager to be alone with him or afraid of it. Who knew what she was thinking and feeling when she squinted like that. He shook his head. She'd be surprised how often and how thoroughly she perplexed him.

"I'll wait here while you check the faucets, the lights, and your radiators. A couple of inches of snow can put this town out of commission, and we've got four or five inches." He slapped her playfully on the bottom. "Hurry up. I've got to get going."

She spun around, her eyes like daggers. "My reaction to that is about the same as yours to getting your nose pinched. So keep your hands to yourself." He didn't care if his laughter irked her as she stood with her hands on her hips glaring at him.

"You're trying to pick a fight—but sweetheart, when we tangle, I'd prefer it to be under different circumstances. Believe me. Now go check your house, because if I do it, that Jaguar may be sitting right out there tomorrow morning." She went, and he figured she could hear his sigh of relief as she walked down the hall. He watched her and wondered what, other than a fire, could make her rush or lose her cool facade. A casual acquaintance might think her aloof and frigid, but he knew better. She was like a fine, rare diamond: cold on the outside and fire on the inside. And he wanted to explore every facet of her.

Eight

Melissa awoke early that morning feeling as a tigress must while prowling and pacing alongside a barbed-wire fence too high to scale. She wanted Adam, and what she felt for him went deep—deep enough to shatter her if he walked away. But he promised her nothing, and if she made love with him, he'd leave his mark on her forever. She didn't want to be like her mother, married to one man and loving another, losing her sense of self because of guilt. But she wanted a family of her own, though honesty forced her to admit that she wanted it with Adam Roundtree. He had all but promised her that they would make love. And soon. Face it, she told herself, you know you're not going to stop him, and he knows it, too. She stepped into the warm shower, but chills coursed through her at the thought of her father's certain reaction when he discovered how far she had gone with Adam.

The municipal workers cleared the snow from her street around noon, and Melissa dressed warmly, put on an old pair of boots, and set out for her parents' home. She leaned into the rising wind and tried to walk faster. Few people greeted her along the way. A five-inch snowfall was rare in Frederick, and everything was closed except the post office. It would be too much to hope that her father would be at his office and she'd find her mother alone, but she felt the need to see her even if it meant a confrontation with her father. Did young girls unburden themselves to their mothers? She didn't know, but she figured women her age didn't do it. It didn't matter. Her new relationship with her mother was precious to her, and she wanted to spend every moment with her that she could.

Emily opened the door and held out her arms. Melissa hadn't felt an urge to cry, but her tears came. She hadn't been cold, but when she stepped into the warmth of her mother's love, her sense of drifting in an unfriendly, frosty environment dissipated. Until she found herself dabbing at her tears with the back of her hand, she hadn't been aware that she shed them. She stepped back and looked into her mother's warm eyes, so like her own.

"I don't remember the last time I cried." Her mother's gentle hands stroked her back, and she soaked in the healing that they generated.

"That's what mothers are for. You can be yourself with me. This just makes me even more remorseful for not always having been here for you when you needed me."

Melissa shushed her. "I have you now, and that's what matters. Where's Daddy?" Her breath hung in her throat as she awaited the answer. She had no desire to grapple with her father's blind hatred of Adam and his family.

Her mother's words comforted her. "Rafer went to his office same as always. I'll make us some tea, and we can talk."

When Emily led them up to her room, carrying a tray of tea and sandwiches, Melissa realized that her mother had a sense of well-being only in her own room—that within her home, she could relax only in her bedroom.

"Now tell me about those tears," Emily soothed. "Have you fought with Adam?"

"No, but I'm not sure I can talk about him. I've got to work out my feelings about him and about us." The look of understanding that met her gaze caused her to wonder how her mother had come to terms with the destruction of her plans for a life with Bill Henry. But she didn't ask her. Instead, she told her of her meeting with the man.

"I gave Bill Henry a ride during that downpour we had early last week. He asked about you, and I thought he was pretty upset when I told him that you had been ill. Quick as a flash, he changed all over. I thought at first that he intended to pounce on me. Said he was very sorry to hear about it." She paused. "He sure was concerned, Mama." Her mother's teacup clattered in its saucer, staining the green broadloom carpet with amber liquid.

"Until I told you about us, I hadn't mentioned Bill Henry's name to anyone in thirty years, and I haven't seen him in nearly as long. How does he look?" She didn't wait for an answer. "Very distinguished, I imagine. When I saw Adam, I saw Bill Henry as he must have been at Adam's age. Does he still live at the old Hayes mansion?"

Melissa told her about Bill Henry's life-style and his little clapboard house. "I thought you knew."

Emily leaned forward in the brightly upholstered wing chair. "Who would tell me? Everybody in our families knows the story, and half the town, too." She sat up straight, looked Melissa in the eye, and spoke in a hoarse, teary voice. "I tell you again, honey. If you want Adam, don't let anybody stop you. Imagine what it's like to live twenty miles from the only man you ever loved, want him every day of your life, know that he wants you, and not be able to have him. Be strong, and don't let them ruin your life."

Melissa sipped her tea, buying time, trying to find a way to tell her mother what bothered her. She chose another, less personal, issue and silently scolded herself for doing it. "Mama, I don't want to be the one to tear this family apart." Her mother's hand rose and fell disparagingly, as though slapping at the air.

"You can't destroy what doesn't exist. After Schyler was

born, your father moved out of this room, and I didn't blame him. The bathroom between us isn't for intimacy, but for show. He had his son, and he finished the marriage. I did everything I could to keep us together, but it was never enough. There hasn't been any intimacy between us for over twenty-five years. We coexist, nothing more."

Melissa knew that her face must have mirrored her sense of horror. "How could you live like that, without love or affection for so many years? How could Daddy do such a thing?"

Emily slipped off her shoes, and her right foot found its customary place beneath her left thigh. "At least he was honest. Don't judge him too severely, Melissa. He's always had to walk in the footsteps and the reflections of other men. His tragedy is that it's always been high noon for him, and he never created a shadow of his own. That can make a man lose perspective, make him desperate."

Trudging back home in the howling wind, Melissa reflected that she hadn't told her mother the real reason for her visit. She loved Adam and wanted to tell her mother. Wanted to tell her that she needed to be with him in the most intimate way. Wanted to tell her mother that she needed advice. She walked through her door as her answering machine was recording Adam's voice and ran to the phone, but was too late. She telephoned him and advised him of his bad timing.

"What did you want?"

"I wanted to know if you were alright."

"I had expected you to say you couldn't live another second without hearing my voice." The minute she'd said it, she wanted to retract the careless statement. But he laughed.

"A modified version of that would be accurate. I'm going to New York this evening, and I wanted you to know. I'll be back in a couple of days."

"Anything wrong?" She had to cover her disappointment that she wouldn't see him perhaps for several days.

"Just loose ends. Stay out of mischief." He hung up before she could retaliate, and she called him back.

"Yes, Melissa. I didn't move, because I knew you'd need the last word. What is it?"

"Some rise by sin, and some by virtue fall," she quipped, quoting Shakespeare. "Have a good trip, Adam." His deep laughter still warmed her long after she'd hung up.

Sunday afternoon, three days later, Adam pushed his right index finger through the handle of his garment bag, dragged it from the carousel, threw it over his right shoulder, and strode out of the airport. He had ordered a limousine before leaving New York, because three days of sparring with employees and competitors had drained him. He'd worked night and day with little sleep and knew better than to drive. He ignored the half dozen newspapers that had been placed there for him, opened the bar, poured himself two fingers of bourbon over ice, and sat back to review the past three days. Melissa had been right—the corporate raiders wanted his best employees, and he didn't doubt that as soon as they weakened his staff, they'd go for his jugular. He had gotten things under control, but the sooner he found the culprit at Leather and Hides and got back to his own business, the better.

He leaned forward to replace the glass in the bar, and an envelope slipped out of his coat pocket. He opened it and read what he'd written. A puny declaration compared to what he felt and what he needed from her. But he couldn't ask for what he needed, and if she offered it, he couldn't accept it. His family's views about him and Melissa didn't matter, but the insidious annihilation of Leather and Hides did matter—and until he solved that mystery, he couldn't allow himself to become too deeply involved with her. He leaned back in the downy softness of the exquisite leather seat, leather tanned as only Hayes/Roundtree Enterprises, Inc., could, and his thoughts drifted to his growing dissatisfaction with his life. He loved his family and his work, but he needed a woman whom he loved and who loved him, and he wanted children. In his mind's eye he saw Melissa in his home with his baby at her breast. "Damn! I must be losing it." He reached for the handle on the door of the bar, decided against a drink, and turned on the radio. But he didn't need to hear George Strait sing "You Can't Make a Heart Love Somebody," so he flipped it off and asked himself why he was so restless. He had the driver go into Frederick and wait while he pushed the envelope into Melissa's mailbox. His heart pounded as he held his hand suspended next to her doorbell, but he resisted, got back in the car, and went home to Beaver Ridge.

"Anything happen here while I was gone?" he asked his mother when she greeted him at the door.

Mary Roundtree bussed her elder son on the cheek. "Not a thing. Looks to me like those dreadful crooks do their devilment at Leather and Hides either when you're out somewhere with Melissa Grant or when you're over at The Refuge. Never when you're home. I guess they didn't know you were out of town." He kissed her quickly, grabbed his garment bag, and headed for the stairs.

"Sooner or later they'll show their hands and trip themselves up," he threw over his shoulder. He would not be drawn into a discussion of Melissa, and if his mother insisted on it, she'd learn exactly what he felt. He hung up the garment bag, his overcoat and jacket, pulled a chair up to the desk that faced the window, and dialed her number. When she didn't answer and had forgotten to turn on her answering machine, he hung up and stared at the wintry scene through his window, stunned at the intensity of his disappointment. He was full of her, day and night, and he had to do something about it. He changed clothes, got his sports bag, took the Jaguar, and set out for the sports center in Frederick.

Melissa put on her swimsuit under her fatigues, added a winter coat, and went to the sports center. She checked her mailbox as she left the house and opened the unaddressed envelope that she found there. A red, silver-tipped feather fell to the floor. She picked it up, looked into the envelope, and found a card on which was printed, "When I saw this, I thought of you. It's unique, elegant, and it's soft—just as you are.—A." Excitement enveloped her. Had he put it there before he left? Or had he stopped by after his return? She had to fight the temptation to telephone him, and she walked less briskly than normal, skipped occasionally, and spun around a time or two.

"Adam." She wanted to scream his name. "Oh, Adam."

Melissa patted the water from her glistening body, threw the beach towel across a lounge chair, and prepared to relax after her vigorous swim. But she sat up abruptly when her eyes caught sight of a flawless male figure, his slim brown hips accented by a yellow bikini, as he stepped up to the diving board and arched his body into a breathtaking dive. Who was he and how could she feel an attraction for a man when she'd seen only his near naked form? Her breath hissed from her lungs as she watched his rhythmic strokes take him to the opposite end of the pool. He reached it, flipped into a turn, and she stood up, feeling his raw masculinity from her brain to her toes. She continued to gape at him as he swam toward her with his head down, impatient to see his face. He surfaced right at her feet and climbed out.

"Adam!"

"Melissa! I didn't know I'd find you here." He must have seen the fire in her, must have sensed her need of him, because his gaze reciprocated what she felt. Want. Hunger. Reluctance.

WE HAVE 3 FREE BOOKS FOR YOU!

(If the certificate is missing below, write to:
Zebra Home Subscription Service, Inc.,
120 Brighton Road, P.O. Box 5214, Clifton, New Jersey 07015-5214)

FREE BOOK CERTIFICATE

Yes! Please send me 3 *Arabesque* Contemporary Romances without cost or obligation, billing me just $1 to help cover postage and handling. I understand that each month, I will be able to preview 3 brand-new *Arabesque* Contemporary Romances FREE for 10 days. Then, if I decide to keep them, I will pay the money-saving preferred subscriber's price of just $12.00 for all 3...that's a savings of almost $3 off the publisher's price with no additional charge for shipping and handling. I may return any shipment within 10 days and owe nothing, and I may cancel this subscription at any time. My 3 FREE books will be mine to keep in any case.

Name _____

Address _____ Apt. _____

City _____ State_____ Zip _____

Telephone ( ) _____

Signature _____ AR0996
(If under 18, parent or guardian must sign.)

Terms and prices subject to change. Orders subject to acceptance by Zebra Home Subscription Service, Inc. .
Zebra Home Subscription Service, Inc. reserves the right to reject or cancel any subscription.

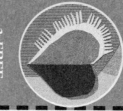

Pain. She saw it all reflected in his eyes, eyes that also bore a sadness she hadn't seen in him. She knew she'd give him whatever he wanted, but could she handle the certain repercussions? She panicked and dove into the water. Within seconds she heard his splash and felt his strong arms about her.

"Get dressed, get your things, and come with me. We've got to settle this." Her breasts tingled, and a shudder shot through her as his strong fingers grasped her bare flesh.

"Come with me," he said, in a voice that soothed and cajoled.

She couldn't calm her runaway heartbeat. "No," she told him, reaching for control though she knew he held the cards.

"Yes. Come with me now. We aren't children playing games, Melissa. It's time for us. It has been for weeks, and you know it."

Melissa summoned her customary cool demeanor and told him in a calm, steady voice, "If I go, it will be because I want to, not because you shoved or wheedled me into it."

Adam stroked her arms and back. "If I have to shove you into it, as you put it, I don't want you to go. It has to be mutual, Melissa. But we can't continue this way." As if he didn't care who came in and saw them, he fastened his mouth to hers without warning. Shivers betrayed her tingling body as his lips took her nectar, his strong fingers roamed over her naked flesh, and she opened her mouth for the sweet torture of his hot tongue. Her senses whirled, and her feminine center pulsated wildly when he slipped his hand into the scant bra of her bathing suit and brought her full breast naked against his hard chest. Her moans filled his mouth, and she felt herself sag against him.

"Come on, sweetheart, let's go."

"Where?"

"Your house. Baltimore. A hotel. I don't care, as long as you and I are the only ones there."

* * *

She sat motionless beside him as the Jaguar raced toward the setting sun. She wondered if its now cool rays, hovering as if in silence over a declining sphere of the horizon, foretold what she would experience with Adam. Would their passion for each other peter out coldly like the dying sun? She thought of Gilbert Lewis, of B-H and her mother and the toll that thirty years with a broken heart had taken on her mother. The doctors hadn't found anything wrong with her mother, because medical doctors didn't have the tools with which to detect a broken heart. She couldn't count on a life with Adam, but she would at least have this one night with him. She remembered the red feather and the note and forgot her fears, her anxiety. She realized that he had stopped the car and cut the motor.

"Aren't you going to ask me where I've taken you?"

"You wouldn't take me anywhere that I wouldn't want to be," she replied, and she meant it.

"You're sure?"

"It's one of the few things I *am* sure of right now." She paused, trying to decide whether to thank him for the feather and his note. Uncertain about it, she didn't mention his gift, but said, "And if I decide I want to leave here or anywhere else you take me, I only have to tell you."

Adam's right thumb and index finger stroked his chin in slow sweeps. "Why are you so certain?"

She stared into his eyes, masculine eyes that mesmerized, that twinkled for no reason, and that demanded confidence. In minutes she would give herself over to his keeping, so she spoke with honesty and candor.

"I'm not positive of much where men are concerned, Adam, but you're the rock of Gibraltar, and I'd go anywhere with you."

She knew from his demeanor that her words had affected him. He spoke in a slow, deliberate manner, as though to make certain of his ground. "You're not setting me up, are you?" He got out and started around the car to open the door for her, but she met him in front of the hood.

"Setting you up? Haven't I always said precisely what I

mean?" Heat coiled in the seat of her passion as he growled deep in his throat and locked his arms around her.

"Tell me more of what you mean."

She couldn't believe that he needed the assurance, that he could be vulnerable. With her head against his shoulder in symbolic submission, she told him, "I mean the earth wouldn't dare quake when I'm with you.

He looked hard at her, picked her up, and carried her into his lodge on the bank of the Potomac River.

She glanced around at her surroundings when he set her down, but he didn't let her dwell on it. His fingers under her chin brought her lips within an inch of his, and she breathed in his words—"sweet, soft"—just before her body absorbed the shock of his tender kiss. On more than one occasion he had let her feel his power, his maleness, and he'd been tender with her, too, but he hadn't drugged her with this sweet supplication. Hadn't whispered loving words of encouragement, assuring her that her beauty beguiled him, that she was all a man could want in a woman.

"I've never known a woman like you," he whispered as she hid her face in his shoulder until he tipped up her chin and kissed her eyes.

"Trust me, sweetheart. I want your happiness more than my own." Her heart believed him, and she slumped against him in submission. "I need to love you," he murmured, trailing kisses over her neck and collarbone, easing off her coat, "but I need to know that I'm giving you what you want, what satisfies you." She held him closer, loving the feel of his lips skimming over her flesh, barely touching her, inflaming her. Unsure of herself and of her ability to please him, she fought her body's urge to twist itself around him, to issue its own sensuous invitation. Fought until her nipples beaded and her hips moved forward in an urgent plea.

"Ah, Melissa. My woman! *I need you.*" She could no longer

resist her body's wild hunger and its searing demand that triggered her frantic undulations when she felt him hot and hard against her belly.

"Slow down, baby, and let me get a handle on this." Out of control now, her hands stroked him inside his shirt in her eagerness to explore him, to know him. And her fingers became bolder, toying with his nipple until his unbridled moan thrilled her with the knowledge that she could excite him so easily. She looped her arms around his neck and took from his mouth the kiss that she needed. Her heart skidded, and she buried her face against his throat as he cradled her to him and started up the stairs. At the top he stepped away from her, giving her a chance to change her mind, and between quick, short breaths, asked her: "Are you sure this is what you want?" Her smile must have reassured him, for he kissed her quickly and by the time they reached his bedroom, she wore only her bathing suit.

He threw back the bed covers with one hand without releasing her, and with exquisite care, placed her in his bed. He undressed himself quickly, removed her bathing suit with gentle hands, laid down beside her, and took her to him. Her body screamed in frustration as his talented, knowing assault on her senses began.

"Your breasts make my mouth water," he murmured, and she cried out as he circled a nipple with his tongue, pulled it into his mouth, and sucked it greedily. She swung her hips eagerly up to him. Seeking, begging. But he retained control of their loving, nourishing himself at her breast while his hand skimmed slowly down her body, tantalizingly, until he reached her woman's treasure.

"Adam, *please!*" she begged. "I think I'll die if you don't do something to me." He released her breast, bringing a groan from her, and with his tongue deep in her mouth, began to simulate the act of love. She couldn't restrain herself any longer, and her hips undulated wildly, as his knowing fingers began their witchery, working their magic.

"Adam," she pleaded, "I need you." He quickened his strokes, heightening her pleasure while he murmured sweet, tender words of encouragement. She shivered as her heart hammered out an erratic rhythm, and an unfamiliar need seared the center of her passion, dampening her for his entry. Her love nectar poured out of her, flowing over his fingers, and she felt the involuntary movement of his steel-like erection against her thigh. Excited beyond reason, impatient to know him, all of him, she reached for him to bring him into her, but he resisted.

"In a minute, baby. This is the most important thing that will ever happen to us," he whispered. With skill and more patience than he'd probably thought he would need, he joined them. Afterward she nestled close to him, shaken by the intensity of her feelings, by the sense that he had become a part of her. She had already forgotten the pain of his penetration, but the awesome control and tender guidance with which he had accomplished the ultimate surrender of herself to him would remain forever with her. Her whole body had quivered uncontrollably in its final submission to him. She wanted to stay with him always.

Adam lay on his back and held Melissa close to his side. His lips brushed her hair as she relaxed against him in trusting slumber. He closed his eyes and suppressed a sigh. How had she come to mean so much to him? He'd controlled his release, because he hadn't wanted her to know how deeply she moved him. Hadn't wanted her to witness the effect that the powerful climax she drove him to would have on him. He'd feared that even in her innocence she would have recognized her power over him. And he had sworn never to give another woman the power to ring his bell. But if he wasn't careful, Melissa could do that.

She threw her left leg over his groin, and he sucked in his breath, his appetite for her whetted but far from sated. He tried to come to terms with her having been a virgin. His first. He wouldn't have thought that would mean anything to him, but it did. When his first affair had crashed around him, he'd been young, still in his teens and, as youth are wont to do, he'd mended easily. This was different. He was no longer a boy, but a man who knew the value of the kind of loving he'd just had with Melissa and who had sense enough to realize that he'd probably never find it in another woman. She wasn't as sophisticated as he'd once thought, and lovely as she was, if she was a virgin at twenty-eight, she had to care a lot to allow him to be her first man.

If he told her about his first sexual encounter, would she forgive him? And what would she say about his misdeed at age sixteen when he got his revenge? He doubted that she would overlook either. Feeling the need to be closer to her, he pulled her over on top of him, and she buried her face in his shoulder and went back to sleep. His grip on her tightened; how could he let her go? But what if she were in cahoots with whoever was ruining his family's business? He wanted her but for how long? Vexed with himself, he laid her on her back and tried to focus on the problem he'd caused himself. Why hadn't he straightened it out, as he'd intended, before he made love with her? Lovemaking so explosive as they'd just experienced didn't end after one session, and a man didn't offer Melissa Grant a one-night stand.

He felt her shift beside him and sit up. "Adam," she whispered as she leaned over him, "we've done a dangerous thing. We could rekindle that awful feud between our families."

"Maybe, but I don't think it'll reach its past furor. It's worth watching, but there's no fertile ground for it."

She nuzzled his neck and ran her hands over his broad chest. "No? Speak to your uncle B-H, and ask him if I'm right."

His hand stroked her tangled curls, and his gaze roamed over her lovely, sepia face. He wanted to know what she felt for him, but if he asked and she told him, he'd have to reciprocate. So he didn't ask her. "If you know something about this feud that you think I don't, tell me."

"Speak to your uncle. I'd rather he told you. You know, Adam, my father rides me constantly about you. He's never had any genuinely fatherly feelings for me, but he hates you and your folks so much that he's suddenly become very protective of me."

Adam propped himself up on his left elbow. "What do you mean, Rafer has no feeling for you. I thought you said—"

She spoke quickly. "I couldn't tell you then, and I hated misleading you. I'm his property, a member of his family, that's all."

He crooked his arm around her shoulder and pulled her close. "It's his loss, Melissa. Any father should be proud to have you for a daughter." He dropped a kiss on her nose. "What about us, Melissa? What do you see ahead for us?" Regret laced her voice as she recited her misgivings, her belief that they'd had as much as they could ever have.

"Do you mean that?"

"I don't want it to be true, but it's what I believe. I don't expect more, because our families come first."

"You're not speaking for me. If you're not prepared to deal with your family, I guess this is it."

She got up. "You can't harness the Atlantic, Adam."

"No," he answered, pulling on his fatigues, "but you can ride the waves. Let's go, Melissa, before we manage to paint this black."

As though upon reflection and with apparent reluctance, he grasped the back of her neck with his large hand and guided her to face him. Standing mere inches from him, she made herself look into his penetrating gaze, and his naked passion. His unshielded want jolted her. Her arms encircled his neck, and her body found its haven in his tight embrace as she molded herself to him.

He held her until her rapid breathing subsided, and she felt his fingers tilt her chin upward until she looked into his twinkling eyes.

"This isn't over, baby. It may never be over. We didn't seek this, and I don't think we wanted it, but it found us and we have to deal with it. And we have to decide whether we're going to do that together or separately." She started to speak, but he shushed her. "We're too raw right now, and there are too many unanswered questions and unsolved problems—at least from where I stand, so let's think about this." He kissed her without passion.

"Adam, one day I tried to list the things that I dislike about you."

Both of his eyebrows arched. "And?"

"Well, while I admire your self-control, it irks the hell out of me that you can turn off your passion at will, as though it were a kitchen faucet."

His eyes lighted with mirth, and she thought his deep laugh held more than humor, that it signified release as well. He pinched her nose and hugged her. "If I wasn't able to turn it off, you probably wouldn't be speaking to me." Arm in arm, they walked to his car.

They spoke little on the drive back. Adam reflected on what had passed between them and on the unpleasant, empty sensation in his chest. He'd thought, hoped, that the fever raging in him whenever he saw her or spoke with her would subside if he made love with her. He'd depended on it. It struck him that if he were so far off in his business dealings, he'd soon face bankruptcy, because she'd gotten into his blood and made herself as much a part of him and the red and white corpuscles that coursed through his veins and sustained his life. But hell! People lived without sight, auditory faculties, limbs, and even a kidney. And if he had to, if she couldn't come to terms with it, he'd live without Melissa Grant.

* * *

But Melissa's thoughts didn't lean toward life without Adam. Monday morning found her slouched in her desk chair, daydreaming. Alarmed at her unusual behavior, she went to the ladies' room to refresh her face with cold water and try to change her mood. She had to get started on the mound of work in her incoming box. She walked into the room and Banks stopped fingering her curls, observed Melissa from the mirror, and smirked.

"What are you licking your chops about?"

Immediately defensive, Melissa asked her, "What do you mean?"

Never one for subtlety, Banks retorted, "You didn't even see me. Whose arms were you in last night? I've never seen a more sated female in my life."

Annoyed at her suddenly hot face, Melissa denied it. "You're imagining things."

"Nooooo kidding. Is he six-feet-four or so with long-lashed, bedroom eyes and a body to die for?"

"That could be anybody."

"You think I was born yesterday? Not in my estimation, it couldn't. That man doesn't even come in pairs. If I'd spent the night in his bed, I'd be walking around with a silly smile on my face, too. Go girl!" She ducked into a booth, and Melissa checked her face in the mirror, but detected nothing different. Still smiling, she sauntered back to her office.

She examined her e-mail and called her New York office for confirmation. She'd read correctly, but the secretary she shared had no explanation as to why she would be the subject of a private investigator's sleuthing. The woman called a few minutes later to know whether Melissa would participate in a roundtable discussion on women in business. She said she'd consider it. She checked her mail again. The Houston lawyer named Cooper hadn't despaired in his effort to hire MTG to find a manager for his two thousand-acre-ranch. She wasn't inclined to take the job, but the man was persistent, and the search would be a big enough challenge to keep her mind off of Adam.

"It ought to keep me so busy I won't have time to daydream," she said, and asked the man to offer a contract. But two hours passed and she'd done nothing but relive those moments in Adam's arms. She'd been afraid to let herself go, but he had soothed, coached, and loved her until she did. Shivers coursed through her as she remembered his sweet urging.

"Give yourself to me, sweetheart. I'm your man, and you belong to me—you'll never belong to anybody else. Give it up, Melissa. I'll make you mine, if it takes me a week." She'd looked up at his perspiring face and into his desire-laden eyes, and he'd twisted his hips and whispered her name. "Melissa, my baby, I need to feel you explode all around me." And she had exploded, had lost her will as though he'd tossed her in a whirlwind of ecstasy. Frustrated, she stuffed some papers into her briefcase and went home.

She answered the telephone after the first ring, hoping to hear Adam's voice. "If you had been home last night, you'd know that somebody shot your cousin Timmy. Louise said he came home with his arm bleeding, and he's sure it was one of the Roundtrees or their men. I guess now you'll stay away from Adam Roundtree. It was probably him anyway, because everything was fine here until he came back."

She tuned him out and realized it was the first time she'd ever done that while her father spoke. She didn't want to hear Adam criticized, but if a Roundtree or one of their men had shot her cousin, she had disgraced herself with Adam.

"What time did it happen, Daddy?"

"About ten o'clock. Why?"

Her adrenaline began a rapid flow, and joy suffused her. "I can't imagine who did it, Daddy," she said, "but I'm certain of one thing. It wasn't Adam."

"You dare defend him when he's wounded your blood relative?"

She could imagine that his eyes narrowed and the veins in his forehead protruded as they always did when his temper flared. It occurred to her that what she'd say next might be the last words he ever heard, but she had to say them.

"Daddy, I was with Adam until midnight. It wasn't Adam."

"You— How could you?" he sputtered and hung up.

"Now I've really done it," she moaned. "There's no way I can continue to see Adam. Daddy will find an excuse to hurt him, maybe even prosecute him."

With reluctance, she answered her doorbell to find her mother, the first time Emily had visited her. Their greeting reflected their newfound warmth, and they walked into Melissa's living room arm in arm.

"This is a wonderful surprise, Mama. Tell me nothing's wrong."

Emily Grant walked around the room, touching little objects, admiring her daughter's taste. She lingered before a group of family snapshots that Melissa had set in little silver frames. "I never realized that you were so well organized, so neat, or that you preferred these muted colors that your father adores."

Melissa laughed. She knew when someone was buying time. "Mama, surely you don't consider green and antique gold muted. You've got these same colors in your bedroom, along with a little hot orange, I should add. Now tell me what's bothering you."

"You're father's up to something. He and Booker—you know the deputy sheriff, that crooked brother-in-law of his— well, they've had their heads together all morning, and for some reason, Rafer didn't take him to the office but brought him home, and they're closeted in his room."

"Just a minute. Let me get the door. You don't think Daddy followed you over here, do you?"

"Hardly. He was trying to convince Booker about something, but I couldn't hear them too clearly."

Melissa opened the door. Adam. Excitement boiled up in her, and her heart started a fast gallop as she looked at him.

"Hi." He didn't speak but bent to kiss her at about the same time as his gaze fell on Melissa's mother, who stood in the foyer a few feet away. Adam straightened up and looked into the eyes of Emily Grant, then he pulled Melissa into his arms and kissed her waiting lips.

Melissa knew Adam wondered why she'd let him give her a lingering kiss in her mother's presence and why she didn't move out of his arms. Still holding on to him, she turned to her mother.

"Mama, you must know this is Adam Roundtree. Adam, this is my mother, Emily Morris Grant." Adam released her, walked over to Melissa's mother and extended his hand. His surprise at Emily's warm response was obvious, and when she continued to hold his hand, he remarked on his delight in meeting her.

"I don't want to interrupt your visit," he added, "I can talk with Melissa later."

"Please don't leave on my account, Adam. I'll just run along. You didn't come over here midday on Monday without a good reason. And when I called Melissa's office and found out that she'd gone home so early even though she wasn't sick, I tell you I was mystified. You two must have something to talk about, and I don't want to get in the way."

Melissa wanted her mother and Adam to be friends, though she doubted that her father would tolerate it, and she knew she'd better seize the moment. "Come on in here and have a seat. I'll get us something to drink," she offered, ushering them into the living room. She rushed to make tea and fresh coffee, fearing that tension might develop between her mother and Adam if she left them together for too long. She returned a few minutes later to find them comfortably engaged in conversation, and her mother's words rang in her ear.

"I don't have any ill will against anybody, Adam. Hatred ruined my life."

She watched Adam scrutinize her mother as if he could see inside of her, and it struck Melissa that Adam adopted that penetrating stare when sizing up his opponents.

Emily must have sensed it, too, because she told him, "I'm not your enemy, Adam. I know Rafer would like to see the last of you and all your kinfolk, but I don't know of anything that he and I think alike on."

Adam patted her hand, crossed his knee, threw his head back as if meditating and then abruptly sat forward. Melissa knew he had just made up his mind about something important.

"Rafer has accused me of shooting your cousin Timothy," he told them, his gaze fixed on Melissa. She knew why he hadn't told her over the phone, that he wanted to watch her reaction.

"I told Daddy that charge was ridiculous, that you were with me until midnight." She carefully avoided looking at her mother.

"Why did you decide to be with me last night? There've been many other times when the situation was just as compelling, just as urgent, and you sent me on my way. But yesterday afternoon you went with me without hesitation. Are you for me or against me?"

Melissa bristled. "How dare you suggest that I'd cheapen myself by taking subterfuge to the point where I'd—" She remembered that her mother sat three feet away and tried to cool off.

"Do you think I haven't wondered whether you were keeping me occupied while Wayne or one of your men went after Timmy? I haven't read any proclamation attesting to the spotless lives of the Hayes-Roundtree clan, so back off."

"Adam. Melissa," Emily began in a troubled voice. "Will

you two stop it? Can't you see what you're doing to each other?"

Adam turned to her. "You're not against a relationship between Melissa and me. Why is that?" Melissa watched in horror as tears glistened in her mother's eyes and prayed that she'd be able to hold them back. She knew that the loss of dignity in Adam's presence would humiliate her mother.

Emily opened her handbag, pulled out a tissue, and blew her nose. "I've been a victim of this stupid feud for the last thirty-one years, and I pray to God I live to see the end of it."

"I've never raised a gun to anybody," Adam assured them, "and I don't know that I could. Life is precious." His gaze shifted to Melissa's face, and she read his silent message. *Precious, as you are precious.* From the corner of her eye, she glimpsed the silver-tipped red feather that she'd placed in a tiny crystal vase and walked over to the mantelpiece where it stood. She handed it to her mother, and Emily remarked on its elegance and uniqueness.

"This is lovely. Unusual."

Melissa was still learning her mother's ways, and Emily startled her when she grinned devilishly, as if she knew Adam had given her daughter the little gift.

Melissa's voice tittered with emotion. "Yes," she answered as her gaze adored Adam. "Someone very special gave it to me." The twinkle in his eyes glowed until it enveloped his face, and his lips moved with unspoken words that she couldn't decipher. She glanced over at her mother, then back at Adam, and fought her need to rush to him and feel his man's strength surround her. As though compelled to touch her, he slid a finger down her right cheek while the impassioned turbulence of his eyes caressed her face. Mesmerized, she leaned into him and gloried in the feel of his strong arms around her.

"I'd better be going," he told them, his tone indicating a reluctance to heed his words. Melissa nodded and opened the door. Adam turned to Emily.

"I'm glad you were here. It was a pleasure to meet you."

Melissa watched Adam brace himself against the wind and strike out for his office and knew she couldn't turn their relationship around nor change what she felt for him. She loved him more today than yesterday. More now than an hour ago. Anxious that she and Adam had disclosed to her mother how intimate they had become, she pivoted sharply, ready for a lecture.

"I know what you're thinking, Mama, and I'm sorry you witnessed that exchange, but I couldn't let Adam take the blame for something I knew he didn't do." Her mother's intense scrutiny irked her, but the words she heard told her that she needn't have been concerned.

"Why apologize?" Emily asked her. "You're twenty-eight years old. When a woman and a man love each other and they're not obligated to anybody else, how they express their passion and their love behind closed doors is their business. The government can't legislate it, and the courts can't ban it. I only wish I'd been as sensible. Well, I'd better leave—your father will be up in the air as soon as he discovers he's in that house by himself."

Adam inclined his head in brief greetings to passersby as he walked swiftly to his office, his dilemma about Melissa's possible culpability mounting with the seconds. He *had* to solve it—far more than his family's reputation and livelihood hinged on it. He wasn't certain he could give her up even if she was guilty, and if she was and if he didn't give her up, he faced a complete break with his family. All except B-H. Somehow he didn't think his uncle would side with Wayne and his mother if— B-H . . . twice in connection with their relationship, Melissa had suggested he ask his uncle about the long arm of their families' feud. He made a mental note to speak with B-H.

As though by agreement, they avoided meeting each other at work or seeing each other outside the building, and they didn't telephone for several days. Adam had decided he needed to at least talk with her when he answered his phone.

"Roundtree."

"Hi, Roundtree. Grant here." He wasn't fooled by her light response, because he figured she'd missed him as much as he'd missed her.

He shrouded himself in his office demeanor. "What may I do for you?"

"I thought you'd like to know that I've found a position for Dan with another real estate firm, and he's willing to accept it."

"I told you I wouldn't object to his leaving my staff since he has good reasons, so why are you telling me this? Is there something else?" He heard the hesitancy in her voice and wondered if he'd been too brusque.

"Sorry, but I thought you'd like to know before I completed the transaction. He's joining one of your competitors, but he's assured me that he won't reveal anything about your business. I do need to talk to you about something else, though." He listened as she told him of her contract to locate a managing officer for a Pittsburgh real estate firm and knew at once that asking him for tips on what to look for in the applicants was an excuse to talk with him. She didn't need his advice, and she must be aware that he knew it and that he'd guess she only wanted contact with him.

"If you need the information urgently, perhaps we could get together for dinner. I'm . . ." He paused, uncertain. "I'm busy just now. Suppose I pick you up at seven?" He'd planned to go more slowly with her until he solved the problems at Leather and Hides, but he'd detected a need for him in her voice and responded to it.

He leaned back in his chair, placed his feet with ankles crossed on his desk and buzzed his secretary to come in. "No calls and no visitors until I tell you." He ignored her inquiring look and glanced at the Jaeger-Lecoutre on his wrist. Three o'clock. He'd see Melissa in four hours. He put his feet on

the floor and got to work. An hour later he was squeezing his
relaxer, annoyed with himself. He was damned if he'd be a
slave to his penis just because he'd found a woman who was
his soul mate in bed. He'd have dinner with Melissa, take her
home, and leave her there. He whistled just to prove to himself
that he'd gotten rid of a burden. After another two hours, he
realized he'd looked at his watch a dozen times, willing the
moments to pass more swiftly. It irritated him. He'd thought
that if he made love with her, that would be the end of it. But
he'd gotten an astonishing surprise, and he'd need the will of
Moses to hold his passion for her in check. But he'd do it.

Bill Henry's telephone call as she began dressing for dinner
with Adam disconcerted Melissa. To her knowledge, he hadn't
previously contacted anyone in her family. Her mother hadn't
heard from him since she'd broken their engagement. Fear
streaked through her at the possibility that something might
be wrong with Adam, but B-H's tone reassured her.

"How is Em— How is your mother?" Stunned, Melissa told
him with all the casualness she could muster that Emily had
recently visited her, apparently well. His deep sigh and audible
release of breath communicated to her his profound relief, jolt-
ing her. Would it be her destiny to love so deeply and lose so
painfully? She hoped not as she tried without success to calm
her mounting excitement at the prospect of being with Adam.

She knew she shouldn't have agreed to go to dinner with
him, but she couldn't contain her eagerness to be with him
and resigned herself to take whatever came. She dressed in a
soft, figure-flattering, berry red, wool knit dress, smoothed her
long curls into a French twist and wrapped a strand of pearls
around it. She slipped on a pair of black suede dress slippers,
dabbed Opium perfume in strategic places, and walked down
the stairs just as her doorbell rang.

"Hi. You look . . . beautiful. Is this all for me?" Blood

rushed to her face, and she ducked her head. He took her hand and entered without waiting for her invitation.

"You . . . you look good, too," she told him. He stared at her, shaking his head, obviously denying something. As if transfixed, she didn't move out of his way. Her gaze feasted on him. Chills twisted through her whole body as the gong of her grandmother's clock announced seven o'clock, and she couldn't shake the thought that it tolled for her and Adam. She knew he could tell that he'd disconcerted her and that he sensed her need for his reassurance, because she read his emotions in that fraction of a second before he blanketed his feelings. She looked up at him, waiting.

His sigh and mild oath fell on her ears like music, but he disappointed her when he didn't take her in his arms. His eyes mirrored his remorse, and she knew he intended to put their relationship on the shelf. She lowered her head to hide her reaction when his deep sigh of regret confirmed it. It wasn't easy to stand casually before him while his eyes adored her and his thumb tenderly stroked her chin, even as his posture sent a different message.

"It's okay, Melissa. We'll survive it." She knew he meant that going their separate ways would hurt, but that it wouldn't kill him. Her smile had never been so brilliant.

Nine

Melissa read Magnus Cooper's signed contract and decided she'd made a mistake. She had quoted the man a very high fee and had expected him to bargain or at least complain. But if her eyes served her properly, he would pay double that if she could find a manager who suited him within two weeks. She telephoned him to bargain for three weeks at one and a half times the fee she'd quoted.

"Are you telling me the president of MTG is a woman? Well, a man I trust told me this was one of the best executive search firms in the country. Who's your CEO?"

"Mr. Cooper, *I* am the president and owner of MTG." Melissa iced her voice to put the man in his place, but to her astonishment, he persisted.

"Well, I don't know, ma'am. I'm not used to doing business with a woman . . . but, well . . . they say you know your stuff. Still, I just don't know."

Annoyed, she told him, "Mr. Cooper, I'm looking at a contract that says you do business with me. I hope legal action won't be necessary."

"Of course not," he cajoled. And she envisioned honey dripping from his tongue as he drawled, "Let's have dinner and smooth over this little misunderstanding." Unimpressed with the offer, she declined—Houston, Texas, wasn't around the corner. Magnus Cooper gave her the three weeks and fee she demanded and told her he'd forward an amendment to the contract. Pleased, she thanked him and said a polite good bye. Later, dispirited over her unsatisfactory relationship with Adam, she accepted Banks's suggestion that they browse in a few antique shops after work.

They walked through Bessie's Yesteryear, looking at old coffee grinders, grandfather clocks, alabaster candlesticks, a Tiffany lamp, an early Shaker rocker. Melissa paused beside an ancient brass scale and lifted one of its weights, thinking that if she polished the scale it would add a nice touch to her kitchen's bay window. She felt Banks jab her in the back and glanced up and into the unfriendly eyes of Mary Roundtree. She couldn't treat Adam's mother discourteously, but the woman didn't invite warmth. Melissa didn't know what kind of response she'd get, but she squared her shoulders and spoke.

"Good afternoon, Mrs. Roundtree. How are you?" For that, she received a stingy "Fine, thank you" and a nod of the head. Perplexed that Adam's mother behaved more coldly toward her than when they'd first met, she nevertheless introduced Banks, who retaliated on Melissa's behalf by accepting the introduction with a frosty "Nice to meet you, Miss Mary." Melissa watched in horror as Adam's mother excused herself and turned away in such haste that she crashed into an 1890 gaslight post and knocked herself out. Alarmed, she knelt beside the woman to assist her while Banks telephoned Adam and called for an ambulance. She gave silent thanks that both were only a few blocks away.

Adam rushed into Bessie's Yesteryear and stopped short at the unbelievable scene. Melissa held his mother's head in her lap and placed a cold compress to her forehead. He knelt beside them and tried to gain his mother's attention, but she didn't respond. The wail of the ambulance seemed miles away and, anxious, he felt for his mother's pulse. Satisfied, he looked again at Melissa and marveled as she continued her careful ministrations. Shaking his head, he sat up on his haunches and fixed his gaze on her face. How could she treat his mother with such tenderness after she had accorded Melissa the barest civility and all but dismissed her when she'd visited her home? He studied the woman who, without realizing it, had made him rethink his priorities and knew an unaccustomed softness in himself. She combined gentleness and tenderness with strength, determination, and efficiency. He remembered Wayne's assessment of her and reached out to touch her face.

"The ambulance is here now. I won't forget your kindness, Melissa."

"Please don't thank me. I'd like to go to the hospital with you. Do you mind?"

His gaze roamed over her face before resting on her eyes. He wished he could read her reasons, because he knew she'd be affronted if he asked her why. He agreed, though he suspected that she detected his reluctance, and it bothered him that he didn't welcome her company.

They waited three hours before a doctor advised them that Mary may have suffered a severe concussion, but that she had regained a fair amount of lucidity. Adam expressed his relief and went to the cafeteria to get coffee for Melissa and himself.

Melissa stepped closer when she heard Mary's weak voice. "What happened? Why are you here?" It struck her that a lack of strength didn't camouflage the hostility in Mary Roundtree's voice. Melissa told her what had happened, her tone devoid of feeling. More alert now, the woman attempted without success to sit up, and Melissa pulled up a chair beside her bed.

"Where is Adam? Are you here because you're after him?"

Melissa couldn't believe the displeasure in the woman's eyes as she turned her face away. "I'm sure you know your son well enough to realize that if he didn't want me here, I wouldn't be here."

"If you care about him, you'll leave him alone," the woman told her with trembling lips.

Melissa tried to push back her annoyance. Being Adam's mother gave Mary Roundtree the upper hand. Melissa told her, "I can't be with him if he doesn't want to be with *me*, so use your influence with Adam. Your words are wasted on me."

Adam returned to find his mother dropping silent tears, her lips pursed in disapproval. "What did you say to her?" he asked Melissa. She looked the man she loved fully in the face, stared him down for several seconds, and told him, "I just answered her questions. Seems I overstayed my welcome here. I'll be seeing you."

"Melissa!"

She kept walking. Her world seemed filled with men who, like Gilbert Lewis, exacted a pound of flesh for every smile they'd given you. She didn't want to believe Adam would think her capable of doing or saying anything to hurt his mother. Deep in thought, she nearly passed Bill Henry without speaking.

"What's wrong, Melissa? You look as though you've just witnessed an execution."

"Maybe I have. *Mine.*" That tired voice couldn't be hers.

"What happened?" He stepped closer and touched her arm. She told him, beginning with her encounter with Mary in the antique store. B-H nodded in apparent understanding.

"Didn't Adam tell you that Mary Roundtree is a consummate actress? For years my sister belonged to the Frederick Players—she can switch from saint to siren in seconds. I can't believe Adam would let her antics rattle him."

"No. He let her rattle me, and with impunity. I've had it with the Roundtrees."

Bill Henry shook his head. "For now, maybe. Well, it's a good thing I'm a Hayes." She felt his soothing pat on her forearm and sensed that he felt a special kinship with her. He walked on, turned, and called her. "Melissa, how is Em— How is Emily?" She walked back to him.

"She's fine, B-H. Lately something about her reminds me of early spring. I don't understand it, but I'm certainly happy about it."

He nodded, and she thought his face reflected a wistful longing. "Are the two of you close?"

"We never were until I came back home, but we are now."

"She needs someone. I'm glad she has you."

"Me, too," she said, as much to herself as to him. She walked back to the phone booth and called Towne car service for a taxi home. She'd gone shopping to escape her thoughts and look what she got as a result. More to think about. She went home and began undressing almost from the front door, not bothering to wonder why a bath seemed the answer to her problems. You can't wash it away, an inner voice nagged.

Adam walked out of his mother's hospital room, displeased with himself for having asked Melissa such a thoughtless question after her kindness to his mother. She hadn't deserved it. But his mother never cried, and he'd thought that . . . It didn't matter—he had mistreated Melissa. His uncle's voice interrupted his mental meanderings.

"What's going on around here? First Melissa walks past me without speaking, and now you nearly knock me down. How's Mary?"

Adam looked into the distance, preoccupied. "She's improving. She'll be home tomorrow."

"Be careful with Melissa, Adam. That girl's very tender."

It struck Adam that his uncle regarded Melissa with a deep affection for which he could see no apparent basis, and he meant to ask him about it. "I know what she's like, B-H, and it isn't my intention to hurt her."

"But you did."

"I know." Adam hastened on without saying good-bye. He had to get to her.

He parked in front of her home and sat in the car considering the charm of her little house nestled among the four swaying pines, cloaked in brilliant moonlight. How much like her it seemed: simple, elegant, uncluttered, and lovely. Frustrated when she didn't answer her bell after five minutes, he went back to the car and called her on his cellular phone.

"I don't want to see you, Adam."

He exhaled deeply. "My question wasn't called for, and you didn't deserve it. My only excuse is the anxiety I felt for my mother."

It would serve him right if I hung up, she told herself. Instead she said, showing more irritation than she felt, "I've had better apologies from strangers. My father is good for a better one than that." She braced herself against her bathroom wall and forced out the words. "It's best we go our separate ways, Adam."

Annoyed with himself for needing her, for caring, he snapped in anger, "You can't see the forest for the trees, Melissa. If that's what you want, I bow to your wish." He remained there, silent, collecting his wits, pensive. The shock of regret pierced his system when he heard the click as she replaced the receiver. He had to accept that she meant more to him than anyone else. More than Leather and Hides. More than finding out who wanted to destroy it. More than any woman he'd ever known. More than he would have believed possible. He laughed derisively—for the first time since his misadventure of over a decade and a half earlier, he couldn't call the shots. He didn't like it, but there it was.

Melissa heard Adam's car as he drove away and lectured herself: no tears, even as she brushed them from her cheeks. She loved Adam, but at the moment she could dislike him. Not for long, she admitted. She had wanted so badly to see him, to hear him say that he cared for her, that he hadn't meant those words, but his apology had been stingy, halfhearted. She called Banks for company, but had a sense of relief when she heard the answering machine. She searched for Ilona's phone number, thinking she'd call her in New York, but before she located it, the phone rang. She raced to it, hoping to hear Adam's voice.

"Sorry to disappoint you, dear," Bill Henry said. "I called to find out how you are, since Adam's at home. Don't think too harshly of Mary. She's troubled about the sabotage at Leather and Hides, and she isn't certain who's responsible." He told her as much as he could about the incidents at the plant, and she knew he detected her shock and her hurt that Adam hadn't told her how serious the problem had become.

"How do you know I can be trusted? Adam obviously doesn't think so, because he hasn't told me much about it."

He ignored the latter comment. "Because I know you love Adam."

"What? How?"

"Melissa, I saw you and spoke with you as you left the hospital. A man couldn't hurt a woman that deeply unless she loved him. Make her furious? Yes. But he wouldn't have the power to break her heart."

She wrapped herself in a bath towel and sat on the edge of the tub. "Oh, B-H, I've done a foolish thing, loving him, and I know I'll pay for it."

"Only if you refuse to accept the truth."

"B-H, I know Adam didn't shoot Timmy. He was with me."

"Would you have been so certain if you didn't have that proof? The hatred between our families runs deep, Melissa. Adam is tough, but he's fair, and he's honest. Money doesn't protect you from everything, and he's had some hard knocks. If you look carefully, you can see that. Don't think you can wait until this clears up and your family is absolved and then let him know where you stand. He'd lose all interest, no matter how much he loves you. My nephew demands loyalty from everybody, and he gives it unstintingly."

"I've told both my parents that he was with me," she replied with a sense of virtue. "I won't let him down."

His next remark gave her pause. "If you won't listen to what he has to say, you're letting him down."

She rose to her feet. Surely Adam didn't discuss his personal life with his uncle. "How do you know? Did he tell you that?"

"Adam isn't a man to unload on another one. I doubt he'd tell anyone what's in his heart except the person involved. I know you didn't listen to him, because he's in his home and you're in yours, and it isn't even nine o'clock. Nothing would convince me that he hasn't tried to apologize."

A heaviness centered in her chest, a sense of dread, as she made herself ask him a question, seeking from him reassurance she had long needed—evidence of a man's great love for a woman. "B-H, I have to know this. Did you love my mother?" His long pause unnerved her.

"How do you know about this?"

"Recently my mother told me that you are the only man she ever loved."

She didn't let him know she'd heard him sniffle, but waited during the ensuing silence while he struggled to collect his composure.

"Yes, I love her. I will always love her, and I thank you for telling me, Melissa. Knowing how she feels means everything to me. Make certain it doesn't happen to you. The feuding, lying, and meanness has to stop. We are all victims of it. Hatred ruins people . . . destroys them. And it will break you and Adam if you don't learn to trust each other. You have only to look at Emily and me to know the consequences." She thanked him, hung up and dialed Adam's number.

"Adam Roundtree."

"Do you still want to see me?" Her pulse raced when she heard his words.

"I'll be there in twenty minutes."

* * *

Melissa slipped into her red velour wrap robe, combed her hair, and dabbed a bit of Opium perfume where it counted. She put on her white fluffy bunny bedroom slippers, started downstairs, and stopped. Might as well go for broke she decided, turned, went into her bedroom and lit the four candles on her dresser, switched off the lamp, and got downstairs just as the doorbell rang. She opened the door, and he walked into her open arms, kicked the door closed and clutched her to him.

"Melissa. Melissa, I need you!" She parted her lips and let her senses succumb to his loving. Her heart raced as his tongue danced against hers and his large hand slipped beneath her robe and captured her naked breast. Her breathing accelerated, and her hips moved voluntarily against him. He put her away from him, his face harsh with desire, and a charge shot through her at his heated gaze and wordless question.

"Yes," she whispered. "Oh, yes. Yes." He didn't need any urging, just tucked her to his side and climbed the stairs to what he knew would be heaven in her arms. Her eyes adored him as he threw back the coverlet and laid her on the lavender satin sheets. With her gaze still locked to his, she slowly loosened the tie on her robe and threw it open. Quickly he took it from her, removed his clothes, and leaned over her as her outstretched arms welcomed him in a gesture as old as womanhood. He bent to her and caressed her lovingly, his hands claiming her body. Her moans of delight must have excited him more, for he rushed her preparation for his entry.

This time, her innocence behind her, she made demands of her own. Her senses sharpened, and his salty flesh and musky scent heightened her desire. She grasped him and stroked him, and his every move, every gesture, told her she'd found the right torch.

"Melissa, sweetheart."

"Yes," she answered, eager for what she knew awaited her. This time they flew swiftly and unerringly to the sun.

He wiped the perspiration from their faces with the corner

of the sheet, and remained within her body, his gaze on her face.

"Melissa, please look at me." His throat tightened when she smiled, and the trust he saw in her eyes sent his heart into a gallop. He hated that he'd held back again, but he couldn't let her know how deeply she moved him. Not yet.

"You said 'please.' We're making progress." Her finger traced his bottom lip, and he felt as if she'd touched his soul. His arms drew her tightly to him, and his mouth sought her soft, pliable lips. He felt himself stirring within her and raised his head. With so many imponderables in their lives, he had to be careful what he said to her, but he couldn't let her think that he would use her.

"I have very deep feelings for you, Melissa, probably deeper than I realize."

"But?"

He knew that his smile must seem feeble to her, considering the explosiveness of their lovemaking. "No buts. There are things you don't know, and other things I have to straighten out—and until it's all clean and clear, I can't commit myself and you won't want to either. Let's try not to hurt each other while I work it out. Will you promise me that?"

"You don't think we're making a mistake? It looks to me like we're going the wrong direction on a one-way street."

He shook his head. "Life is what you make it, sweetheart. We can let the folly of our parents and grandparents ruin our lives, or we can put that feud behind us and make our own way, base our decisions and what we do on merit. I chart my own course. What about you?"

"I've learned the value of that since I've been back here, and I've stopped begging for my father's approval. I'm my own person, and my mother supports me in that."

"Alright, it's settled. We stand together until we have reasons not to, reasons that concern only us and have nothing to do with our families. Agreed?" She smiled and wiggled beneath him.

"Vixen. I'll teach you who to tease."

* * *

Melissa rolled over and hugged herself. Adam's good-bye kiss lingered on her lips, and she pulled his pillow over her head to blot out the fast-breaking daylight. If she didn't get up, she'd probably oversleep and get to work late. She heard him close the front door and snuggled deeper under the covers, her nostrils tingling with his heady masculine scent and the lingering aroma of their lovemaking. Thoughts of her mother alone in her room, her love denied her, brought Melissa upright. "Back to reality, kiddo," she advised herself, scrambling out of bed. She padded over to her window to look at the birds and glimpsed a bluebird among the swarm of blackbirds. But she lacked her usual enthusiasm for them and went about preparing herself for the day. Leaving home later that morning she had a consoling thought: Adam didn't accept defeat; if he wanted them to have a life together, he'd move mountains for it. She knew, too, that if he came to a different decision, what she wanted wouldn't matter. "So I can stop worrying about it," she muttered to herself.

Adam drove into his garage as the first streak of dawn shot across the horizon. Teased with the stirrings of desire one moment and in the next irritated by uncertainty, he knew he had to take action. If he couldn't solve the mystery at Leather and Hides soon, he'd get more professional help. It was hell making love to a woman whom you wanted all the way to the recesses of your soul and holding back because you were suspicious of her.

Adam selected a red and gray paisley tie to wear with his gray shirt and gray pin-striped suit that morning. He remembered that whenever Melissa saw that tie, she fingered it absentmindedly, though she never said she admired it. He hadn't been alone with her since he'd left her sleeping in bed four days ago. Lunch at a restaurant wouldn't afford them much privacy, but it allowed them to be together without the temptation of lovemaking.

He stopped by her office just before one o'clock.

"She has a client with her, Mr. Roundtree," her secretary told him.

"For the tenth time, Cynthia, my name is Adam."

"Yes, sir, Mr. Roundtree."

Adam sighed. He believed in hiring seniors, but getting them adjusted to the changing social norms could be difficult. He didn't sit but leaned against the doorjamb to wait for Melissa. Within minutes, handsome Magnus Cooper stepped out of Melissa's office wearing his ten-gallon Stetson and alligator boots, drawling his appreciation and his wish to see more of her. Adam had the satisfaction of hearing her say she didn't date her clients, but Cooper dismissed the comment with a laugh. Fury shot through him, constricting his throat and burning his chest. By what right did that cowboy hit on his woman?

Her smile when she saw him helped him to calm himself. He and the man had height in common, Adam observed, then noticed the Texan's two-inch boot heels with mean satisfaction. He nodded at Melissa's introduction, but didn't offer to shake hands. Then he pointedly asked her, "Can you take off the rest of the day? I thought we might run over to Baltimore. The Great Blacks In Wax Museum is having an open house." He hadn't planned to ask her right then, maybe Saturday, but it served a purpose. Magnus Cooper had been warned that Adam Roundtree didn't tolerate another man on his turf.

He glanced at Melissa, figured he'd irritated her and didn't much care. The more she understood him, the better. He knew he hadn't fooled her, and that her professionalism wouldn't let her take him to task in front of Cooper. He watched her get rid of the man, and it amused him that she drew out their good-byes, obviously to deny him assurance that she had no interest in the Texan. They spent the rest of the afternoon in

Baltimore, first at the museum and then wandering around the Inner Harbor.

"Those Maryland crab cakes were worth battling this weather," she said, referring to the fierce wind blowing off the Atlantic over the Chesapeake Bay.

He rested an arm around her shoulder. "I'm glad you think so. The food was delicious, but I'd wondered whether this breeze might be too much for you." They approached a toy store inside the mall, and he ducked into it, pulling her with him, bought a tiger-striped kitten, wrote Adam on its tag, and gave it to her. Then he asked himself why he'd done that, but the joy he saw in her eyes placated his guilt for having encouraged her.

They walked on, browsing in little shops and gazing at spectacles that held no interest for them. He took her hand and urged her into a quaint coffee shop, where he got a table off in a corner. He needed to clear up a few things, and he couldn't do that amidst the distractions. He ordered the coffee and pastries that she selected, but he didn't want to eat. He wanted to know whether she remembered her promise to preserve their relationship until he'd solved some issues.

"Melissa, do you like that man I met in your office this morning?"

She must have misunderstood his question, he decided, when she replied.

"So far I do. Why?"

He knew she'd revolt if he showed anger and did his best to contain his temper and his impatience. "I'll put it differently. What I mean exactly is this: *do you want him?*" He tried to ignore the mirth reflected in her eyes.

"He's just a client, Adam."

"That's your view. His differs substantially." He swallowed his annoyance. Melissa could give the appearance of naivete whenever it suited her.

"You saw him for only a little while this morning. Why don't you like him?"

"What was there to like? He's rich—but honey, money doesn't part rivers, not from where I sit. I can usually judge a man by what he laughs at, and I didn't like his laugh nor what he found funny."

"You ought to know how much money impresses people," she scoffed, "considering how much of it you've got."

He didn't smile as he looked at her. He was serious, and he wanted her to know it. "Yeah. I'd probably make out better with you if I didn't have a cent. This guy I met this morning—is he the one you found a ranch manager for?"

"I'm finding one for him. Yes."

He put his elbows on the table, made a pyramid of his ten fingers, and searched her face. "I thought it was your policy to take the executive to the employer. What was Cooper doing up here in Maryland?" He knew that if he kept it up, she might lose her customary cool, but he didn't let the thought stop him.

"We talked a few times, and I guess he got curious about me."

Adam straightened up and glared at her. "Curious, eh? Remind him for me that curiosity killed the cat." He watched her clutch the little tiger kitten as if it were a security token, though she stuck out her chin in defiance. But he refused to feel guilty for having goaded her. He didn't want Magnus Cooper within miles of her.

They left the coffee shop, and he looped her arm through his. An old-fashioned gesture, he realized, but one that he liked. "Say, didn't Harriet Tubman once live around here somewhere?" he asked as they left the harbor area.

"I'm not sure," Melissa told him. "Imagine a woman born into slavery in the first quarter of the nineteenth century managing to get her freedom and organize an escape route for other slaves. She was something."

He squeezed her arm in a gesture of affection. "Sure was.

In those days people depended upon their wits for survival. I'm curious," he said. "Are you a feminist because of the men in your life or in spite of them?"

"Both," she said, as they reached his car. He buckled his seat belt, turned to her, and with his arm around her shoulder asked her, "Why did you let me make love to you that first time? You were a virgin. Why did you give me that honor? The question plagues me, Melissa."

He could feel her withdrawing from him. "If you have to be told, Adam, the answer wouldn't help you."

He put the key in the ignition, but didn't turn it. "If you'd rather I reached my own conclusion, I can certainly do that."

She reached over and rubbed his nose with her index finger, surprising him, because she hadn't previously shown him such familiarity. "You will do that, no matter what I say." He noticed that her hand fell casually into her lap, that she sat in the bucket seat, quiet, serene. He thought of Keats's poem and the silence "upon a peak in Darien." Might as well accept it, he thought. I may not be able to let her go no matter what she's done and no matter how badly I want to forget her.

He felt her delicate fingers pinch his thigh and smiled. "Feeling your oats?"

"Just testing the water."

"What's it like?" he asked.

"Hot." He stared at her. Twice that afternoon she'd goaded him, and he liked her new familiarity with him, her shy possessiveness. Her fingers walked from his knee halfway up his thigh while she hummed "Frère Jacque" in accompaniment. They reached her house, and he tipped up her chin with his right index finger, excitement wafting its way through him as she continued her play, running her fingers up his left arm. His gaze steady and unfathomable, he stated, "I'll pick you up tomorrow morning at seven thirty."

She squinted, as though not believing what she'd heard. "What for?"

He didn't make her wait for his answer. "The weekend. If you want to test the water, I aim to accommodate you."

"You asking, or telling?"

He grinned sheepishly. "I suppose I can learn to crawl if you force me to it, though right now I'm having trouble envisaging such a scene."

Melissa laughed. "It's giving me trouble, too."

Adam took Route 340 toward Harpers Ferry to where the Appalachian Trail hit the Potomac River, bore left onto an unmarked gravel road, swung up a bumpy strip and stopped at his lodge, twenty-four miles from Beaver Ridge. The overcast skies and the air, warm and stifling for mid-November, warned them not to expect beautiful weather. Adam went about storing their supplies, but her quiet demeanor and obvious wariness began to disturb him, and he sat in a straight-back dining room chair and pulled her between his knees.

"What's the matter? If you want to go home, I'll be disappointed, but I'll take you." He breathed deeply in relief when her hands wound around his neck.

"I don't want to leave, but this feels strange."

He put her away gently and stood. "Maybe we should have done this a while back. I don't want you to be uncomfortable, so if you want to leave, just tell me." He meant it, but he didn't expect to have to keep that promise, because he knew how to get the response from her that he wanted, and he'd get it. They ate the breakfast he'd cooked and cleaned the kitchen together. Domesticity wasn't so bad, Adam mused, turning on the dishwasher. He could even get to like it.

The sun peeked through the clouds, and they put on light sweaters and jackets and hiked along the Appalachian Trail. They strolled into the forest, amidst trees of golden and rust-colored leaves that waved among the green pines.

"I could get used to being in this place with you. I come here to find peace, to shut out my problems, to rejuvenate as it were. And I always come here alone. But having you here with me feels good. Feels right." He let his gaze roam up the trunk of a tall elm. "Are you glad you came?"

"Yes," she whispered. "Yes, I'm glad." His heartbeat raced wildly when she reached up and tucked his scarf closely around his neck but wouldn't look at his face.

"Come on—let's walk," she said, though she grasped his arm and faced him, making it impossible for him to take a step. His fingers guided her face upward until he could see the passion glittering like soft lights in her eyes.

"Oh, honey. Sweetheart, we're insane," he said softly. Immediately her arms reached up to caress his broad shoulders.

"I know. Oh, Adam, I know." He watched, captivated by her soft, yielding manner, as she raised parted lips for his kiss even as the words left her mouth. He covered her mouth with his and drank in her sweetness. He needed her closer, and he needed all of her. She moved against him, but he stilled her. He needed all of her, to *know* her fully, to communicate with her at the deepest level. But how could he, when the level of trust that he needed eluded them? He tucked her to his side and walked on. Unsatisfied.

"Time to go," he told her abruptly after seeing a brown bear dash into the thicket. They walked swiftly through the high pines, white ash, and oak trees that thrived there. Riffling excitement, akin to fear, alerted Adam to danger, causing him suddenly to sniff the wind and look up at the black sky. He released her hand.

"Let's get out of here. We'll have to make a run for it." Drenched and shivering, they reached the lodge.

"Too bad we didn't wait an hour to take that walk," he lamented, as the storm moved on, and the sun peeked through the clouds.

"You're t-t-telling m-m-me."

"You're shivering. I'll get something warm for you." He removed her jacket and shoes and wrapped her in a woolen blanket.

"T-th-thanks."

"I think I'd better call a doctor."

"No d-d-don't. I'm scared to death of electrical storms—it's just nerves," she told him, and he stared at her, incredulous. He took her in his arms and rocked her until the tremors stopped. She'd shown no sign of fear while she sprinted a half mile in that electrical storm.

He reflected on Melissa's behavior as he set about preparing lunch. He'd never seen her so vulnerable as when she'd trembled uncontrollably because of fear, not even when she had lain beneath him and splintered in his arms, and he realized he felt a new tie to her, a feeling that she needed him.

After lunch he made a fire in the fireplace to ward off the sudden chill that followed the thunderstorm. They sat before it, and he took her hand.

"What do you want from life, Melissa?" He could see that she'd rather he'd phrased the question differently.

"A girl and a boy in whatever order they decide to show up."

He took no offense at her attempt to downplay its importance to her, because he knew she had a tendency to squirm whenever their conversation became too personal. "And?"

"Well, I don't want to conceive them by artificial insemination, and I don't want to be an unmarried mother."

Adam couldn't help laughing. She refused to admit that she wanted a husband. "Anything else? What about a father for those kids?"

A brief wistfulness flashed in her limped eyes. "He can be part of the package." Her manner changed. "Are we talking serious, here?"

"Not as serious as we might, but I need to know something about you apart from your intelligence, efficiency, wit, sexy beauty, and earth-shattering lovemaking." Her raised eyebrows and skeptical look said that he might have overstated it. Heat flooded her face, and she shrugged, her diffidence adding to her allure.

"Seventy-five percent of the men in this country wouldn't need to know any more than that," she said, "and the other twenty-five percent wouldn't know what to do with that information if they had it."

He hadn't thought her shy or so tender. Getting her to reveal herself proved as simple as getting blood from a turnip. His eyes narrowed as he remembered his first encounter with her father. "What—besides your father—makes you cry?"

"Adam, that's behind me. If I hurt, it's for my mother."

He rolled over, clasped her in his arms, and she spoke more readily of her life. They talked, holding each other until sleep claimed them.

Hours later they awakened in a chilled room beside a cold fireplace. Melissa snuggled closer to Adam. The tender protectiveness he'd shown her bound him more closely to her, and she forgot the reasons why she should avoid him. She wanted to tell him she loved him, but even in his loving, protective mein, when he'd held her while she trembled uncontrollably in fright, he'd withheld something. She looked down at him, his arms behind his head and his eyes closed for emotional privacy, and thought of his masterfulness under pressure and his awesome passion for her. Yes, he charted his own course, and he hadn't committed himself to her because he hadn't accepted their relationship. Something or somebody stood between them, and she had an eerie feeling that the chasm they faced involved her family. A deep intimacy had developed between them as they'd sat before the fire talking and sipping coffee, but he had told her little of himself and nothing of what he envisaged for them. Yet he'd filled her heart with himself. She had to hold back—she didn't want to, but she had to.

Ten

Melissa unpacked her small weekend bag and dropped the soiled garments into the hamper. A glance at her watch confirmed that she didn't have time to get to Sunday morning church. Who would have thought their weekend would pass as it had—first a storm in which they'd nearly drowned and then an afternoon and night of the deepest intimacy she'd ever experienced. They'd shared affection and their minds, but not their bodies. If they had spoken words of love and given of their bodies, too, she doubted she could have left him for any reason. But he'd kept their temperatures low, though she knew that wasn't what he'd intended when he took her there. She understood that their feelings for each other had changed, that they'd come to a reckoning point and had opted for caution and restraint. She hadn't been hurt nor had she attempted to seduce him when he bluntly suggested they leave early, because he couldn't spend another celibate night there with her.

She answered the phone reluctantly, since Adam had no reason to contact her that she could imagine. Her father's voice roared through the receiver.

"Where were you yesterday and last night? Your mother stayed in her room all day. I told you she's not well, and I thought you came back here to look after her."

Why hadn't she realized that her father manipulated her, using her mother, her brother, and one phony situation after another to control her? "I spent the time with friends," she said, and let her voice proclaim her right to do as she pleased. She hadn't lied, she'd been with Adam and the little creatures she'd met near the brook. For the first time his taunts had no effect on her. Loving Adam had made her strong, and her new-found relationship with her mother made her less dependent on her father for parental affection. She didn't want to hurt her father, though, so she didn't share with him her suspicion that Emily remained in her room to avoid him. She changed the subject.

"What do the police have to say about Timmy getting shot?"

"Your uncle Booker is dealing with it, and he'll bring Adam Roundtree to justice. Mark my word. You'll rue the day you turned your back on your own people." When she didn't answer, he added, "So you're ready to agree that he did it."

Annoyed, she told him in icy tones, "You'd save a lot of breath and energy, Daddy, if you'd get to know your daughter. I hold integrity inviolate, and I won't lie for a Grant or a Roundtree or anyone else." He hung up, dissatisfied with her as usual, but she shrugged it off, put on a top coat, and went out to buy milk. On an impulse, she stopped at a public phone and called her mother. Her father had just gone out, she learned, and decided to pay her mother a short visit.

"You're just glowing, darling," her mother said. "Were you with Adam this weekend? Rafer swears you were."

Surprised at the question and uncertain how to answer, Melissa only nodded. But Emily assured her that she hoped Melissa had been with him.

"Mama, are you suggesting—"

"I'm saying what it sounds like. I was a prude, insisting to Bill Henry that we wait until after we married. That was the fashion in those days. But we didn't marry, and I never knew him. A thousand times I've bemoaned the day I exacted that promise from him. Melissa, I've had thirty-one years to wonder what it's like to make love with a man who loves and cherishes me. Rafer and I both got cheated."

She noticed the quivers in her mother's voice and asked if she felt ill. "I don't feel sick, just weak all the time. Not a bit of energy. If I complain, Rafer takes me back to the doctor for more tests. I've been scanned so much I feel transparent. That's all these doctors do: tests and more tests and feed whatever it is they find into the computer. How the devil will the computer know what's wrong with me? It hasn't been to medical school." A wide grin spread across Melissa's face, and soon, peals of laughter erupted from her throat. Her mother had a devilish sense of humor, and all these years she hadn't known it.

In recent weeks she'd noticed an absence of the invisible weight, the aura of defeatism that she had always observed about her mother. She looked at her mother's rich brown, wrinkle-free face, naturally black hair, and svelte figure. Who'd guess she had lived for fifty-two years? The doctors wouldn't find her mother's illness in her bloodstream nor her vital organs. The name of Emily Grant's disease was despair, lack of a reason for living.

Melissa walked over to her mother and began to massage the back of her neck and her shoulders, all the while thinking and putting her mother in perspective. It should have been obvious that Emily's listlessness and myriad of complaints stemmed from discontentment with her life, that her total submissiveness to her husband was unnatural and partly phony, that she just didn't care enough to fight hard for her rights, that her reclusive behavior had the earmarks of a power play, a defensive tactic. Her fingers stilled, and she pulled a small footstool to the front of her mother's chair and sat down.

"Mama, why don't you get out of the house, volunteer at one of the shelters, teach in the Head Start program, tutor, read to the blind, anything except stay in this room. You have a college degree, Mama. And you're too young to fold up like this." Her heart constricted at the expectancy, the eagerness, mirrored on her mother's face, and hope welled up in her as they walked toward the foyer.

"Honey, I've never gone anywhere much without your father, except shopping, and I certainly haven't done a thing unless he wanted me to. Your grandfather wouldn't rest until I married Rafer and gave him some grandchildren, so I bowed to his wishes. You know the rest."

"Well, it's time you did something for yourself, Mama."

"I hear what you're saying, and I may try it, but you and I both know that nothing will give me back Bill Henry. And that's my problem. You make sure you don't ever have one like it."

"If I have a choice, Mama, I won't take the one that will make me miserable. So please don't worry about me, and get out of here and do something about your life."

Adam walked through the recreation room of the Rachel Hood Hayes Center for Women, talking to the women who had taken refuge there. Small children clung to several of them, fright still mirrored in their young eyes. He took pride in The Refuge, as it was popularly known, and he hurt for the women whose hard lives and cruel mates had forced them to leave their homes for a communal shelter. He had intended that the one being built in Hagerstown would have only private rooms and small apartments, but the continuing fiasco at the leather factory threatened to get out of hand, and since he used his Leather and Hides shares to finance his charities, including The Refuge, he'd had to retrench.

The crooks had struck again on Saturday night while he'd been at the lodge with Melissa. He forced himself not to think of her in connection with it. His heart dictated forbearance, but his common sense counseled him to challenge her. Reorienting his thoughts, he shook hands with a woman who had arrived at The Refuge so badly battered that he'd had her hospitalized for more than a week, patted an older woman, there for the third time, and headed for his small basement office.

Adam didn't wait for an elevator. He opened the door to

the stairwell and stopped just short of colliding with Emily Grant.

"What?" They spoke simultaneously. Adam stepped back and held the door for her.

"Mind if I ask why you're here." He didn't care if she detected suspicion in his tone.

"I'm a volunteer. Why? Is something wrong?"

Adam braced a hand on each hip, took a deep breath and pierced her with an accusative gaze. "Did Rafer send you here? He isn't satisfied with the damage we're getting at Leather and Hides and wants to start on The Refuge, is that it?" She appeared at first to wilt under his stern rebuff, but he could see her back stiffening.

"I don't know any more about Leather and Hides than what you just said, and I have no idea what Rafer is doing." That comment made him realize that Emily didn't know his relationship to The Refuge. Nothing on the door identified the place by its correct name, the Rachel Hood Hayes Center for Women. He took her arm and walked with her to his small office.

"Emily, I don't suppose you knew that I'm the founder of this place and its sole support. It's a memorial to my maternal grandmother." She told him that she hadn't.

"Melissa suggested that I do some volunteer work, Adam, but she doesn't know I've actually started. I needed something for myself and when I saw these women, I knew I could help them. My body hasn't been battered, but my brain certainly has. I've been happier here these past four days than at any time since . . . well, it's meant everything to me. I feel like a different person. Please let me stay, Adam. I know that when Rafer finds out, he'll want your neck and mine, too, but I have to do this and I'm not turning back."

He opened two of the soft drinks that he kept in a tiny refrigerator beneath his desk and handed one to her. "I want you to stay here as long as you like." He rubbed his chin reflectively. "Do you mean to tell me your husband doesn't know you're doing this?"

"It's a long story, Adam."

He forced himself not to glance at the elegant watch strapped to his left wrist. "I've got plenty of time." She gave him what he figured was a well-censored account of a troubled marriage, careful to omit mention of the main reason for it, and they spoke at length. He thought over what she'd told him and released his signature whistle.

"There's going to be hell to pay," he warned. Emily sipped some ginger ale and leaned back in her chair with all the serenity of a reclining Buddha.

"So what? I've always had hell to pay." He tapped the rickety wooden desk with the rubber end of a pencil and laid his head to one side, watching her carefully. He ruled out the possibility of her presence there as an effort by Rafer to manipulate him.

"And you say Melissa doesn't know about this?"

Emily leaned forward, as though to beseech him. "She suggested I do something, but she didn't mention this, and I haven't told her about it."

He nodded. According to the facts he now had, the cleavage between the two families didn't appear as great as he and other people thought. Yet it went deep. Wayne might feel strongly about it, but he wouldn't be unfair. And B-H disassociated himself from the feud. Its main keepers appeared to be Rafer and his mother, but two more fierce or more committed fighters he didn't care to meet.

"I'm happy to have you with us," Adam said, and walked with her a few paces down the hall to the elevator.

"Are we going to be friends?" she asked him, when he held the door open. In that moment, it cheered him that he'd adopted the habit of smiling.

"I think we are," he said with a smile and meant it. He went back to his office, feeling as though he and Melissa had a chance at happiness. He pulled the sheet from his fax ma-

chine and read, "Somebody mixed the chrome and zirconium
samples, and we've got some useless fluids and a hell of a
stench here.—Cal." So much for that, he muttered. He figured
he'd just spent twenty seconds in a fool's paradise. Too much
dirty water flowed under the bridge—seventy years of hatred,
the sabotage, and the things about him that Melissa didn't
know and for which she might not forgive him. They didn't
stand a joker's chance.

A few days later, the Saturday after Thanksgiving Day,
Melissa sat in Banks's kitchen while her friend altered a dress
she'd recently bought.

"This is a great color for you," Banks said. "Turn around.
It doesn't fit because your waist is too little for the rest of
you." Melissa waited for the words that would follow Banks's
melodramatic sigh and groaned when she said, "But I guess
Adam likes it."

"Throw out all the bait you like, kiddo," Melissa said, "but
this fish isn't biting."

"Come on. If he was my guy, I'd hire a blimp and trail a
mile-high streamer behind it proclaiming 'Adam Roundtree is
my man,' and, by damn, I'd sign it."

Melissa laughed. "You're hopeless."

"The least you could do is let me enjoy him vicariously."

"I don't kiss and tell, Banks, and I don't ask you about
Ray."

Melissa knew her friend shrugged mainly for effect—she
enjoyed attention and got a laugh when she said, "What's to
ask about Ray? He fills the bill for the moment."

With the dress finished and pressed, they got into Melissa's
car and went to look for antiques. Melissa saw an old, sterling
silver apple designed with a bite taken out, teeth prints evident,
and a loop at the bottom for a key chain. She had it wrapped

and sent to Adam, ignoring Banks's raised eyebrow but not her succinct words: "What's he supposed to do, conquer or surrender?" They bought apple cider at a farm and stopped for lunch at the adjoining restaurant.

Melissa nodded toward an adjoining booth and asked Banks, "Do you hear what I hear?" They listened as two men aired their views on women working. One didn't want his wife to work, but the second disagreed on principle. He wanted an independent, interesting woman with a career of her own, one who stayed with him because she wanted him and not because she'd rather not work. His voice grew more persuasive when he admonished his companion, "Keep your ego out of the way and get a woman who's your equal. Who the hell cares whether bag carrots taste as good as the ones on a bunch or the kid's Reeboks last a week longer than some other brand? You can't stay in bed all the time, man. Then what do you do?"

Melissa glanced toward the familiar voice as she and Banks left their booth. Wayne Roundtree. She hoped Adam was as far ahead of most Frederick men on the issue as his brother appeared to be.

"Isn't that Wayne Roundtree?" Banks asked. "If I were a little younger . . . well, I could go for a man who thinks like that."

"You're always seeing a man you could go for."

"I'm not promiscuous, honey, but I'm not dead either," Banks assured her. "Take a hint and give Adam something to mull over. A man shouldn't be too sure of a woman." Melissa's deliberate smile denoted the contentment of a cat licking her whiskers. Let Banks think whatever she liked.

Adam pushed a shopping cart full of used books into The Refuge's small library and began shelving them. Ordinarily he didn't go to the place on Mondays, but he knew the volunteers—mostly older women—needed his help following the weekend's Thanksgiving celebrations, and he'd do as much as he could during his lunch hour.

"Let me do that, you must have more important things to do."

He turned toward the familiar voice and greeted Emily. "Thanks, but this will only take a minute. Do you still enjoy it here?"

"Oh, yes. I'm happier than I thought I could be. These women and girls are so grateful for the little care we give them that I'm humbled."

"Hasn't Rafer discovered this, or have you told him?" His left hand remained suspended above the cart, holding an old cookbook, while he awaited her answer. In the past few days, the sabotage at Leather and Hides had stepped up, though the incidents weren't major disasters, but small yet destructive acts. He had begun to look everywhere for clues and to suspect a widening circle of people.

"If he knew, he'd have said something." Emily's voice halted his musing. "Rafer isn't one to keep his peace about a thing that displeases him." Adam released a deep breath. How could a man not know what his wife did for four hours every day of the working week?

As if she'd sensed his unspoken question, she said, "We live separate lives, Adam. At least *now* I'm living a life." He told her that her health seemed improved, and she replied, "It's my mind that's finally working. Never let anybody force you into leading a double life." At his raised eyebrow, she added with a laugh, "Just listen to me. Nobody *could* force you to do that or anything else. All these years I've accepted public adoration and private scorn from Rafer—but like that old song 'New Day In The Mornin',' that's all behind me. I'm not living like that anymore."

Adam's hand grazed her shoulder in a tentative gesture. "Be careful. Don't provoke him unnecessarily." He finished shelving the books and glanced at the wall clock. Twenty-five minutes before he had to be at his office in the Jacob Hayes

Building. He phoned a take-out shop to have a hamburger and coffee delivered there, told Emily good-bye, and strode briskly down Court Street, deep in thought. Rafer had accused him of shooting his nephew but had taken no legal action. Authorities hadn't even questioned him about it. Emily had been a volunteer at his charity for over two weeks, and Rafer didn't know it or pretended that he didn't. Meanwhile someone had found a nearly indecipherable way to destroy the very foundation of Leather and Hides. And that someone knew his moves and had the run of the factory. Melissa knew his moves, and Calvin Nelson had the run of the factory, but somehow they didn't fit, and the possibility of their disloyalty grew increasingly more remote.

He fingered the symbol of man's surrender to woman that he kept in his pocket. Almost every time he touched it, he laughed. Only a very secure woman with a riotous sense of humor would send a man a silver apple out of which a generous bite had been taken. Lord! He hoped she was innocent. He'd hate to give her up—at least not before it suited him.

Adam sipped his coffee, gripped his private phone, and listened to his brother.

"You remember that I ran a piece in the paper about industrial sabotage in general and hinted at our problems at Leather and Hides. Yesterday I got a call. The guy said that if Leather and Hides went down the drain, the Roundtrees deserved it, and that it was too bad Jacob Hayes wasn't alive to see it. I'm having difficulty believing that Cal is involved in this."

"So am I. Anything else?"

"What about Melissa, Adam? Are you holding back because you're passing time with her?"

Adam swung out of his chair and paced as far as the telephone cord would let him. "Wayne, don't make me tell you this again. Melissa Grant isn't time I'm killing."

He heard his brother snort. "Well, at least you recognize it. I don't suppose you'd be willing to enlist her help with this?"

"Leave it to me, Wayne."

"Alright. Alright. I haven't mentioned to anyone that you hired a private investigator."

"And don't. I'll keep you posted." He hung up, called Melissa, and invited her to dinner.

Bill Henry's visit around six o'clock surprised him. His uncle used that time to prepare his healthful meals, which he ate without fail at six thirty. "Noticed Wayne's short piece in *The Maryland Journal*. I see you still got problems at the plant. What do you make of it?"

"Inside job, but I think it's someone in cahoots with the Grants. Problem is who and why."

"Did it start before or after you began this thing with Melissa?"

"You're saying I started something with Melissa?"

"Yeah. And you're knee deep in it. Son, I hope you're not following in my footsteps. But then I don't suppose you will. I doubt that even the Grants and your mother could bring you to your knees, and they're masters at it."

Adam rubbed the back of his neck, remembering that Melissa had twice suggested he speak to B-H about their families' feud. He stared at his uncle.

"You want to explain that?"

"I thought you knew." He related to Adam the tale of his ill-fated engagement to Melissa's mother.

Horrified, Adam braced his hands at his hips and whistled. "That explains plenty." Emily's behavior toward him. Rafer's hatred of him and his family. B-H himself, his bachelorhood and reclusive behavior. He walked with his uncle to the family room, opened the bar and poured a ginger ale for B-H and a shot of bourbon for himself.

Adam looked at the man who had played such an important role in his youthful development and for whom he cared deeply though he hadn't wanted to imitate him. Less so now.

"Emily volunteers at The Refuge four hours a day, Monday through Friday, and when Rafer finds out—"

B-H interrupted him, his face hard with incredulity. "Don't tempt me, Adam. She's still wearing Rafer Grant's ring on the third finger of her left hand."

Adam set his drink aside, gazed at his uncle, and then shook his head. His words bore a soft, funereal quality. "After all these years? Three decades?"

He went back to his room to sort out his thoughts. He ought to call Melissa and cancel their date, but he couldn't disappoint her. And he admitted that he needed to see her. His mother's footsteps in the hallway forced him into action, and he quickly left his room, greeting her in passing before loping down the stairs. He knew she'd read Wayne's article and had primed herself to speak to him about Melissa and her family. He barely heard the rain pummeling the roof of his car as he steered it against the windy gusts. Bill Henry still loved Emily Morris after thirty years. Could what he felt for Melissa become so powerful? And would it do to him what loving a woman had done to his uncle? Would it drive him into himself?

Melissa finished dressing in a black velvet pants suit just as the doorbell announced Adam's arrival. Breathless with anticipation, she swung open the door, but her smile quickly disappeared and her face lost some of its glow.

"Hi."

She didn't know how to respond to this no-nonsense, harsh, and businesslike Adam, the one she hadn't seen since before they'd first made love. Scanning his face, she greeted him with a careful smile, the kind she'd give a client.

"Hello, Adam. Won't you come in."

Adam followed her into the living room, declined her offer of a seat, and ambled with deliberateness from one end of the room to the other, his overcoat open and his hands stuffed in his pants pockets. She sat in a comfortable chair, perplexed at his pacing, but certain that it allowed him either to rein in his temper or to deal with his feelings for her.

She opened her mouth, aghast, when he stopped before her and asked in a voice devoid of emotion, "Why did you make love with me that first time? A twenty-eight-year-old virgin doesn't do that without solid reason. Why?" Stunned at the bluntness with which he'd asked that intimate question, and for the second time, too, and annoyed with herself for having spent the afternoon longing and waiting to see him, she replied in like manner.

"You're Wall Street's boy wonder. If you can't figure it out yourself, my explanation wouldn't mean anything to you, either."

He pulled her up from the chair and into his arms. "You tell me. I want to hear it from your lips."

She couldn't bear having his arms around her in that impersonal way—she wanted more of his warmth, the gentle caring of which she knew him capable, but she was damned if she'd show it.

"Tell me," he urged, his tone dispassionate.

"If you just came here to get your ego stroked, I'm sorry to disappoint you. Mine's been out of sorts since the last time I saw you. So nothing doing."

"What do you mean?" She knew he'd remember that when they'd last been together, they'd spent the night at his lodge, she on the sofa and he on the floor nearby. He'd reached up and held her left hand in his right one until they'd fallen asleep. She'd wanted to sleep in his arms, but he'd said they needed to wait until he resolved some undisclosed problems before becoming more deeply involved, that they already risked more that he thought wise.

"I think you know the answer, and I also think we shouldn't see each other anymore until all of these problems you mentioned are cleared up. If ever they are." She had to look away from the lights twinkling in his eyes, challenging her to give

in to him, to tell him what he demanded to know. "I want you
to leave, Adam."

"This is another first. You're the first—and only—woman
to give me her feminine truth and the first woman or man
with the nerve, or perhaps I should say the chutzpa, to invite
me to leave anyplace whatever." She twisted out of his arms
and turned toward the foyer as though expecting him to follow,
but his hand heavy on her shoulder detained her.

"You don't think I'm leaving here before you answer my
question, do you?"

Her nose lifted upward. "What was your question?"

He grasped her shoulders, drew her to him, and looked into
her eyes. "If you won't say it, I'll tell you, and I dare you to
deny it. You gave yourself to me because I'm the only man
you've ever wanted. Ever loved. Deny it, and you lie. Unless
of course you want me to believe you used yourself as a decoy
while your relatives trashed my leather factory."

She gasped, appalled. "How dare you accuse me of such a
thing!"

"I didn't. I gave you the choice."

"I don't care what you believe," she bluffed.

He pulled her closer. "Oh, but you do. You care, alright."
She thought his demeanor softened. He'd never before made
a deliberate effort to seduce her. When they'd made love, he
had led her, but only where she indicated she wanted to go.
She knew he meant to push her over the edge, but she didn't
intend to accommodate him.

"Which is it?" he murmured. "Tell me."

Loving him as she did, she cared what he thought of her
and how he felt about her, so she threw caution aside though
she knew she'd regret it. "You know I didn't throw myself at
you. How could you think I'd make love with you because of
some feud?" His heated gaze toyed with her.

"Adam, what do you want? Please!"

"If what you say is true, you did it because you love me.

Which is it? Tell me," he persisted, never taking his eyes from
hers, his breath harsh and uneven.

"Yes. Yes, I love you. Yes. Yes." He wrapped her to him,
kissed her tears and hugged her until she hurt. Her whimpers
must have alerted him to his use of strength, because he loosened his hold and soothed her with gentle strokes over her
back and down her arms.

He wanted to tell her that he felt as if her words would
cause his heart to burst, but he couldn't bring himself to di-
vulge the two episodes in his life that she might not forgive,
and worse still, there remained the slim chance that he'd have
to prosecute her.

"Alright." He walked them over the couch, sat down, and
patted his lap, inviting her to sit there. "My questions may
make you angry, but I have to ask them." He hugged her to
him and blurted, "Tell me what you know about Timothy's
gunshot wounds." He'd expected her to attempt to get up, and
he restrained her, nibbling on her ear to soften the gesture.

"You're wasting your time and mine," she threw at him,
bitterness lacing her voice. "I haven't seen Timmy since that
happened. We're not friends, Adam. He thought I could find
a cushy job for him, though I suspect that was Daddy's idea.
I referred him to a bus company in Hagerstown, but he hasn't
reported back to me on it. Anything else?"

"Bear with me in this, please."

"Why should I? You got the confession from me that you
wanted, and of course it didn't occur to you that I also need
reassurance about your feelings for me. I want you to leave."
He put his arms around her and held her close, needing her
with every atom of his being, needing to make love with her,
to make certain that she belonged to him. But he'd lost the
moment. Her pride wouldn't let her allow him that intimacy,
and he didn't want to see her without her elegant sense of self.

"Are you going?" she asked, though her voice didn't convince him of her sincerity.

He caressed her arms, inhaled her woman's scent, and let

his gaze roam over the warm, feminine body that reclined in his arms. Shudders plowed through him, and in a voice hoarse with desire, he said, "I care. Dammit, you know I care. Why do you think I don't stay away from you? It isn't because I'm a masochist, though I'm beginning to wonder about that." He felt her relax against him, and sensed a giving of her trust.

"Melissa, I asked you about Timmy, because you know your father accused me of wounding him. But did you know that I haven't been officially charged with it, and I can't find out whether anyone has been formally accused? Did it actually happen?"

She nodded. "Mama says it did." He had to ask her about Leather and Hides, but considering how she reacted to the question about Timothy, he didn't care to risk it.

"Adam, tell me what's going on at Leather and Hides." His astonishment must have been mirrored in his face, because she explained that B-H had mentioned it to her. "Hadn't you planned to tell me about it?"

He stood but resisted the urge to pace. "I tried several times, but I couldn't represent it to you as it really is, because I didn't want to hurt you." He saw her back stiffen, and it occurred to him that he ought to be grateful for Melissa's even temper.

"What's it got to do with hurting me? I don't have anything to do with it."

Adam considered his words carefully. "There are some who think your family may be involved, though I'm certain that the culprit has help from at least one of our employees."

She leaned forward, squinting, and he could almost see her mental wheels spring into action. "Do you believe I'd knowingly hurt you?"

"I don't want to believe it." He watched her rise from the sofa as a woodland sprite would drift up from a spring, though her vacant eyes belied serenity.

"But you do?"

He couldn't lie. He considered her guilt in the sabotage unlikely, but he hadn't exonerated her, either. "I'm a cautious man, Melissa, and I—"

She interrupted him, walking out of the living room as she did so. "I'm going to the kitchen, and I want you to be out of my house when I get back here."

Her words stabbed him. He'd hurt her, and for once he knew that special kind of pain, a deep agony that only one woman could relieve. He walked into the hallway and looked toward the kitchen. He couldn't see her, turned in that direction, and stopped. Until he cleared up the mess at that factory, what could he say to her? He had no choice but to do as she'd asked.

Melissa wouldn't have believed she'd allowed herself to be duped a second time. He'd numbed her senses, coaxed her into submission with tenderness and with his blazing heat, and she'd spilled her longing, told him her heart's secret. Lost herself in him. He'd said he cared, but he'd confessed it grudgingly, and minutes later he had implicated her family and all but accused her of aiding the ruination of his business. If any member of her family had a hand in it, she'd find out.

Adam sat at the desk in his bedroom, planning his strategy to trap the culprits, when he received a call from his private investigator.

"I'm certain it was Melissa Grant," the man insisted, when Adam suggested that he might be mistaken. "I saw her here at the factory about an hour ago, but she only looked around outside the gate and left. I waited for any follow-up before calling you."

"Thanks. Stay there, and if she comes back, call me." He didn't welcome that news. He had discarded the idea that she might be involved—now he had to rethink his strategy. Had she intended to meet someone? If not, what had she sought? He called his manager.

"I secured the gates myself, Adam, but someone gained entrance, and that person must have had a key. I can't even guess who it might have been. This time the damage involved finished shoe leathers. The criminal has realized that it is more damaging to attack after we've spent the money and time tanning the leathers. Damned if I know what to make of it." Adam thanked him and hung up. He wouldn't call local authorities. Why waste the energy? Rafer had the deputy chief of police or deputy sheriff, as he preferred to be called, in his pocket. He'd deal with it tomorrow.

He got to his office around nine o'clock the next morning and called the Physicians' Registry. A young doctor named Grant practiced in Hagerstown. On a hunch, he called the office, and without hesitating the unsuspecting young receptionist gave him the information he cleverly wrested from her. He taped their conversation.

Next he headed for The Refuge, where he knew he'd find Emily, engaged her in casual conversation, and satisfied himself that she had no part in the crimes at his factory.

He'd begun to like Emily Grant. "Are you sure you're up to this work? It's mentally as well as physically demanding."

Her smile reminded him of Melissa when she teased him. "I love it. And I'm not frail, Adam. That's what I've been led to believe for over thirty years. Not a bit of it's true. I'm strong."

He squeezed her shoulder in a gesture of affection. "I'm glad you've joined us. I like your spirit. Have you discussed this with Rafer yet?"

She hadn't, she told him without any apparent regret, and asked him to let it be.

"What about Melissa?"

She shook her head. "This is my own. I'll share it when the time comes. When I have to." He patted her shoulder and headed back to the Jacob Hayes Building. Emily Grant could grow on a person. He could appreciate his uncle's passion for her: a lovely, giving woman. She must have been captivating in her youth, for she remained a beauty, and she could charm a mouse away from its cheese.

Adam called his New York office. He'd have to get back there soon, but he couldn't leave Frederick so long as his relationship with Melissa hung in limbo, and to straighten it out, he'd first have to unravel the mystery at Leather and Hides. A short conversation with Jason Court assured him that, for the time being, he needn't worry about his New York office. He had two detectives working in the plant and had hired a private investigator, but the criminal who wrought destruction in the factory seemingly at will remained undetected.

Impatient with their lack of progress, Adam dressed in jeans, a sweater, leather jacket, and sneakers after dinner that evening, and to avoid the noise and headlights of his car, rode his bicycle to the factory. The moon had shone brightly all week, and he considered himself fortunate that it settled behind the clouds as he left home, affording him the cover he needed. He secured the bike and leaned well hidden against a large oak tree. A red Corvette appeared, and its driver parked and waited. Very soon, another car arrived. Apprehension gripped him as the door of the familiar car opened, and stark, naked pain raced through him when he saw Melissa get out of the car and walk around to the driver's side of the Corvette. He watched, motionless, as she stood there and talked with the driver for at least ten minutes, before the Corvette drove off and left her standing there alone in the darkness. Minutes later she, too, drove away.

As if he shouldered the weights of Atlas, Adam moved with slow steps toward his bicycle, numbed with pain. He mounted the bike just when a third car arrived. The intrigue heightened as the driver cut the motor, turned off the lights, and waited for thirty minutes before driving. Whoever it was didn't get out of the car. Crossed wires, Adam decided. Melissa would answer to him for her part in the scheme.

Eleven

Melissa sat in her office the next morning, tortured by what she'd discovered and bleary-eyed from the sleepless night it had caused her. She hadn't answered her phone nor the loud knocks on her door the night before for fear of reprisal or that she might get into a hassle with her father. Her head lolled against the back of her chair, and she tried to concentrate in spite of the intruding noise. She hadn't realized that it was she who kept up the consistent, rhythmic rapping until she noticed the wooden letter opener waving up and down in her hand. She laid it aside and attempted to make notes for her regular morning calls to her satellite offices in Baltimore and New York. But no sooner had she begun to gather her thoughts than Adam burst unannounced through the door, and she'd never seen a colder, more furious and feral expression on a human face.

"What's the matter?" she asked before he could speak.

"You ask me what's the matter?" he growled. She couldn't imagine what her facial expression had imparted to him, because his anger evaporated, and a sad, bitter expression cloaked his handsome face.

"You want to know what the matter is? I'll tell you." He spoke slowly and with deadly softness as though killing his feelings, shredding his emotions. "Have you known all this time who was ruining my business, trashing my factory? Why didn't you tell me, Melissa? Don't you feel that you owe me *any* allegiance?"

"You're out of your mind," she protested, trying to figure out why he seemed so certain.

He leaned over her desk, his face inches from hers. "I was, but not anymore. Just two nights ago you swore innocence, and you curled up in my arms and told me you loved me. You defended me against the charge that I shot your cousin. Was that a screen?"

She pushed her chair back and braced her palms against her desk. Horror gripped her at the depth of disappointment in his eyes. "You're wrong, Adam," she said in a strong voice, but one that held such sadness that she barely recognized it as her own.

He didn't give quarter. "Oh, no, I'm not. I saw you there last night. The three of you got your wires crossed, didn't you? Your other partner, whoever he was, drove up right after you left and waited a full thirty minutes for you. Did they meet at your house later? Is that why you didn't answer your door and ignored your telephone?"

She wouldn't have believed that she could endure such pain. She took a deep breath and told the man she loved—the man who still leaned toward her, his anger less apparent now and his face warped with sadness—that she'd done nothing for which she felt ashamed and that if he believed her guilty of so heinous a crime, nothing she said in her defense would matter.

Melissa sat tongue-tied, stunned, while he walked out of her office without another word, leaving the door ajar. Her glance fell upon the framed portrait reproductions that hung on her office walls, and she winced as every eye seemed to accuse her. None of them would have tolerated such an unfounded accusation without a history-making defense. Frederick Douglass wouldn't have, nor would Sojourner Truth, Thurgood Marshall, Martin Luther King, Jr., or Eleanor Roosevelt.

She'd heard that a thin line often separated love and hatred and took some solace in knowing that Adam could not have expressed such bitterness, such disillusionment, had he not cared deeply. He would discover the truth, she hoped, but in her present mood, she didn't give a snap what he found out about that factory.

She reviewed events of the night before and wondered whether she should have told Adam. She buzzed her secretary with the intention of asking her to dial her New York office, but to her amazement her mother walked into the room. Emily had visited her at home once, but had not come to the office. She was about to tell her mother of Adam's accusations, but Emily Grant had her own agenda.

"You don't know it," she began, "but for the past few weeks, I've been volunteering four hours a day at The Refuge. That's the shelter for abused women and children that Adam operates over on Oak Street," she rushed on, as though oblivious to her daughter's air of incredulity. Melissa ushered her to a chair.

"Sit down, and tell me what you're talking about." Still trying to adjust to the effects of her earlier episode with Adam, she all but reeled under the impact of her mother's words.

"I'm talking about your father found out that I've been volunteering at Adam's charity, and he packed his personal things and moved out of the house."

"He what?" Melissa reached for the corner of her desk to steady herself. She'd had about as much as she could handle for one morning. First, Adam's rage, and now this. "Are you sure?"

"Of course, I'm sure. He raved at me for two hours last night, and when I got downstairs this morning, he'd already packed two bags and put them in the foyer. He said he's moving into an apartment."

"Oh, Mama, I'm so sorry." She watched in awe as her mother tossed her handbag into a chair, jerked off her coat, braced her hands on her hips, and stood akimbo.

"I don't want anybody's sympathy. I don't need it," Emily told her. "I want a divorce, and I'm going to get it. I've spent

over half of my life letting people walk over me, behaving like
a nincompoop." Her pacing increased in speed. "That's my
house, and I'm the one with the prestige and the clout in this
town, and it's time I acted like it."

Melissa advanced toward her mother as though reluctant to
disturb her. "Mama, why don't you sit down while I run to
the machine and get you some tea." She blanched from her
mother's withering look.

"I forgot to add, honey, that I'm not going to let anybody
patronize me and that includes you, much as I love you. Your
father's done me a favor, and I'm getting out from under his
heel. He walked out of the door grumbling that the whole
thing was a Hayes-Roundtree conspiracy, that they inveigled
me into working at The Refuge just to humiliate him. To hear
him tell it, they're the reason his party didn't nominate him
for mayor, then for congress, and finally passed over him for
governor. Damned if I'd admit anybody was that powerful."

"Mama!"

"What's the matter?" Emily asked her. "Didn't you ever
stop to wonder where you got your spunk? You didn't think
you got it from your father, did you?"

"I can't believe Daddy left you. He's always so concerned
about what people think."

Emily shrugged with apparent disdain. "It isn't the first
time. He left me once before, and you were born while we
were separated. I think it's the reason he always treated you
as though you were his stepchild, rather than his own blood
daughter. I thought that after you grew to look so much like
him, he'd behave differently, but you can't teach an old dog
new tricks." She reached for her coat. "Well, I thought you
should know, and tonight I'll call Schyler and tell him. We'll
talk this evening. I've got an appointment with my lawyer in
twenty minutes."

Melissa watched her mother swish out of the door, plopped
down in the nearest chair, and expelled a long breath. *What
next?*

"I might as well get this over with," Melissa told herself, dialing her father's office number. She identified herself, and it annoyed her that his secretary nevertheless asked him whether he'd care to take the phone.

"I suppose you and your mother have been talking," he said by way of a greeting. "I can't stand any more of their humiliating tactics, Melissa, and I won't live with a woman who's in their pay." Melissa attempted to explain that her mother volunteered at The Refuge and received no pay.

"I don't expect you to understand," he said. "You're having an affair with him, and she's working for him. A man can take just so much. Both of you seem to have forgotten that those people stole your birthright. Old Jacob Hayes bilked your grandfather, and you're consorting with his rich descendants. I'm ashamed of both of you." He hung up.

Tired of the tale and the excuse it provided, she decided the time had come to face him down. She drove to his office building, went in, and started past his secretary.

"You can't walk in there, "the woman hissed. "Visitors have to be announced."

"I don't need your permission to see my father," Melissa replied, still miffed at the way in which the secretary had treated an earlier phone call. She opened his door, and he glanced up, then continued writing. She hated that his refusal to acknowledge her presence drained her of her anger. She attempted to reason with him.

"Daddy, why do you hold on to that myth? You know it isn't true. You know my grandfather withdrew his money from that venture and nearly ruined Adam's grandfather. Anyway, it isn't your feud, it's mama's, and she dropped it years ago."

"How dare you speak to me about that?" She didn't ask him what he meant, but assumed he referred to her mother's broken engagement and shifted the subject to a more pressing concern.

"You know how Timmy got shot and who did it, don't you Daddy? And you know the Roundtrees had nothing to do with it, don't you?" She ignored his sputter and said what she should have said days earlier. "I told you Adam was with me that night. Well, if you accuse him publicly, I'll tell the town of Frederick where we were."

She heard the sadness in her father's voice and saw the grimness that lined his face, but she couldn't let that sway her. He had no interest in upholding the truth, only in besting the Roundtrees and Hayeses.

"I never thought I'd live to see the day one of my children would take sides with those people against me," he told her in the weary voice of one facing defeat. "Why do you defend him? He's nothing to us."

"You're mistaken, Daddy," she told him, her voice strong and sure. "Adam Roundtree is my life, and if you force him to go to court, I'll stand with him." What had she said? She stood looking at the man for whose love and approval she had begged most of her life and felt as though she had suddenly flown free of him. He—a lawyer sworn to uphold the law—would ruin a man's reputation in order to shield his nephew from what she was certain involved some kind of crime. He didn't deserve her blind devotion. Perhaps no one deserved that.

Rafer Grant stared at his daughter. "Just like your mother. Hot after the Hayeses." He picked up his pen and returned to his writing. "Well, both of you can have them." She stood there long after he'd dismissed her, giving him a chance to soften his blow, but he continued to ignore her. She left, thinking him a lonely man.

Adam despaired of getting any work done, and for the remainder of the morning, roamed around in his office shuffling in his mind his unsatisfactory conversation with Melissa. She hadn't attempted to defend herself, and he had seen the honesty in her shock and outrage at his accusation. He couldn't imagine why she would drive out to the factory alone on successive nights if not to meet someone. And she had met someone. Yet when he'd confronted her with it, she'd withheld information that he needed. He slapped his right fist into the palm of his left hand. Alright, so he'd gone about it wrong; he'd accused her. He'd try another tactic.

When he walked into Melissa's office early that afternoon, Adam brushed past Magnus Cooper as he left. Angered beyond reason, he skipped the greeting and demanded, "What's he doing here?"

"We have a contract. Remember? I've just found a ranch manager for him." Relieved that she ignored both his temper and his audacity, he said in a more even tone, "I thought you made it a policy to take the employee to the new boss, but at least you avoided that long trip to Houston."

"Magnus thinks I ought to have an office in the capital of every state. He wants to invest in my business."

Adam tried to shake off his annoyance at her use of the man's first name. "And what do you think?"

"He's impressed with my work, and he made a good case for a bigger operation," she said, letting the words come out slowly as if to keep him dangling.

"And?" She squinted at him and, in spite of himself, he softened toward her.

She shrugged. "Then he or somebody else would own my business. I said no thanks. He was very disappointed."

Adam blew out a deep sigh. "I'll just bet he was—he won't have an excuse to come up here to see you." He ignored her silent censure. "He may fool you with his trumped-up reasons for hanging around you, but he isn't fooling himself and definitely not me." He noticed that her voice lacked its usual verve and color and told himself to lighten up.

"Am I interrupting something private?" Banks asked, surprising them since neither had heard her approach. "Your secretary must have stepped out," she explained to Melissa.

"Bessie called me. She just got in a load of stuff at Yesteryear, and if we get down there this afternoon, we can have our pick before she does her Christmas ads." She must have noticed their preoccupation, Adam decided, when she exclaimed, "Oops! See you later," and ducked out of the door.

"Melissa, we have to talk, but not here. We need to speak openly and honestly with each other, and we need privacy for that. Can we get together this evening?" He suspected from her deep breath and the way in which her fingers had begun to drum her desk that she intended to refuse.

"I'm not about to let you harass me the way you did this morning, so whatever you have to say, you may say now."

"Fine. Lock your door." She stood and moved toward it but stopped when he said, "Not even your friend, Banks, would resist broadcasting the fact that you locked the door with only the two of us in here."

He had the advantage, but that didn't mean he'd keep it. "Well?" He persisted, standing to leave.

"Alright, Adam," she said, with obvious reluctance. "I'll be home around eight tonight." But at seven o'clock that evening she called him, canceled their date, and refused to give an excuse.

"I can't see you tonight."

"That's it? No reason?"

"That's it."

Melissa hung up, threw off her robe, and crawled into bed. She had no appetite and hadn't bothered to eat dinner. The day's happenings crowded her thoughts. Her mother had filed for a divorce, and her unrepentant father pouted somewhere, sad and alone. She'd telephoned her brother, thousands of miles away in Kenya, in an effort to understand how it could have happened. His summation had astonished her.

"I used to wish they'd split up, because I didn't know which one of them to sympathize with, and they both needed it. Maybe they'll salvage the rest of their lives. I hope so."

The day's events had undermined her sense of identity, and she lacked the strength to endure another of Adam's interrogations. Tangling with him that morning had left her raw, and after that, the dam had burst. If she could have expected him to greet her with love and understanding, she'd have run to him. But he wouldn't come prepared to meet her needs, only to wring from her what he required for his own peace of mind. No. She couldn't see him.

Adam rose from his bed and stared out at the still dark morning. He had to see Melissa, to arrive at an understanding with her and to find out what she knew about the incidents at Leather and Hides. Although he'd seen her there and witnessed what appeared to be her collusion with people intent on destroying his property, he didn't want to believe her capable of it. Yet what was he to think? Why hadn't she defended herself? He dressed in woolen pants, a long-sleeved knitted T-shirt, crew-neck sweater, and leather jacket and drove into Frederick. He parked four blocks from Melissa's house in order to thwart the local gossip mongers and strode briskly through the darkness to her front door. She probably wouldn't appreciate a visit at seven o'clock in the morning, but if her night had been as rough as his, at least he wouldn't awaken her.

She answered after several rings, and he wondered why she seemed relieved to see him.

"You could have been someone intent on mischief," she explained in response to his question.

He didn't wait for her invitation to enter, and once inside surprised himself by asking, "What about Magnus Cooper?" He hadn't realized that her relationship with the man bothered him that much.

She tightened her robe, walked into the living room, and sat on the sofa. "Where is it written, Adam, that I have to explain my behavior to you?" He wished she wouldn't squint—every time he saw her do it, she all but unraveled him. He pulled off his jacket and tossed it near her on the sofa.

"It is written in the tomes of common decency, Melissa. You've been in my arms, and I've been inside of you. That gives me some rights."

She sucked her teeth and waved her hand as though to say, Don't fool yourself.

Adam took a chair opposite her. "Let's not bicker. The problem at the factory is getting out of hand, and if I don't find out who is responsible, we may lose it. Who did you follow there? And who shot Timothy, Melissa? Tell me what you know. If it weren't for you, I'd go to the FBI about this, but I'll level with you. My list of suspects includes three members of your family. Tell me you're not involved, and I'll believe you."

"If you need my verbal assurance, there's no point in my giving it."

He saw her lips quiver and her composure falter as she fought tears, and he told himself he wouldn't let her tears influence him, but he couldn't remain unmoved by the sight of water glistening in her eyes.

"What is it? Don't. I don't want to cause you pain." He'd never seen her cry, never seen her lacking the calm assurance that defined her character. Alarmed, he stepped to her and put his arms around her. "What is it?" he whispered, bending to hear her broken words.

"My family's falling apart. My father has left my mother, moved out of their house with all of his personal belongings, and Mama's actually happy that he's gone. She retaliated by filing for a divorce. Schyler stays as far away from our parents as he can get, because he can't stand to see them live out their farce, making the best of their painful marriage. And Daddy attributes every misfortune he's ever had to the Hayeses and Roundtrees. No matter how remote the issue, if it didn't go his way, he holds your family responsible. He's a failed man,

Adam. He wanted to play football but couldn't make the varsity. He wanted my mother, but although she married him, in her heart she belonged only to Bill Henry Hayes. And he wanted a career as a politician, but he lost the most celebrated legal case this region's ever witnessed, one that he should have won, but for his own inefficiency. After that, he could never win his party's support."

Adam eased her out of his arms. The time had come—he'd known it would. But he hadn't expected that he would have to confess responsibility for something that weighed so heavily on her and to do it at a time when she needed his strength. And at a time when he questioned her role in the attempted ruination of his family. With his hands lightly on her shoulders, he urged her to sit.

"I have to tell you something, Melissa—something I've postponed mentioning because I didn't know how to broach it to you." He stopped talking and thought for a minute, aware that she didn't press him to continue though she scrutinized his every gesture. "That isn't quite accurate," he amended. "The truth is, I knew I should have told you the first time I took you to my lodge, but I wasn't ready to take the risk that you wouldn't forgive me. I'm not ready for that now, either, but I don't have a choice. When I was sixteen, I found a lawyer's briefcase that contained court papers in the men's room at a local restaurant, but I noticed that it belonged to Rafer Grant, and in an act of vengeance I left them there without telling Rafer about them. I hadn't cared what the next finder did with them." He paused, his voice softening as though in regret. "I later learned that the brief pertained to the defense of a prominent person, and that because he didn't have the papers, Rafer's summary to the jury had been sloppy and ineffectual. He lost the case."

He shifted his stance, uncomfortable in the silence that hung between them. He got the impression that she wanted to recall something that eluded her, and he waited with as much patience as he could muster. At last she spoke.

"I've heard about that case Lord knows how many times. Daddy's excuse was that he'd misplaced his brief." Her cynical laugh jarred him. "And that's probably the only thing that happened to him after he married Mama that he didn't blame a member of your family for." She folded her arms, running her hands up the wide sleeves of her robe. "You couldn't have been more than fourteen or fifteen at the time. What could have upset you so badly that you'd do such a thing?"

"I can't tell you without reflecting upon someone else. Remember that I didn't hide it or take it—I just didn't tell him I'd seen it. But I didn't care if someone else took it. I hated the word Grant."

Her eyes widened. "But you were a child. Why?"

"I had a reason, a personal one, but looking back, I admit that I didn't behave honorably. It taught me a lesson, too: I never carry important papers in a briefcase unless I've stored a copy elsewhere." The slow shake of her head, her pensive expression, were not the reaction he'd anticipated. She didn't show anger.

"I don't know what to say to this. Whatever made us think we could have a normal relationship as other men and women do? There's too much bad blood between us."

He wondered if she felt as ill fated, as resigned, as her seemingly careless shrug suggested. No matter, he had no intention of landing on his face because Rafer Grant hadn't shown guts enough to fight adversity.

"A man doesn't allow a single incident to bring him down, to circumscribe his whole life. Such a man will use any excuse, any crutch."

Melissa opened her mouth to defend her father, but remembered that she had stopped doing that. She spoke mostly to herself. "Do you know what it means to spend your life trying to please someone, only to have the scales fall from your eyes, only to realize that such blind devotion is undeserved?"

"Rafer?"

She nodded.

"Blind devotion is never deserved." He kicked at the carpet, looked down at her, shook his head, and walked toward the opposite end of the room.

"Adam, will you please stop pacing. It's unsettling." He did as she asked, but his close scrutiny told her that he wanted to gauge her mood, to figure out what had prompted her remark. She didn't enlighten him. Why should she tell him what she felt when she watched his muscles ripple, or that the sight of his tight buttocks and long masculine legs cased erotically in his pants challenged her sense of propriety?

He returned to his seat, leaned forward, and said, "You're your father's only daughter. How could he not love you? How could *anybody* not . . ." He didn't complete the sentence, and she refused to raise her hopes by doing it for him. He sat with his right sneaker resting on his left knee, and her gaze caught his long slim foot, his tapered ankle, and her mind's eye recalled that foot sockless and unshod and the circumstance in which she'd seen it. Her mouth watered. Her right hand went to her tingling breast, and she shifted her position on the sofa. Flustered, she locked her gaze on a group of snapshots that rested on her mantelpiece and swallowed the saliva that accumulated in her mouth.

"Melissa!" She resisted the pull of his voice and wouldn't look at him.

"Look at me," he purred with the soft growl of a great cat preparing to mount its mate. As if programmed to do so, her eyes found his beloved face, and she drew in her breath when her gaze locked into his seductive stare, his knowing look.

She glanced away. Good Lord! She nearly panicked at the realization that she still wore her robe and her bikini panties. Did he think she'd sat with him dressed in that way just to entice him? She stood, tightening the robe as she did so. She'd greeted him in that robe once before, she recalled, and he'd spent the night with her. Not this time. She started toward the door.

"Where are you going?"

"To get dressed."

"Why?" The sizzling hot, steely expression in his eyes told her that her robe was more than she needed. She tugged it closer to her body.

"Come here and sit on my lap, honey." With a hand in each of his pockets, he uncrossed his knee, spread his legs, and leaned back in the chair. "Come here, sweetheart." Liquid legs propelled her to him.

"I don't want this, Adam. We can't solve anything between the sheets." He reached up, gathered her in his arms, and lowered her to his left knee. Tremors of anticipation raced through her at his deep, masculine laugh.

"That's the only place we ever solve anything. We want each other, so don't bother to deny what you're feeling."

She shrugged to display an air of indifference. "I've decided to deny myself. Self-denial builds character."

"And guarantees sleepless nights. Come on, honey. Open your mouth for me."

Her stubbornness gave way to compliance when she felt him rise strong and rigid against her hip, and she eagerly sought his lips. She reeled under the impact of his loving kiss. As soon as she returned his fire, his kiss gentled, and he showered her with tenderness, feathering kisses over her lips and eyes. Cherishing her. She reveled in it. Oh, it felt so good to be in his arms.

She wanted to hold him forever, but his reason for being there flitted through her mind, and she couldn't help withdrawing and knew that he sensed it. He held her away from him, studying her countenance.

"I need to make love with you, but I need more. I can't give myself to you halfheartedly, and I don't want you to do that, either. You're important to me, Melissa. Do you know anything about the problems we're having at the factory?" He curled her to him as one would hold a baby. "Can't you understand that I have to solve that problem, and that as long as

I don't know where you stand in this, my loyalties are split and I'm unable to do my job effectively?"

She took a deep breath, mused over his words, and sought middle ground. "I can tell you that I don't know who shot Timmy. The other thing I know is that Timmy's daddy is the deputy chief of police, and Mama says he's always taken care of Timmy's numerous brushes with the law. I know that much, Adam." She leaned back and looked him straight in the eye. "But I will not exonerate myself for you. Not now or ever."

She welcomed his audible sigh of relief. At least she could give him that much without compromising her integrity.

He released her, stood, and walked to the far end of the room. "Will you lose any sleep knowing that I intend to seek the help of the FBI?"

She couldn't hold back the smile that curved her lips. "Not one wink. Crafty rascal, aren't you?" He ran his right hand over his hair, not taking his eyes off of her.

"So I've been told. You won't yield on this, and neither will I, but you've given me something and for now I'm satisfied."

She yawned. "Would you like some coffee?"

He slid his hands into his pockets and propped his foot on the rung of an antique chair. Then he laid his head to one side and cocked an eyebrow. *"Coffee?* You're kidding. I want *you."*

Adam lay on his back, his left arm securing her to his side. He'd made love to her twice, and the first time he'd been able to hold back as he had with every woman since, as a boy of fifteen, he'd gotten the strength to walk away from the one who taught him to crave her and then humiliated him for it. With her every move, Melissa had asked him for more than he gave her, but still he'd been able to withhold a vital part of himself. And with all her sweet giving, he'd been left unfulfilled, knowing he'd brought that on himself. She seemed to have sensed that his war with himself didn't involve her, and she'd stroked and soothed him as he rested above her spent, but unsatisfied.

Minutes later, still sheathed within her warmth, he had reached full readiness again. He'd kissed her with all the tenderness he felt for her, and with his eyes had asked her permission to continue. Her sweet smile of acquiescence had sent his heart soaring, and he'd cherished her, because it was what he felt, and she'd suddenly gone wild beneath him. Her body demanded that he give her all of himself, and at her zenith she'd repeatedly whispered her love for him and stunned him by telling him she needed his love more than she needed air. He'd lost it then. A feeling he'd never known. And he'd given himself because he wanted to, needed to, and finally because he couldn't help himself. His control had shattered, and he would never forget that feeling of scaling the heights, of having the earth move beneath him and the stars shooting all around him. She had pulled down his walls, blasted his safe, and left him vulnerable to her. If he discovered that she had a hand in the mess at Leather and Hides, it probably wouldn't make a damned bit of difference.

He leaned over her, clasped her in his arms, and feathered kisses over her cheeks. He knew he had strength, that his toughness had made him a success. But he didn't fool himself. The woman he held in his arms had a strength equal to his own. She had considered one of his "secrets" of little consequence. But he knew she wouldn't treat the other one lightly, and that she had the guts to walk away no matter what she felt for him.

Adam showered in Melissa's lavender-scented bathroom. He had thirty-five minutes in which to go home, change into business clothes, and get to his office in time for his first appointment. He hooked a towel at his waist, stepped out of the bathroom, and began to dress.

"Where did you park?" He glanced over at her lying on her belly, her chin supported by the heels of both hands, and told himself to think about blackened redfish, the Indonesian rain

forests, or poison ivy—anything except the sleepy woman between those sheets. He had to be in his office in minutes.

"I parked four blocks away. Don't worry, I wouldn't do anything to make you the main topic of discussion at Martha
Brock's 'Monday evening tea to help the homeless.'" Happiness flooded his heart at the sound of her infectious and uninhibited laugh, the laughter of a well-loved, sated woman.

"Don't forget Miss Mary's Wednesday night prayer service,"
she added, mimicking the old woman. "They'll race right
through it so they can get to the good part, the coffee and
gossip part of the service."

He sat on the edge of the bed, pulled on his socks and
sneakers, and felt her hand stroke the back of his head.

"Do whatever you have to do about Leather and Hides,
Adam. You would regardless of what I said, but I want you to
know that I'd never want you to compromise your integrity—
and no matter what you discover, do what you have to do. If
I were in your big sneakers and faced what you do, I'd go for
the truth and let the chips fall—"

He turned to face her. "Thank you . . . I think. It's easier to
say that than to live through it, Melissa. I don't want to make
a move against you or anyone dear to you, and I hope it won't
be necessary. But I can only be who I am and what I am. I'll
do what I know is right, no matter how much or who it hurts,
and this ridiculous feud won't weigh in my decisions. We may
face some difficult days. If we mean anything to each other
after I get this mess settled, call it a miracle." He hugged her
quickly, shoving his desire for her under control.

"Aren't you going to work today?" Desire stirred in him as
the backs of her fingers trailed down his cheek and stroked
his neck.

"I don't think so. A dear friend will be staying with me for
a few days, and I'm going into Baltimore shortly to get her."

He allowed a raised eyebrow, but inwardly he felt relief that
she didn't expect Magnus Cooper. "Anyone I know?"

"I don't think you've met her, but she'd love to make your acquaintance."

"What does that mean?" He stood, looked around for his jacket, and remembered that he'd left it downstairs. She rolled over, dropped her feet off the bed, and tucked the sheet around her.

"It means she's normal."

"Are you getting testy?" He had a feeling the look she gave him had been used repeatedly and to maximum effect.

"Not yet, but give me time. I just remembered that Magnus Cooper is coming here today. Business, he said. He thinks this town is ripe with investment opportunities."

Adam's hand remained suspended above the doorknob. "Remind him for me that when the great warriors of history lost a battle, they were usually on foreign soil. I'll call you tonight." He didn't wait for her reaction.

Melissa dressed, put in a call to her secretary, and left for Baltimore. She'd had the car tuned up and cleaned inside and out. What she'd consider an ordinary mishap, Ilona would view as a major disaster. Her friend didn't pamper herself to the point of being a bore, but she expected life to flow smoothly. She parked along a narrow street that ran perpendicular to the west side of the Pennsylvania Railroad station and walked the short block. A neatly attired older woman fell in step beside her.

"You look so nice, dear. You remind me of myself when I was your age."

"Well, thank you," Melissa answered, trying not to break her stride.

"I love to see our young people looking so prosperous," the woman went on. "Where're you headed?" Melissa told her that she was meeting a friend.

"I sure hope he's nice, and I hope you appreciate him," the woman droned. "Don't do like I did. I was going to be an opera singer, come hell or high water. Well, it was high water, because it turned out I didn't have the talent for it. The man I gave up in order to chase that windmill married my sister, and every holiday I have to watch him being happy with her and my three nieces and nephews. Now I'm fifty with a cracking voice, fading looks, and myself for company."

Melissa slowed her steps to a halt. "I don't know what to say. I . . . I'm sorry, ma'am."

"Don't be," her companion said. "I make a very good living with my tarot cards, and the older I get, the more people seem to trust me." She shook her head, as if in sadness. "If I could just stop dreaming about him and waking up thinking he's with me." The woman drifted into introspection, and Melissa touched her shoulder, waved, and strode to the information booth. Her encounter with the stranger had lowered her spirits. She feared that she would love Adam Roundtree forever, just as her mother still loved Bill Henry hopelessly after three decades, a marriage to another man, and two children. But the next move wasn't hers to make.

She bought a copy of *The Baltimore Sun* and found a seat in the waiting room. But the newsprint danced before her eyes until she saw only Adam's face above hers. Adam in ecstasy, shattered, vulnerable, and bare. She had finally touched him. For the first time he'd given all of himself, had belonged to her completely. She wondered about the other times they'd made love. Best not to speculate, because she would never know unless he told her. But she'd keep the memory of it close to her heart. For those few moments, if never again, Adam Roundtree had been hers. Perspiration dampened her forehead as she recalled the fire-hot tension he built up in her, refusing her the quick and easy release she begged him for until at last he hurtled her into a star-spangled otherworld. And then he'd joined her.

"Melissa, darling, you must be thinking about this man. I've been standing here a full minute. Darling, it must be awful to sit in these wooden seats. How long have you been waiting?"

A wide grin spread across Melissa's face, and she quickly stood to hug her friend.

"I didn't wait long." She picked up Ilona's bag and started for the car. "I thought we'd have lunch in the Inner Harbor before going to Frederick."

"Whatever you say. I'm in your hands." Ilona pointed to her new low-heeled shoes. "I bought these just for the trip. I wouldn't be caught dead in these things on Fifth Avenue."

"Well, at least you'll have some respite from your sore feet while you're here," Melissa commented, unable to resist needling her friend.

After lunch Melissa gave Ilona a quick tour past the Johns Hopkins University and along Charles Street and walked with her through the famous Lexington Market.

"I haven't seen so much meat since the last time I shopped with my dear mother in the Great Market in Budapest almost forty years ago," Ilona exclaimed. "Don't they have strawberries down here?" she asked, when they wandered through the produce section.

"Ilona, this is December. If you want strawberries, I'll stop by a specialty shop." Ilona told her not to bother.

"But darling, you should have strawberries to feed your man—one at a time," she explained, pausing for effect. "But we could get some grapes. Grapes are good for that, too, except then you feed him the whole bunch. Just make sure he doesn't choke—some men don't know the purpose of that." Melissa resisted asking her to explain it.

"Are you expecting company, Ilona?"

"No darling, but you must be. I'm going to be here four days, and no real vooman would let so much time go by without seeing her man. So when do I meet him? Tonight?" she asked, hope caressing her accented tones.

Melissa glanced at her rearview mirror when she backed up to park in front of her house and saw the gray Towne car ease to the curb right behind her. She counted to three under her breath, and turned to Ilona.

"We're home." She opened the trunk to retrieve Ilona's bag and the few items she'd bought. She knew that the male hand on her arm didn't belong to Adam, and suppressing annoyance, looked up into the hazel brown, expectant eyes of Magnus Cooper.

"You broke our appointment," he reprimanded in a gentle voice.

"I've been waiting to meet you," she heard Ilona say, mistaking Magnus for Adam. "But somehow, you're not what I expected. You're more my style than Melissa's." She looked him up and down. "I've had less pleasant surprises." Melissa watched Ilona's fun and felt some of her antagonism toward Magnus ebbing. His car parked in front of her door would be a feast for her nosey neighbors and fuel for Adam's temper. He wouldn't believe that a man of Magnus Cooper's sophistication would visit a woman unless he knew she would welcome him.

"Ilona Harváth, this is Magnus Cooper. Mr. Cooper lives in Texas and is here on business. Magnus, Ilona is a dear friend visiting me from New York." He nodded.

"Mmmm. How do you do?" Ilona's raised eyebrow and suggestive shrug told them what she thought of Cooper's business in Frederick. Melissa asked him to excuse her and promised to see him at her office the next morning.

Inside, Ilona looked around, complimented Melissa on her home, and got down to business. "Melissa, darling, if this man you are so taken with doesn't look as good as the one who just left here, I will kill you." She shook her head and rolled her eyes skyward as though savoring the tenderest fresh truffle. "Darling, this Cooper is a real man. If I was ten years younger, I'd separate him from the pack in a minute."

"You could do it now." She took Ilona's bag and walked upstairs with her to the guest room.

"Darling, don't make jokes." That expression always amused Melissa, as did the withering look that accompanied it. She raced to answer the phone in her room.

"Did your friend arrive?" She flopped down on the side of her bed, kicked off her shoes and swung her legs up on the coverlet.

"Yes. She's here. You want to run by for a couple of minutes after you leave the office? I'd like you to meet her." And she longed to see him, to reassure herself that what she'd experienced with him that morning had been real, that she hadn't dreamed it. She couldn't understand the long silence nor his seeming lack of enthusiasm when he replied.

"Why not? See you in a half hour." She combed her hair, refreshed her makeup, and dabbed a little perfume behind her ears and at her temple. She arrived at the top of the stairs simultaneously with Ilona.

"Don't tell me," Ilona said, folding her arms about her chest in a gesture of satisfaction. "That was *him,* and he's coming over. Let me get my heels. I wouldn't be—"

"—caught dead around a man wearing those flats," Melissa finished for her.

Melissa tried not to rush to the door when he rang, and she had to muster an air of casualness when she opened the door.

"Hi." He didn't speak but stood looking down at her, his gazing roaming over her upturned face. And after what seemed to her endless minutes, he opened his arms and folded her to him. Unable to wait longer, she leaned back and fastened her gaze on his mouth in a silent request, and he gave her what she wanted, crushing her to him and shivering against her when she opened her mouth beneath his in sweet union.

He eased her from him, and tugging her to his side, turned toward the living room.

"Where's your friend?"

"Is somebody asking for me?" Ilona queried as she strolled down the stairs from her perch where she couldn't help but witness their kiss. Melissa couldn't suppress a hearty laugh. She should have known that Ilona couldn't wait to see Adam. She introduced them, and Adam went to greet her before she reached the bottom of the stairs.

Ilona accepted the introduction with the comment, "Melissa, darling, this is God's country. I'm living in the wrong state."

Melissa needled her, "But we don't have a ballet here, remember?"

"Who needs the ballet? From my experience since I've been here, I can't see how you'd have time for it." She shook Adam's hand. "I'm happy to meet you, Adam. You mustn't mind my continental manners."

Adam's grin seemed to please her. "I doubt the continent has much to do with your manners. I know a free spirit when I see one. Welcome to Frederick, Ilona."

Melissa sensed his forced manners. She'd felt a distance between them during their phone conversation and when she'd opened the door for him. And she sensed it now.

"Would you join us for a drink? Ilona drinks only espresso coffee, but I'd like some wine. What about you?"

He glanced at his watch. "Thanks, but I've asked Jason Court to come down here, and I want to meet him at the airport this evening." He bade Ilona good-bye, and they walked to the door.

"I sense a problem. What's wrong?"

"Did you enjoy your visit with Magnus Cooper?" The question surprised her, and she suspected from his closed expression that he hadn't planned to ask her that. She wondered how he'd known that Magnus came to her house, but she ignored his sarcasm and his audacity.

"We didn't visit. I made an appointment to see him at my office tomorrow morning. Anything else?" He ran his right hand over the back of his hair and looked at her intently for a few seconds without saying anything. She knew when he made up his mind to tell her about it.

"Sometime between six o'clock and eight this morning, someone sprayed red, oil-based paint on a batch of leathers that Cal had planned to ship today. He's threatened to resign if this sabotage continues. I'll be busy with this for the next few days, but I'll be in touch." He kissed her quickly and left. Melissa forced a bright expression on her face and went back to get Ilona's extended verdict.

"What's the matter, darling?"

Melissa countered with another question. "Why do you think something's wrong?"

Ilona shrugged first one shoulder and then the other. "Am I a lamb born today? This man is fighting a war with himself, and he's strong enough to win it. He wants you, but something's dragging him back. Pull out the stops, Melissa, and don't give him a chance to breathe without thinking of you first. What a man! Hmmm. If I had to choose between him and Cooper, I'd probably lose my mind." She lit a cigarette. "My one vice since I gave up rummy, darling. As far as Adam's concerned, you belong to him. Well, that's something. Cooper's only hoping."

"What are you talking about?" Melissa had headed for the kitchen to start supper and beckoned Ilona to follow her. Ilona tried without success to blow a smoke ring.

"Don't make me spell it out. I saw you with Adam, darling. You've made each other happy. Very happy. Keep it up." She sat down and crossed her knees. "I'm not going to offer to cook—it's not my style. But if you want to eat out, I'll pay. Cooking is for servants. I don't know why you do it." She sipped the hot espresso. "I see you remember I like it in a little glass. Listen darling, all fun aside. You love Adam, and he thinks an awful lot of you, but he's a man who can put you behind him. You know what he needs, so give him plenty of it. Don't let anything or anybody get between you, because you won't find another like him."

Twelve

Adam drove home for lunch with Jason Court. He'd invited Jason to stay with him in Beaver Ridge, rather than at a hotel in Frederick, reasoning that if he was seen with a stranger of Jason's description—big, tough, jaded, and possibly a crime buster—the criminal or criminals might be alerted to the ring tightening around them. His intention had been to have his assistant bring him up to date on affairs at his New York office, but he remembered that Jason had been a police detective until he'd quit after having been wounded. He told Jason about the problems at the leather factory.

"I suppose you've planted one or two specialists there whom you can trust."

"Yeah. But they're poor detectives—these incidents take place all around them."

Jason interlocked his long brown fingers and leaned back in his straight chair. "Adam, this thing could involve people in more than one state. Maybe you should contact the FBI."

"I've thought of that, and I've postponed doing it, but if nothing else, the Feds could give me some advice." A smile creased Adam's face when his mother walked in the dining room with a huge chocolate bombe, his favorite dessert, and a pot of coffee.

"You're a lucky man, Adam, getting this kind of home cooking," Jason said. He smiled at Adam's mother. "I wonder how you knew I'm a chocaholic."

"Chocolate is usually the safest dessert to offer men, if you don't know what they like," she replied in a softer than usual voice. Adam glanced sharply at her. He'd lived for almost thirty-five years and hadn't guessed that his mother was what he thought of as a man's woman. His fifty-four-year-old mother bloomed in a soft, womanly response to Jason's compliment. He scrutinized the man who sat across from him, lustily enjoying the delicious dessert, a man who commanded respect as much for his masculinity as for his abilities. He recognized a similarity with his father and smiled to himself.

Melissa walked to her office door with Magnus Cooper, told him good-bye, and prayed that Adam wouldn't meet him in the hallway as he left. She liked and respected the genteel Texan and appreciated his business. He had divined her interest in another man and hadn't been surprised to learn the man's identity.

"From what I've seen and heard, you've chosen well," he'd said, removing himself from the picture with consummate grace.

She checked her calendar for the day, hoping to have the afternoon free so that she could show Ilona the town of Frederick and the little picturesque villages nearby. Friday had always been one of her busiest days, and this one was shaping up similarly. She punched the intercom and dictated a short letter to a woman in Atlanta who needed a florist to baby-sit her nursery while she took a long-anticipated tour around the world. Melissa declined the job on the grounds that she couldn't be responsible for damage or loss that the nursery might sustain in the owner's absence.

She'd asked her secretary not to disturb her, but she accepted Adam's call. "Hi."

"Hi." Pleasure enveloped her at the sound of his deep velvet voice. "Have I seen the last of Cooper?" Melissa couldn't resist a chuckle.

"Search me. Your sight seems to pierce walls and dart around corners. I wouldn't be surprised if you did see him. Making any progress?" She must have asked the wrong question, because his silence seemed almost palpable. "Are you there, Adam?"

"I'm here. I haven't made any moves. What is Ilona doing to entertain herself while you're at work?"

Adam didn't invite a person to butt out—he merely changed the subject. "You never see a need for subtlety, do you?" she asked, a tinge of testiness in her voice. But with his self-confidence, she thought, he didn't have to resort to that. He ignored her taunt, and she thought it just as well.

"Like any vacationing New Yorker worth the name, Ilona is probably sound asleep," she told him. "She asked me to set the coffeepot for eleven thirty, and I did." She waited, wanting him to tell her why he'd called, needing his admittance that he just wanted to talk to her.

"I was in a rush when I left you last night, but like I said, I had to get to the airport. I could have done a better job of telling you good night."

She settled into her chair and felt her lips curl into a slow smile. "It isn't too late. Want to make up for it right now?"

His laugh warmed her. "Seeing through walls is nothing compared to what you're asking me to do now."

"Do you know something I don't? Why should making up for last night be such a chore? Especially for you?"

"You pick the damndest times to toy with me, always making sure you're out of sight. The manner in which I should have preferred to tell you good night cannot be executed through these telephone wires," he said in exaggerated Oxford English and with a hint of belligerence. She didn't try to suppress her delight nor the wickedness with which she communicated it to him.

"Oh, you're up to the task," she teased. "I can't imagine

there's anything you'd want to do that you can't manage. Don't let a couple of telephone wires deter you. 'A man's reach should exceed his grasp, Or what's a heaven for?' " she quoted from Browning. She couldn't figure out whether her deviltry excited him or annoyed him. All she had to go on was his cryptic reply.

"If heaven is in a receptive mood, the telephone wires be damned. I can burn up the distance between us in no time. Say the word."

"Oh, dear, did I say something wrong?" She put her hand over the mouthpiece. If he heard her snicker, he'd be there in short order, and she wouldn't bet on what he'd do.

"Never pull a tiger by his tail, baby. I'll see you tonight."

"What? I have to entertain Ilona. I may not be home."

"Oh, yes, you will—and nothing would delight your friend more than to watch you take your medicine."

"Adam!"

"See you at seven, babe." He hung up.

She hugged herself and swirled her chair around in delight as her heart raced in anticipation of the evening. Whatever medicine he'd planned for her, she couldn't wait to taste it. Her euphoria evaporated when Emily appeared in the doorway, her face the picture of anger and determination.

"Your father backed a truck up to the house and took out everything he'd put there. He must have kept a list. You know, it struck me as strange that he'd do that when he didn't seem to want to leave. If Schyler was here, he could talk to him. Go see if he's alright. I have to make some plans, and I can't do that if he's having a breakdown."

"Okay. Do you think he's home?" Melissa's deep sigh bespoke her reluctance to speak with the man as daughter to father, but she promised her mother that she would. "Come on. I'll drop you off at home."

Rafer Grant did not welcome his daughter's interference. "You know why I moved out. Your mother has sold out and

gone over to them. Both of you have, and I'm not going to
hang around and watch you throw yourselves at my enemies."

"I just came to see if you're alright, Daddy."

"Of course, I'm alright. Are you sure you didn't come here
to protect Adam Roundtree?" He gritted his teeth apparently
in disgust at having to mention the name.

A surge of anxiety washed through her. "What do you
mean? Protect him from what?"

His smile was that of a man who held the trump cards. "He
has alienated my wife, causing an irreparable breach between
us and, even if you get on your knees and beg, I'm still going
to sue him for that."

"Daddy, that's ridiculous. Mama told me that the two of
you have lived separate lives for twenty-five years. Adam
didn't alienate Mama, and he didn't shoot Timmy." She regretted the words when he stammered and sputtered, unable to
articulate his rage. She'd only fueled his passion for revenge.

"I warn you," he finally managed to say. "If you betray
your family, you'll regret it. You'll lose your clients, and Adam
Roundtree won't be so anxious for you when he learns that
you instigated the sabotage of his leather industry." She
couldn't contain her loud gasp. How did he know about the
problems at Leather and Hides?

She left her father and walked down the hall to his lawyer's
office. "My cousin doesn't have a case against Adam," she
told the man. "On the night of the shooting I was with Adam
from around seven until midnight, and I'm prepared to give
public testimony to that effect. And it was I and not Adam
who urged Mama to begin volunteer work."

"Why did she choose The Refuge? Plenty of places around
here need volunteers."

"Mama had never associated The Refuge with Adam or his
family. I didn't even know Adam had any connection with it
until after Mama went there."

"You'd go against your father?"

"I will if he goes ahead with this attempt to embarrass my mother."

"You're pretty resolute about this."

She hesitated to say more, but she didn't want the lawyer to doubt her. "Yes, I am, and I won't omit the damage he's done to her psyche. He has treated her as though she were incompetent, deprived her of self-confidence. She can't drive a car, has never been allowed to go anywhere without him except the hairdresser, and he has insisted on choosing her clothes. Yes, I'll tell it!"

"I find this hard to digest." The man walked over to the window and looked down toward the street.

"He robbed me, too. All these years I thought my mother preferred my brother to me, that she didn't love me, but she was only trying to please my father. I was no better—I begged for his approval and didn't try to understand my mother. He manipulated both of us."

"I'm surprised."

She shrugged. "He probably isn't aware that he's done these things or, at least, of their effect."

"Rafer said you'd witness for him."

"Tell me—do I look as if I might do that?" Her face must have mirrored her sadness, because he shook his head in sympathy.

"I'd say, not."

She walked to the door and turned. "And you'd be right. Good-bye."

Melissa laid back her shoulders, plastered a smile on her face, and unlocked her door. She found a well-rested Ilona fresh from her scented bath doing her nails to the tune of Jimmy Lunceford's "Uptown Blues."

"I love your records, darling. Who'd believe that blues could be so sexy? I always thought they were supposed to be depressing. You know, somebody crying about losing their lover. That's the only thing worse than death that I can think of."

Melissa laughed and hugged her friend. One couldn't remain dejected around Ilona—she didn't allow it. "Adam will be over at seven."

Ilona beamed. "Want me to take in a movie?"

Melissa cast a dark glance in Ilona's direction and started up the stairs. "Thanks, but no thanks. I'm wearing an avocado green silk sheath an inch above the knee. Can you handle that?"

"Of course, darling. Mine's red, four inches above, but don't worry—I don't have your height or your legs."

Adam arrived at Melissa's home promptly at seven. He'd brought Wayne along as company for Ilona, and they'd dressed in dark business suits.

"What's she like?" Wayne had asked about Ilona.

Adam had replied, "You can't describe Ilona—she has to be experienced. But not to worry, she'll be good company."

He rang the bell and waited, wondering what kind of curve he'd get from Melissa after his audacious taunt and thinly veiled promise of earlier in the day.

My God, he told himself when she opened the door, she can still take my breath away. The ball is in my court, she seemed to say when she stepped up to him, ran her arms up his chest, grasped the back of his head, and kissed him.

"Hi. You're right on time."

"Hi." He looked down at her feet, getting a grip on his senses after her surprise assault. "You're very tall tonight. How high are those heels?"

"Three inches. Gives me an advantage, doesn't it?"

"Depends. I thought Wayne would like to meet Ilona." Melissa looked over Adam's shoulder at his brother.

"Oops. I didn't see you. Come in."

Adam watched Wayne kiss Melissa on the cheek and sup-

pressed a flicker of annoyance. He had no need for jealousy
and wanted to kick himself for feeling it. They walked into
the living room, and Ilona stood as they entered. Adam enjoyed
the smile that lit her countenance: here was a female who took
pride in her womanhood. He introduced her to his brother.

"Now I know I'm moving down here," she joshed.

Adam suggested a restaurant in Baltimore. "Want to drive,
Wayne?"

Wayne laughed. "Do I have a choice?" He nudged Ilona.
"They want to make out in the backseat. What do you think?"

She grasped his arm. "Wayne, darling, never get in the way
of lovers. It's not sporting."

Adam positioned himself in the right corner of the backseat,
knotted his fingers through Melissa's and urged her closer.
"This car is bigger than the Jaguar," he said of Wayne's car.
"You've put three feet of space between us. What's the matter?
Scared you'll have to back up that greeting you gave me this
evening?" He urged her all the way into his arms and held
her close.

"I'm on to you, sweetheart. You're full of pranks when I'm
not around and you can get away with them." He let a finger
trail from her cheek down to the cleavage that her dress exposed.

"How sassy do you feel right now?" he teased. She didn't
answer, but to his surprise urged his face down to hers with
the tips of her fingers and parted her lips. Caught off guard,
he had to do battle with the unsteadiness that he knew she
sensed in him as his blood coursed wildly through his body.
Her lips moved beneath his, seeking, demanding that he lose
his self-control and, however fleetingly, belong to someone
other than himself. With effort, he eased the kiss and moved
her away from him.

"Are you staking a claim?" he whispered, trying to come to

terms with the depths to which she had embedded herself in him.

Her calm response that she didn't know what he meant didn't fool him. She trembled against the arm that he slung around her shoulder, and he wondered for the nth time if his uncle's fate would be his own.

Melissa watched Ilona slip off her gold earrings, unfasten their matching bracelet, lay them in her jewelry box and lock it. She didn't take chances. Melissa wondered what role chance had played in her relationship with Adam. Had Ilona not chosen that weekend to visit, and if she hadn't admonished her to be more assertive with Adam, would she know that her kiss alone could make him tremble?

"You should have sent me to the movies," Ilona said as if aware that Melissa's thoughts rested on Adam.

"Didn't you have a good time?"

"What a question! Darling, if a vooman couldn't enjoy herself in the company of those two men, she should see a psychiatrist. You can get Adam, if you don't make any mistakes with him. But that's easier said than done. He's a tough one."

Melissa bade Ilona good night and went to her own room. She moved about absentmindedly, her thoughts on Adam's reaction each time she'd kissed him without warning. She undressed and slipped into bed. Ilona's words bruised her mind: "He's a tough one." Yes, Melissa mused, he is that. He had been hers when she'd kissed him unexpectedly, but only for moments before he reasserted his self-control. He'd kissed her good night at her door, looked at her solemnly, and had spoken in an unmistakably serious voice.

"I assume Cooper has already left for Texas. If he hasn't, give him a reason to do that." Then he'd walked off without waiting for her answer. "He doesn't like the word 'no'," Jason Court had once said. Well, she thought, frustrated at his continued refusal to declare himself though he could tell her to cut ties with another man, he's going to hear it if he doesn't take the same chance on me that he's demanding I take with him.

Adam read his private investigator's report a second time. Nothing in Melissa's behavior the previous Friday night nor when they spoke during the weekend had prepared him for what his eyes saw. He rose from his chair, paused and sat down, not trusting himself to enter her office. He picked up his private phone and dialed her number.

"Melissa, what have you done?"

"I don't know what you mean."

"Yes, you do." His breathless tone betrayed his emotions, and he paused in an effort to control his voice. "You've risked everything in order to protect me from personal damage, threats, and accusations that I didn't even know about. Why did you do it, Melissa. I have to know." His breath trapped in his throat while he awaited her answer.

"How did you find out?"

"Nothing remains a secret for long in this town—you know that. Why did you do it?"

"I didn't have a choice, Adam. I acted in the interest of decency. There've been too many lies, too much misunderstanding and suffering because of this feud, and I won't contribute to it. I want it laid to rest." Her disappointing words hurt him.

"You're asking me to believe you risked relationships with your family, everything you've worked for, your business for such an impersonal reason? Tell me the truth, Melissa. You've lain in my arms and told me you love me. Can't you trust me enough to level with me now? The truth, Melissa. I need to hear it."

"And my needs, Adam. Does it matter what I need?" He pushed back his chair when he detected a hint of tears in her voice, hung up, and raced down the hall and up the stairs. He strode past her secretary, opened her door, and closed it behind him. She sat with elbows on her desk, holding her bowed face in her hands. Without breaking his stride, he knelt beside her chair and cradled her in his arms.

"I care for you. I feel for you what I've never felt for anyone else, but I can't name it."

Her arms tightened around him, and as though exhausted by a traumatic experience she rasped out the words: "I couldn't let him destroy you. I couldn't let anybody do that."

He hooked his foot under the platform of her chair, dragged it away from the desk, and sat with her in his lap. His heart swelled and his breath quickened. How had he ever doubted that he could trust her? She would give up everything for him.

"I care," he repeated, stroking her back, tangling his fingers in her dense curls, and spreading soft kisses over her face. "I care, sweetheart." Love and contentment flowed through him and with eyes closed, he rocked her, cherished her. For the first time in his adult life, he knew total vulnerability to a woman and, at the moment, he didn't care.

Later that evening Melissa sat in her living room addressing Christmas cards, a chore that she always tried to finish by the fifth of the month. Her house seemed empty without Ilona. She reflected on her friend's philosophy that a great love made the pangs of birth and death worth experiencing. Ilona had known such a love with her husband, but had lost him to Hungary's political madness of the time and had since refused to settle for less. She flipped through the stack of cards looking for one suitable for Bill Henry. She couldn't understand her affection for the man, having spoken with him only three times, but she suspected that his love for her mother and hers for Adam bound them. She found one, addressed it, and put away her writing.

She tried to control the happiness she felt, to subdue it so that if Adam walked out of her life, she wouldn't have a painful letdown. Adam hadn't committed himself, but she'd felt his love, sensed the change in him, and had known that he cher-

ished her. She knew their differences wouldn't be resolved until Adam had satisfied himself that the person sabotaging his
factory had been apprehended. But she had hope now that he'd
give them a chance.

She crawled into bed, turned out the light, and the telephone
rang.

"Hello."

"I called to tell you good night. Sleep well."

"Adam," she mumbled. "Good night, honey." He hung up,
and she fell asleep and dreamed that he kissed her in a field
of early spring lavender.

Around noon the next day Adam lifted the receiver, swung
his alligator-shod size twelves up on his desk, crossed them at
the ankle, and cleared his throat. "Are you sure?" he asked
Wayne.

"The announcement didn't come by mail, but by Federal Express. Emily Grant wants the world to know that she and Rafer
Grant now live under separate roofs and that she has filed for
a divorce. What do you think we should do with this?"

He didn't hesitate. "Print it."

Adam welcomed Wayne's presence at dinner that evening,
grateful that he'd driven in from Baltimore to ease the strain.
Both expected their mother to explode with rage at Wayne's
decision to print the announcement in the family paper.

"What else is going on behind my back," she asked them,
then turned to Adam. "Doesn't this have something to do with
you and Melissa Grant? The whole community talks of nothing
but the two of you."

"Mother, I'm sure I don't have to remind you that the community's reaction to my friendship with Melissa doesn't concern me. Besides, this had nothing to do with her."

"Of course it does," she stormed.

"Hear me out, Mother. It seems that Timothy Coston was
shot, and Rafer has decided that only a Hayes or a Roundtree

would have done it. He gave me the credit. But I haven't seen a newspaper account of it. It hasn't been reported to the police, and I can't get any details. I didn't do it, but he intends to indict me. I expect he hopes such a suit will distract attention from his wife's divorce suit."

Mary Roundtree's lips quivered in anger. "If he dares to charge you, I'll keep him in court until he doesn't have a cent. I don't suppose I have to remind you of my advice that Melissa Grant is poison. Now that you've found out for yourself, I hope you'll leave her alone. When we finish with them, they'll know who we are."

Adam left the table and walked from one end of the dining room to the other in a move that Wayne and his mother recognized as one intended to cool his temper. Oblivious to their silence, he paced the floor, embattled with an inner turbulence not unlike the Atlantic in the clutch of an angry storm. He stopped at the head of the table, the place vacant since his father's death, and took a seat. He was head of the family, and it was time his mother accorded him that respect.

He looked into his mother's eyes. "Melissa Grant risked her relationship with her family, her clients, and her business to stand up for me and deny that I had any part in the deeds with which Rafer wants to charge me. If any of you thinks that I won't stand up for her, you don't know me."

"But what if she's engineered that situation at Leather and Hides and went to your defense as a ruse to cover it up," Mary asked.

He leaned forward. "Mother, that woman loves me as surely as any woman ever loved a man. I told you once that I didn't want to hear another word against her, and I don't. She's important to me. I will make my move after I find out who is trashing Leather and Hides."

"Emily is behind this," he heard his mother say. "She's still chasing B-H after all these years."

"Emily Grant is a respectable woman. She may have thought of B-H for the past thirty years, but she hasn't chased him."

"How do you know her well enough to defend her?" Wayne asked.

Adam sipped the last of his cold coffee and stood. "Mrs. Grant has volunteered four hours each day, five days a week, at The Refuge for the last month and a half. That's how I know her." He excused himself, put his leather jacket over his sweater, threw a long cashmere scarf around his neck, and set out for Bill Henry's house.

"What brings you here tonight, Adam?" B-H relaxed in his rocker and inhaled deeply. Adam had long enjoyed his uncle's habit of roasting sweet potatoes and peanuts in the hearth while he sat before the blazing flames.

"I take it you haven't spoken with Wayne today," he said, preparing him for the conversation's potentially explosive nature.

"Can't say that I have. What's up?"

Adam looked directly into Bill Henry's eyes. "Emily Grant and Rafer have separated, and she's officially announced that she has filed for divorce." Something akin to pain settled around Adam's heart when his uncle jerked forward as though blown to the position by a cannon.

"Don't lie to me, Adam."

"You still want her?" His uncle looked steadily at him, not blinking an eye until his expression assumed a far-off, lost look.

"Oh, yes. I want her. I doubt that even death could put an end to it. Just let me know when the decree is final. There isn't a Grant or a Roundtree alive whom I'll allow to get in my way this time, and that includes Emily." Adam sought to lower his uncle's expectations.

"You think she'd still—"

Bill Henry interrupted. "I don't think. I know. At times I've actually felt sorry for poor Rafer. A morsel of bread is worse than having none at all. Emily Morris loves me—she has never loved anyone else, and she never will."

Adam shook his head in wonder. "All these years. It must have been difficult for you."

Bill Henry picked up the poker, knocked a few peanuts away from the coals, and fanned them. "It hasn't been easy, Adam—but I had solace in the knowledge that she loved me, that no matter what appearances might suggest, it was me that she loved."

"You're sure of yourself." Adam stroked his chin with his right thumb and index finger.

"And if you want Melissa, you should be, too. You'd better bind her to you. She's a fine woman, and I'd hate to see you lose her." Adam didn't ask B-H why he was so certain he wanted Melissa, because he wouldn't discuss her with anyone, not even his beloved uncle.

He held out his hand for the peanuts he knew his uncle had pushed aside to cool for him and which he'd nibble on the way home.

"I'll let you know when the decree is final, B-H, and I hope things work out for you."

"Thanks."

Adam forgot the nuts as he walked home in the pitch darkness. His thoughts centered on his uncle and Emily Morris. A love that strong could bring a man to his knees, even flat on his face. Could he withstand what B-H had gone through if Melissa sided with her family, or worse, if she turned her back when he told her what he knew he had to reveal—a secret he'd kept from her far too long. His steps slowed, and unfamiliar tentacles of alarm made him shiver: suppose he couldn't get along without her. Then what?

At noon the next day Wayne walked into Adam's office and handed him a copy of *The Maryland Journal*, the family newspaper. The society columnist's phone had rung constantly that morning, he told Adam, and Rafer had called disclaiming the pending divorce and threatening suit. He sat down and faced Adam, his demeanor more solemn than was normally his bent.

"Adam, do you think it's possible that your affair with Melissa might have opened Pandora's box?"

Hot anger lit Adam's eyes, and his quelling look wasn't one that his brother had witnessed before. His lips thinned as he spoke with frosty softness. "I am not having an affair with Melissa, but if I were, it would be my business and hers and not a matter for discussion."

Wayne's careless shrug didn't mislead Adam. He sensed his brother's worry and annoyance at the turn of events, as he watched him hunch his shoulders and walk out of the office. Adam leaned heavily back in his chair, himself displeased. He had never spoken so sharply to his brother, and he feared it was only the beginning. What would his passion for Melissa cost him?

Adam remained in his office until six thirty that evening in order to have the privacy he needed. Never before had the folly of mixing business with pleasure been clearer. He had to choose between two things dear to him: his family's best interest and his relationship with Melissa. He thought of her warmth, the way she molded herself to him whenever he put his arms around her. Hell! He lifted the receiver and dialed her office number.

"Hello."

"What are you doing here so late?" he asked. And before she could answer, he whispered, "I'd like to see you, Melissa. Tonight. Now. Will you have dinner with me?"

Her immediate reply warmed his heart. "Could we go to that little place where we went that first time?"

"Yes. I'll pick you up in a couple of minutes." When he reached her office, he found her standing outside the locked door. For the last few hours he'd thought of nothing but the feel of her warm and soft in his arms, sweet and loving. Easing the torment he felt over that angry exchange with his brother, and calming his apprehension about their relationship. He'd needed to hold her.

"What's this?" he asked, his frustration barely suppressed.

"I was going to meet you." She stood on tiptoe for his kiss. He kept it light—he had to, or they'd be a spectacle for whoever passed them.

He drove past the Taney house on South Benz Street, and Melissa seemed to spit in its direction, mystifying him.

"It's a small pleasure I allow myself whenever I pass here," she explained. "Now that we have school integration, I wonder whether our children still learn that, as chief justice of the Supreme Court, old Taney in the Dred Scott Case of 1857 upheld the tenet that slaves and their descendants were not citizens of this country and couldn't sue in Federal courts, and that congress couldn't forbid slavery in the United States or its territories. I refuse to forgive even his memory. Pursing my lips as if to spit at the place isn't very ladylike, but it's oh so satisfying."

A deep chuckle rose in Adam's throat. "The lady's a bag of surprises. I never know what to expect of you." He glanced over at her after pulling into the interstate. "You're like a brilliant comet shooting through a bunch of ordinary stars." He had the pleasure of seeing her settle down in the soft leather seat, fold her arms in contentment, and smile as though she possessed the secrets of the ages. Maybe she did, he mused, as she rested her head against his shoulder—she certainly had the key to his closet.

At the little restaurant they got seats at a small table in the rear, away from a group of happy revelers.

"What's so amusing?" he asked as the waiter approached.

"This red tablecloth clashes with my fuchsia suit, don't you think?"

"Do you really think I'm looking at this tablecloth?"

"Oh!" Crimson tainted her cheeks, and he observed her more closely when she ducked her head.

"You seem a bit down tonight. Anything wrong?" The shake

of her head denied it, but he soon realized that she'd been waiting for the chance to share her concerns.

"We both knew way back when . . . when this started that if we got close there'd be turmoil in our families. I barely have one left. Earlier today my father begged me not to continue seeing you, to testify in support of my cousin, and to dissuade my mother from getting a divorce. Adam, I can't do any of those things. I can't give up my integrity, and I don't know how he can ask me to. All my life, he drummed into my head how important it is to be faithful to the truth and to myself, that I should never compromise on those things. Do you think he's sick?"

He stroked the back of the hand she rested on the table. "No. But I think Hayes-Roundtree may be his Achilles' heel."

"It isn't his feud, and I told him so."

"Maybe not, but it's the excuse he uses. The thought of Bill Henry makes him feel like a whipped dog, and he didn't do anything to deserve getting the short end." Adam didn't think it a matter for grinning, but when she squinted at him, he couldn't avoid it.

"He isn't guiltless, Adam. Daddy went into that marriage knowing that Mama didn't love him." Adam stared at her in surprise.

"Oh, I was blind about their relationship," she said, "but since I've been back home, I view a lot of things differently. I hate to see him so desperate, though. He told me I'd be sorry for standing against him, but if I regret anything, it will be my loss of faith in him."

Adam seized the opportunity to press his point. "If you're standing against him for me, you're pretty quiet about it, because you still haven't told me what you know."

"We've already had this discussion, Adam. I want you to succeed, and soon. But you have to find out on your own. When you do, I won't deny the truth."

She couldn't be different, and that suited him. He'd met too many women and men who didn't have a conscience and who had a price. She knew that he was scrutinizing her right then, but she sat unruffled, letting a smile play around her lips so he'd know she didn't mind that he looked at her. He wanted to take her to his lodge, away from everybody and every unsolved problem, to lose himself in her. He needed her to bind the wounds he'd inflicted on himself when he blew up at Wayne. But he'd never run from anything, and he'd never used another person. As long as his thoughts were only of himself, and he had no right to touch Melissa.

A full moon lit their way back to Frederick. Tall, leafless trees cast eerie shadows across the highway as they sped through the night. And Adam's thoughts drifted to the night he'd first kissed Melissa and how he'd spent the rest of it, sleepless, preaching to himself that nothing but disaster could come from a romantic involvement with her. But he'd paid no attention to his common sense, and the damage lay all around them. Quickly he threw out his right hand to protect Melissa as he slowed down abruptly and swerved to avoid a doe. He noticed how she tensed, and at the next rest stop he parked, walked around to her door, and gave her a hand getting out of the car. He held her loosely, stroking her back, but keeping her far enough away to make sure he didn't succumb to his feelings.

"I'm sorry I frightened you back there, but I didn't want to hit that deer."

"I'm alright. I realized you knew what you were doing."

He urged her closer. "I wish I did. Ah, Melissa, I wish I knew where we're headed." They got back in the car.

"Moral of the story is don't speed," she teased.

"Or leave woolgathering to sheep shearers," he added with a chuckle. "It's early yet. Let's stop by the Watering Hole for a few minutes." They remained there for about an hour, watching the strange night pairings, the loners, and those afraid to be alone.

"This scene is wearing on me. Are you ready to leave?"

She nodded and drained her wineglass. He held her hand as they walked out, leaving their audience gaping. He felt good, and her comment that they had just made Miss Mary's Wednesday night prayer meeting a success brought a chuckle from him. They walked arm in arm in the brilliant moonlight to his parked car. Adam stood at the passenger's door, looking at her, wanting and needing a resolution of their relationship. A pain of longing shot through him, and he bent down to kiss her. She welcomed him lovingly, her embrace strong and her lips open for the thrust of his tongue. He gave in to his feelings and admitted to himself the joy he felt when she molded herself to him and clasped him to her.

A niggling thought that he'd had early in their relationship began to plague him again, telling him to walk away while he could, to remember his vow never to let another woman control him, to let her go before she reined him in and had him at her mercy. The words "I can't" exploded from him, and Melissa stared at him.

"Can't what?"

"Shhhhh," he whispered. "Just let me hold you." He hadn't ever asked her for tenderness, though he'd been tender with her. He felt her discipline her own want and, instead, let him take what he needed from her as she reached up to receive the kiss that tenderly possessed them both. He raised his head to break it off and looked beyond Melissa and into the eyes of Louise Grant Coston, Rafer Grant's sister. He held Melissa away from him, and as though ice suddenly flowed through his veins, he stared at the woman he'd detested for more than half of his life.

Thirteen

The following Sunday morning, Emily fell into step beside Melissa as they left church service. They had both dressed warmly for protection against the biting winter wind, and Melissa smiled inwardly when her mother tugged the luxurious fur more tightly around herself. She was learning that her mother loved beautiful things.

"I've never enjoyed walking so much as now," her mother told her as she hunched her shoulders against the cold. "I can almost appreciate this coat. Rafer always insisted on driving, and you know how he hated for me to go anywhere by myself." Melissa looked at the woman beside her. Her face and figure seemed to have lost years in a few short weeks, and her whole being seemed to proclaim the sweetness of life. Her rich brown skin glowed, and her eyes sparkled.

"You are more beautiful every time I see you, Mama. It's the most amazing thing."

"Well, I don't know about that, honey," Emily demurred, "but if it's true, it isn't that I'm happy—maybe it's because for the first time in years, I'm free to do as I please." She glanced down a narrow side street that jutted off Court. "I haven't tasted a cloud nine in over thirty years. They used to serve them in the Watering Hole. Let's stop there." She took Melissa's arm and steered her toward the popular bar. "When I was young, this is where we hung out. But the Banks family bought the place, changed the policy, and the older crowd took over. I don't know where the young people go these days."

"Mama, are you sure you want to go to the Watering Hole right out of church? It'll be crowded. And what's a cloud nine, anyhow?" Her mother's laughter heightened Melissa's spirits.

"In my day, every young person knew what that was. A cheap champagne cocktail. A cube of ice, a jigger of cheap champagne, and ginger ale to the top." Melissa's grimace brought another laugh from Emily. "Honey, sophistication is a matter of definition. Sojourner Truth or Phillis Wheatley would probably have been shocked at such carrying-on, but what they did stuns me." They talked amicably until they reached the local gathering place. Melissa knew that her mother couldn't even contemplate the reaction that her presence in that place would generate. A hush and gaping stares greeted their entrance, but to Melissa's astonishment her mother ignored it and strolled confidently to a vacant table.

She watched her mother sip the harmless drink with relish but contented herself with coffee, though she hated the chicory with which southerners delighted in ruining its taste. She glanced around when her mother nudged her and asked, "Isn't that Timmy sitting over there staring at us?" Melissa suppressed a catch of breath, nearly choking herself—she'd never known anyone to look at her with such distaste.

"He looks as if he'd like to murder me," Melissa said. "But why? I haven't done anything to him."

"I know Timmy's a coward, and I know his mind has never been infected with common sense, but he isn't that crazy," Emily assured her. "I never could figure him out. I was mother to him for almost a year, and you watch. He won't even walk over here and ask me how I am." She drained her glass. "A long-stemmed glass should be handled with white gloves." Emily strolled over to Timothy.

"I haven't seen you in ages, Timmy, not since I heard you'd had an accident. Are you alright now?" Emily asked him.

Melissa remembered that her mother had always been able to coax him into being gracious.

"I'm fine," he said grudgingly.

"Good," Emily said, patting him on the shoulder. "You come see me sometime, now. You hear?" A scowl marred his face as he looked up at her.

"Aren't you lost, aunt Emily?" Melissa marveled at the new Emily Grant, who favored Timothy with a dazzling smile, and informed him, "Not anymore, son. *Not anymore!*"

Melissa smiled at the devilish twinkle in her mother's eyes and turned to leave. "Mama," she said, pronouncing the word distinctly, "you're having fun at everybody's expense. Come on, let's go." Melissa paid, and they left with even more attention than they'd gotten when they walked in. They soon knew why. Rafer Grant had entered the bar in the meantime and seated himself near the door. He attempted to intercept his estranged wife.

"Don't make a spectacle of yourself, Rafer," Emily admonished with apparent disdain for his status as one of the town's leading attorneys. "If you want to talk, come on outside. We don't have to be the sole source of town news. You go on home, Melissa; I'll call you." Melissa nodded to her parents, feeling oddly alienated from them both, and walked on home.

"You either drop these ridiculous proceedings, or I'll make certain that Melissa and Adam Roundtree won't want any part of each other. The state of Maryland isn't as big as the space they'll want between them."

"You wouldn't do that to your own daughter," she gasped.

"You go ahead with that divorce, and you'll see. That man has been nothing but trouble to us."

"I love my daughter, Rafer, just as you should, but if the feeling she and Adam have for each other won't withstand whatever it is you plan to tell one of them, then I'm sorry. I only have one life, and I've wasted too much of it already.

I'm going to try and live the rest of it on my own terms. Do what you like."

"You asked for it." He left her standing there, bemused, wondering what he knew. Rafer was too much the attorney to engage in idle threats.

Snow banked high around her house prevented Melissa from opening her kitchen door Monday morning, so she eased up the window and threw seed out to the birds. She tested the phone line, found it operating, and relaxed. She knew she couldn't get to her office through that heavy snow, but she didn't mind working at home so long as she had access to her on-line services. She dressed in jeans and a sweatshirt and sat down to her computer just as her phone rang. Her father didn't waste time on small talk, but went right to the reason for his call.

"I thought you ought to know that you aren't the first woman in this family to have an affair with Adam Roundtree."

Melissa sucked in her breath. If her father heard her, he ignored it. "Your aunt Louise tells me she had an affair with him years ago. I guess he just can't resist Grant women." When she didn't respond, he needled her. "What have you got to say to that, young lady?"

"I don't believe you."

"Really?" he snorted. "Then ask him."

Melissa wrapped her arms around herself and paced from one end of her den to the other. Twice she started toward the stairs leading down to the second floor and twice she remembered that she probably couldn't open her front door. She had to talk with Adam, to know if her father's story had any truth, but she wanted to be with him when she asked him about it. Right then, she needed the reassurance of his arms around her, holding her. She didn't know what she'd do if he admitted having had an affair with her aunt, a woman known among the local people for her beauty and her feminine figure. Beauty that she had envied as a young girl.

She whiled away most of the day, unable to focus on her work, almost uninterested in it. When she could stand it no longer, she telephoned Adam at home in Beaver Ridge only to have Mary Roundtree tell her that Adam went to his office on weekdays, snow or no snow.

"How did you get to the office?" Melissa asked Adam as though hers was a casual call. "I don't think I can open my front door."

"Hi," he chided for her failure to greet him. "If you can't get out of the house, I'll come over and dig you out. I hitched a snowplow to my dad's old Chevy truck and got in here with no difficulty. I'll be over there in about an hour."

Melissa changed into an off-white denim jump suit and prowled aimlessly about the house until she glimpsed Adam digging his way to her front door. Four or five inches of snow wasn't much in New York, but it stilled the town of Frederick. She watched him for a minute, dropped the curtain, and went to the kitchen to make coffee. She could at least be hospitable, she told herself, if he cleaned her walkway and steps. And any way, a man was innocent until proved guilty. Wasn't that the American way? She resisted the temptation to serve the coffee in porcelain cups, laid two paper napkins on the table, and set two mugs on them. She rubbed her hands together, caught herself doing it, and dropped them to her side. Then she rubbed her thighs. When he finally rang the doorbell, she walked to the door on wooden legs.

"Hi. What took you so long to get here?" He stepped in, pulled off his gloves, and took her into his arms for a kiss. He must have sensed her resistance, for he leaned back and looked into her face.

"What's this? You don't want me to kiss you? After digging out there in the cold for the last half hour, I deserve some warmth, don't I?" His arms tightened around her, but she turned her head.

She knew that she'd gone about it all wrong, but she couldn't help her feelings, and she wouldn't pretend. His reaction did not surprise her. She sensed at once the psychological distance he put between them, knew that if he proclaimed innocence she trod on dangerous ground. But she had to hear him say it.

"Would you like some coffee?"

He looked her straight in the eye, the twinkle that she loved devoid of warmth. "You don't feel like offering hospitality, and I don't want any. Why did you call me?"

She locked her hands behind her to still her fingers. "Let's go in the living room."

"I'm fine right here." He leaned against the front door and folded his arms. "Say whatever you've got to say, Melissa. I'm going back to work."

She took a deep breath and slowly expelled it. "My father is accusing you of having had an affair with my aunt Louise. I told him I didn't believe it." She glanced up hopefully, but received neither confirmation nor denial from his hard, unfathomable stare.

"What's the question? I see you've already made up your mind."

"I told you that I denied it to him."

"But not to yourself." He straightened up, walked a few paces away from her, and walked back. "I refuse to defend myself, Melissa. I realize that I should have told you about this months ago, before we got so deeply involved, but I anticipated that you'd react this way, and couldn't bring myself to mention it." He stopped pacing, shrugged with an air of indifference, and stared at her when she brought her hand to her chest as though to regulate her heart.

"If you're interested in the truth," he went on, "I was fifteen years old, and your thirty-year-old aunt seduced me deliberately and vengefully. And she made it very pleasant," he told her in a voice hard with bitterness. "I didn't know what had hit me. She built my ego to the heavens to make certain that I'd go back to her and I—a boy with no previous experience—

went back for more. I can still hear her laughing at me. Is that what you wanted to know?"

She turned her back and knew, when he walked around to face her, that he intended to have his say. Only she didn't want to hear another word. *Adam had slept with her aunt.*

"How could you? How could you?"

"Weren't you listening? Don't you know that a fifteen-year-old boy who hasn't had any experience is no match for a thirty-year-old woman? Especially one like Louise Grant. She flaunted her sexuality, and she had plenty to show off. It wasn't until long afterward that I realized she'd done it for the pleasure of belittling me—a member of the Hayes-Roundtree family. I hated her, and I still despise her. I wanted vengeance against her and her whole family, and I got some a year later when I didn't tell Rafer that I'd seen his briefcase with his court papers in the men's room at the Harlem Restaurant."

Pain seemed to squeeze her heart, and she put both hands to her ears and shook her head, denying what she knew to be the truth. "And was that the end of it?"

He glared at her. "Weren't you listening, or aren't you interested in the truth?"

She turned her back. The old jealously of her sensuously beautiful aunt—who had once suggested that she, Melissa, was the family's ugly duckling—returned nearly to suffocate her. Louise had had everything that she as a gangling teenager had lacked; she had even been Adam's first woman. She knew her reaction was unreasonable, but she couldn't help it.

"I want you to leave, Adam."

"Are you saying you hold me responsible for something that happened when I was fifteen years old? For your own aunt's criminal act of child molestation?" he asked, clearly incredulous. She looked up at him, tall and proud, lacking even a semblance of warmth toward her.

"Adam, please, just—"

"I'll leave when I've had my say. You know you're wrong, but you're looking for an excuse to get back into your father's good graces. If you don't care enough to see through his scheme, I'm glad he told you. You could overlook my deliberate act of vengeance a year after your aunt seduced me, when I was sixteen and more responsible. You could ignore an act that ruined your father's political career, but you haven't the heart to understand that a boy is most any woman's easy victim." The fierceness, the coolness of his gaze made her heartbeat accelerate, and she suddenly hurt so badly that she knew she wasn't ready for him to walk out of her life. But she refused to absolve him.

"You said you went back to her, that you wanted it to continue. You should have told me before . . . you should have let me choose whether to— You don't know what she was like when I was a 'plain jane' teenager. My own aunt. Beautiful. Voluptuous. All of my dates talked about her, boasted about her. And now you tell me this."

He reached for the doorknob. "This is all my mistake. I wish you well, Melissa."

She gazed up at him as he moved to open the door, apprehension thundering like wild horses in her head. She backed away from the door, disbelieving that he would leave without another word, that he'd walk out of there as though she no longer existed.

"Is that all you have to say?" she mumbled. He stepped toward her and tipped up her chin with the tip of his right index finger, as though to be certain that she understood.

"What else do you want me to say? You don't believe in me." He opened the door and left.

Adam drove the truck into the garage adjacent to his family's home, parked, and sat there. During the drive from Frederick, he hadn't let himself think over what had just happened. How long had Rafer known about him and Louise and why— Louise's glacierlike look a few nights earlier as he'd bent to kiss Melissa flashed through his mind's eye. So she was going for the kill. She'd tried repeatedly and without success since he'd been an adult to get at him, to coax him into an affair, and he'd tired of her shenanigans and told her that she didn't measure up to the women he'd known as a man. He knew she hated him, but he hadn't dreamed that she wanted revenge badly enough to reveal her own indiscretion.

He got out of the car and paced around it in an effort to walk off some of the anger building in him. He'd been willing to sacrifice more for their relationship than Melissa could imagine. Even face down his mother. But Melissa hadn't believed in him. He stopped himself just as his right fist drove toward the truck's windshield. Her rejection had hurt him. He got a shovel and walked around to clean the snow from the steps of the combination sundeck and greenhouse that his father had built on to the exterior of the dining room wall. But he felt no better after the vigorous exercise. Up in his room he locked the door, fell across his bed, and began planning for his move back to New York.

Melissa stopped by her mother's house the next morning on her way to work. She'd never done that before, and her mother would guess that something was troubling her, something unpleasant. Emily waved a hand when Melissa tried to talk in a voice muffled with tears.

"I know. I know. He told me Sunday morning that when he'd finished, the two of you wouldn't be speaking. I tried to warn you, but you didn't answer your phone. Your father won't stand by docilely and let Adam have you. He's wrong, but I know the pain and humiliation he feels where that family is concerned. The feud is a screen—that was never his battle. Knowing that his wife would always love another man ate him up inside. Melissa, his hatred of the Hayeses and Roundtrees has had thirty-one years to harden and fester. Tell me what he did."

"Melissa recounted it, and encouraged by her mother's stunned expression, she went on.

"Adam was taken with her. He said so himself."

"When did it happen?"

"When he was in his early teens. Oh, it doesn't matter." The tears that pooled in her eyes failed to fall, so startled was she when her mother grabbed her shoulders and shook her.

"My God. It *does* matter. Louise is fifteen or sixteen years older than Adam. You mean to tell me you've fallen into the same kind of trap that I did? You've put family above your love. You made up your mind to believe Rafer and Louise before you heard what Adam had to say. Don't you know about Louise's reputation when she was younger? How could you be so foolish?"

Melissa opened her mouth, closed it, and repeated the action, amazed at her mother's harshness.

"Adam won't dance to your tune," Emily told her. "And he won't swear off of women the way Bill Henry did. He'll go on with his life, and you'll be an unpleasant memory. I never could understand why you allowed Rafer to worm himself and his influence into everything you did. I was glad when you left town, even if I didn't see my own role in it."

"I only wanted his approval. I wanted him to feel the same way about me that he did about Schyler."

Emily reached up and put an arm around her daughter. "And he knew that and used it as a weapon to bend you to his will. Now that it doesn't work, he first tried strong-arming you and then blackmailing me. We both defied him, so he took revenge. But he couldn't have done it without your help, Melissa. Oh, yes. You helped him. I thought you loved Adam. Didn't you learn anything from my life?"

"I don't know why I stopped by here this morning. I just couldn't seem to go anywhere else. I think I've upset you, and I'm sorry, Mama."

Emily Grant shook her head as though in wonder. "Honey, you came to me because I'm your mother. But you didn't learn anything from my stupidity. Well, maybe you'll learn something from this: if Bill Henry will have me, I'm his. As soon as my divorce is final, I'm going to him, get down on my knees, and beg his forgiveness. Beg him to let me live my last years with him, married or not. I don't care. And I couldn't care less about the gossip mongers of Frederick and Beaver Ridge. I need him. I just want to go to sleep and wake up in the same bed with him."

Melissa's eyebrows shot up, and she stared in mute astonishment at her mother. Appalled. Was this what she had done to herself in letting Adam go? Why hadn't she listened to her heart? She found words, but it wasn't easy.

"Mama, how can you feel this way about him after all this time? It's been thirty-one years." She watched the tears gather in her mother's eyes.

"Thirty-one? It seems to me like thirty-one hundred."

Melissa hadn't expected to accomplish much work that morning, and she didn't. The pain of knowing she'd lost Adam was almost more than she could tolerate. Why, she wondered, had Magnus Cooper chosen that morning to call? She hadn't been able to summon either her normal professional demeanor nor to act her naturally cool self. Just when she'd feared her ability to continue the conversation, he'd asked her about her relationship with Adam, and she hadn't been able to lie.

"Any chance you'll give him the boot if he shows up?" Magnus asked her with a nonchalance that she realized was clearly forced. She thought of her mother and B-H.

"Not as long as cats scratch."

"What?"

"There's not much likelihood of that," she amended.

"Then I hope you've got sense enough to go to him. It's been my experience that pride isn't good company, Melissa. And it sure won't keep you warm. Roundtree impressed me as being a fair man. If he's responsible for your misunderstanding, he'll come to you. But if you're the one who messed up, honey, he won't budge. Invite me to the big event, and I'll send your first kid a thoroughbred pony."

Melissa hadn't needed Magnus's lecture. She was in the wrong, and she knew that Adam wouldn't come to her. He'd said his last word on the subject. She wanted to go to him, wanted him back in her life and in her arms, but he'd never given her a reason to think he wanted her to be a permanent fixture in his life. Twice she'd told him she loved him, and he hadn't yet said he loved her. Only that he cared. She knew he cared, otherwise she'd have to conclude that he had a streak of promiscuity.

Melissa welcomed Banks when she sauntered in around a quarter of ten with two cups of coffee and her usual box of hot, powdered doughnuts.

"Here," Banks said, holding out the coffee. "This won't cure what ails you, but it'll at least warm your tongue."

"Why do you think something is the matter with me?" Melissa asked her, reaching for the paper cup and realizing simultaneously that she would have been smart not to ask.

"Is this the first time you've seen me today?" Banks asked.

"Yeah. Why?"

"You've just answered your own question. You met me once in the hallway, and you stood almost on top of me in the ladies' room. You took your comb out of your purse, looked at yourself in the mirror, put the comb back where you got it, and left the place."

A flash of annoyance gripped Melissa momentarily at having exposed her emotions without realizing it. "Why didn't you speak to *me?*" she asked Banks in what she meant as a reprimand.

"I did, but it didn't penetrate." Melissa set the cup on her desk and waited for what her friend would say next. Banks always had a punch line.

"At least you didn't bump into me without apologizing, the

way Mr. Roundtree did. I'm thinking of writing a manual on common courtesy and distributing it to some of the people in this building."

"I'm sorry, Banks. I didn't intend to be rude."

Banks sent a perfect smoke ring toward the ceiling. "I know. But you'd better get it together with Adam. The word's out that he's making plans to move back to New York, and that's strange, because a couple of days ago, he was over at Jack Pettigrew's place ordering a new desk. They sell those in New York, don't they?" Banks didn't give Melissa time to answer. Just picked up the remainder of her doughnuts, sauntered to the door, waved, and left.

Adam threw his briefcase in the back of the Jaguar, decided the engine had been warmed up sufficiently, and pulled out of the garage. A good rain that night had melted the remainder of the snow, and he figured on getting to Baltimore in thirty minutes. How could so much have happened in less than an hour? For months he'd thought of himself in relation to Melissa, and now he had to change that. He hadn't wanted to involve the FBI in the sabotage of Leather and Hides, because he hadn't wanted to risk an escalation of the antagonism between the two families. He didn't want that now, but the break in his relationship with Melissa had added urgency to his getting away from Frederick and back to New York. He had to get her out of his thoughts, and he wouldn't do that easily if he had to see her unexpectedly a half dozen times a day. He had wrestled with his feelings for her the whole night—even when he finally slept, she'd been there to mock him in his dreams. He pulled into the right lane to let a nervous driver pass, slowed down, and decided to remain there.

He'd have sworn that she loved him. She probably did, but— He took a deep breath, turned on the radio, and whistled along with a singer whose name he didn't know. When had Melissa become so important to him that he needed her trust? He'd never given a damn whether people had confidence in him. He'd never needed to—he knew he was trustworthy. He pulled up to the Federal Building, put a couple of quarters in the parking meter, and went inside. When he left an hour later, the Feds knew everything about the sabotage of the Hayes/Roundtree leather factory, and Adam had the name of an FBI contact who would serve as undercover agent at Leather and Hides. Adam marveled at the thoroughness of the man who interviewed him; he held everyone suspect who had any connection to the factory. Adam drove next to the office of the secret agent.

"Shouldn't take long," the man told Adam. "Crooks tip their hand without knowing they're doing it."

"These are slick, and they're greedy," Adam replied. "They want to bring me down. How much time will you need?"

"From what you've told me, I'd say a week at most, but probably only three or four days. One thing. No one—not even your manager—is to know about me."

"Right."

"I'll check in tomorrow."

"Check in at my home." Adam handed the agent his card. "And make it after dark. I'll be expecting you." The man read the card, dropped it in an ashtray and struck a match to it.

"By the way, who lives there with you?"

Adam looked at the man in surprise. It hadn't occurred to him that a secret agent would suspect members of his family. "My mother and, on weekends, my brother. He's managing editor of *The Maryland Journal*." The man nodded.

Adam left feeling as though the man had violated his privacy. But that didn't compare with what he'd experienced when he walked out of Melissa's house four days earlier. He still carried the sense of abuse and abandonment that he'd felt when she withheld her trust. But he vowed he'd get over that. He'd liked her a hell of a lot, but that was all, he assured himself. He was going back to New York and put her in his past.

He telephoned Emily that night and made a luncheon date with her for the following day at noon. She declined a drink.

"My ladies at The Refuge need me to have a clear head, Adam."

She didn't seem surprised when he failed to mention Melissa, and he supposed she knew that he and her daughter had broken off their relationship.

"Emily, I'm going back to New York soon, and I want you to know how much I appreciate the work you're doing at the shelter. I hope being there hasn't caused you any pain or regrets." He lifted her hand, and her delicate fingers reminded him of the times he'd held Melissa's hand while they talked, or laughed. Or fired each other with desire.

"My only regret, Adam, is that I didn't do this years ago. And my pain hasn't ceased, but it got noticeably duller the day Rafer decided he'd be more comfortable living somewhere else." She looked at him steadily, and he saw the truth in her clear, honest eyes. "If I get another chance at a pain-free life, just one more chance at a little happiness, I'll grab it and hold onto it with all my might as long as I live."

Adam took Emily back to The Refuge, where she'd switched to volunteering full time. He hugged her and realized that he had developed a deep affection for Melissa's mother. He made his way to his cubbyhole in the basement, checked his incoming box, and hurried back to his office in the Jacob Hayes Building. He'd gotten the information he wanted. His uncle had been right; Emily Morris still loved him. He was glad for B-H, but the realization that two people could care so deeply after so long a time and under such circumstances didn't console him about his feelings for Melissa.

At dinner that Friday evening, Adam told Wayne and his mother that he planned to move back to New York.

"But you can't go before we solve the problem at the factory," Wayne complained.

"I didn't say that I would, but as soon as that's settled, I'm leaving." His mother asked whether he planned to leave before Christmas.

"I'll be here for Christmas, but I'll be leaving the following morning." He knew he sounded curt and detached. Well, so be it. He had already begun to distance himself from Frederick and from Melissa. What might have been didn't interest him. And he wasn't sorry that he'd kept a tight rein on his feelings for Melissa, that he had resisted the temptation to let go and let himself love her. He might be many things, but he knew he was a survivor. You got to be that way by protecting your flank, and in this case that meant removing himself from wherever Melissa happened to be.

"What about Melissa?" Wayne dared ask.

Adam threw the remainder of his cognac to the back of his throat and stood. "That's in the past." He ignored their stunned expressions, strode to the hall closet, got his leather jacket, and headed for the little clapboard house down the road.

Adam walked up the modest steps and caught himself wondering whether he could be content to live as B-H did—a semi-recluse who rationed his ventures out among people, avoided ties with all but his family, and did as he pleased. Why the hell should I? he asked aloud, annoyed at having let himself contemplate that easy solution to his life. He heard familiar pops from the big stone fireplace in his uncle's living room as he let himself in the house.

"You roasting peanuts?" he asked by way of a greeting.

"Naaah. These here are pecans. Nothing like a hot roasted pecan." Bill Henry raked a few nuts away from the coals and put them in a wooden bowl that he'd bought in Haiti years earlier.

"Come on in. How's Mary? She didn't look so well when I saw her yesterday."

Adam sat down, stretched out his long legs, and crossed his ankles. "Mother's fine, B-H. When you saw her, she was probably practicing the technique she'd use to cut down Melissa without my riding herd on her. When she first learned about Melissa and me, she behaved as if I was a grown man, although

I knew she hated the idea. But she's gotten desperate and careless of late, and it's just as well that I'll be leaving soon."

"You're leaving Melissa here to deal with Rafer and that bunch by herself?"

"Why not? They're all cut from the same cloth; birds of a feather. It's over between Melissa and me, B-H, and I expect that within a week we'll have whoever's committing those crimes at the factory behind bars. My place is in New York running my own business." He could appreciate his uncle's stare of disbelief, because he was still unable to reconcile himself to the reality of not having Melissa in his life.

"I don't believe what I'm hearing. What happened?"

Adam rubbed the back of his neck with his left hand and tried to figure out where to begin.

"It's a pretty long story, B-H, and I'm not sure I want to tell it."

"I want to hear it." Bill Henry didn't speak until Adam finished. His uncle listened attentively, nodding occasionally and sometimes frowning. Adam remembered that Bill Henry's careful attention to his childhood dreams, stories, and complaints and his way of withholding harsh judgment were the traits that had bound the two of them for as long as he could remember. In a rare outward gesture of affection, he reached over and patted his uncle's hand.

"Adam," B-H began, as though bearing a heavy weight, "didn't you and Melissa learn anything from history? Do you think life has been so beautiful for Emily Morris and me that you'd like to walk in our tracks?" Adam didn't want to talk about Melissa and himself, yet he knew that he'd gone there to give B-H a chance to say what he thought.

"Do you love Melissa? Don't answer, if you don't want to. I know you love her."

Adam reached down for a couple of roasted pecans, cracked them together, and shook them around in his closed fist. Distracted.

"What is love, B-H? If it's the willingness to let one's entire life slide by for want of another person, I'm not in love and never will be." He sat forward at the sound of Bill Henry's soft, almost pitying laugh.

"You're a strong man, Adam, but you're not Goliath enough to rid your soul of Melissa. You've got the will to do just about anything you set your mind to. You had that trait at the tender age of five, and I've always admired your tenacity. But, son, I'm sorry to tell you that you've met your match." His disbelieving stare must have amused his uncle, for Bill Henry's lips curved into a smile that flickered across his face.

"What do you mean?" Adam asked him, disliking the turn of conversation.

"I mean love isn't something you can order around, arrange to suit yourself or just banish. It will greet you at breakfast, glare at you when you're in a business meeting, and laugh at you in the dead of night. And I'll tell you something else. What you feel for Melissa will defy you to take another woman to bed no matter how much your head tells you that's what you want. Yes, sir. You've met your match."

B-H laughed aloud, and Adam knew he'd been caught with a rueful expression on his face. "You think so, do you?" he asked.

"I know so."

"I've got to be going." He bit into the pecan, savored it, and relaxed. "Cook a few more of these. They're good. By the way, I had lunch with Emily Grant today." Bill Henry jerked forward, as though his five senses had just come alive, turned and looked into his nephew's eyes. He said nothing, and no words were needed. Adam saw in his expression the hopes of a man about to glimpse the light after years in darkness. He dropped his gaze. No man should see another's naked soul.

"Emily will be a free woman in a matter of days, and she wants to see you. She didn't call your name, but she left no doubt that seeing you was foremost in her thoughts." The two of them stood, and Adam wrapped an arm around his uncle.

"I wish you luck, B-H. If you need me, you always know where I am."

"Thanks, Adam. I can't hope yet. I won't believe this is happening until I've got her in my arms again."

Adam struggled against the wind, stronger now than when he'd left home an hour earlier. He had an urge to get Thunder and ride hell for leather until he and the stallion exhausted themselves. But he didn't dodge his problems; he faced them. And he'd face this one. He hunched his shoulders when the wind increased in velocity, and dry leaves and small sticks swirled around his feet. The bright moonlight cast his long shadow ahead of him, and as he walked faster, he swore, disliking the implication. An intelligent man did not chase his shadow.

Clouds raced over the moon, but none obscured its light, and he thought of his uncle's warning that no matter what he did, where he went, or whom he met, Melissa would always live inside of him. How could a man love a woman so deeply as B-H loved Emily Grant? Grant. Bill Henry never acknowledged her married name, he recalled, but referred to her as Emily Morris, discounting Rafer's importance in her life. And she loved Bill Henry. Her simple declaration of it had moved him, and he wondered what he'd do if Melissa loved him like that.

Melissa sat in her dining room, checking her Christmas gift list. Several times that evening, she'd walked to a telephone, lifted the receiver, dropped it back into its cradle, and walked away. She sat dispirited among the glistening papers, ribbons, and gift tags.

"I don't care about any of this," she declared, wiping her eyes. "Why did I do it? Why did I let Daddy manipulate me like that? I don't care what Adam did. I want him." She wrapped her arms across her breasts and walked the floor. Finally she went over to the window and looked up at the thin clouds that whisked past the full moon. Where was he, she wondered, and what was he doing right then? She looked back at her boxes and wrappings, went over to the table, and sat down.

"I'm not going to let this or anything else throw me," she vowed, and lifted a pair of green and gold tassels and attached them to a box intended for B-H. Her mother had remarked during a rare moment of reminiscence that Bill Henry had a fondness for blue jays, so she'd bought him a book about them and a little house said to encourage them to nest. She'd bought something for everyone on her list except Ilona and Adam. She planned to give her friend a pair of tickets to an American Ballet Theater performance of *Swan Lake.* That left Adam. Maybe he didn't want anything from her.

She raced to the phone and picked up the receiver after the first ring, praying that she would hear Adam's deep voice.

"Hello." She knew that her voice betrayed her anxiety.

"Hi, sis. What's the matter?"

"Schyler! Where are you? Is anything wrong?" She clutched her stomach with her left hand, anticipating the worst.

"Nothing's wrong, at least not with me. I'm in Nairobi. Daddy just phoned me and told me to talk to you. He had a string of complaints a mile long. What's going on over there? Are you having an affair with Adam Roundtree?" Before she could answer, he continued with a litany of their father's grievances.

"Slow down, Schyler. Are you Daddy's advocate? If you are, I'm hanging up right now." A warm glow spread through her at the sound of her brother's deep, familiar laugh.

"Are you suggesting that I've slid back into ancient times? I understand Daddy better that you ever did, Melissa. Now tell me what this is all about. You and Adam. I'll be damned!"

She told him only that she loved Adam and that she'd let herself be victimized by their father's clever machinations.

"I don't understand. Tell me everything. It's my dime."

She told him everything, including Louise's abuse of Adam as a child, Adam's revenge, their mother's love for Bill Henry and his for her. Their parents' divorce. The problems at the leather factory. Her mistrust of Adam. Everything.

"Well, hell! I'd better go home. I'm starting to understand a few things that always bothered me. Let's deal with you first. I take it you've cleared the sawdust out of your eyes, and you can see that Daddy's a user. It must have knocked him for a loop when you stopped worshiping him. Melissa, I don't have anything against Adam Roundtree. He's doing his thing and I'm doing mine, and I never did give two hoots for that feud. But if that guy hurts you, look for a revival of it."

"He hasn't done anything to hurt me, Schyler. I did that to myself—and to him. I'm history with him."

He disagreed. "Not necessarily. Tuck in your pride and go to him, but don't wait until some other gal starts easing his pain. Now, what about Mama? You think she'll make it with Bill Henry Hayes?" Melissa caught the anxiety in his voice and wondered whether he disapproved.

"I don't know, Schyler. I hope so. At least she's going to try—I'd bet MTG on that." She heard the long breath that he expelled and waited.

"I'd better call her and tell her what I think. Thirty-one years! She deserves every bit of happiness she can get. You do, too, sis. Go talk to that guy. And don't worry about Daddy—he may come out of this a new man. Maybe even a happy man. I hadn't planned to go home for the holidays, but I think I will."

She hung up and went back to wrapping her gifts. Abruptly she shoved the boxes, paper, and ribbons haphazardly into a shopping bag and started upstairs, her taste for Christmas gone long before the season began. She didn't know how she'd stand it if she had to wait thirty years before she could feel Adam's arms around her again.

Fourteen

Adam jumped up at the buzzing sound of his beeper. A glance at the iridescent numbers of the clock on his night table informed him that it was nearly one o'clock in the morning.

"Roundtree."

"This is your agent. Two cars rendezvoused near that pine grove behind the factory for twelve minutes and left. That was three minutes ago. I'd planted a couple of mikes around, but not out there, so I couldn't monitor their conversation. We can probably expect somebody to make a move tomorrow night."

"I take it you didn't get a license plate number."

"No, but every time a criminal gets away with something, he gets more daring, a little more careless. I'll get him. Trust me."

Adam didn't try to disguise his furor nor his eagerness to get the crooks behind bars. His heart thudded rapidly at the thought that one of the cars might have belonged to Melissa, but if she were guilty, she would have to pay. He asked for a description of the cars and held his breath until the agent said that one was an old model, but that he couldn't see the other one clearly.

"Don't arrive at any conclusions yet though—this may have been a ruse to distract us while action was going on somewhere else. And I have to check out a couple of men here tomorrow. Stay close."

Adam hung up. An old-model car. Melissa's car was eight or nine years old. Hell. He got back in bed, but didn't sleep. He didn't want it to be hers. He sat up in bed and dropped his head in his hands. Anything but that. He could take anything but that. Before breakfast the next morning, he phoned his brother in Baltimore.

"Can you come home tonight? I may need you."

At eleven o'clock that morning, the agent had further news. "Your deputy manager just gave one of your men instructions that would have destroyed seven hundred and fifty pounds of hides if the man had done as he was told. Fortunately he just pretended that he'd done it. If the men know this is going on, why haven't they told you?"

"Probably because a man's word doesn't count for much sometimes, unless he has a witness. Find out whether Nelson knows about this."

"He doesn't. I've made sure of it."

"Alright. I'll be out there tonight. Let me know where you'll be."

Wayne joined Adam in the family room after dinner. "Who do you think we'll get?" Adam leaned against the mantelpiece and ran his hand over his hair.

"Beats me, Wayne. I can see that one of our men might do this out of anger if he had a grudge against us. And what better time to get away with it than when a new manager takes the job and I blame it all on his incompetence? But if a Grant's in it, that's more puzzling. I can't believe Rafer would encourage or shield a crime and lose his license to practice law. He wouldn't do it—he's too proud of his standing in the community."

"How can you be so sure?" Wayne asked. "He covered up Timothy's accident, and I've got a premonition that there's a connection with us. Otherwise, why did he accuse you of it?"

Adam shrugged first one shoulder and then the other one.

"Rafer doesn't need an excuse to go after one of us. The man wallows in hatred. He's been consumed by it for so long that he's forgotten what it means to be charitable, and he's paying for it." Adam sensed his brother's discomfort. He had to repair the breach between them that he'd brought on with his harsh words in support of Melissa. He loved his brother and disliked seeing him feel his way through their conversation, making sure that he didn't say anything offensive.

"I said some harsh things to you the last time we discussed Melissa, and you're still smarting over that. I can't say that I blame you, but neither can I swear I wouldn't do it again if the circumstances were the same. Don't let it come between us." He shrugged off the annoyance he felt when Wayne laughed.

"Let me in on the fun, will you?"

"As far as I know, that's the closest you've ever come to offering an apology. I'd as soon forget that argument, but thanks for mentioning it." Relief buoyed Adam, but only momentarily. Wayne hadn't wanted him to become involved with Melissa, and he'd been right.

"We'd better take our bikes out to the factory tonight. If we drive, we might as well send a fax saying we're coming."

"Fine with me," Wayne said, tapping one of the brass andirons with his booted foot. "I guess you'll be leaving in a few days." Adam nodded. Wayne looked him in the eye and asked, "What about Melissa, Adam? Are you really going to give her up?"

Adam squashed the irritation that he knew was unreasonable. His brother cared about him, and he had a right to ask. He straightened up, started toward the stairs, and stopped.

"Nothing new. That ought to please you." He heard Wayne's chuckle and cocked his ear for the wisdom that their father used to say always followed.

"Please me? Oh, I don't know. If I were in your place, I'd tell the family to butt out."

"Make sense, Wayne," Adam said more sharply than he intended. "The family was never in this. You know very well my personal life is my own business. This was between Melissa and me. Now it's over."

"If you say so, brother. Don't ever tell me I didn't warn you that you're making a mistake. I always envied your clear sight and your ability to make the right moves. But I never thought I'd see you make an error of such gargantuan proportions, and I do not envy you the consequences."

"Wayne—"

"Alright. Alright. Those are my last words on the subject." Wayne scrutinized him as though puzzled. "At least for now, Adam. Well, let's get ready. You got an extra helmet?"

Adam pressed the switch on his beeper. "Roundtree. Yeah. The tanning room, you think? Alright, but station yourself somewhere nearby. I'm after an arrest. Tonight." He switched off and said to Wayne, "That was our agent. He's fingered two of them. We'd better hurry."

"Right on. Adam, does it ever occur to you to say which Roundtree is speaking? I don't mind getting credit for your brilliance, but—well, you get the idea."

Adam didn't pause. "It's an office habit, but not to worry. I don't criminally implicate you, because I usually stay out of trouble."

Wayne touched his brother's shoulder as he passed on the way to his own room. "But like you said, that's in the past. Man, you won't know what trouble is until you head out of here and leave Melissa behind."

"How would you know?"

"The voice of experience."

An hour later Adam worked the combination lock on the iron grill securing a window that overlooked a marshy pond and was sheltered by a clump of high pine groves. He and Wayne slipped into the factory through the window and made their way to the basement. Armed with a powerful walkie-talkie, Adam waited alone in the darkened "finishing" room where the tanned leather was polished, while Wayne leaned against the doorjamb of an adjoining packing room, closing a potential escape route. A surge of anger gripped Adam as the smell of chromium sulfate wafted closer and closer, alerting him to the criminals' steady approach. The men set the heavy drum on its bottom and started to attack each other.

"You're going too far, now, Mack. If nobody's mentioned any of these accidents to you, it's because you're a suspect. After all, you're the assistant manager and you're supposed to know what goes on here. Man, if you burn holes in these hides, the jig'll be up. I don't want to risk any further involvement in this thing."

Adam couldn't place the voice. He waited for the other man's words, knowing now who would utter them.

"You getting cold feet again? You're repeating yourself, buddy. I'm reminding you for the last time that this was your idea, and that makes you as guilty as the one who does the job. You sold me on it, and I paid you for it. Of course, like I said, you can bail out anytime you give me the twelve thousand dollars you owe me."

Adam struggled to control his anger. So Mack was the one. He'd passed over him in favor of Cal, because Mack never got to work on time. Why hadn't it occurred to him that this one man had a reason for wanting revenge? Mack had been in his family's employ for a quarter of a century. He'd been right in not promoting him to manager. They began stacking the hides.

"Instead of whining all the time," Mack went on, groaning as he heaved the drum to its side, "you ought to be thanking me. If I drop you, who'll save your neck from that gang in Baltimore?"

Adam shook off the tension clawing his insides as he folded and unfolded his fists and finally rested his elbows on his knees, ready to spring. Patience, he told himself. In a minute, you'll know it all.

"They could have killed you," Mack said. "That shot in

your arm was just a warning. If you ask me, you ought to get into therapy. One of these days, your gambling habit is going to be the death of you."

Adam didn't need to hear more. He reached over and clicked the light switch, flooding the room and stunning the two men. Mack started to lunge toward Adam, but Timothy, the bigger man, restrained him.

"Do you want to make things worse, man? Adam Roundtree didn't come in here by himself. Unarmed."

"Smart thinking, Coston," Adam told Timothy as Wayne and the agent rushed into the room.

"If you book them here in Frederick, the sheriff will release them in minutes," Adam told the agent.

"Why?"

Adam could appreciate the agent's obvious annoyance as he rocked back on his heels, and a scowl transformed his face.

"This is a small town," Adam said. "The deputy sheriff is this man's father." He pointed to Timothy.

"Then Baltimore it is," the agent said, walking off with the two in handcuffs. "I'll call a cop from Hagerstown and take them in."

Adam stood by his bedroom window, his foot resting on the rung of a dining chair that had been in the first house Jacob Hayes built. He'd kept the chair in his room since boyhood, but he couldn't remember ever having sat in it. Yet it had a special place in his life. Would it be that way with Melissa? He knew he wouldn't forget her. How could he? Shudders ricocheted within him at the thought that he'd never know what she might have been to him. He looked at his left wrist and remembered that he'd pulled off the expensive watch before leaving home earlier that evening to go to the leather factory. Anyway, he knew it was too late to call her.

"You can talk to her now," an inner voice counseled.

"You've got the perfect excuse." Tomorrow. He promised himself.

Just before noon the next day, Melissa glanced up from the mound of papers demanding her attention and saw Banks standing in the door. Nothing unusual about Banks standing in her office door, she thought, but it alarmed her to see Banks wearing a troubled expression on her face.

"Come in. What's the matter?" Melissa got up and closed the door. She couldn't imagine what had precipitated such an obvious difference in Banks. "What happened?" Melissa noticed that Banks didn't cross her knee, nor did she light a cigarette, but sat forward in the chair with her palms pressing her kneecaps.

"Janie just picked up Adam's plane ticket. He's dropping his car off at the rental agency in Baltimore, and taking the seven forty flight to New York Saturday night." Banks drew a deep breath and expelled it slowly, her expression pitying. "You didn't make it up with him, did you? You still have time, Melissa. If you let him go, you'll regret it forever."

"Thanks for being my friend, Banks, but it's already too late. If he can leave without telling me good-bye, I doubt I'd accomplish anything by going to him. It wasn't meant to be."

"Since when did you become a fatalist?" Banks snorted in disgust, more in keeping with her normal demeanor. "By the way, I was hoping you'd introduce me to Wayne. I get a funny sensation, like stars exploding all through me, every time I see that man."

Melissa's lower lip dropped. "Are you serious?"

"I wish I wasn't, 'cause I don't think he's noticed me. But, hey, we're talking about you. Get with it, girl."

She doesn't have her usual saunter nor her crusty self-possession, Melissa thought as she watched Banks leave her office. She shoved aside a feeling of depression, turned on her computer, and got to work. If she had to live without Adam, she might as well start.

Melissa clipped a metal bookmark on page 192 of Sandra Kitt's book *Sincerely* and turned out the light. Joanna Mitchell would get her man by the end of the book, but as much as she enjoyed the story, she couldn't bear the thought of anybody else's happy ending. She felt ashamed at the tears that cascaded down her cheeks, mortified that she'd let herself love a man who could walk out of her life without a word of good-bye. Yet she admitted that it was she who bore responsibility for their breakup. She'd known that Adam would not beg, that he'd state his case . . . maybe a second time, and you could take it or else. She'd turned him away, and he wouldn't give her a chance to do it again.

Excitement gripped her at the sound of the telephone. "H-Hello."

"Melissa, this is Adam. I'm calling to let you know that last night we caught Timothy Coston and Andrew MacKnight destroying cowhides in the leather factory. They're both in a Baltimore jail. That finishes my work here." Melissa later asked herself why she responded as she did when she hadn't cared about the answer.

"Who arrested them?" She wanted to bite her tongue, for she knew that with those words she'd completed what she started the afternoon that he cleared the snow from her walk and doorsteps.

"An agent of the FBI. You don't think I'd hand them over to your uncle Booker, do you?"

"Adam, I—"

"I wish you the best, Melissa. I'm leaving in a few days for New York."

"Aren't you staying for the dedication of the Gardens for the Physically and Mentally Challenged?" Anything to keep him there, to postpone hearing the sound of that dial tone.

"That's set for noon on Friday, and I'm leaving Saturday night. Incidentally my mother has renamed the gardens for my father. She's calling them the John Roundtree Gardens. We already have over a hundred applicants, some from as far away as Baltimore and Washington."

"I see," she stammered, feeling powerless to curb what she saw as the inevitable. With each passing second, the gap between them broadened, and he didn't give her an opening. She couldn't have begged her case if she'd wanted to. And she didn't. She'd give up a lot for him, but not her pride.

"Well, I— Good-bye, Melissa."

Just before noon that Friday, Melissa joined other Frederick and Beaver Ridge notables in the heated, plastic-domed garden plot that covered three acres not far from the Monacacy River. The gardens were to serve as therapy for handicapped children, who would be encouraged to tend their own small plots. From her place in the front row, Melissa watched as Mary Roundtree rose from her seat between her two sons on the makeshift dias and told her audience how proud her husband would have been to see the project he loved so much completed. A rumble of noise overhead distracted her, and she didn't hear Adam's mother introduce him. Shivers crept up her arms when she heard a second, closer and much louder burst of noise above that she recognized as a clap of thunder. A glance at Adam told her that he'd fixed his gaze on her, and she braced herself. She wasn't going to let him see her fall to pieces.

The lights went out, and she knew from the noonday darkness and the unseasonably warm weather that a wild storm threatened them. She wrapped her arms around her middle as though to shield herself from it, but a brilliant streak of lightning and a sharp clap of thunder completely unnerved her as rain pelted the roof with the force of golf balls. Shaking, she stood up. She had to get out of there. Flashes of lightning illuminated the domed garden, and she covered her mouth with her hand.

"Melissa, what's the matter?" Banks asked her. Her breath lodged in her throat, and her lips formed a mute gasp. Another burst of thunder ripped the silence, and flashes of lightning seem to burst into the dome. Her mouth opened in a soundless scream just before she felt a pair of steel-like arms cuddle her to the haven of a man's chest.

The scent of his skin, the rough texture of his jaw against her temple, and familiar feel of his hands eased her terror. Adam held her. Then the sharpest flash of lightning and the loudest clap of thunder she thought she'd ever experienced filled the domed garden. Petrified, her arms tightened around his neck, and she couldn't hold back the wrenching scream.

"It's alright. I'm here and I've got you—I won't let anything happen to you. Just take a few slow breaths." He hurried to the entrance and put his coat around her. She didn't ask him what he intended to do. She didn't care—she was with Adam, and he would protect her. She didn't offer resistance nor question him when he picked her up, dashed through the pelting rain, and put her in his car.

"Give me your door keys." She fumbled in her pocketbook and placed them in his hand.

"Try to relax, I'll make some tea," he stated after removing their coats from around her. Melissa wanted to tell him that she didn't want tea, only his arms around her. She leaned into a corner of the sofa while he left her to go into the kitchen. Another clap of thunder shook the house, and she clasped her hands tightly over her mouth and put her face between her knees. He handed her a cup of tea and placed his own on the glass coffee table.

"How do you manage these storms when you're by yourself?" She felt his arms around her and, thought she knew it was childish, she suddenly welcomed the storm.

"I'm sorry to drag you into this, Adam, b-b-but this is the worst one I've experienced in years. One of the reasons I liked

New York is that there aren't many storms like this one." She snuggled closer, but his arms remained loosely about her. "I don't know how to thank you for getting me out of there. I was scared, and I didn't want people to know it." He stood, and she looked toward the window. His gaze followed hers.

"Appears to be over. You'll be alright now."

"You—you're not leaving?"

"Yes, I am. Mother and Wayne need transportation home." Fear shot through her. He didn't intend to patch it up with her. He could walk away just like that. He had acted the part of a gentleman, helped someone in distress. She could have been anybody. She looked from his shuttered eyes and his impersonal manner to his wet clothing and led the way to her front door.

"Thanks for helping me." She tried to form the word "good-bye" but couldn't.

He nodded. "I couldn't have done otherwise." She opened her mouth to speak, but she couldn't make a sound, and her right hand didn't obey her command to reach out to him, but dangled at her side. She watched, helpless, as he saluted her in a gesture that struck her as sarcastic, stepped out of the door, and sprinted to his car. Gone.

Her heart pounded at the sound of the Jaguar's engine taking him away. She grabbed her chest as though to slow down her heartbeat and leaned against the front door. After a few minutes she could take deep breaths and managed to calm herself. She took his untouched cup of tea to the kitchen, emptied it into the sink, and washed it along with hers, wondering if she'd ever do anything else for him. After an hour during which she distracted herself with "Oprah," she got a pencil and sheet of paper and began to list the things she had to do before she could consider her slate with Adam clean. Their relationship had ended, but her responsibility to him had not. She finished writing, typed it on her word processor, printed it out, and climbed the stairs.

The next morning Rafer summoned Melissa to a family conference, and she alerted her mother, certain that Emily hadn't been included.

"I don't know who else will be there, but I want you to come along. There's no telling what he's up to." She told her about Timothy's arrest.

"I was afraid Timmy had gotten in with the wrong crowd. When he was a boy, he was always into something unwholesome."

Melissa found her aunt Louise, Louise's husband, Timothy, and her father speaking in hushed voices when she arrived. Seconds after her father began to speak, her mother walked in wearing a chic Armani pants suit and her fur coat draped on one shoulder. Emily Grant could have passed for a fashion model had she been a few inches taller. She marveled that her father could camouflage his surprise so well, and she suspected that she alone knew how angry he was. Her mother paid him no attention.

"Adam Roundtree has gone too far," Rafer exploded. "Blasting a hole in Timmy's arm wasn't enough for Mr. Roundtree. He's framed our Timmy and had him arrested. I bailed him out an hour or so ago." He nodded toward his nephew. "Well, we've indicted Adam for the shooting and for defamation of character. I won't have our family name smeared by Adam Roundtree." In answer to Emily's question, Timothy revealed that he had been charged only with trespassing, but that MacKnight had been booked on a far more serious charge. Melissa saw Adam's lenient hand in that.

"He could have thrown the book at you, Timmy," Emily told the man. "Don't you think you ought to tell us truthfully who shot you? We know Adam didn't do it."

Melissa regarded the players in their little family drama. Her father glared at her mother though she thought she detected his admiration for her as well, and to the irritation of all present but herself, her mother sat relaxed with the serenity of a bejeweled regent surrounded by her loyal subjects. Melissa smothered a laugh. Adam's mother wasn't the only consummate actress of her generation in Frederick—Emily Grant could hold her own with any of them. Among those present, she didn't doubt that only she and her mother cared about the ruination of an innocent man. Adam. She stood to leave.

"I think I ought to tell you, Daddy, that I just mailed the district attorney my sworn affidavit that Adam was with me at his lodge on the Potomac when Timmy was shot, and I also sent Adam a notarized copy. I'm prepared to say the same thing in any court. Adam did not shoot Timmy, and I won't be party to a frame-up." Emily stood as though preparing to join Melissa, but instead she walked over to Timothy.

"How'd you get mixed up in this? Might as well tell the truth—it will come out anyway."

He shrugged before mumbling, "I've been gambling, and one thing led to another. When I tried to quit and didn't go to the gaming tables, one of the gang took a shot at me. Said it was a warning. Mack paid off a couple of my debts."

Rafer's voice rang out. "I don't believe you. Are you saying that because you're afraid of Melissa? Have you forgotten who I am? Your attorney, that's who."

Melissa looked her father in the eye. "And for a gambling debt, you're ready to sacrifice a man who's made a unique contribution to this town, a citizen in the fullest sense. Come on, Mama, I'll drop you off at The Refuge on my way to work." To her amazement, her father followed them out of his office and stopped them in the hallway.

"I thought you'd be through with this volunteer work by now, Emily. I thought you'd have gotten it out of your system. I want us back together, but not while you're playing up to those people."

Emily's face bore an expression of astonishment before

laughter spilled from her throat. "Be serious, Rafer. Only a chicken is stupid enough to rush back into a cage after having been free all day." She looked at her watch. "My divorce will be final in fourteen hours and one minute. Our farce is over." She reached out to touch his hand, but he quickly withdrew it.

"We made a mess of our lives, Rafer, and I'm sorry for my part in that. I intend to get mine straightened out, and I hope you do, too. Schyler has avoided the curse of this feud, because he got away from here and didn't let any of it touch him. And when Melissa hurts badly enough, she'll go to Adam and undo the mess she's made of their lives. But she'd better hurry."

Adam packed for his return to New York. He didn't want any of his mother's questions, but he knew she'd stay with him until he left, so he reconciled himself to the inevitable.

"What are you doing about Melissa?" He didn't answer at once, but picked up a brush and used it to clean a pair of soft leather moccasins while he thought.

"You asked me that two or three days ago, Mother. Nothing has changed." If he sounded a bit testy, she should expect that. He tucked the shoes into a sack, turned, and went into his private bathroom. He propped his left foot on the edge of the tub and rested his left elbow on his knee. He'd finished the job and caught the troublemakers, but the letdown he felt was a new thing, as though he lacked completeness. As if he'd lost something of himself, something on which he had unwittingly relied. He looked at his watch, went back in the room, and resumed his packing. As he expected, his mother remained where he'd left her, sitting on the side of his bed. If he had to talk about Melissa or listen to his mother talk about her, he knew he'd succumb to his urge to call her. He'd done that last night, and her first thought had been of her family. Had Booker Coston arrested his own son? She hadn't said the words, but that was what she'd implied. He walked back into the room and resisted kicking the side of the armoire.

He'd never express to anybody what he felt when he walked out of her house that afternoon. He had wanted, needed her words—that he'd done nothing wrong, that her aunt Louise bore responsibility for what had happened between them. Melissa had wanted affection, maybe lovemaking. He didn't know. Who the hell could figure out her mind? But she hadn't taken that first step, and he'd figured she wouldn't. So he'd left. He'd handed himself something akin to a death sentence. But he'd left, and he wasn't sorry.

"Just tell me this." His mother hadn't been in the habit of nagging him, and she wouldn't do it now, he decided, if she didn't need satisfaction about her son's well-being. She didn't want a Grant in his life, but she didn't want him to be unhappy, either. Could she be mellowing? He gave her his full attention.

"Were the Grants involved in the trouble at Leather and Hides? You said Mack engineered it. Who helped him?"

"Timothy Coston was the lookout, but he's guilty only of trespassing. Poor fellow—he let himself be blackmailed into it. The Grants had nothing to do with it, Mother." He stopped packing and sat beside her.

"I'd rather not talk about this, but you seem compelled to get the details. Melissa had no part in MacKnight's havoc at Leather and Hides." He tossed the affidavit to her. "She's gone to some lengths to support me against Rafer's accusations."

"Then why are you leaving like this?"

He got up and locked his suitcase, uncomfortable with her queries, but unwilling to hurt her by refusing to answer. In three hours he'd be on the plane, and nobody he knew in New York dared question him about his behavior.

"Let's just say I've paid for an innocent, youthful indiscretion. Nobody can screw up your life for you, Mother. You have to do that yourself."

She frowned. "Is yours screwed up?" He released a grudging smile. His mother hated that word.

"Is it?" she persisted. Adam dropped a hand lightly on her shoulder, at once consoling her and attempting to stop her. She shook it off, and he knew that she'd have her say, but he didn't have to answer her.

"Why can't you wait until after Christmas?"

How could he tell her that he needed distance between Melissa and himself, that he had to push aside temptation? How could he tell her that Melissa had erased from his consciousness every other woman he'd ever known? That he'd come close to loving her?

"I'll fly down Christmas Eve and spend the night," he threw out as he set a case down in the hallway. Mary unfolded the paper that he had handed her and read its contents.

"Adam, do you love her?" Her voice sounded less firm than it had a little earlier, as though she fought tears. He was about to tell her he didn't think so, that he wasn't certain, when Wayne walked in and saved him the necessity of a reply.

"We'd better get moving, if you want to stop by B-H's place." Adam kissed his mother's cheek. "Don't worry about me, Mother, I can take care of myself." He noticed her somber expression and the absence of her usual confident air.

"You always could do that," Mary said, "but you haven't ever hurt like you're hurting now." He felt the heat of his blood burning his face.

"Let's go, Wayne." They didn't speak during Wayne's demonic drive the short distance to Bill Henry's house. Adam got out of Wayne's car, glad to be alive, and wishing he'd driven himself in the Jaguar as he'd originally planned.

"This thing won't fly no matter how much gas you give it, don't you know that?"

"Thought you could use a little diversion," Wayne answered, obviously unperturbed by the faint rebuke.

"Like having my heart plummet to my knees? You're so considerate."

They sat around the fire on either side of their uncle, prepared to tolerate one of the latest herbal teas Bill Henry had received from Winterflower. He did hand Wayne a warm glass fragrant with rosemary, but he opened a bottle of fine VSOP cognac, gave Adam a glass, and poured him a drink.

"I expect you'll be full of this stuff by the time you get to New York. If I were in your place, I know that's what I'd do. The day Emily married Rafer Grant, I stayed sober until after the wedding, making sure the deed was done, you might say. But an hour later I was three sheets to the wind and stayed that way for two weeks. Then I sobered up, and signed on for Vietnam. I must have been the only man in the service who didn't want to go back home." He changed the subject so quickly that Adam had to laugh. His uncle knew just how far to go with him.

"Run over to see Winterflower first chance you get and tell her what's happening with me. 'Course I expect she knows. Go anyway. Westchester's beautiful this time of year with its hills and snow and the Christmas lights decorating the houses and lawns. And I like the peace—it's so quiet there." He raised his head as if to bring himself back from a dream. "You go and see her. Maybe she'll put some sense into you."

Adam sipped the drink, savoring its flavor and aroma, but he remained silent. When Bill Henry wanted to say something, he said it. He was that much like his sister, Mary.

"I hate to see you walk away from something you want, Adam. There's no virtue in useless martyrdom. If life has taught me anything, it's that one lesson." Adam turned toward his uncle to announce that he was leaving, but the faraway look in the eyes of that strong man stopped him.

"I didn't pressure Emily enough to stand up to Mittie and Moses Morris, and I should have. I've paid for that every day since."

Adam downed the remainder of his drink, stood, and signaled Wayne to join him, but his brother remained seated. "I know what you're saying and what you're trying to protect me from, B-H," Adam said, "but don't let it bother you. I can handle it."

"Then you're a better man than I am, son."

Adam's eyes widened, their often luminous twinkle dulled by his vision of the future. For the second time since he'd left home for college, indeed in the last five days, his uncle had called him "son." Somewhere in that was a message. He slapped B-H on the shoulders in a gesture of affection.

"You're making too much of this. I feel like I've had more lectures today than in my first week as a college freshman. Hang in there, B-H, and if you want me for—well, for whatever, call me." He brought himself up short. B-H didn't want his hopes raised, and he had almost offered to be his uncle's best man.

Wayne drove through Frederick, past the Taney house, and Adam felt his heart constrict when he glanced out of the window and remembered Melissa's funny and foolish little habit of spitting in its direction. He spread his knees and slid down in the soft leather seat.

"Want me to drive by there? Just for a minute?" Adam didn't ask where, and the negative movement of his head sufficed for an answer.

Sitting at last in an aisle seat in front of the curtain that separated first class and cabin class of his Piedmont flight, Adam released a deep breath and surrendered to the fatigue that had dogged him for days. He'd been hoping that he wouldn't have a seatmate, but one arrived and immediately attempted to press him into service. Would he put her carry-on in the overhead bin? He would and did. Would he excuse her so she could go to the lavatory? He did. She returned, sat in her seat beside the window, and decided she needed a magazine. Would he—? Adam turned to face her.

"Madam this is a fifty-minute flight. Please resist the temptation to spend the entire time getting in and out of your seat."

When her scowl failed to move him, she offered her feminine charm. Adam laughed.

"Lady, I've had it up to here with women." He sliced the air above his head. "You're wasting your time."

She crossed a pair of long brown legs, adjusted her suit jacket to avoid wrinkling the hem and leaned back in her seat. "That's no surprise. I'm out of practice." She opened her lizardskin handbag and took out a deck of cards. "How about some blackjack? I usually play against myself, but it's nice to have a real game for a change."

He didn't want a conversation with her, and he didn't want to play blackjack, but she had aroused his curiosity. A good-looking woman, around thirty-five, he supposed, who dressed with taste and money. And she'd just admitted to not having a man in her life for some time, at least not one susceptible to her brand of allure.

"Deal."

She dealt him two jacks, and he thought of the song about new fools. "I'm really not interested in a game," he told her, and turned away. She pushed a business card toward him.

"You wouldn't happen to need an office manager, would you? I just got fired from a big insurance company, and I have a child to support."

He tried not to listen, but compassion was as much a part of him as his skin. "What for? What were you accused of?"

"I refused to lie for my boss. I could fight it in court, but I need the money. Besides, I wouldn't win—it would be my word against his. I worked there for ten years, and I can't get a reference."

Adam sat up straight, adjusted his pants at the knees, and looked her over. He asked her the name of the company and what her duties had been. The flight attendant offered drinks, and he took a bourbon and soda, but she declined. One in her favor, he noted. He steered the conversation to other areas while he wondered how an office manager could afford such expensive clothes. She answered his unasked question when she told him, "Half of my salary went for clothes, because my boss demanded that the women working there dress like socialites."

Adam heard the change in the thrust of the engines and

made up his mind. "Come to see me Monday morning." She looked at the card he handed her and drew back.

"You're—I didn't know who you were, honest. I mean, I wouldn't have—" Her hands dropped into her lap. "Mr. Roundtree, please don't build up my hopes for nothing." The pilot turned off the seat belt sign, and Adam stood and took her bag out of the overhead bin. "And to think, I asked you to . . . I don't know what to say."

"I know. I'll see you Monday morning at eleven." He looked back at her. "The women who work in my office wear whatever they like."

Adam walked rapidly through LaGuardia Airport. If the energy pulsing around him was an omen, he wouldn't have time to think of Melissa. And at least he wouldn't have to go back to her for another office manager.

Melissa opened her door reluctantly, hoping she wouldn't have to deal with her father. She stared, tongue-tied, at Bill Henry until he asked her if he could come in.

"Why, yes. Yes, sure," she stammered.

"I know you're surprised," he said, "but probably not much more than I am. I've been sitting home counting off the hours, and it just got to be too much. About the only other person whose company I could stand right now is Adam's, and he's not here." When Melissa's raised eyebrow allowed him to see her skepticism, he explained.

"I wouldn't want to be near your mother, either, until after midnight tonight, because I've never yet put my hands on another man's wife and the temptation to do that would be too great. Three more hours."

"But that's nothing compared to how long you've waited already." He took the chair she offered and stretched out his legs. So much like Adam, she thought.

"Melissa, don't you believe that. I could bear it before, because I didn't think of Emily in relation to the passing time.

She was lost to me forever. I came to terms with it, but now I have hope. I trust I'm not intruding—I just wanted to while away the time with a friend."

"I won't ask if you'd like coffee, because Adam said you don't drink stimulants, just those teas that Winterflower concocts. How about some mint tea?" He accepted her offer, and she brought large mugs of the fragrant tea for them both. He took a few sips and set the cup aside.

"Melissa, have you decided to give Adam up? Is there a chance that you two could learn what happened to your mother and me and let the same thing occur to you? Adam told me Emily bloomed into a different woman when Rafer moved out, and I know how much more like a live and breathing man I've felt since then. Looks like we both just shriveled up inside, and I hate to think that the same thing will happen to you and Adam. Did he call you before he left?"

"Yes, but only to tell me about the arrests." His look of disbelief disconcerted her.

"Come, now, Melissa. He wasn't obliged to do that. Sounds to me as if he used it as an excuse to call you. Didn't you talk?"

"Not really. I was so surprised and pleased to hear from him that I blurted out the wrong thing, and I knew it. He didn't call me again, just left town without another word."

"You're a businesswoman, and I hear you swing some heavy deals. So use your head. Adam is strong, and he's tough, but you can bend him with your little finger. Just apply what you already know." He stood to go, and she walked with him to the front door.

"B-H, I'm glad you stopped by. I'll pull out of this, but it may take me a while." He bent and kissed her cheek, and she stood with the door ajar until he reached the sidewalk. Ten o'clock. She hadn't known a night could be so long, and it had only begun. She went to the kitchen, put the mugs in the dishwasher, doused the downstairs lights, and started up to her bedroom. She got the phone on its fourth ring.

"Melissa, darling. Tell me you're watching this beautiful black dancer with the long neck right now on the public television station. She is exquisite. Such a ballerina!" Melissa told Ilona that she hadn't been watching.

"Then you are with Adam. Hmmm. What eyes this man has!" Melissa tried to pull herself together before Ilona sensed her mood, but she didn't succeed. "He isn't with you?"

"Ilona, Adam is in New York, maybe four blocks from you. We've split." Ilona's silence told her more than words would have.

Finally her friend asked her, "Is it over for good? It can't be."

- "He didn't tell me good-bye."

"I'm sorry"—then after a minute—"but darling, turn on the ballet. You can be unhappy and still enjoy this wonderful ballerina. Call Adam and tell him you made a mess of things and you want to make it up."

"How do you know it's my fault?" Melissa huffed.

"Because I'm sensible. He didn't give you up voluntarily, darling. I saw him with you. Remember? You're the one who needs to have the head examined."

"Alright, I'll watch the ballet. And don't worry, I made my bed hard, and I won't complain about lying in it."

Ilona snorted. "Big words, darling. Just think how much more fun it would be if the bed was a little less hard and you weren't in it by yourself."

Fifteen

Melissa closed her desk drawer and opened the wrapper of her fifth Snickers since she'd returned from lunch an hour and a half earlier. She stared at her blank computer screen while she devoured the miniature candy bar. She had dialed her mother and hung up before the first ring. Her walk up to Banks's office had been without reward, and as she stood looking at Banks's empty desk chair, she remembered belatedly that her friend had gone shopping when they separated after lunch. At the other end of the long hallway, she found that all of the paper cups had been used, and she had to drink from her hand. Where was everybody on Monday afternoon, she wondered, though she ordinarily wouldn't have noticed the desolateness, because she, too, would have been busy. She trudged back to her office suite.

"Just a minute, Mr. Roundtree, she just walked in." Melissa's secretary punched the hold button, and she went into her office and closed the door. Her heart fluttered and excitement flared up in her as she anticipated the sound of his voice. Maybe this was it—maybe this time he'd tell her he cared, that he couldn't wait to be with her. She calmed herself.

"Hello, Adam. How are you?"

"Hello, Melissa. I'm just fine. I'm calling to tell you that I have decided not to extend Lester's contract. We all agree that he's competent and efficient, but we—my staff, from Jason to the new messenger—dislike him. You're entitled to know why I'm letting him go. It's his officiousness. Olivia threatened to quit, and that settled it. She's indispensable."

"Are you planning to hire another office manager?"

"I've already done that." He said it too quickly, she thought, as though being able to do so held a measure of triumph. "I didn't use a search firm this time. I met her on the plane coming up Saturday night, and I think she's exactly what we need." You mean what *you* need, Melissa surmised as she fought a feeling of melancholy, but she refused to allow him the pleasure of knowing it, and her response concealed her real feelings.

"I see. MTG is glad to have been of service, and I hope we may continue to count you among our clients." She found his silence aggravating, but it was his call, his next move, and she remained silent, refusing to ease the way for him.

"Have you ever done anything that you later regretted?"

"Hasn't everyone?" she asked, wondering about the question and stalling because she couldn't figure out what had prompted it.

"You're not everyone," he told her in a voice that was a little rough and lacked its usual authority. "I'm interested only in you. Have you?"

"Of course. Why?" She picked up a pencil and began tapping its eraser rhythmically against the phone.

"How did you manage to forgive yourself, Melissa? Or did you?" She stopped the tapping.

"How did I—?" He interrupted and spoke rapidly as if anxious to release something he'd held for a long time, to finish an unpleasant task.

"Something else I've wanted to ask you ever since we met."

"What?"

"What do you think of masquerade parties? Do you like them?"

At first she thought he might want to invite her to one. Then she wondered if he was accusing her of some pretense.

"Adam, this isn't the best day I've had recently, so would you just say whatever it is that's bothering you?"

"Sure. How about answering my question?"

"I can take masquerade parties and most other kinds or I can leave them. Some of the most unforgettable ones have been distasteful, but I remember others because they brought pleasure that I least expected and that had a lasting impact." She tried to fathom his sigh of obvious dissatisfaction at her remark.

"Tell me about it!" he said, affirming his frustration. His pause led her to expect more, something he'd forgotten, something more personal. But he only added, "Give my regards to your mother, Melissa. I'm glad I got to know her. Take care."

"Adam—"

"What is it?"

She thought she detected hope in his voice, but he'd been so distant in recent days that she couldn't risk more evidence of his disinterest.

"Adam, I— Take care." She hung up.

Melissa struggled with the turmoil into which her conversation with Adam had plunged her. She couldn't decide what his questions implied. The man with whom she'd just spoken had not displayed the tough candor that she thought of as such an essential part of Adam's makeup. Furthermore, he hadn't even mentioned the affidavit, and she knew that the document was of importance to him. The oversight bordered on rudeness, a trait that she couldn't associate with him. She wished he hadn't called her.

"I'm not sitting here moaning over that man or any other one," she lectured herself. She went to her lavatory, splashed cold water on her face, applied a touch of makeup, and went back upstairs to look for Banks.

"Let's go look for some antiques after work," she suggested to her friend. Banks lit a cigarette and took a few draws, looked

Melissa up and down, and declared, "You sure won't find him wandering around in Bessie's Yesteryear, honey. Adam's in New York. For good, I heard."

"I know that, Banks. Do I ever."

"What are you planning to do about it? Just sit around here and dry up?"

"Right now, I just want to make it through today. I didn't send him packing—he left."

Not many people could match Banks's expressions of disgust, Melissa decided, watching her arched eyebrows and tired shrug.

"He's still breathing, isn't he?" It was more a statement than a question. "But if you like being miserable, you won't find a better opportunity. Let's call it a day." Everybody told her that she had to go after Adam, but she didn't know how she could. "Everybody" didn't know that Adam had never professed to love her, and without that armor she couldn't make herself approach him.

Why did he continue punishing himself, calling her under any reasonable pretext in the hope that she'd tell him what he wanted to hear? He'd spent one night in his apartment, and already he hated it. Not that he minded living alone; he didn't. But he'd gotten used to looking forward to seeing her every day, often many times. The last two weeks hadn't been easy ones. He needed her, and he sensed that she wanted them closer, but he couldn't compromise on the issues of trust and faith. He stood on his balcony looking toward the Hudson River and the building where she'd lived. Once, he hadn't doubted his ability to walk away from her and stay away. But he hadn't counted on the pain he felt when she showed him that she didn't have faith in him, didn't trust him.

A harsh wind swirled around him, bringing below freezing air that penetrated his heavy cashmere sweater, and he walked back into his living room. Why couldn't he get her out of his mind, out of his system, out of his— He sat down on the oversized leather sofa, spread his legs, and rested his elbows on his knees. Was she really in his heart? He cared. He cared a lot. But did it really go that deep? He walked into his den, picked up the phone, held it, and returned it to its cradle. He wasn't about to whip himself again, getting his hope raised and his libido unruly from the sound of her voice.

"Damn! I've got to get on top of this thing. I promised myself that I wouldn't give another woman the upper hand with me." He looked at his watch. "And that includes Ms. Grant."

He picked up the phone again—and dialed. "Hello, Ariel," he said when she answered on the first ring. He resented that habit of hers even before he greeted her. As he expected, she commented on his long absence and wanted to know when they might get together. But to his surprise, he demurred, telling her that he'd just gotten into town, that he was only touching base and would call her in a few days. His uncharacteristically inconsistent behavior disgusted him, and what he considered a softness in himself made him uneasy.

He tied a scarf around his neck, threw on his coat, and went out. Twenty minutes later he stood in front of Carnegie Hall. It hadn't been his intention to go there, but he figured the Preservation Hall Band might be just the thing. If he concentrated on Dixieland jazz, he couldn't stew over Melissa. He paid thirty dollars for the remaining forty minutes and went in. Twenty minutes later he left. The last time he'd heard live jazz, the fingers of Melissa's left hand had been entwined with his right one. He pulled up his coat collar and headed up Broadway. He loved New York. Hell, no, he didn't. He couldn't stand it.

Melissa steadied herself and took her mother's arm as they entered the district attorney's office where an attendant directed them to seats behind her father, Timothy, and his mother,

Louise. The chairs had been arranged to make the office resemble a courtroom, with rows on either side of an aisle that led to the DA's desk. Before she succumbed to the urge to look for Adam, she put on the dark glasses that she'd bought for the purpose—to shield herself from his knowing looks and the seductive twinkle in his eyes. He sat with Wayne on the other side of the aisle, and she knew at once that with the seating arrangements putting her in her father's camp—against him—the gulf between them would widen the minute he realized it.

And as if by a magical ability to read her mind or to divine her concerns, he looked back and locked his gaze on her face, nodded briefly, and turned around. Less than a week had passed since he'd gone back to New York, but those few days had given her a glimpse of what forever without him would be. She recognized the gentle squeeze of her mother's hand as a gesture of support and wondered how she'd ever gotten along without the wonderful woman at her side.

The assistant district attorney breezed in with an air of importance greater than that to which her status entitled her. She stopped to shake hands with Adam and Wayne, nodded to Rafer, who sat away from the aisle, and began the proceedings.

"Mr. Grant, as Mr. Coston's attorney, would you repeat the charges, please."

Rafer made the accusation, but Melissa thought he lacked his usual verve, that his heart was no longer in it.

"Miss Grant, would you please read your sworn affidavit." The clerk brought the document to Melissa, and she stood and read from it. When she finished, she had to look at Adam, had to see his reaction to her public confession that she had spent half a night with him at his lodge. Their first time together. Her first time. She brushed away the tears that coursed down her cheeks. He had turned to look at her while she read it, and he didn't alter his gaze. But from where she stood, she couldn't see his expression, though she did know that the twinkle in his eyes seemed to remain still. Dull.

Suddenly Timothy stood, resisting Rafer's efforts to make him sit down and be quiet. "I don't want to go on with this," he said. "I never did want to accuse him." He nodded toward Adam. "He didn't have anything to do with it. I got into some trouble in Baltimore, and the guys warned me with that shot. That's all." The DA's office concluded the proceedings, and Melissa hurried out, pulling her mother with her. Adam and Wayne stopped them in the lobby.

"Thank you for the affidavit, Melissa. The DA had assured me that it exonerated me, so even without Timothy's confession, I wouldn't have been indicted." So cool and formal, like a dash of cold water, she thought.

"I only did the decent thing," she said, adopting what she took to be his demeanor. She watched Adam hug her mother in a warm, tender greeting and felt an unreasonable tinge of jealousy.

"I'm glad to see you, Adam," Emily said. "By the way, have you met my daughter?" Neither Wayne's laughter nor Adam's indulgent grin sat well with Melissa.

"My mother's a comedienne, now," she said to no one in particular. Adam introduced Emily to Wayne, and the two stood there making conversation, while Adam and Melissa gazed at each other. She wanted to reach out to him and couldn't understand why he didn't respond to the longing he must have seen in her eyes. She swallowed the bitterness she felt at his determination to withhold himself from her, to be oblivious to the needs he had cultivated in her. Needs that he alone had fulfilled. She waved at them and left.

Twenty minutes later she walked into her office, pulled off the dark glasses, and threw them across the desk.

"Oh, dear," she sighed, awareness dawning, "how could he know what I was thinking or feeling? He couldn't see my eyes." With a humorless chuckle she tipped her hat to herself—she had outfoxed Melissa Grant. Her purpose in wearing the glasses was to protect her emotions while she read that paper, and when she'd looked at him, he hadn't seen her, only her glasses.

She switched on her computer, lecturing to herself while it checked itself out. "I will not wonder when he arrived, whether he'll call before he goes back, or when he's leaving. I will not give a hoot." She looked at her e-mail and enjoyed a provocative message from Magnus Cooper.

"I suppose by now the men of Maryland are in mourning, having lost you to Roundtree," he wrote. "But if I'm wrong and you're slower than I think, drop me a note."

"You're wrong, and I'm slower than you and everybody else think," she answered, switching to her "talk" mode in the hope that he was at the computer and she'd get an immediate answer.

"Come down here for the holidays, and give him something to think about."

She laughed. He was there. "Sorry. That's family time. I'd have to bring my mother," she teased, enjoying the fun.

"Fine with me. If she's half your equal, don't hesitate to bring her."

"The question is whether I'm half her equal. Emily Grant is a beauty."

"This machine doesn't transmit whistles—I'll have to get another one. You coming down?"

"Maybe another time." She signed off.

By five o'clock she knew she wouldn't hear from Adam. She trudged home, went through the motions of eating and, completely out of sorts, crawled into bed and counted sheep, butterflies, horses, and cows until she fell asleep around two o'clock.

Melissa arrived at her office a half hour earlier than usual the next morning. If she couldn't be with Adam, she wanted to be alone, and she couldn't manage that unless she'd closed her office door before the tenants on her floor arrived for work. She missed Banks. Not that her friend wouldn't happily provide company, but Banks had fallen hard for Wayne Roundtree—and apart from work, didn't allow herself to think or speak of anything except her schemes to make Wayne reciprocate.

I've got my own problem with a nonreciprocating Roundtree, Melissa grumbled to herself. She got up and went over to straighten Eleanor Roosevelt's picture that hung on the wall facing her desk, and the door burst open bringing a whiff of fine French perfume. And Emily Grant.

She gaped as her mother strutted forward, waving her left hand before her. "Mama. What on earth—? Mama?" Emily swung round and round, her head thrown back and laughter spilling from her lips.

"Look. Look at it. Look!" She held her left hand within inches of her daughter's face. Melissa's shrieks of joy filled the room, and she gripped her mother in a loving embrace.

"Oh, Mama, I'm so happy for you. When? You didn't call or say a word, and yesterday morning you acted as if nothing had happened between you two. And I was scared to ask you. Tell me, when did—?"

"He gave it to me this morning, the same one I took off thirty-one years ago."

"But when? I mean, how did you get together?"

"My divorce became final midnight last Friday, and nine o'clock the next morning, I knocked on Bill Henry's door. I didn't have to get on my knees and beg; he was waiting for me. I didn't leave him until yesterday morning when I had to go to that hearing. And I left the courthouse, went home and put some clothes in a suitcase, and went right back to him. Are you really happy for me?"

"You know I am. I don't think anything could make me happier."

Melissa marveled at the swiftness with which her mother's sparkling face sobered with concern. "Nothing? *Nothing?* Oh, honey, go after Adam. Now I know what you're throwing away. At last I know what the fuss is about. Don't lose the chance to love him in the bloom of your youth. 'Of all sad words of tongue or pen—' "

"I know, Mama. 'The saddest are these: "It might have been!" ' When is the wedding?"

"New Year's Eve at five o'clock. I've already hired a caterer, and I'm going to get married in white satin. Don't look so shocked. I don't care about tradition. Bill Henry said he used to dream of seeing me coming up the aisle to him dressed in white satin and lace and carrying white calla lilies, and I'm going to make his dream come true."

Melissa quickly wiped the frown from her face, though she doubted that anything she did or said could diminish her mother's joy. Yet she couldn't resist adding, "Won't people think that you and B-H— I mean, so soon after the divorce?" Melissa stared, aghast, when her mother arched her eyebrows and shrugged with disdain.

"I know better. So do B-H, Rafer, and my children. I couldn't care less what the gossip mongers of Frederick and Beaver Ridge think. What people might think circumscribed my life for over a quarter of a century, thanks to Rafer." What's come over this woman, Melissa wondered, when Emily suddenly beamed and told her, "Sorry I can't have lunch with you—we're going to see an architect. B-H wants us to start fresh, and he's going to build us a home just off that grassy slope near his little house. Oh, honey, I'm so happy. Get a dusty rose gown made to match my wedding dress. You're going to be my maid of honor."

Melissa finished wrapping her Christmas gifts and held the one she'd bought for Adam, a silver business card case that bore his initials, and wondered what to do with it. At last, unable to decide, she placed it under her brightly decorated Christmas tree. She stared for a few minutes at the twinkling lights that reflected off red and gold bells, trying to summon a modicum of Christmas spirit. Finally she threw up her hand in frustration and ran up the stairs to shower and dress.

Around five o'clock, as dusk settled over the brightly li town, she joined Banks and her sister, and the three went i search of carolers. With other singers, they stopped at home decorated with a Christmas tree or wreath, sang a verse o two, and walked on. Melissa had thought that their tour of the hospital wards and at the seniors' center would depress her and she couldn't understand how she could feel uplifted and unhappy at the same time. At home later she dressed and waited for her mother and B-H. She knew why she prowled from room to room, glanced frequently at the silent telephone and in frustration shook her fist at the air. Her affidavit should have told him where her heart laid, but maybe he'd had enough of her. Enough of the Grants.

She opened the door to B-H and her mother, both radiant and had to squash her jealousy of their happiness.

"You two could light up a dark night," she told them ashamed that she'd envied her mother the joy that had been denied her for so long.

"If you and my nephew ever come to your senses, you'l outshine us, believe me," B-H said. Melissa waved a hand gainsaying the thought.

"Don't worry, dear, they'll get together as soon as one of them hurts badly enough," Emily said, gazing at him in adoration.

"When did you get a car, B-H?" Melissa asked as they reached the Lincoln. "What about the air pollution?" she needled.

"It was a trade-off. I figured I'd looked after the environment for thirty years. Now I'm going to take care of Emily, and I need a car for that. I've got a list of places I want to take her right around here. Then we'll take one of those African-American heritage tours, go down to New Orleans for some real jazz, see the Metropolitan Opera, and the museums in New York City. Ah, Melissa, there's so much." He put an arm around Emily, love shining in his eyes. "I've got to make up for lost time. And after I've showed her the United States, I'm going to take her around the world." Melissa wiped her tears with the back of her index finger.

"Adam's in town," Bill Henry said as they neared the church.

"I figured he would be." But I won't let him get me down, she swore to herself. They entered the little church from a side door, and her heartbeat escalated as soon as she glimpsed Adam sitting with Wayne opposite the entrance. She had to pass close by him and wondered if Bill Henry knew he'd be in that pew and had taken that route to force them to notice each other. She managed a smile when he looked her way and nodded, but he didn't touch the hand she'd left dangling at her side, and she kept walking. Emily and Bill Henry could follow her or not—she was doggoned if she'd be manipulated into such a convenient arrangement. Her companions joined her, and she soon felt her mother's elbow.

"I think I'm disappointed in you."

"You'll get over it," Melissa told her and turned her attention to the program. Her mood soon changed into one of well-being. The little church glowed with hundreds of candles nestled among beautifully arranged red poinsettias, and carols sung by the local community choir filled the sanctuary. At the end of the service, she left the building by the front door and waited alone beside Bill Henry's car for him and her mother.

"I didn't see Mrs. Roundtree," she remarked to Bill Henry as he drove away from the church. "I would have thought she'd go to church with Adam and Wayne."

"Mary can't even tolerate the House of God if Emily and I are in it together. But that's her problem. I enjoyed the service, but she's so full of bitterness that she had to miss it."

The next morning, Christmas, Melissa started out of her front door and rushed back to answer the phone, hoping to hear Adam's voice.

"Schyler! Where are you?"

"I'm home. I got in here late last night. Would you believe I found a note from Mama telling me she's in Beaver Ridge and I should go out there. Now I don't have a car, don't know the address, and there's no phone where she is. I take it Hayes is some kind of a recluse."

"You can borrow my car after I run by to see Daddy. I was on my way there."

"Drop by here, and I'll go with you."

Melissa couldn't help being nervous while they waited for her father to answer the door.

"I'm glad you're with me, Schyler. I was not looking forward to this meeting."

"His bark is louder than his bite."

Rafer Grant opened the door, dressed as though he was going to his office, and stared at his offspring. Melissa clutched her chest as she waited for his words. To her surprise, his smile didn't dim when his gaze moved from Schyler to her.

"Well, this is a nice Christmas present. Come on in."

Anything is possible, Melissa mused, when her father made coffee and served it along with Oreos. She'd forgotten his passion for those cookies. He questioned Schyler about his activities in Nairobi and his trip home, and she began to wonder when he'd get around to his favorite subject. Schyler hinted that they had to leave, and Melissa handed her father his gift—a pair of initialed cuff links. She knew he'd have to say something to her then and braced herself for the worst.

"I didn't expect to see you. I thought you'd be with your mother"—his head dropped—"and with Adam."

"Daddy, I told you almost three weeks ago that Adam and I aren't seeing each other anymore."

"Yes, you did, but I didn't believe it. What happened?"

She shrugged. "We had a misunderstanding. I don't know what it was exactly, but we can't breech it."

"That's strange," her father said, his expression one of amazement. "He doesn't strike me as foolish. After what you did for him, he must know how you feel about him. Well, I thank you for coming and for my present." He handed each of them an envelope and looked at Schyler. "I hope I'll see you again before you go back."

"Of course, Daddy. I'm staying until January third." Rafer walked with them to the door and opened it with apparent reluctance.

"Merry Christmas, and thanks for coming to see me."

Melissa clutched her brother's arm as they left. "Was I seeing a ghost in there, Schyler?"

"Don't ask me. I was wondering the same thing, but ghost or not, it sure was refreshing. I can enjoy being with him if he stays like that."

She nodded, rushing along to match his long strides. "Me, too."

Adam savored his lemon custard pie, the finale of a flawless Christmas dinner, and reflected on the emptiness he felt. For the first time in his memory, Bill Henry hadn't joined the family for the holiday meal, and throughout it his mother hadn't mentioned his uncle's name. Worse, he'd been within inches of Melissa last night, but she'd been miles away from him. He couldn't pretend to enjoy himself.

"Do you need your car for the next hour?" he asked Wayne.

"I'll be here for the next hour and a half." Wayne reached in his pocket for the keys and handed them to Adam.

"Dinner was delicious, Mother. I'm going to Frederick." He didn't pause at the clatter of her demitasse spoon against the saucer. He'd upset her, but he couldn't help that. He wouldn't allow her or anybody else to control his life. Twenty minutes later he knocked on Melissa's door.

"I couldn't leave without telling you Merry Christmas." His breath caught in his throat when she squinted at him, parted her lips, and then seemed at a loss for words. "Are you inviting me in? Or should I leave?" She opened the door wider.

"I'm kind of surprised. Merry Christmas." He stepped through the door, and she turned and walked into the living room.

"I took a chance coming here without calling. You might have had a date." She seemed disconcerted, and his gaze swiftly searched the room. "Are you alone, Melissa?" He nearly laughed. Her chin jutted out, and she surveyed him with the cool detachment that he had always admired and which he knew she'd forced. He handed her a small package, asked her to open it after he left, and accepted the lone one under the tree when she handed it to him.

"I'm glad I decided to come—at least I know you've been thinking of me." He watched her eyes widen in obvious amazement before she frowned and gave him a mild rebuke.

"My father said this morning that you'd never struck him as a foolish man. Wonder what he'd say to that remark." In what he'd come to recognize as an unconscious gesture, she moistened her lips and dropped her head slightly to one side. Stunned, he realized that he was learning her all over again. The peculiar little habits that he'd gotten used to seeing . . . hitting him now. Fresh. And the smell of her perfume that had been in his nostrils since the night before when she'd drifted by him, and that brought saliva to his mouth right then. And her eyes. Sparkling and sad at the same time. Why couldn't she tell him she believed in him?

He heard the guttural sigh that filled the soundless room and knew it came from his soul. He reached out and felt her warmth in his arms. He'd meant to vent his frustration and to torture her as she tormented him. But she parted her lips for his kiss, and current after current zinged through him. He lifted her until her mouth was an easier target, and his fire pressed against her fire. He tried to banish the loneliness he'd felt without her, to ease the pain of her rejection, and to cushion himself against her failure to understand what he needed from her. Her whimpers were the sounds she made when she needed him inside of her, her love call, and he felt himself answering her. She moved against him, her demand becoming more insistent. Why am I holding out, he asked himself as he felt his ardor begin to cool. Memory flooded his thoughts. He had vowed that until she told him she'd been wrong, that she didn't believe he'd had an affair with her aunt, that she believed him and believed in him, there could be nothing between them. He needed her trust and her faith in him, and he couldn't accept less. She must have sensed his withdrawal, because she released him at once. But her eyes clouded with unhappiness. He couldn't leave her that way.

"I shouldn't have let things get out of hand, Melissa, but you know what happens when the two of us are together." He tried to manage a smile and knew he failed.

"Yes, I know," she said, and with her eyes she begged him for an answer to their predicament. If you'd only say it with words, he wanted to tell her, we could at least work toward a solution. But she said nothing. The next move was his, and he walked to the door and stood there for a minute. Then he clasped her within his arms—more roughly than he'd intended—and kissed her on the mouth.

"Merry Christmas." He heard her close the door, and he walked faster. He had to put some distance between them and to do it quickly. Even a shift in the wind could send him back to her.

Melissa walked up the stairs carrying the small rectangular red package, resplendent in its gold-speckled green silk bow, and laid it on the table beside her bed. He'd asked her to open it after he left, but she dreaded knowing its contents. She needed a token of his love, something more than the pulsing fire of his kiss, the kiss he later regretted. She supposed that he was in as much of a dilemma as she about their relationship, but he at least had control of his feelings. Not that that surprised her. From the beginning she had been impressed with his mastery of himself and his refusal to allow others that role. She sat on the side of her bed, her gaze fixed on his gift, and thought back to their happier times. Maybe she'd squandered a precious moment with him—she didn't know, but something had made him withhold his love.

When she'd seen him at her door, joy had suffused her only to be extinguished by his cool manner. They had been as strangers. Polite. Careful. And then he'd reached out for her, and she didn't remember how she had gotten into his arms. Only that she nestled where she knew she belonged. His harsh kiss had quickly turned worshipful, and she'd thought her prayers had been answered. Maybe he didn't love her, but he couldn't deny that he wanted her. She turned out the light and swung her feet beneath the cover, leaving the gift unopened. She could wait until morning for another letdown.

"Mrs. Roundtree's residence."

Melissa assumed it was the maid who spoke, gave her name, and asked for Adam.

"Sorry, ma'am," came the reply. "Mr. Adam already left for New York." Melissa fingered the little book of verses, a selection of poems that Adam had chosen and had bound in leather with gold tooling especially for her. Each one brought to mind something of their relationship, pleasant and painful. But not one contained the phrase 'I love you,' though she couldn't swear that each wasn't an ode to love. *I'd better not assume too much,* she admonished herself and decided to write him a thank you note.

Adam stood by his window, looking across at the snow-blanketed promenade of Lincoln Center, holding Melissa's note crushed into a ball. What had he expected? He moved away from the window and wandered aimlessly around his apartment. Discontented. Drifting for the first time in his adult life. "What the hell's gotten into me?" he asked the silence that surrounded him. None of the things he usually enjoyed doing on Sunday mornings in winter attracted him. He thumbed through the books on his shelf, books he longed to find the time to read, and walked away. Disinterested.

It's this apartment that's getting to me, he decided. An hour later he was on the train to Westchester. Winterflower opened the door before he rang. He accepted her generous hug and marveled at the sense of calm that he immediately experienced.

"You're troubled. What's brought you here?" she asked him.

"I needed a dose of your company." He followed her to the basement and leaned against the edge of a wooden sawhorse while she unveiled a clay mural.

"Perfect timing," she told him. "I want this to dry in the garage. It's less humid there." He stored it as she wished, walked out into the sunlight, and stood transfixed by the idyllic scene. The great trees stood burdened with icicles. Evergreen shrubs peeked through the snow, and birds darted in and out of the birdhouses that hung from branches and porch eaves. A blackbird tripped across his foot, unafraid. He couldn't hear a sound, and he knew he'd come for the peace and for Flower's calming presence. How different the setting from his last visit—a time when his body had just begun to churn with desire for Melissa. He looked in the direction of the rock on which she had sat with her hands in her lap. Relaxed. Serene. He turned quickly to open the porch door, but as he reached for it, it swung open and he looked into Winterflower's knowing eyes.

"Why can't you admit that being without her is tearing you apart? You've tallied some superficial reasons why you can't go to her and just give yourself to her. The problem begins with you, Adam. Not Melissa. She told you that she loves you." He cocked an eyebrow, remembering her ability to see beyond the ordinary.

"Yes," she continued. "And she risked her standing with her family and the community for you."

"There are things you don't understand, Flower."

"Like what?" she scoffed. "The fact that you're fooling yourself? You are a realist, a man who rejects sentimentality, who despises the shortcomings that afflict most of us mortals. A man who demands the truth of his associates. But not of yourself, Adam?"

He frowned. The assistant district attorney had been more understanding. "What are you getting at, Flower? I want it in English."

"Your complaints against each other are excuses, though hers make more sense." He tried to associate her words with what he felt. "You're both scared to go the other mile," she went on, leading him into the kitchen. "You'll give fifty percent, but not fifty-one. There's virtue in self-pride, Adam—but none whatsoever in self-centeredness. You can't expect Melissa to bare her soul to you when you've never told her that you love her."

"Why are you so certain that I love her, that I want a permanent relationship with her?" He watched, amazed, as Winterflower threw up her hands in exasperation, the closest to being disgusted that he'd seen her.

"When did a man, especially one such as you, tie himself into knots over a woman he didn't love?"

His gaze swept over her, but his thoughts were of how badly he'd wanted to include Elizabeth Barrett Browning's sonnet— *"How do I love thee? Let me count the ways."*—in the collection that he gave Melissa at Christmas and how dissatisfied he'd been when he'd forced himself not to do it. A rueful smile played around his lips.

"See what I mean?" Flower changed the subject. "B-H must be bursting with happiness along now."

"Yes," was his quiet answer as he recalled her special talent. "He's a lucky man. Emily is a wonderful woman."

"Not more so than her daughter."

Five o'clock in the afternoon, three days later at the Good Shepherd Presbyterian Church in Frederick, Melissa started up the aisle as the organ began to play, but her steps faltered when she saw that Adam stood beside Bill Henry as he waited for his bride. He turned slightly until he saw her and locked his gaze with hers. She hadn't thought to ask her mother who would be best man, but what would have changed if she'd known? No wonder her mother hadn't needed a rehearsal. She fought to hold her tears in check, but she couldn't banish the heartache that threatened to rob her of the self-possession she needed in order to make it through the rest of the day. Her hands trembled as she passed him, her eyes diverted, and took her place on the other side of the groom.

She saw Bill Henry throw custom aside and turn fully to the front to watch Emily Morris approach him, escorted by her son. Melissa didn't doubt his happiness, for her mother had given him his dream and dressed in a white beaded satin and lace gown with a headdress of beaded lace, and she carried his white calla lilies. She didn't think she'd ever heard a couple repeat their wedding vows so clearly and so loudly. Amused, she glanced over to find Adam watching her, the twinkle in his eyes aglow. After Bill Henry kissed his wife and walked up the aisle with her, Melissa saw Adam approach and offer her his arm. She had to fight a feeling of giddiness—what a time to experience a bout of hysteria!

Adam must have sensed her feelings for he tugged her a little closer and said, "That was almost enough to make a man cry. They're very happy." She looked up at him and knew that her face mirrored her surprise, but she only nodded, unable to speak.

"The bride is beautiful," he went on, "but not more so than the woman on my arm." Her shoe heel caught in the red carpet that Bill Henry had ordered laid down for his bride's satin-slippered feet, and Adam stopped, removed her other shoe and carried both of them in his hand. At the door he knelt and put them back on her feet.

They followed the bride and groom to the reception, and after the newlyweds drank a toast, cut the three-tiered cake, and began the dancing, Adam rose and extended his hand to

Melissa. Custom demanded that she dance with him. She'd be
lost, she told herself, hoping that she alone knew how her
body quaked.

The band played a fox-trot, but he danced the one-step. She
looked into the distance, past his shoulder, but he lifted her
chin with his index finger and forced her gaze to his own. She
missed a step, and he held her closer.

"Adam . . . Please . . ." She couldn't avoid his eyes, as
fiery as she'd ever seen them.

"I love you, Melissa. You're my life. Everything." She
missed several steps and had to cling to him for support.

"Do you still care for me? Or have I killed what you felt?"
Her heart thundered in her chest and she couldn't help trembling in his arms. She fixed her gaze on his mouth and moistened her lips.

"Melissa, what do you feel for me?" He had stopped dancing.

"I love you." He bent closer to hear her words. "I love you,
too, Adam."

"Come on. Let's go." His hoarse voice sent trills of excitement through her. He turned and started for the door just as
the bride's beautiful calla lilies brushed Melissa's chest. Grateful for her good reflexes, she caught them, looked around the
room for her mother, and when she found her, waved and
grasped Adam's arm.

Wayne met them at the door. "Where to?"

"Thanks, buddy. Thirty-eight Teal."

"Right on."

Adam didn't speak again until his shoe heel kicked her front
door shut.

"I'll put the flowers in some water. You wait here." She
removed her coat, hung it in the closet, and stood with her
gaze on the hallway, waiting for him. She made up her mind
to accept the explanation he gave her, to take whatever he
offered. He loved her—that was enough, all she would ever
need. She raised her arms when he stopped in front of her.

The twinkle in his eyes danced in a lover's smile as he looked into her eyes before he lifted her and sprinted up the stairs, his arms tight around her.

Her impatience for his possession mounted as he stood beside her at the foot of her bed. "I expected more from you than I was willing to give, Melissa. I know that now. Subconsciously I asked for proof that you loved me, while I withheld that from you." She placed a finger over his lips. She didn't need the words, but realized that he might and gladly gave them.

"Shhh. I didn't have any basis for believing that you had an affair with aunt Louise, that you would lie to me. I was wrong in not listening to my heart, in not believing in you. When I . . . when I read those poems, I looked for one that said you loved me, but—"

He interrupted her. "How could you not know? Why do you think I carried you out of that garden in the presence of half the population of Frederick, defying my mother when I was there to support her? Why would I wrap my coat around you and allow myself to get drenched in that icy rain? Why do you think I sat on the edge of your sofa, chilled to my bones, and drank cold, sugarless tea—which I hated—while I waited for you to calm down?"

She sucked in her breath and shivers raced through her as she beheld the storm that suddenly swirled in his eyes. "Nothing and no one is as important to me as you are," he said. She heard the unsteadiness of his voice and saw desire blazing on his countenance. Her mouth opened beneath his, and she clung to him, nearly delirious with happiness and reveling in her womanhood, when the movement of his tongue in and out of her mouth reminded her of the way he could make her feel. With eyes that had become pools of warmth and blatant desire, he asked permission to love her.

"Yes. Oh, Adam. I've waited so long for you. So long." He reached behind her and released the zipper of her dress, while she held his face lovingly between her hands. The touch of his fingers trailing down her spine triggered her feminine heat, and her body arched to his in unmistakable demand. He turned back the coverlets, laid her in bed, and quickly joined her. Pleasure radiated through her when he covered her body with his own, and she felt his love flowing in her and through her until she lost herself in him.

Adam lay on his back, holding Melissa in his left arm. "Let's talk, sweetheart. I want to begin the year with nothing between us hidden or unsolved, with everything out front. I once asked you how you felt about masquerade parties, but I didn't get much of an answer. Tell me where you were five years ago tonight." She sat up in bed, and he had the impression that he'd triggered her memory.

"What was I doing? Let's see. I went to a party, a masquerade party. Why?"

"Where?" Her face clouded as though she had an unpleasant memory. I won't stop now, he told himself and waited.

"The Roosevelt Hotel in New York. It was an AKA sorority affair. Why?"

"Why did you run away from me?"

"That was *you?*"

"Yes. I want to know why you ran."

"A few minutes before I met you at that party, I broke off with a man whom I had believed loved me; he'd just proved that he didn't. I had walked away from him and stumbled right into you. I left you, because I didn't want another man's kiss."

"Did you get over it?"

"Long ago."

"I looked for you, and I never forgot you. Occasionally I'd think you were the same person, but she was much shorter."

"I wore flat shoes that night. Ballerina slippers." She grazed his shoulder tenderly with her fingertips. "I didn't see your mother tonight. Was she at the wedding?"

"I'm sorry to say that she wasn't, but her absence didn't

mar my uncle's happiness, Melissa, and her attitude toward
you won't influence my feelings." He pulled her down beside
him and leaned over her.

"Will you marry me? I'll love you forever, Melissa. I swear
it. And no matter what my mother and your father think, we
can't permit them to wreck our lives. We may not be as fortunate thirty years later as Emily and Bill Henry. Will you take
me for your husband and the father of your children?"

She squinted at him. "Shouldn't you be on your knees right
now?" He reveled in the laughter that poured out of him, release that he'd learned through her and because of her.

"Don't keep me hanging here, lady."

"How about Valentine's Day? That should give me time to
have a dress made. Oh, Adam. I'm so full of love for you."

Epilogue

Adam leaned against the doorjamb of the room he shared with Melissa in the family home at Beaver Ridge and wondered when again his wife would have a chance to hold her son of ten days. They had come back to the family home after Melissa's delivery, so that their child could spend its earliest days among their families. Grant Roundtree had already found his niche as a force for peace. Mary Hayes Roundtree cooed at him from her chair on one side of the chaise lounge on which Melissa reclined, and Emily Morris Hayes made goo-goo eyes at him from the other side. Wayne, who was currently in possession of the little prize, insisted that he saw a clear likeness to himself. A five-foot teddy bear and a Lionel train bore testament to the love of Grandfather Rafer, who used his lunch hour to visit his daughter and grandson, and Schyler had come home from Nairobi for the event. Wayne had been so impressed by the changes he saw in Melissa on his visits to New York, and with his nephew, that he had stopped running from Banks and had begun to see her in a different light. Adam stood straighter when a hand rested on his shoulder, glanced around, and saw that his uncle B-H had joined them.

"Feels good, doesn't it, son?"

"Yeah. Unbelievable!"

Dear Reader,

I hope you enjoyed meeting Melissa and Adam and following their joys, conflicts, passions, and triumphs as much as I enjoyed giving life to them. I fell in love with Adam and developed an affection for three of the other male characters, especially Magnus Cooper. I'd love to know which of these men—Wayne, Jason, or Magnus—you would like to read about in his own story.

Against All Odds is my second novel for Pinnacle/Arabesque. I was delighted beyond measure when my first one, *Sealed With A Kiss* (ISBN 0 7860-0189-5), was published to rave reviews in October 1995. You may still find it in your favorite bookstore. The numerous letters of congratulations that I have received from readers have warmed my heart. I am happy to inform you that my novella, *Christopher's Gifts,* will be included in the Arabesque 1996 end-of-year anthology *Silver Bells* as the Christmas entry.

I love to receive mail, so please write me with SASE at P.O. Box 45, New York, NY 10044-0045, and I will send you an autographed bookplate.

Gwynne Forster

About the Author

Gwynne Forster, a demographer formerly with the United Nations, was chief of the Fertility Studies Section of the Population Division when she left to form a working partnership with her husband. She has traveled extensively around the world, she is an avid gardener, chef, and singer. She lives happily with her husband on Roosevelt Island, New York.

Look for these upcoming Arabesque titles:

October 1996

THE GRASS AIN'T GREENER by Monique Gilmore
IF YOU ONLY KNEW by Carla Fredd
SUNDANCE by Leslie Esdaile

November 1996

AFTER ALL by Lynn Emery
ABANDON by Neffetiti Austin
NOW OR NEVER by Carmen Green

December 1996

EMERALD'S FIRE by Eboni Snoe
NIGHTFALL by Loure Jackson
SILVER BELLS, an Arabesque Holiday Collection

SENSUAL AND HEARTWARMING
ARABESQUE ROMANCES FEATURE
AFRICAN-AMERICAN CHARACTERS!

BEGUILED   (0046, $4.99)
by Eboni Snoe
After Raquel agrees to impersonate a missing heiress for just one
night, a daring abduction makes her the captive of seductive Nate
Bowman. Across the exotic Caribbean seas to the perilous wilds of
Central America . . . and into the savage heart of desire, Nate and
Raquel play a dangerous game. But soon the masquerade will be
over. And will they then lose the one thing that matters most . . .
their love?

WHISPERS OF LOVE   (0055, $4.99)
by Shirley Hailstock
Robyn Richards had to fake her own death, change her identity, and
forever forsake her husband, Grant, after testifying against a crime
syndicate. But, five years later, the daughter born after her disappear-
ance is in need of help only Grant can give. Can Robyn maintain
her disguise from the ever present threat of the syndicate—and can
she keep herself from falling in love all over again?

HAPPILY EVER AFTER   (0064, $4.99)
by Rochelle Alers
In a week's time, Lauren Taylor fell madly in love with famed author
Cal Samuels and impulsively agreed to be his wife. But when she
abruptly left him, it was for reasons she dared not express. Five years
later, Cal is back, and the flames of desire are as hot as ever, but,
can they start over again and make it work this time?

FUN AND LOVE!